# PRAISE FOR ONE OF SCIENCE FICTION'S MOST HONORED SERIES

## NOW, LEARN THE SECRETS BEHIND THE SERIES ...

# BAEN BOOKS by
# LOIS McMASTER BUJOLD

# The Vorkosigan Companion

Edited by
## Lillian Stewart Carl
## & John Helfers

THE VORKOSIGAN COMPANION

This is a reference work about works of fiction. All the characters and events portrayed in this book are fictional, and any resemblance to real people or incidents is purely coincidental.

A Baen Books Original

Baen Publishing Enterprises
P.O. Box 1403
Riverdale, NY 10471
www.baen.com

ISBN: 978-1-4391-3379-8

Cover art by Darrell K. Sweet

First paperback printing, September 2010

Library of Congress Control Number: 2008032556

Distributed by Simon & Schuster
1230 Avenue of the Americas
New York, NY 10020

Pages by Joy Freeman (www.pagesbyjoy.com)
Printed in the United States of America

# · CONTENTS ·

## Part Three: Appreciations

## Part Four: The Fans

## Part Five: The Vorkosiverse Itself

# · COPYRIGHTS ·

## "Gosh, is it midnight already?"

There are many memorable firsts in a writer's career.
First story started—first finished. First submission.
First rejection. First sale! First review, good/bad. First
public speech about one's writing, urk. First fan letter! First time meeting one's editor face-to-face. First
award nomination—first win! Maybe, a first film option.
First time on a genre best-seller list—first time on
a *general* best-seller list, though this is a much rarer
prize. First career award—what, already? but I'm not
finished yet! First book *about* one's books.

I'm not just sure where we've arrived, but we're
definitely here.

Head down and pedaling as hard as possible, it's
not often that working writers have a chance to look
back and see just how far they've traveled. Much of
my biography and literary biography are covered in the
articles and interview that follow, so I won't linger to
recap it all here. But in this year, 2007, and in 2008
upcoming, have fallen a couple of firsts that force me
to pause and put it in perspective.

My first career award came last month from the
Ohioana Library Association. Literary awards generally, by nature intrinsically subjective, are mysterious

gifts bestowed upon writers; it is something done to us, not something—like finishing a novel—that we do. Career awards seem to be awards for winning awards, a suspicious circularity. (That said, this year's Ohioana memento takes the prize for being the prettiest ever, a gorgeous piece of art glass looking like a transparent blue jellyfish. Lead glass apparently looks extremely strange on airport X-ray machines, however. Someone could write a whole essay on the sometimes-deadly designs of the various awards and the challenges of getting them home.)

Next year, as I write this (though it will be a done deal by the time this book is published) I have been invited to be Writer Guest of Honor at the 2008 World Science Fiction Convention in Denver, Colorado, which is very much a career award in its own right. I put pencil to paper for my first science fiction novel in 1982; from there to this in a mere twenty-six years. Seems . . . fast.

Writing stories, using words to sculpt other people's thoughts, would appear to be the most evanescent of arts. Writers make and sell dreams; the vast publishing industry that conveys those dreams between the writer's head and the reader's seems a lumbering vehicle for such a light load. And yet, of all the many tasks I've undertaken in my life—apart from bearing and raising my children—it's my books that have best lasted and carried forward, the main thing I have to show for all my efforts. The lineup of first editions on my office bookshelf seems a procession of captured years, my basement full of books like an array of vintages laid down in a wine cellar.

A certain branch of linguistics and culture studies has a catchphrase—"time-binding"—to tag those inventions, including writing, that allow humans to carry their culture and achievements forward, through time that otherwise destroys all things each instant. I would quibble a little with the phrase, since it's not actually time that is bound. "We can neither make, nor retain, a single moment of time," as C. S. Lewis remarks somewhere. But for a little while, time's grinding teeth may be eluded. Most of my life's labors were consumed almost as soon as committed—all that housekeeping plowed under, all those meals I cooked gone in a day, all the forgettable daily tasks duly forgotten. But "Words," as another writer said, "can outlast stones." I'm not sure mine will go that far, but they definitely outlast meals.

I'm a bit bemused by this present volume. Why spend precious time reading *about* books—or worse, about the author—when you could be reading the *actual* books? But I presume the main audience here will be those who have read parts or all of the Vorkosigan Saga already, a reflection which allays my writerly anxiety. For you all, I trust that many amusements and some lively discussion follow. So I will get out of the way of the text—as writers should—and bid you all have fun.

—Lois McMaster Bujold
Edina, Minnesota,
November 2007

*Creator of the Vorkosiverse*

• • • • •

# Putting It Together:
# Life, the Vorkosiverse, and Everything

### LOIS MCMASTER BUJOLD

Fans have dubbed my science fiction universe "the Vorkosiverse," after its most memorable and central (but far from only) character and his family. Science fiction and fantasy are the only genres I know where a series is defined by what universe it is set in (making mainstream fiction, looked at with the right squint, the world's largest shared-universe series).

The series is a family saga, as it has grown to center around one family where all the stresses of their changing worlds intersect. The tale begins in *Shards of Honor* (which I have also described as "a gothic romance in SF drag") where Cordelia Naismith, a survey scientist from the advanced planet of Beta Colony, first meets Aral Vorkosigan, soldier from war-torn Barrayar. Barrayar, settled early by humanity, had been cut off from the rest of the worlds by an astrographic accident, and regressed culturally and technologically in what they call their "Time of Isolation," until rediscovered in Aral's father's time. It has been scrambling to catch up ever since, an effort sabotaged by both external invasion and internal civil conflict. And so I can have my swords 'n' spaceships in a way that makes both historical and economic sense.

In that early work, when I was still feeling my way into such basics as how to write a novel at all, I used elements ready in my head. One such was the setting for what later came to be named the planet Sergyar, which was based on the landscapes and ecology I'd seen on a biology study tour of East Africa back in my college days. I never became a biologist, but it was nice to think the experience wasn't wasted; one of the best things about writing is how it redeems, not to mention recycles, all of one's prior experiences, including—or perhaps especially—the failures.

But, now that I'd hit my early thirties and had two small children in tow, failure was no longer an option. With a rather large amount of help from my friends, including the present editor of this volume, I clawed my way through the learning experience of writing that first book. These were pre-word-processor days, so it was all produced, first, with pencil and paper, then on a typewriter with carbon copies. The book went through a lot of revisions, including the title—its original working title was *Mirrors*, both a name and a theme that I revisited later.

Miles Vorkosigan grew out of the world and situation created in *Shards of Honor*. He came as real people do—from his parents. I have a catchphrase to describe my plot-generation technique—"What's the worst possible thing I can do to these people?" (Others have pointed out that this should have an addendum, "that they can survive and learn from.") Miles was already a gleam in my eye even when I was still writing *Shards of Honor*. For his parents, Aral and Cordelia, living in a militaristic, patriarchal culture that prizes physical perfection and has a historically driven horror of mutation, having a handicapped son and heir was a major life challenge, a test worthy of a tale.

Miles has a number of real-life roots—models from history such as T. E. Lawrence and young Winston Churchill, a physical template in a handicapped hospital pharmacist I'd worked with, most of all his bad case of "great man's son syndrome," which owes something to my relationship with my father. But with his first book, *The Warrior's Apprentice*, he quickly took on a life of his own; his charisma and drive, his virtues and his failings—and he has both—are now all his.

My initial ideas for *The Warrior's Apprentice* actually centered on Miles's complex quasi-filial relationship with his bodyguard Sergeant Bothari; Bothari's death was the first scene I envisioned, and the rest of the book was written, more or less, to get to that point and explain it satisfactorily to myself. Other characters and events happened along the way and rather hijacked the tale, as sometimes occurs, often to a book's benefit.

I had heard of brittle bone disease before inflicting it on my hero Miles, of course. However, I took care to give it another cause, in his case a prenatal exposure to a fictional poison gas called soltoxin; this allowed me to authorially adjust his disease to the needs of my plot. His bones have a slightly suspicious tendency to break only when I need them to. Their realism is more psychological.

One of the things about being disabled is that you are disabled every damned day, and have to deal with it. Again. So this aspect of Miles's character has necessarily followed him into all his stories. And yet, the theme isn't just Miles; we have Taura, the genetically engineered super-soldier-monster, Elli Quinn of the reconstructed face, Bel Thorne the hermaphrodite, Miles's clone-brother Mark, the list goes on. While it's possible all these people were got up as plot-mirrors for Miles, the quaddies appear independently of him. So disability, and difference, have become ongoing subjects, directly or obliquely.

I've sometimes wondered if this theme is a personal metaphor. I grew up in a family with a remarkable father, strong older brothers, a close grandfather who'd been widowed in 1916 and never remarried, no sisters, and a mother whose attempts to feminize me I fought from age two onward. I had no extended family nearby to provide alternate models for women's lives, nor did the culture of the Fifties and Sixties offer much relief. In the lexicon of (some) feminist critique, disabled Miles becomes "codedly feminine": he's smaller than those around him, can't win a physical fight, is in a "wrong"-shaped body—has lots of medical problems—and has to beat the bastards using only brains, wit, and charm. The sense of being "wrong" is deeply inculcated in females in our society; I recall a pretty woman of my early acquaintance who wouldn't go out without her makeup on. "I have to put on my face," she explained. Sad, and scary. But regardless of gender, almost everybody harbors some cripplement, emotional if not physical. You can't judge anybody—you never know what backbreaking secret burdens they may be carrying. There is scarcely a more universal appeal to the reader.

The most important feedback I've received from handicapped (and non-handicapped!) readers is the sense that my fiction is energizing for them. Somehow, watching Miles operate gives them the emotional edge they need to tackle, as I described it above, just one more damned day. I think it's a variant of the Dumbo-and-the-magic-feather effect. When I reflect how much Miles's world is stacked in his favor, and how much their world is not stacked in theirs, the idea of anyone trying to use Miles's life as a blueprint gives me cold chills. Yet it seems to work. Miles models success.

I also note in passing that the definition of a handicap goes by majority rule. The fact that I cannot flap my arms and fly is not considered a handicap in Minnesota, because nobody else here can, either. On another world, in some avian evolution such as constructed by several wonderful SF stories, this disability would severely limit my social opportunities.

But, of course, since Miles lives in the future, one must allow that future medical technology will be better and cleverer than our own. In general I see technology as an annihilator of handicaps. I am increasingly convinced that technological culture is the entire root of women's liberation. But technology, outside of science fiction, is as awkward as any other bit of reality. It arrives sideways, it never works right at first, the interface problem is always a bitch, and for every problem it solves, several more are created. Still, I adore technology, medical and most other kinds.

Prior to the time his books open, Miles has already undergone many invasive repairs. I had a curious conversation with a fan once, comparing and contrasting the childhoods of Miles and his clone-brother Mark, one of the contrasts being the degree to which Mark was abused and Miles was not (it's a long story, spread through two novels). "But what about all that medical treatment Miles had to endure?" my bright fan inquired. "Oh," I said. I hadn't thought of it like that, but she had a point. There's a scene somewhere in *The Warrior's Apprentice* where Miles remembers how his father extracted cooperation from him when no one else could: "You must not frighten your liege-people with this show of uncontrol, Lord Miles," his father earnestly addresses the hysterical child-Miles. A consummate politician, that man.

Over the course of the next decade of his life, and several books, Miles gradually acquires more and more repairs; by age twenty-eight, almost all of his original bones have been replaced with synthetics. He's still short, but can scarcely be described anymore as handicapped. This invited new challenges.

Miles's inferiority complex and bad case of Great Man's Son syndrome give him an enormous amount of drive, which is both attractive and gets him into a hell of a lot of trouble, particularly when he drives first and looks later. (He simultaneously has what is popularly called a superiority complex. I figure you can't be that smart and not know it.) As his author, I find his drive an enormously valuable characteristic for kicking my plots into motion, but I'm pretty sure any people who have to live with him in book-world (his cousin Ivan, for instance) find him pretty obnoxious at times. Miles has a dangerous tendency to try to turn the people around him into his annexes, a trait most spectacularly resisted by his clone-brother Mark. It's the main reason feminist scholars trying to construct Miles as codedly feminine get about halfway through the analysis and go, "Um, but..."

I didn't write the volumes about Miles Vorkosigan in strict chronological order. *Shards of Honor* and *The Warrior's Apprentice* are the first two novels I ever wrote. Nevertheless, the proper direct sequel to *Shards of Honor* is actually *Barrayar*, written six years later—they are literally two halves of one story—and the proper sequel of *The Warrior's Apprentice* is *The Vor Game*, also written years later.

The series grew organically as I scrambled from book to book; neither I nor my readers—nor Miles—have known what would be next. Quite like real life, that way. I admit, by the time I'd finished *The Warrior's Apprentice*, the structural model of C. S. Forester's Hornblower books had entered my mind. In this series about a British navy captain in the Napoleonic Wars, Forester began in the middle of Hornblower's life and career, then jumped forward and back as the spirit moved him. Each book stood alone as a complete and independent novel, yet when you put them all together, they turned into something larger than the sum of their parts, the character's overarching biography—stories within a mega-story. That structure gives a great deal of creative freedom, on a book by book basis. I've also found it allows each book to comment thematically and in other ways upon all the others, via a sort of literary hyperspace; an extra reward for the series reader's faithful dedication.

However, I have found by experiment that prequels suffer from certain constraints. The ending of the tale told has to not disrupt or contradict events that come later, and a character cannot grow beyond the bounds the writer has already shown. And there needs to be some explanation of why events are not causal in the intervening books, why an episode important enough to write a novel about is never subsequently-in-book-time thought about by the point of view character. Tricky. Lately, I've been sticking more to chronological order for these reasons.

My advice to new readers is: Begin reading the series where you are, and go on as you can. Which is not bad advice for life generally, come to think of it.

The next novel to be written wasn't about Miles, except very indirectly. It was *Ethan of Athos*, about an obstetrician from the planet forbidden to women. Charming fellow. Thereby hangs a tale that could only be science fiction. . . .

*Ethan of Athos* had two mainsprings: consideration of what extra-uterine gestation might do to human society, and reaction to earlier SF works from the Fifties and Sixties, when I grew up and imprinted on the genre, that dealt with gender relations in the future, particularly the "Amazon planet" meme, which I now take (with half a century of hindsight) as that era's attempt to grapple with the impending issues of women's lib. *Ethan* was my contribution to the SF gender argument. The future universe in which all my SF plays out is not culturally uniform, and so I can explore more than one take on all these intertwined issues. Settings in the future also allow one to detach the underlying issues from current events and their emotional baggage, a standard useful SF hat trick.

At the time I wrote *Ethan of Athos*, I had not yet

sold any novels, though two completed works were making the rounds of New York publishers. I had, however, made my first short story sale, and on the boost to my morale so provided, I embarked on this third novel. I was groping around for the magic trick by which I might break in, and among the advice I collected was "Try something short. The editors are less daunted by thinner manuscripts on their slush piles, and maybe they'll read it sooner!" So I was determined to keep the length under strict control. I still wasn't sure I would be able to sell the books as a series, although I quite liked the universe I had begun to develop, so I also wanted the next thing to be series-optional, not dependent on the two prior books but connectable to them if some editor did see the light. But more importantly—in the course of *Shards of Honor* I had tossed off as a mere sidebar the idea of the uterine replicator. Upon consideration, this appeared to me more and more a piece of technology that really did have the potential to change the world, and I wanted to explore some of those possible changes.

Extra-uterine gestation is not a new idea in SF. Aldous Huxley first used it way back in the early Thirties in *Brave New World*, but being who and where he was, used it mainly as part of a metaphoric exploration of specifically British class issues. I was a child of another country and time, with a very different worldview, and other issues interested me a lot more. Primary among my beliefs was that, given humanity as I knew it, there wasn't going to be just one way any new tech would be applied—and that the results were going to be even more chaotic than the causes.

One obvious consequence of the uterine replicator was the possibility of a society where women's historical monopoly on reproduction would be broken. All-male societies exist in our world—armies, prisons, and monasteries to name three—but all must resupply their populations from the larger communities in which they are embedded. This technology could break that dependence. I discarded armies and prisons as containing skewed or abnormally violent populations, and instead considered monasteries as a possible model for an all-male society both benign and, provably, viable over generations.

About this time—the winter of 1984/85—I went to a New Year's Eve party given by a nurse friend, and fell into a conversation about some of these nascent ideas with two men. One was an unmarried and notably macho surgeon, the other a hospital administrator with two children of his own. The two men took, interestingly, opposite sides of the argument of whether such an all-male colony could ever be workable. The macho surgeon rejected the notion out of hand; the man who'd actually had something to do with raising his own children was intrigued, and not so inclined to sell his gender short. (The surgeon, note, did not perceive that he was slandering his gender; in bragging about what he could not possibly do in the way of menial women's work, he was positioning himself and his fellows as ineluctably on the high-status end of human endeavor.) It was clear, in any case, that the topic was a hot one, of enormous intrinsic interest to a wide range of people.

My reader reaction has been pretty positive—or they wouldn't be my readers, QED. A somewhat circular proposition, there. *Ethan of Athos* has not been my top seller, and I do get echoes of negative response from unreconstructed homophobes now and then, who bounce off the very idea of the book. (A quick scan of the reviews on Amazon.com can give a self-selected slice of response from the general public.) But in general, if a straight person is open-minded and bright enough to read SF in the first place, they don't have a problem taking that book in stride. My gay readers like it that earnest physician Ethan was a fairly early positive portrayal (the book was first published in 1986), and that he's a fully-rounded person, not just an agenda with legs.

*Falling Free* came to be written as a result of a phone conversation with Jim Baen. I had written my first three science fiction novels "on spec," that is, without a prior contract or even contact with a publisher, which is pretty much the norm for first-time novelists. They'd sold on one memorable day in October 1985, in my very first phone conversation with Jim, when, after reading *The Warrior's Apprentice*, he called me up and offered for all three books. I was then faced, for the first time, with writing a novel with a known publishing destination, and intimidating expectations.

I had been thinking of following up a minor character from *The Warrior's Apprentice* named Arde Mayhew, a jump pilot afflicted with obsolete neural implant technology who would be on a quest for a ship that would fit him. I pictured him finding his prize among a group of people dwelling in an asteroid belt whose ancestors were bioengineered to live in free fall, and who were eking out a living, among other ways, as interstellar junk dealers. Jim was not much taken with Arde, but he seemed to perk up when I came to describe my proto-quaddies, and opined that a tale about them might be more interesting and science-fictional.

The quaddies' reason for being, or rather, being made, would be knocked asunder when a practical artificial gravity was developed. As I researched what was then known about free-fall physiology, it seemed to me that most of the obvious changes wouldn't necessarily leave people unable to return to a gravity environment. I came up with the notion of a second set of hands to replace legs after conversing with a NASA doctor about the dual problems the astronauts faced of leg atrophy, and their hands growing excessively tired as they took over the task while working of bracing oneself in place that on Earth is done by gravity. Having reasoned my way backward to their two-hundred-years-prior genesis, I decided to begin the quaddies' tale at the beginning, came up with the main characters, and from there, just followed their actions to their logical conclusions.

I decided to make my protagonist a welding engineer because I knew the type—my father was a professor in the subject, and one of my brothers had taken his degree in the specialty. This also seemed to handily solve my technical research problems; wrangling preschool children at the time, I knew I wasn't going to be able to get very far-from home to do research, or much of anything else. This would have been early 1986.

I was about five chapters into the tale when my father died of a long-standing heart condition, in July of that year. At the timely invitation of then senior Baen editor Betsy Mitchell, I took a needed break to write my first novella—also the first work I'd ever sold before I wrote it, a scary step into a larger world for me as a writer. "The Borders of Infinity" had its start in about four pages of notes I'd scratched out for a potential Miles tale that drew on my early reading about WWII military prison camp breaks, an interest I shared with this volume's editor—Lillian lent me *Escape from Colditz* and other works on World War II way back in high school. Then there was the copy of *Bridge Over the River Kwai* that surfaced in my house. My notions didn't support a novel, but turned out to be perfect for the shorter length. Updating the technology of confinement—but not its psychology—provided the rest of the plot.

It found its place in Betsy's novella collection series in *Free Lancers*, along with tales by Orson Scott Card and David Drake, which may well have served as the first introduction of this new writer Bujold to some of their readers. After a few months, I was able to return to work on *Falling Free* and, my confidence boosted, send it to contract.

I then turned for technical research answers to my brother, and through him, to an engineer friend of his named Wally Voreck, who sent me the fascinating material on ice die formation, which is a real industrial process. With such a cool (literally) gimmick, I reasoned my way backward to a plot development that would use it as a solution. (Writers cheat with time, you know. We can run it both ways.)

But I did manage to sell the novel to *Analog* magazine as a four-part serial, which ran from December 1987 through February 1988. This brought my work to the attention of a whole pool of new readers who might not necessarily have picked the paperback (which came out in April of 1988) off the bookstore shelves. This was the first of several happy sales to *Analog*, one of my dad's favorites back in the Fifties and Sixties, and one of the first SF magazines I'd read when I was discovering the genre in my early teens. Since *Falling Free* was very much a tribute (if slyly updated) to the science fiction of that era, it felt much like coming full circle. The serial also was splendidly illustrated by Vincent di Fate; I still have five of the scratchboard originals, my first real art purchase. (He kindly adjusted his rates to my budget.)

Back in *The Warrior's Apprentice*, Miles was forced to split himself into two personas, the constrained Lord Vorkosigan and the active Admiral Naismith. (I leave it as an exercise for the reader to figure out how this relates to Mrs. Lois Bujold, housewife, and Lois McMaster Bujold, successful science fiction writer.) When in *Brothers in Arms* it became apparent to outsiders that there was going to be more than one of these books, I had a conversation with Jim Baen over what to dub the series in the little red banner on the front cover. He was voting for "A Miles Naismith Adventure," correctly identifying the admiral as by far the more charismatic of the pair. I held out for "A Miles Vorkosigan Adventure," and then wrote the novella "The Mountains of Mourning" to demonstrate to him why. I heard no complaints about the choice thereafter.

That novella was also a chance to explore mystery elements with an SF setting, in which Miles, a new-minted ensign, is sent up to his own District's backcountry to investigate a case of infanticide for mutation. This brings him face-to-face with those uglier aspects of Barrayar that he would most like to avoid, and foreshadows his future need to reintegrate himself, and, through himself, Barrayar's past and future.

Inherent in Miles's split into his two sub-personas— something that was vital for his growth at the time (and most useful for my adventure series)—was the necessity for his ultimate reunion into an integrated maturity. In *Brothers in Arms*, which may otherwise appear a mere adventure series sequel, I began my first halting exploration of these ideas, where Miles, trapped on Earth, meets the clone who was made to replace him in a political plot aimed against his father. Miles's clone-brother Mark represented yet another mirror-split, of the dark and light aspects of a fully rounded person, as is traditional for doppelgänger suspense tales, but those were precisely the traditions I wanted to explode. In one of the many triumphs of the personal over the political in my books, Miles instead frees him.

"Labyrinth" was the last-written of the Miles-adventure novellas collected in *Borders of Infinity*. With two rather dark tales already in the bag, I decided to make this one something of a comedy, for balance.

The novella allowed me to ring changes through still another social milieu: in this case, Jackson's Whole, and what it might do with the new biological options. On this planet, laissez-faire capitalism has gone completely over the top, as the rule of law enforced by governments with guns is replaced by the rule of guys with enough money to hire guns. Here, the only limits of biotechnology are "whatever money can buy." For chaotic results, this serves up a smorgasbord to make an adventure author's mouth water. Since Miles is the master of chaos, this was a character and a setting made to bring out the most in each other, and indeed they did.

In every society, no matter its response to technology, the test of humanity comes out the same, and it has nothing to do with genetics. No one can be guilty of their own birth, no matter what form it takes. We need not fear our technology if we do not mistake the real springs of our humanity. It's not how we get here that counts; it's what we do after we arrive.

The character of the quaddie Nicol in "Labyrinth," though a rather minor player, got me thinking again about the quaddies and my lost promise to complete their saga, and how their exodus might have come out. But other stories were crowding for my attention, and the impulse slipped away yet again.

Usually, I can't reliably trace where my story ideas arise from, but in one case I can. The first element to trigger the "Weatherman" sequence that opened *The Vor Game* was a memoir. T. E. Lawrence (better known as Lawrence of Arabia), after his WWI adventures left him with what we would nowadays call a bad case of post-traumatic stress disorder, attempted to change his identity and life by enlisting in the British air corps as a grunt under a pseudonym ("Aircraftman Shaw"). He wrote a memoir about going through enlisted basic training, titled *The Mint*, which pretty much summed up the dismal horrors of army basic upon a nervy, intelligent man. I read this, heavens, sometime back in the early Seventies; it went into the bag of authorial data and lay there pretty much dormant.

The second element was a story from Roman times.

A Roman legion was deployed in, I believe, Dacia,
somewhere off the Black Sea that had horrible cold
winters. The high command was going through flip-
flops over whether Christianity was to be an allowed
religion among the troops. They decided it wasn't,
and the order came down that everyone who had
become Christian must recant. Forty men refused.
To punish them, they were sent to go stand on the
ice of a frozen lake naked until they changed their
minds. One man broke, and decided to come back
in. The other thirty-nine stood out on the ice, and
one of the watching Roman officers was so impressed
with their fortitude that he went out to join them, to
make up their numbers. They all died together, and
so became the early Christian martyr story known as
"The Forty Martyrs of Sebastiani."

The third element goes back, again, to my father.
He had a moonlighting job as a television weatherman
in Columbus, Ohio, when I was growing up. And he
was very good at this. His weather reports—analyses
and predictions—were better than the military weather
reports that the Strategic Air Command pilots at the
local Air Force base were getting, as he discovered
when they began to call him for forecasts. In addition,
one of the things I had from my father was a picture,
which hung on his home office wall for years, of an
arctic weather station. It was a stylized watercolor
print of a man in a parka who has come out into the
snow and is checking his instruments. (I still have this.)

I was doing the dishes and listening to music, a
tape by the Irish singer Enya, and on the tape was
a song she sang in Latin. Now, I don't understand
Latin, and I really have no idea what the song is really

about, but somehow the sort of military-ecclesiastical rhythms made all the ideas cross-connect in my mind for the first time. And so I thought, "Ah, I know! I will send Miles to a miserable arctic army base as his first assignment, where he'll be assigned to be a weather-man and get in all kinds of trouble and replay 'The Forty Martyrs of Sebastiani' and he'll be the fortieth man." That would be the opening of the story and how he gets into trouble and gets reassigned back to ImpSec, all this in aid of eventually reconnecting him with the Dendarii Mercenaries.

The novella was actually an outtake from the larger *The Vor Game*, rather than the novel being a later extension or continuation; but the rest of the tale involved such large shifts in tone and setting, I've often wondered since if they really ought to have been two separate books. Too late now.

In the case of *Barrayar*, a direct sequel to *Shards of Honor*, the first part of the tale was already written. I'd cut off the last six or eight chapters of *Shards* because at the time I didn't quite know how to end a book and had rather overshot the ending, and had to back up to find a good stopping place. I set this fragment aside in my attic for several years. So about the first third of the book was already written when I was moved to go back and explore those themes and characters. I think it was a stronger, better book for the wait and the extra writing experience I'd accumulated in between—and certainly with a somewhat different plot—than if I had gone on to write it directly instead of turning my attention to *The Warrior's Apprentice* instead.

*Barrayar* explores what happens after the "happily

ever after," which in real life is usually where the unglamorous long-haul work starts. Since Aral's work is a rather deadly brand of politics, the failure of which devolves into civil war, the action plot was obvious. (Well, by then it was. It hadn't been when I'd set it aside back in '83.) But in this early example of my many explorations of the personal versus the political, the biological versus the social, which are still ongoing in my work, the real subject of the tale is reproduction through adversity, political and otherwise—and, of course, through technology, compared-and-contrasted through several parallel couples and their different choices and chances.

*Mirror Dance* is most truly Mark's book, in which I came around again to complete what I'd merely attempted when he was introduced back in *Brothers in Arms*. But in that first pass on the problem, I realized in retrospect, I undercut myself by not including Mark's point of view, so that was the very first thing I corrected in the next try. In order to give Mark his chance to grow onstage it was also necessary to ruthlessly suppress Miles, which proved not without its satisfactions, and fruitful consequences. But here Mark finally obtained the viewpoint, the voice, and the story he needed to step out of his progenitor-brother's shadow.

*Cetaganda* was a prequel that had been kicking around for a while in the idea-form of "Miles and Ivan go to the Cetagandan state funeral, and…" with no idea of what happened next. When I finally came to write the tale, it just seemed to call for younger and more naïve characters, so I set the way-back machine to their early twenties. The story might have fallen elsewhere in their timeline, but would have been a rather different tale.

In *Cetaganda*, I explored disparate consequences of the Vorkosiverse's reproductive technologies in a very different social milieu. The Cetagandan haut use replicators and associated genetic engineering to construct their race's entire genome as a community property under strict central control. Although spread among many individuals, the genome becomes conceptualized as a work of art being consciously sculpted by its haut-women guardians. Where this is finally going, even the haut women do not have the hubris to guess—one of their few saving graces.

In addition, *Cetaganda* allowed me to do something a writer can pull off especially nicely in a series—critique or comment upon the assumptions of earlier books. I had originally tossed off the Cetagandans as mostly-offstage and rather all-purpose bad guys to stir up some plot action for my heroes. But the Barrayarans had started out as bad guys too, from a certain point of view. The closer I came to them, the more complicated their picture grew. No one is a villain in their own eyes; when I brought the story closer to the Cetagandans, they, too, became more complex and ambiguous. I was very pleased with the effect.

*Memory* was pretty much a direct result of *Mirror Dance*. I didn't think a person should undergo so profound an experience as death and a return to life with no consequences or without learning anything, although I downplayed these at the end of the prior book so as not to alarm my publisher.

In *Mirror Dance*, Miles gets killed—and cryonically frozen, and eventually revived and repaired. But the cryo-freeze does him subtler damage than brittle bones, resulting in an idiosyncratic (i.e., literally convenient) form of epilepsy. The reward for a job well done is another job. After watching Miles overcome every physical setback in his passionate pursuit of his military career, in *Memory* I set him a problem that really would throw him out of the military, one inside his own brain, one he couldn't get around—and then sat back to see what would happen. What happened was that he grew up, in some extremely interesting ways. The epilepsy is surely a metaphor for something, in Miles's life; that his handicap has mutated from something external to something internal as he matures surely has significance, and if I ever figure out what it is, I'll let you know.

I had my eye on the reintegration aspect of *Memory*, in its essences if not in its accidents, since at least *Brothers in Arms*; in fact, it was inherent from the moment Miles popped out his desperate creation of Admiral Naismith back in Chapter Seven of *The Warrior's Apprentice*. I knew that Miles's eventual destiny was to reassemble himself whole, sometime before age forty. How this was to come about was much less apparent.

Somewhere I have a penciled outline of about seven chapters of a book involving Miles dealing with Simon Illyan's memory chip going glitchy. It was the oblique result of encounters with my sister-in-law's aging mother, who was undergoing a protracted Alzheimer's-like debilitation. While visiting, I stayed with her one afternoon while my brother and his wife ran errands. I found it was possible to carry on an oddly satisfactory conversation with her, if I didn't care where the conversation went. She still had interesting things to say, in a fragmentary sort of way; they just weren't in any order, and I had to take them as they came up, and maybe string them together later.

To me, whose identity is so bound up with intellectual achievement and value, Trudie Senior's situation seemed boundlessly horrific, and Trudie Junior's unfailing day-by-day care of her rather more heroic than anything I'd ever put one of my fictional characters through. And so the idea came to me in techno-metaphor of Simon Illyan's eidetic memory chip failing, and Miles somehow coming to his rescue. One of the deep appeals of fiction is the ability, as my friend Lillian here once put it, "To heal with the stroke of a pen."

I had a choice between starting that book, or doing the one where Miles reencountered his clone-brother Mark. Patricia Wrede, after listening perhaps once too often to my set speech about prequel determinism versus sequel free will, talked me into doing the Mark book first, rather than writing it as a prequel later, even though I was rather excited about the memory-chip idea. I am exceedingly grateful to Pat for that. Because the book that resulted changed Miles and his world.

It had been plain to me, if not to my chief protagonist, that for a long time Miles had been getting along by living a lie, and at some point in his life, this ought to turn around and bite him. Miles was living his adolescent dream, which once had given him vital growth, but now was proving increasingly sterile; it was time for him to grow up and move into a more fully adult, fully rounded life. But he was also getting an enormous amount of validation out of his

Naismith persona; it was equally clear that he would not willingly give that up, even if another part of him was, almost literally, dying to move on.

*Mirror Dance* supplied the missing pieces for both plot and theme in *Memory*, in the form of Miles's own cryo-revival damage and subsequent seizure disorder, and it finally achieved critical mass.

In *Memory*, Illyan's loss of his military career is closely contrasted with Miles's loss of his. (Parallels, spirals, and reflections are some of my favorite literary patterns.) Illyan gets to dump, after thirty grueling years, a job that had eaten his life. He was mortally tired, and ready for the change, however high the ransom he had to pay for himself.

When Illyan gives up being Chief of Imperial Security, it's as if he has a thousand-pound weight lifted from his shoulders. Punch-drunk, he is. No wonder he warbles a bit. Illyan's losses are great—removal of the chip returns him to normal temporal perception, but too dangerously absentminded to continue as an officer—yet there are surprising compensations. His emotional side that his job required him to suppress for years finally gets a chance to flower. And it's contagious; relationships that had been frozen in place for years thaw and change when he changes.

And there's another variant on the book's theme; even after such profound change, as another character remarks, what you get back is "... your life again. What else?" Illyan was ready to be finished with that earlier part of his life, and move on. Miles both was and wasn't; part of him had to drag the rest of him, kicking and bitching the whole way, onto higher ground. Watching Illyan adjust, Miles and his maniacal drive for achievement get a valuable nonverbal but very sharp critique from the man who was his most revered mentor. Trust me, it's very good for him.

*Memory* was published a couple of months before Trudie Senior's long, long death came to an end. I sent a copy to the dedicatees. Trudie Junior said: "I showed it to her...You do what you can."

I really, really wanted to write a lighter book after *Memory*. I didn't think I could, or should, attempt two thematically "big," emotionally draining books in a row. It's like spacing pregnancies too close together; it leaches the minerals out of your bones. But *Komarr* lay across my path to everything else; it had to be done first.

*Komarr* is the romantic drama; *A Civil Campaign* the romantic comedy. After all, Miles had two births, and will have two deaths, why shouldn't he have two romances? On a practical level, the split of the emotional plot of story into two halves was to solve a problem of tone. I could not have combined the material I dealt with in *Komarr* with a comedy of the goofiness I desired in the same book. It would have been too schizophrenic even for me.

Again, with military plots knocked out of the menu, mystery and suspense—and romance—took up the load. Miles is sent to Komarr, a planet his father helped conquer a generation before, in the unenviable position of a hated occupier, to investigate the possible sabotage of a solar mirror designed to help terraform the planet, a very long-range project. There he meets Ekaterin, his female opposite in most ways, whose life has been as restricted as his has been adventurous. Each, it turns out, has value to offer the other, this time across boundaries of culturally mandated gender splits. The backdrop of a cold world requiring decades of dedication to bring to fruitfulness is not accidental.

Meanwhile, I'd been itching to write a Barrayaran Regency romance ever since I realized I'd given Barrayar a regency period. I dedicated it to four inspiring female writers. I'd read Charlotte Brontë's *Jane Eyre* fairly early on, but I only came to Georgette Heyer and Dorothy L. Sayers in my twenties, when my reading branched out, and I've only picked up Jane Austen fairly recently. Heyer remains my favorite comfort reading—*A Civil Campaign* is very much a tribute to her—though there was a period when her inherent class-ism got up my nose. Sayers's work, even more than that of C. S. Forester and Arthur Conan Doyle, is a model for the kind of wonderful character development that can only be done over a long series.

The tale offered many delicious levels of play, not least that of dissecting a lot of romance tropes under a true SF knife. What happens to the old dance between men, women, and DNA when new technologies explode old definitions of, well, everything? What happens to a tradition-bound society whose channels of property and power assume gender divisions and functions that new science throws into a cocked hat? Just what rude things do those butter bugs symbolize? What happens to two supposedly immiscible genres when you put them both in a bottle and give it a good shake? What can each say about the other? Chamomile tea and blasters: give me both!

The butter bugs in *A Civil Campaign* have several sources. First, I was a biology major back in my college days, and my faculty advisor was an insect toxicologist.

He raised various strains of cockroaches in his lab to test poisons and resistances. (For some reason, the animal rights people never hassled him. ...) His most interesting strain was one which, when he sprinkled roach powder in their plastic boxes, would stand up on their hind two legs with their front four legs on the sides, a behavioral adaptation. I also did a great deal of insect photography during that period.

Second were some wonderful old Robert Sheckley tales read in my youth about a pair of down-on-their-luck spacers and their misadventures with live cargo. Thirdly was the movie *Joe's Apartment*, and fourthly, at about the same time, was a trip to the Minnesota State Fair where I saw, among other things, a large apiary exhibit. I was scratching around for an idea for a short story when the notion of entrepreneur Mark's adventure in bioengineering with Doctor Borgos and his yogurt-barfing bugs first began to take shape. It quickly became apparent both that the idea could not be crammed into the length, and that it was much too good to waste on a mere short story, and so the Vorkosigan House butter bug scheme was born. Or hatched.

The butter bugs have proved very popular with the readers, generating butter bug hand puppets, at least two fan-written songs, and a great deal of specula-tion as to their future. (Fans have written well over a hundred songs about my stories, to date. And then there are the limericks...)

Life went on, for me and my characters. The opening situation of the book that became *Diplomatic Immunity* called for Miles, in his brand-new hat as a Barrayaran Imperial Auditor (a kind of high-level troubleshooter),

to become involved in straightening out an imbroglio
with a Barrayaran fleet at a deep-space station. I had an
entire wormhole nexus to choose from for this setting,
and it occurred to me that this gave me the long-awaited
chance to visit Quaddiespace and finally see how *Falling
Free* had come out. Because I rather wanted to know.
It was unfinished business that still niggled, though the
time and impulse for anything like a direct sequel was
past and long past.

A subplot featured the free-fall quaddie ballet. It's
my favorite part of the book. I am pleased to note
it, too, has inspired a filk song, and a good one; it
seems a just reward that a chapter which is in effect
an essay on the nature of art as an expression of cultural identity should garner a critique which is itself
a worthy piece of art. That these most wonderful of
dancers have neither legs nor feet, and after a short
time neither their audience nor my readers notice,
was another plus.

Over and beyond the quaddie Nicol, several of
the novel's other precursors are found in "Labyrinth."
Most especially, of course, the tale of Bel Thorne, the
Betan hermaphrodite, although some of the unfinished
business with Bel stems most directly from the end of
*Mirror Dance*. But I found a certain pleasing round-
ness to connecting the first tale in this universe to,
if not the last, the latest.

I'd also known I wanted to do something with the
possibilities presented by the Cetagandan child-ships
ever since I came up with the idea for them back
when I was writing *Cetaganda*. And I've long wanted
to play a bit with yet more varieties of bioengineering on humans in Miles's universe, so this tale also

gave me a chance to introduce Guppy, the somewhat hapless prototype of an amphibian human species.

So *Diplomatic Immunity* drew mainly on information I had in hand, or in brain, rolled with the usual themes: biology, bioengineering, we have met the aliens and they is us, plans not surviving contact with the enemy—or with one's friends, for that matter—and, above all, the transactional nature of parenthood.

I'm asked frequently where I'm planning to go next with the Vorkosiverse. Have I written myself into a corner with Miles?

Well, one of the things I like to do is take non-standard heroes and run them through the wringer and see what happens. So coming up with a plot of the right weight for Miles in his current situation is an interesting challenge.

Given powerful characters, there are still a lot of ways that the writer can play with them. The protagonist can be given a more powerful adversary, but then one gets into kind of a hero-villain arms race that ends up with the Superman–Lex Luthor scenario. A more interesting plan of attack is to look for the hero's uncorrected flaws, and focus on them. The hero may have all these new strengths, but he or she still has other weaknesses. One can separate a powerful character from his matrix of support, isolate and drop him back into a less-powerful position. Since Miles is a character sent out on galactic missions, that approach has a lot of scope for him.

The possibilities just have to become more ingenious. The kind of simple physical plots that test younger characters are now not appropriate for Miles—not that he has ever dealt with anything but curve balls.

The story has to find a different realm or level of challenge. For example, moral problems are not going to be particularly amenable to a character's having more power, because that's not the kind of thing that solves them.

The wormhole structure of my universe gives the advantage to the defense. It requires and rewards interplanetary cooperation. But it also means that any planet has a limited number of immediate neighbors to conveniently have conflicts with, and Barrayar's neighborhood is pretty quiet at the moment. So if I want to stir up trouble for Miles I may have to stir it up someplace else than near his homeworld.

The Vorkosiverse has eons of future history—a thousand before Miles, plus after. What's his world going to look like ten thousand years down his timeline, when this human speciation has exploded? I envision all these different aliens that were once us.

I've thought about setting a story in another era, but these are ideas without characters and if it doesn't have a character it's not a story that picks up and runs. The Miles universe is presently snagged on Miles. He's such a pivotal character, such a world-changer, that I don't know where the universe goes after him—unless I jump so far ahead it becomes a matter of indifference whether he lived or died. Which is a rather sad notion.

More people ask about whether Ivan is going to get married than how human evolution is going to go ten thousand years down the timeline (although, when you think about it, the two questions are profoundly related). We see Ivan a lot through Miles's eyes, and Miles is . . . opinionated, let's say, but beneath Ivan

Vorpatril's lazy facade is a real lazy man. When we finally saw Ivan through his own mind, as a viewpoint character in *A Civil Campaign*, some people were disappointed because there wasn't more there. They had constructed Ivan as this man of mystery.

But the Ivan that you see is pretty much the Ivan that you get. He could be challenged, and he would rise to the occasion. Without the challenge, he would just lie there. Nothing is more life-disrupting for a hapless character than to accidentally stumble into one of my books. When I was writing *A Civil Campaign* and it was time for one of Ivan's scenes, I always had the feeling that he was hiding out from me much the way he hid out from his mother when she had unpleasant chores for him. He whined pitifully whenever I dragged him back onstage. Clearly, I'll have to think about something special for Ivan. He'll hate it, but he doesn't get a vote.

Addressing some of the more common general questions about the Vorkosiverse's roots: Miles's world, Barrayar, is steeped in Russian culture, while their rivals the Betans are more Californian. It was likely my Cold War milieu that inspired me to create a world peopled by the descendants of Russians—plus, it must be admitted, the lingering influence of *The Man from U.N.C.L.E.*'s most personable hero, Illya Kuryakin. When I started the work in late 1982, it looked like the Cold War would go on forever. But in a moment of canny something-or-another—I know it wasn't foresight—I did not make my future Russians necessarily descended from the Soviet Union. I was more strategically vague than that, which put me ahead of the curve when the Soviet Union fell in 1989. Vor society is not based on Soviet society. Its

Time-of-Isolation social structure had devolved to a species of neo-feudalism, for the same reasons of poor communications that the original feudalism evolved to address. I've selected bits and pieces of social inspiration from sources as diverse as Meiji Japan, Imperial Russia and Germany, and whatever other historical sources came my way, building up my own mental picture about how the real world, and therefore fictional worlds, work.

I don't know whether the planet is called Barrayar in honor of the ruling family VorBarra or vice versa. I make up my backgrounds as needed for the tale I'm writing, and I don't fix the details until they are needed (they might, after all, need to be something else). So we won't find out until I set a tale in an earlier period, which doesn't look likely to happen any time soon.

Whether the Galaxy common language is English or not depends on the region. In Miles's neck of the woods, it appears to be English. Some English-descended dialect may be the interstellar lingua franca the way English is the language of international air traffic, for the same practical reasons (it got there first, everybody needs to be able to communicate with everyone else for safety reasons, whatever). I haven't explored the probable effects of really good automatic/computerized real-time translations that we may presume would be developed by then, except in passing at that dinner scene in *Brothers in Arms* where the earbugs were late arriving.

There is the usual rainbow of human races in the Vorkosiverse, too, beyond Barrayar and Beta Colony. The homogeneity of those rather suburban planetary settings is simply a result of their colonization histories. Both were, in quite different ways, "lost" colonies. The original colonizing groups were likely up to eighty percent Caucasian, and the minority racial phenotypes present among the founders were subsumed over time. The mixed genes are still in there, which is why the most common coloration on Barrayar is black hair, brown eyes, and olive skin. "Race" is an arguable concept anyway in a universe where anyone can alter any genetic trait at will in their offspring, and, with rather more medical difficulty, even in themselves. Even "species" turns out to have fuzzy borders.

I tried to use as many ethnic names as possible to reflect Barrayar's colonization history. French, Russian, Greek, and British names thus should appear a lot, with an odd smattering of names of totally unrelated ethnic origins depending on who chanced to be among the fifty thousand Firsters.

I'm occasionally asked whether Miles's mother Cordelia could be a secret agent of Beta Colony. I think while she is certainly not an agent of the Betan government, she is a vector of Betan culture. She feels that her homeworld has many strengths that Barrayar can learn from, not least a great deal of practice at living with what advanced technologies and biotechnologies can do to a society. So, she is an agent of change and for progressive thinking. Although that's plenty enough to work up a great conspiracy theory with, and I'm sure those Barrayarans who resent and resist change have.

As to how Cordelia, a soldier of an enemy planet, could not only get access to Barrayar but thrive there, several factors contributed. First of all, Aral wanted her, and he has a certain amount of power in this situation. Aral was also expected to marry and have a son, since Barrayar is one of those cultures where it is part of one's social duty as a member of the aristocracy to create the next generation. His father Piotr certainly wanted Aral to get on with the job, and Piotr is also a man with a great deal of clout.

Cordelia also created her own status by being an enemy soldier, and a successful one. She became admired, rather the way some American military history buffs admire General Rommel ("The Desert Fox" of WWII fame in North Africa), who although he was the enemy was good at what he did and had some interesting positive qualities. It is quite possible to admire an honorable enemy, especially if one is a militarist and attached to the military virtues oneself. And most critically, Emperor Ezar wanted Aral married so that he would not be trying to stage a coup by marrying Kareen, the dowager crown princess. Cordelia might not have been Ezar's first pick, but she was the woman on the spot.

As for villains in the Vorkosiverse—I have some realistic ones and a few extraordinary ones, and I have to admit, the more over-the-top sorts are very handy to have around. Though I've always wondered, looking at the high-end villains in James Bond movies for example—if they have all the resources they display in the course of the plot, why haven't they just invested them all in mutual funds and retired? They clearly don't need to be villains in order to meet any rational need they could have. Few real people just go out and say "I'm going to be villainous today!," barring the sort of resentful unbalanced loser who has become wound up in his own personal status emergency, which he has decided to share with everyone around him. There is a natural preference for the high-end villains in adventure fiction, however, because the satisfaction of defeating them is unimpaired by messy ambiguities. Waxing the bad guy fixes the problem simply and cathartically, and now the reader can close the book, turn out the lights, and go to bed.

But for the majority of ordinary people not in books who find themselves doing evil things, it's because they've fallen into a situation that they don't understand, didn't predict, didn't anticipate. Sometimes they get drawn into evil just because they don't realize that they can say "No!" Or the cost of saying "no" means that they will be shot. That sort of situation is especially ambiguous and difficult. There are hundreds of ways people can be psychologically manipulated into acts they would never have thought they could or would do, both good and bad—it happens all the time, in wars, in political or economic crises, in domestic violence. Army basic training is an example; so are propaganda and atrocity stories and news spins and religious indoctrination, and on and on. Human beings are immensely malleable. But these realistic sorts of resultant evil are more usually in the background than the foreground in my action-oriented tales, being much harder to bring to closure.

The very last Miles story I wrote before breaking off, or out, of the SF milieu to try my hand again at fantasy was the novella "Winterfair Gifts," set against the backdrop of Miles and Ekaterin's wedding. I came to it after completing *Diplomatic Immunity*, violating my rule against prequels, but not by much. Like "The

Borders of Infinity" novella, it had its seeds in some ideas and images I'd been kicking around earlier that did not seem to support the weight of a whole novel. And like the prior work, their right-sized container found them when I was approached by an editor, in this case Catherine Asaro. She wanted to try some crossover blending between the usually immiscible genres of F&SF and Romance, a project that appealed to me on many levels. (Reintegration across boundaries, again.) The tale gave me a chance to follow up on Sergeant Taura, and explore the character of Roic, whose development had intrigued me in *Diplomatic Immunity*. A wedding seemed a fitting, if not end, resting place for the series, symbolic as it is of the triumph of the comic, the domestic, and the personal. And the universal.

* * * * *

# A Conversation with
# Lois McMaster Bujold

## LILLIAN STEWART CARL

LILLIAN STEWART CARL: Let's begin as all biographies begin. To paraphrase Bill Cosby—whose 1960s records we almost memorized—you started life as a child.

LOIS MCMASTER BUJOLD: Yep. I was born in Columbus, Ohio, in 1949, third child and only daughter of the family. My parents were originally from Pittsburgh; they graduated from high school in 1930 straight into the Depression. My father, through work and scholarships, put himself through night school and, eventually, graduate school at Cal Tech. He ended up teaching welding engineering at Ohio State University. So I grew up in the white-bread suburb of Upper Arlington in the Fifties and Sixties.

My father gave me a model for the writer-at-work; one of his projects during that period was editing the *Nondestructive Testing Handbook*, a major work in his field that was the world standard for twenty years. He did this largely at home in his upstairs office and in the spare room, where a secretary labored to track and collate the pounds of paper and worldwide correspondence. Memories of my dad center around the clack of his IBM Selectric, the scent of professorial pipe smoke, and the constant strains of classical music (WOSU-FM) from his hi-fi.

*Falling Free* has an engineer character based loosely upon my father and his work, and was dedicated to him; Lord Auditor Vorthys owes much to his professor-emeritus mode.

LSC: Your father was a remarkably patient man, letting us use his recording equipment and his typewriter for our own projects. Or we'd just sprawl in his chairs and read.

LMB: I fell in love with reading early, but hit my stride in third grade when I discovered that I wasn't limited to the thin "grade level" picture books they laid out for our class during library periods, but could take any book from the shelf. I fell ravenously on Walter Farley and Marguerite Henry (this was my horse-obsessed period), and never looked back. I started reading science fiction when I was nine, because my father read it—he used to buy *Analog* magazine and the occasional paperback to read on the plane during consulting trips. With that introduction, no one was ever going to fool me into thinking SF was kid stuff!

LSC: Kid stuff?

LMB: Well, one must·admit, SF has roots in boys'-own-adventure genres; I dimly remember reading SFnal tales in my older brother's copies of *Boy's Life* (a Boy Scout magazine) back then. But the term "adolescent" when applied to SF is not necessarily a pejorative, in my later and wider view. The great psychological work of adolescence (in our culture, anyway) is to escape the family, especially the mother but in some families the father, depending on which parent is more intent on enforcing the social norms, in order to create oneself as an autonomous person. This is why, I theorize, so much fantasy and SF is so hell-bent on destroying the protagonist's family, first thing, before anything else. Villages must be pillaged and burned, lost heirs smuggled off to be raised elsewhere, SFnal social structures devised that eliminate family altogether—because before anything at all can happen, you have to escape your parents. It's their job to prevent you having adventures, after all.

When I was a kid, my favorite writers included Poul Anderson and James H. Schmitz—who had great female leads in his tales—the usual Heinlein (the juveniles, not his later work), Asimov, and Clarke, Fritz Leiber, L. Sprague de Camp, Mack Reynolds, Eric Frank Russell, Zenna Henderson; toward the end of that period there was Anne McCaffrey, Randall Garrett, Roger Zelazny, Tolkien, Cordwainer Smith, and so on. There was a lot less SF on the library shelves in those days; you could read it all up, and I did.

I discovered the SF sections at the public libraries I could occasionally get to. Since we lived on the outer edge of the suburbs, and there was no public transportation, getting to a library involved getting my mother to drive me the ten or twenty miles there, which became easier when I reached age sixteen and could drive myself.

LSC: For a while you were getting around on a bicycle. That's devotion to reading, risking getting run off a narrow black-topped road in order to reach the library. But that was after I entered your life—or you entered mine—thanks to some faceless bureaucrat who put us both into Section 7-2 at Hastings Junior High School in Upper Arlington.

LMB: Dear God, you even remember the section number? Scary...

LSC: Do you remember trying out for the school talent show by singing Tom Lehrer's "Poisoning Pigeons in the Park"? The silence after we finished could have swallowed a planet.

LMB: I'm so glad we didn't make the cut. . . . The experience of making the attempt was likely good to have, I suppose. Maybe. Actually, I still don't like getting up on stage, come to think.

LSC: It's a good thing we found each other—no one else could have put up with us. (Although I must admit to having been immensely gratified at sitting around a conference recently, singing Lehrer songs with the other writers!)

LMB: Well, we didn't know fandom existed till after high school. In junior high we shared our love of books, watched favorite television shows and fell in love with their heroes together (*The Man from U.N.C.L.E.! Star Trek!* The short-lived TV version of *The Wackiest Ship in the Army!*), and became each other's first readers for the (mostly highly derivative) stories, scripts, and poetry that boiled up in both our heads—we were inspired to write because we loved to read, and because stories poured through our heads, welling up uninvited from wherever these thoughts come.

I introduced you to SF and fantasy, and you introduced me to history and archaeology. This was the early 1960s, and American television was filled with World War II shows. It was all around in the culture. We shared books like *Escape from Colditz*, which was about WWII prisoner of war camp escapes in Germany. I think it is because we were trapped in high school and the idea of breaking out of the prison camp was a very captivating idea. "Maybe if we dig a tunnel we could get out of the classroom. . . ."

LSC: One of our history teachers was a big fan of the movie *Stalag 17*, so I suppose the thought of breaking out wasn't exclusive to the students. I well remember writing a brief piece where I was magically transported from the crowded halls of the high school to the Pelennor Fields, hearing the horns of Rohan in the dawn.

LMB: My Tolkienesque epic, embarked upon at age fifteen and never finished, at least has the dubious distinction of having been written in Spenserian verse, the result of having read *The Lord of the Rings* and *The Faerie Queene* twice that year.

LSC: It was you who introduced me to Tolkien, something for which I'm profoundly grateful.

LMB: I bought an Ace pirated edition of *The Fellowship of the Ring* on a family vacation to Italy, and found the ending to be a huge disappointment; it just sort of trailed off. Oh, lord, I thought, it's one of those darn dismal British writers.... There was nothing on the cover, spine, blurb, nor after the last page that indicated there was more, except for a brief reference buried at the end of the "about the author" paragraph to it being a heroic romance published in three parts. Marketing was more primitive in those days, I suppose.

Half a year later, it was with overwhelming joy, still remembered vividly, that I found its two sequels. I don't remember the names of most of my high school teachers, mind you, but I can still remember where I was sitting when I first opened up *The Two Towers* and read, with a pounding heart, "Aragorn sped on up the hill..." My father's home office, the air faintly acrid with the scent of his pipe tobacco, in the big black chair under the window, yellow late-afternoon winter light shining in through the shredding silver-gray clouds beyond the chill bare Ohio woods to the west. Now, that's imprinting.

The chair, the room, the man, the world are all gone now. I still have the book. It has stitched itself like a thread through my life from that day to this, read variously, with different perceptions at different ages; today, my overtrained eye even proofreads as it travels over the lines, and sometimes stops to rearrange a sentence or quibble with a word choice. Is it a perfect book? No, doubtless not. No human thing is. Is it a great book? It is in my heart; it binds time for me, and binds the wounds of time.

"And he sang to them...until their hearts, wounded with sweet words, overflowed, and their joy was like swords, and they passed in thought out to regions where pain and delight flow together and tears are the very wine of blessedness" is no bad epitaph for a writer. I could crawl on my knees through broken glass for the gift of words that pierce like those.

LSC: It grieves me to hear someone say, "I don't have to read *The Lord of the Rings*, I've seen the movies"— even though the movies are amazing accomplishments. And had the side effect of allowing us to get back in touch with our inner fan-girls.

LMB: It all comes back around, doesn't it? I tried sporadically to write through early college, but then got sidetracked—although there was a period during college when several of the members of the local SF club I'd discovered (in Columbus, Ohio) met at the house of a graduate student in English Literature who was himself trying to become a novelist, and who eventually succeeded, too. He went on in academia—I ran into him again a few years back at a con.

LSC: Then my family had moved to Texas. We didn't see each other for five years, during which time real life overwhelmed the murmurs of our muses.

LMB: Ray Bradbury, in a speech he gave at a Nebula banquet in the late eighties, told a tale of having one day decided he needed to "grow up"; endeavoring to put away childish things, he burned his comic book collection. About a month later, he woke up to himself and said, more or less, "What have I done?!" I was a slow learner; it took me about a decade to find that lost real self again. I married, worked for several years as a drug administration technician at the Ohio State University Hospitals, and finally had my two children.

During that same period you'd had your kids and began writing again, and made your first short story sales. I'm half-willing to swear that there's something about completing one's family that frees up women's energy, as though we're subconsciously holding something in reserve till then. Stuck in a small town with two preschool children and no job (or rather, no money—don't get me started on how our society devalues "women's work," or I'll still be ranting come sunset), I was inspired by your example. It seemed to me this might be a way to make some money but still get to stay home with my kids. Which eventually proved to be true, but it took a good long time getting to that point.

LSC: How did you get started?

LMB: I count the beginning of this effort as Thanksgiving Day, 1982, when, visiting my parents, I wrote a paragraph or two on my dad's new Kaypro II to try out the toy. I dimly recall that the fragment of description actually had its genesis from a writing exercise done for a couple of visits to a local Marion writer's group. They were mostly middle-aged and elderly women who met in a church basement and wrote domestic and religious poetry; after a hiatus, I found them again the following year when they'd moved to a bank basement, and inflicted much early SF on them. They were a very patient, if wildly inappropriate, audience. The fragment generated, the following month, my first story, a novelette eventually titled "Dreamweaver's Dilemma," although the actual paragraphs were cut from the final version.

Later, I found a much more useful (and younger) group of aspiring writers further away in Columbus, including some SF, fantasy, and mainstream people. Another influence that certainly deserves mention is Dee Redding, the wife of the minister of my parents' church. She used to let me come and read to her from my scrawled penciled first drafts while she darned socks, and say encouraging things. Lots of people were willing to tell me things. Dee was one of the few who was willing to listen.

Even though I never did formal workshops or took a degree in literature, I still found the honest and competent feedback I needed to test and hone my skills. Which was fortunate, because no editor then or now has time to be a writing teacher.

LSC: Meanwhile, at the 1982 Chicago Worldcon, I met another new fantasy writer, Patricia C. Wrede, who lived in Minneapolis. Her first novel had just been published; I had at that time sold only short stories. She said she'd be glad to critique my work, and anyone else's I happened to know—she's teased since then that *your* manuscript arrived in her mailbox at approximately the speed of light.

LMB: The three of us fell into a sort of writer's workshop by mail, sending chapters of our assorted novels back and forth to each other for critique. With your and Pat's help and encouragement, I finished my first novel and started on my second, *The Warrior's Apprentice*.

Somewhere about the middle of Chapter 5 of *Apprentice*, in the late fall of '83, I stopped to pop out the short story "Barter." It was a side effect of reading Garrison Keillor, partly. It took only two or three writing sessions, no more than ten hours. I'd jotted the opening line in a notebook earlier that summer, based on personal observation at assorted breakfasts, without anything to attach it to at the time. "Her pancakes were all running together in the center of the griddle, like conjugating amoebas..."

It was easy work. The setting of "Putnam, Ohio" had been developed in seed form for an earlier tale, "Garage Sale." (Marion was a Revolutionary War general, so was Putnam, hence the transference.) The cats, the kids, the house, the Smurfs, the desperation, and the Christopher Parkening record, if not the peanut butter on it, thank God, were all lifted nearly verbatim from my life at the time.

The news of the sale came on a little teeny personally typed *Twilight Zone Magazine* letterhead postcard, almost lost in the bottom of my mailbox, which I still have. I was ecstatic. The meager money was soon spent, but the morale boost was critical to power me through the following year and third novel until my final vindication, when I sold the three completed manuscripts to Baen Books.

LSC: In tribute to your first professional sale, I appropriated your Putnam as the setting of my romantic suspense novel, *Ashes to Ashes*. I suspect the secondary character of Jan was based on "Barter" as well, in the backhanded sort of way these things develop.

LMB: Speaking of conjugating amoebas. The sales saga of "Barter" had a sequel, a success story—not to mention a cautionary tale—in miniature. The story was seen by a producer from the TV series *Tales from the Darkside*, who threw me into total confusion, in my pre-agent days, by calling and offering to buy the story rights for scripting for the show. The episode that resulted bore almost no relation to the original. Their scripter not only eliminated almost every element I'd invented and reversed the outcome, but used it as a hook to hang an *I Love Lucy* pastiche upon, a sitcom I'd loathed utterly even back in the Fifties when I'd first seen it. Since *Tales from the Darkside* didn't play in my viewing area, I've never seen the episode broadcast, a non-event I do not regret. But I was very grateful for the money.

LSC: I saw the episode. You didn't miss a thing. In fact, I had to call you and ask you if it was indeed based on your story!

LMB: Only on its title, apparently. Anyway, in the fall of 1984, I finished my second novel and started on the third, in the meanwhile sending the first two off to New York publishers, where they languished on assorted editors' desks for what seemed to me very long times. It was a difficult period, financially and otherwise, and as a get-rich-quick scheme writing did not seem to be paying off. But in the summer of '85, my second novel, *The Warrior's Apprentice*, had returned rejected. You suggested I send it next to the senior editor at Baen Books, Betsy Mitchell. Tell again where you met?

LSC: Standing in line for the bar at the 1983 Baltimore Worldcon. Although it was at the Austin NASFiC in 1985 that I suggested to her she might enjoy your work.

LMB: Your Worldcon attendances have proved awfully useful for my career, I think. So I followed your advice. That October, Jim Baen called and made an offer on all three finished manuscripts.

LSC: And you immediately called me, asking me to use my resources as a SFWA member to determine just who these people were and if they were legit! Admirable caution, considering you were tap-dancing on the ceiling at the time.

LMB: Baen Books actually started at nearly the same moment I first set pencil to paper on my first novel, and were still new in 1985, so I may perhaps be forgiven for having barely heard of them. I had no idea how long or if the company would last, but hey, they wanted my books. Through a succession of phone conversations—me bewildered and slightly paranoid, Jim very patient—I gradually learned the ins and outs of how editing was done, how royalty reports were done, how books were marketed, how cover art happened, and a host of other professional skills.

I first met Jim face-to-face in an elevator crush in the lobby of the Atlanta Marriott at the '86 Worldcon. I rather hastily introduced myself, and as he was borne away into the elevator with the fannish mob he called back something like, "If you can write three books a year for seven years, I can put you on the map!" To which my plaintive reply was—and I can't now remember if I voiced it or not—"Can't I write one book a year for twenty-one years?" I don't know if he ever knew how much he alarmed me with that.

LSC: I knew. You spent that whole convention looking like a deer in the headlights. Although it was quite obvious to me, as my friends asked me to introduce them to you, and assorted strangers elbowed past, that you were already on a map of sorts.

LMB: I was frantically trying to figure out this whole pro-writer thing. On the fly, terrified of putting some fatal foot wrong.

LSC: Which may be one reason it took you a while to realize you needed an agent.

LMB: I was figuring it out by then. I had contracted my first seven books before I acquired an agent. This was bad in the short term, in that I was really ignorant about contracts, and also had no way to reach foreign markets. But it was good in the long run, because when I did finally go shopping for an agent, I was able to make a more informed choice—and I was able to get my first pick, the estimable Eleanor Wood. One of the things I discovered through this was that one's early mistakes need not be permanent. As new books came up, we were able to trade back to Baen for rights I had foolishly given away; in other words, we used new contracts to fix the old ones. Although this only works if one is selling to the same house, I suppose; there are also other ways early errors can be rectified by a good agent acquired later.

LSC: We've mentioned starting our families. The thing about starting them, is that then you have to live with them for years on end. It's no accident that the Vorkosigan books give a lot of importance to the role of family.

LMB: Family is a strong influence for everyone, one way or another. Either your experience of family has been good, and you recognize and relate to the emotions, or it has been bad, and you long for something better even if just in the pages of fiction. It's one of those fundamental needs built into human biology, as universal as "boy meets girl." Which also, of course, connects with family.

LSC: Many readers make the assumption that you have to sacrifice family for your art, or vice versa.

LMB: This gives me an inner vision of a writer with her family staked out on an altar at midnight, their bodies covered with cabalistic symbols, her knife raised to dispatch them in exchange for All Worldly Success. Would that it were so simple. The run on black candles would clean out the shops.

More seriously, I don't see that being a writer is all

that more demanding of sacrifice from one's family than any other career or job, and in some ways less. I started writing when my kids were ages one and four. I had more time, and much more flexible time, with my kids by working at home what amounts to part-time, than I would have had putting in eight to ten hours a day at some office, factory, or hospital. I never had to negotiate with the boss for time off when a kid was sick; I was always there when they got home from school, no need for latchkeys or complicated child-care arrangements; vacation and holiday schedules were variable at will. Yes, I had to call on help from relatives or sitters now and then, particularly when running out to do publicity things like conventions, but the total of time taken was still much less. And for whatever the experience has been worth to them, as they grew older I was able to take the kids along on a lot of travel opportunities. They met a wide variety of creative and interesting people.

On the minus side, writers have no backup, in the form of a boss or organization, to lend them credibility or clout in defending their working time. With an outside job, the boss, safely absent, gets to be the bad guy who is blamed for taking you away. If you work at home, you have to be your own bad guy. No one will give you working time; you have to learn to take it. (This leaves aside the little point that no one but you can possibly know when you are mentally ready to sit down and write.) And most other breadwinners are given sympathy and credit for having to go off to work; work is not regarded as a privilege for which they must beg and negotiate time. But a writer's family may suspect (rightly, as it happens) that she's really secretly having fun, and tend to treat the demand for respect as well as some sort of attempt at double-dipping.

LSC: Writer Ardath Mayhar talks about writing an entire novel while one of her sons banged on the typewriter with a spoon.

LMB: I know another who typed her second novel one-handed while nursing her baby. (It was probably her best chance to sit down uninterrupted.) It actually may be less confusing for the kids to have a parent who makes a clean break and leaves the house to work, than to have one who's there, but not paying attention. One of the problems of being a writer is in identifying "time off." If the book is always running in your head, niggling at your brain, you're never quite altogether present to the people you're with. I suspect this can become frustrating after a time, but the people you really need to ask about the effect of this absent-mindedness are writers' family members themselves.

But all that said, on the whole the experience of being a parent, watching real kids grow, has given me back human content for my work a hundred times the value of the time it's taken away.

LSC: If your family has given you content for your stories, so has your reading—and not just fiction but lots of nonfiction as well.

LMB: A nearly universal trait among writers—if we didn't love to read, why else would we want to make more books? I pick up a lot of ideas from historical reading—to paraphrase, history is not only stranger than we imagine, it is frequently stranger than we can imagine. Real life provides jumping-off points for my fictional ideas, but they are frequently turned inside out or upside down before they land on the page, re-visioned, revised. Reading, observation, music and songs, experiences people tell me about, my own life and emotions—it all goes into the stew. But inspiration isn't just knocking into an idea—everyone does that all day long. It's hitting the idea, or more often cross-connection of ideas, that sets off some strong resonance inside one's own spirit, that hot pressure in the solar plexus that says, *Yeah, this is it; this matters!*

Sometimes inspiration falls freely from the heavens; sometimes you have to hunt it down and kill it yourself. Then there is reverse-inspiration, that restless discomfort that says an idea is just wrong for a story. Over time I've come to regard that sort of warning writer's block as almost equally valuable.

Not everything I read triggers an idea-rush. Or does so right away. My reading falls roughly into two categories. The first is general cultural filter-feeding, where I just sop up whatever randomly catches my eye, which then goes into the mental compost, sometimes never to be seen again. It's a sort of Drunkard's Walk through whatever aspects of my world impinge on me. Later, when a set of ideas is beginning to form up into a potential book, I'll do much more directed reading.

LSC: I've said that history is like gossip, or like real-life soap operas.

LMB: The fundamental question of history is "What were these people *thinking*?" The chains of disasters that real people have visited upon each other can scarcely be equaled by anything one could imagine—in fiction things have to make sense. I must be eternally grateful to you for turning me on to history as reading matter, back in junior high.

It's all in the footnotes, all in the details: the diaries and the stuff that gets down to the way people actually lived, not general economic theories of faceless forces at work. In building a world, you want those telling details that hold more than they appear to hold. Every object you put into a story tells you something about the background, potentially. If you have a character wearing a nylon jacket, it's implied that you have a petrochemical industry around there somewhere. You can't use any metaphors from a technology that doesn't exist in that world, and so on. But that kind of thoughtful attention to what all your details imply can allow you to get more bang for your buck, more information than appears on the page.

Effects must have causes. That's deeply inculcated into the modern mind and so we want to see these causes, these costs. That's what storytelling is all about. For all the physical action, eventually it always comes down to someone making a choice somewhere, to do one thing and not another, and those choices are the turning points, if you like, of history. Historians tend to fall into two camps. You have the people in the Impersonal Historical Forces camp, who want to say that all history is these great movements—vast things happen but no people ever do anything. And on the opposite pole are the Great Man theorists, who want all of history to be the effects of certain individual acts by a rather limited cast. I think the actual truth lies somewhere in between. It's far more chaotic. Small causes can have enormous effects and it's very fractal, really.

LSC: For the want of a nail, the horseshoe was lost, and so forth.

LMB: What if—and there's the beginning of many a story—what if at certain key critical junctures, certain things had happened differently; might some of the horrors of history have been averted or healed? In real life, we can't know. In books, healing becomes possible.

LSC: Healing is one of your themes. Do you do much research into the science, medical and otherwise, in your science fiction?

LMB: Sometimes; sometimes I draw on what I already have in my bag. And I've several times had real doctor-readers review both my fantasy and SF manuscripts for medical accuracy. But foregrounding the characters, necessarily, entails backgrounding the technological speculation, however much those new technologies are in fact affecting characters, settings, and plots all three. Because the tech is mostly in the background, some readers don't seem to notice how much is actually there, mostly in biology and medicine.

But I'm interested in the impact of technology on the characters' lives, the new moral choices and dilemmas it presents them with. Sometimes the details are important. When I was writing from an engineer's viewpoint, and he was facing an engineering problem in *Falling Free*, I had to provide enough to give some sense of how the problem-solving was going on inside of his head. But the reader doesn't usually retain all that anyway, so why clutter the page? The stuff should work, and the implications should be displayed, ideally. I don't do this across the board—some of my technologies are complete hand waving, such as the faster-than-light travel. Other technologies, like the design of the uterine replicator as described in *Ethan of Athos*, are very carefully thought out, and would actually work, more or less, as described.

So it depends on the focus of the story. If the plot turns on the tech, or the viewpoint character thinks in detail about it, then one needs to give it more attention.

LSC: Paying attention to the plot. And the characters, and all the rest of the package.

LMB: All at once, all the time, yep.

LSC: But the words have to go down in a row. What's your particular method of developing the story and getting it down?

LMB: I will start to work up ideas for a story from all sorts of sources—other reading, history, film, television, my own life experiences, my prior books, debates with friends about ideas or other books. When my eyes or brain burn out on reading, I'm quite fond of all the nonfiction DVDs I can get from the local library or, now, Netflix, science and travel and history. At some point, all this will spark or clot into notions for a character or characters, their world, and the opening situation, and sometimes but not always a dim idea of the ending. I will start jotting notes in pencil in a loose-leaf binder. By the time I have about forty or fifty pages of these, I will start to see how the story should begin.

I use a sort of rolling-outline technique, largely as a memory aid, and work forward a small section at a time, because that's all my brain will hold, up to what I call "the event horizon," which is how far I can see to write till I have to stop and make up some more. This is usually a chapter or three. I'll get a mental picture of what scenes should go in the next chapter, and push them around till they slot into sequence. I then pull out the next scene and outline it closely, almost a messy sort of first draft. I choreograph dialogue especially carefully.

Then I take these notes to my computer and type up the actual scene, refining as I go. Lather, rinse, repeat till I get to the end of the chapter and, my brain now purged and with room to hold more, I pop back up to the next level to outline again. Every scene I write has the potential of changing what comes next, either by a character doing something unexpected or by my clearer look at the material as it's finally pinned to the page, so I re-outline constantly.

Making up the story and writing down the story are, for me, two separate activities calling for two different states of mind.

LSC: Whereas for me, they're virtually the same thing—the writing generates the creation. But everyone's muse has his or her own idiosyncrasies.

LMB: Yep. For me, creation needs relaxation; composition is intensely focused. I do the making up part away from the computer, either while taking my walks or otherwise busying myself, or, when I get to the note-making or outlining stage, in another room. I do not compose at the computer, although I do edit on the fly, and the odd better ideas for a bit of dialogue or description do often pop out while I'm typing. Sometimes, they're sufficiently strong that they derail what I'd planned and I have to stop typing and go away and re-outline; sometimes they're just a bonus, an unexpected Good Bit, and slot right in.

I do most of my writing either in the late morning, or the late evening. Late afternoon tends to be a physiological downtime for me.

LSC: I know from hard experience that some books come out a lot faster than others.

LMB: For me, it's varied from nine to sixteen months. The amount of time I've taken between books has varied from six weeks to six months. In the absence of distractions I write at a fairly steady rate—about two chapters a month, on average—but then there are the major life-interruptions, which pick their own times. Convention travel, much as I enjoy it, also takes a big bite of time each year. I lose one to two weeks of writing time/attention/energy for each three-day convention I attend.

My writing schedule, too, has varied over the years. In the beginning I wrote during my kids' naps and after they were in bed, but then they stopped taking naps and started staying up later. The younger one hit school as I was starting my fifth novel, *Brothers in Arms*, and then I began writing in the mornings and early afternoons, school hours, though I am not by nature a morning person. Since I have at last moved to a house with my own office, I sometimes get in an evening or late-night session. But my prime time is still school-hours.

If I have the ideas marshaled, I can write in much less than ideal circumstances. If my inner vision is a blank, it doesn't matter how much peace and quiet I have, nothing comes out. During the sticky bits of a novel, I've sometimes found it useful to fool myself with the "five hundred words a day" trick. Five hundred words is not very much, just a couple of paragraphs. A few days of lowering the bar, and I'll get past the bad bit, and it flows again. Other times the blank stays blank, and a good thing too.

LSC: And then there are the several stages of editing, combined with the hair-pulling and head-desk-banging.

LMB: Structural editing almost all takes place at the outline stage, for me, as I shove the scene sequences around and at last into place. Very seldom do I add or delete whole scenes after the first draft. When I complete a day's work I usually print it out and take the pages away to read in the new format (in a different room and chair, which my body desperately needs by that point), and mark it up with line-edit and copy-edit stuff—fixing syntax, improving word choice, adding some forgotten bit or cutting something excess that impedes the flow. At the end of the chapter, it goes out (by e-mail, now) to my inner circle of test readers; those who are syntax-and-grammar sensitive and/or rhythm-and-word-choice sensitive are pearls beyond price. They help me identify a lot of problem spots on the sentence level.

When I agree with their critiques, I enter changes and print out the chapter that goes into the accumulating three-ring binder. I look back over this material fairly frequently as I continue to write, and mark up any problems that catch my eye. At the end of the book comes the vast appalling task of going back over the whole thing, and making all necessary changes on all levels. I enter all these, print it out again, read it again, make any other changes that seem required (by this time I'm cross-eyed and thoroughly sick of it all), and produce the first submission draft, which goes to the editor. She returns her comments, I make what responses I'm going to, and back it goes to the publisher. After that there will be the copy edit to read and approve or fix, and, finally, the galleys.

LSC: After all these years, does it come any easier?

LMB: Well, I'm more skilled at the mechanics of everything. I'm not intimidated or bewildered by the business anymore. There are things I haven't tried yet, so I haven't developed the chops. I've never written anything in omniscient viewpoint. I've never written anything in first person, so those are challenges yet to be met. A whole novel is this very complex pattern which would really have been too vast for my feeble logical mind to have figured out in advance, but something in my back-brain assembles it. I've learned to trust this aspect of myself as a writer.

This doesn't mean I don't whine about my book in progress. In fact, I whine my way from beginning to end. First I whine that I can't get any good ideas, then after an initial rush I whine my way through the whole middle, which can run from Chapter 2 to Chapter 22 of a twenty-three-chapter book. And then my whining rises to a crescendo during revisions, which I hate above all other parts of the process. And when it's all over, I dither about how people will like it. The outside observer mustn't mistake normal creative whining for dislike of the work. To test this, see what happens if you try to take the book away from its author while she's whining about it. Trying to take a baby bear from its mama would be much less dangerous.

LSC: The shelves in your home are lined by copies of your books translated into—how many languages is it now?

LMB: Let's see if I can come up with the whole list: Spanish, French, German, Dutch, Italian, Greek, Croatian, Serbian, Czech, Bulgarian, Hungarian, Polish, Russian, Lithuanian, Hebrew, Japanese, Korean, Finnish, Chinese traditional-characters, Chinese simplified-characters, and I'm still missing a couple somewhere. British is a foreign sale but not—quite—a foreign language.

Some of these are very tiny markets, mind. Our old fanzine had a bigger print run than some of them.

LSC: Have you any explanation for your universal appeal?

LMB: Miles does seem to survive translation well, much as he survives everything else thrown at him. A lot of other SF authors are also translated into other languages, though, so I'm just a part of the picture. I have noted with bemusement that some countries and cultures seem to be "science-fiction-friendly," and others less so. The most avid overseas markets for SF and fantasy at present seem to be Japan and Russia, then Australia and New Zealand, Europe and Eastern Europe, and a very little in South America. There does not appear to be as much SF activity in the rest of Southeast Asia (although I once received e-mail from a fan from Vietnam, he read in the original English), India, Africa apart from South Africa, or the Islamic countries, but that may be changing.

Part of the problem, I think, is that SF has been so America-centic and Britain-centric (with a nod to Jules Verne, here). If people look at a type of literature and don't see anyone like themselves represented in it, they tend to put it back on the shelf, thinking it isn't addressed to them. This has posed a problem for SF in our own country in the past with respect to women readers and black readers, whose selves and concerns seemed excluded from earlier works in the genre. In all the places where SF is popular, the cultures and countries in question seem to have taken up the genre and made it theirs, with the local writers assimilating the foreign model, but then taking off with it in their own directions with their own voices.

LSC: Your work has been packaged as military SF. I don't recall this ever being your intention, though.

**LMB:** At the time I wrote my first books, I don't think the sub-genre had split out yet; I certainly was not aware of it as a thing separate from adventure tales in general. Properly speaking, milSF as a label should be applied to works whose central concern is an exploration of the military in action, doing its job (well or badly, depending). My Miles-centric books, really, are explorations of the psychology of a fellow from a deeply conservative culture who starts out as an army-mad youngster, and grows out of it (well, partially), and along the way encounters other people who occasionally have to deal with the military as a human cultural artifact in the course of a larger story. The military adventures are sometimes occasions for my tales, but they are seldom the point of my tales, which are more usually about what's going on inside people's heads, and in their wider lives. "What are these people thinking?," again.

**LSC:** The Vorkosigan series covers a lot of genres, and was doing so before genre-blending became marketable.

**LMB:** I don't stick to one mode, which confuses people who think series books should be cut to standard shapes like cookies. Genre conventions—which I see as another term for reader expectations—are fun. There're so many things you can do with them—twist them, invert or subvert them, bounce things off them, ignore them, or even play them straight. Like the form of a sonnet, genre forms don't really constrain content, emotion, or meaning—you can write a sonnet about anything from love and death to HO-gauge model railroading, although I'm not sure anyone has done the latter, yet. Surprise, for example, is a literary effect that almost depends on the readers having expectations shaped by prior reads.

My personal definition of a genre is, "Any group of works in close conversation with each other." As readers, we tend to encounter only the polished result of that uproar, as the book alone appears in our hand and the context drops away. Classics are particularly at risk of seeming to have been hung in air, having escaped the death of their original surround. But the reading context matters, since the ground changes the figure.

I've long imagined the sort of SF critics who claim "We want to see writers stretch the boundaries of the genre!" taking one look at my work and crying, "No, but not like that!" (I suspect they really want to see SF link upward to genres of higher status, like mainstream, and not, say, sideways to mystery, or worse, downward to romance.) Within the Vorkosigan series, I've played with romance, coming-of-age, mystery, military fiction, Golden Age engineering, thriller, and satire, for starters—SF is a very malleable genre, rather like whichever blood type is the universal receiver (AB, if I remember correctly), able to accept transfusions from all sources. How many genres can I fit in one series? Well, let's see...

LSC: Ah yes, romance. Girl stuff. When we were kids we'd knit little sweaters for our Barbie dolls and also build spaceships for them to pilot. I don't think many little boys knitted sweaters for their G.I. Joe action figures.

LMB: Poor deprived tykes, missing out on all that small muscle development and pattern-recognition practice. . . . I have noticed, over time, the allergy of many SF readers—male and female, mark you well—to romance; not just lack of interest, an "I don't care for that" response, the way I feel about horror as a genre, but genuine, almost hysterical hostility, which I shorthand as, "Girl germs! Girl germs! Run away!" In my view, nobody gets that heated up over a mere book. They get that heated up because, on some level, their identity or status seems threatened. Why should a reading choice do that?

And then there's the parallel reaction to SF by many romance and mainstream readers. "Ick!" would probably be the politest shorthand. Whatever underlying identity thing is going on, it runs both ways. Why do these women (and men) reject (in an almost medical-organ-transplant sense) SF?

Status-based arguments about ejecting the abject would seem to fall down, here—except that these women don't see SF readers and writers as having status. They see us as geeky dweebs stuck in permanent adolescence. At a book fair once, I talked to one such woman about this perception thing—to her, it was as though SF were some sort of disease vector for social dweebishness, and if you read that stuff, you'd turn into one of them, spontaneously sprouting rubber Spock ears and Nintendo thumbs through some sort of Lamarckian devolution. This is a war with two sides. And SF doesn't actually have any manifest destiny to win it. Indeed, in many—most—cases, in an SF story, the woman's traditional agenda is either totally ignored, or clearly loses, which may be something else that's putting off all those women readers.

LSC: So why is there a literary gender/genre war? What does this systematic put-down of the romance genre really mean?

LMB: You'd think males would line up to applaud a genre that works so hard to interest women in men—after all, wouldn't the relentless celebration of heterosexual relationships seem to increase their chances of getting laid? And yet, it is not so. . . .

In my view, the key to the romance/women's fiction genre is, the woman's agenda wins. Her situation, her personal responsibilities, her life, her needs, and above all her emotions, are made central to the reader's attention. (And if there is anything in the world more thoroughly diminutized and dismissed than women's emotions, I can't think of it right now.) In the end, she gets what she wants, or needs—a committed guy who will stick around to help raise children. In short, in the course of the plot the hero, however much a rake he is initially presented, is transformed into a guy who will do the chores, personally or by the proxy of servants. No wonder adolescent males—and some females, too—of all ages run screaming. . . .

To heck with sex, women, squishy stuff, and liquidity. The real phobia at the bottom of all this gender/genre allergy is to chores, I'm absolutely convinced.

LSC: It's another status thing. Whoever cleans up is the abject. Your mother used to collect your *Analog* from the mailbox and hide it until you'd cleaned your room.

LMB: This whole dialectic presents particular problems for women, and especially for women SF writers. Women in our culture are given the duty and responsibility (though not the power, of course) of "molding" our kids; we're drafted willy-nilly into the Cultural Gestapo, and woe betide us if our kids "don't turn out right." How can we become mothers, yet not become *our* mothers? We are SF writers in the first place only because, like our brothers, we resisted being assigned many of the chores of womanhood, handed out from our culture via, usually, our moms. Instead we went off and read disapproved books. And then, by damn, we even started writing them. (I can still hear my mother's voice, echoing from my own adolescence—"If you don't stop reading those silly science fiction books and get out of bed, you'll never get anywhere!" Now I sit in bed writing silly science fiction books, and my career has given me the world. Ha!) So, which side shall I be on? Must I choose, and lose half my possibilities thereby whichever choice I make?

LSC: But since you write "guy stuff," too, you're respected. By the earnest young (male) fan, for example, who told you that you "write like a man."

LMB: To which I should have replied (but didn't, because I don't think fast on my feet—that's why I'm a writer, the pencil waits) "Oh, really? Which one?"
  I'm still trying to work out whether or not it came to a compliment. In all, since I write most of my adventure books from deep inside the point of view of a male character, Miles Vorkosigan, I've decided

it's all right; if I'm mimicking a male worldview well enough that even the opposition can't tell for sure, I'm accomplishing my heart's goal of writing true character. The comment worried me for a long time, though. A trip through the essays of Ursula Le Guin also shook my self-confidence. Was I doing something wrong? But then I wrote *Barrayar*, returning at last to the full range of a female character's point of view, and I haven't been troubled by such comments since.

LSC: What does it mean to "write like a woman"?

LMB: Not one damned identifiable thing, as far as I can tell. As any competent statistician can testify, from a general statement about any group of people (such as a gender), nothing reliable can be predicted about the next individual to walk through the door.

I once ran a selection of my work through a supposed "gender-identifier" algorithm-machine found on the Net. All of the scenes written from the point of view of female characters came out as "written by a woman." All the scenes written from the point of view of male characters came out as "written by a man." I concluded that I wrote like a writer.

I see plenty enough female SF writers not to feel unusual. When I start naming them, it adds up pretty quickly—Willis, Cherryh, Asaro, Moon, McCaffrey, Turzillo, Czerneda, Zettel, Kagan, Kress, Le Guin for heaven's sakes, and dozens more. I don't know why journalists and critics and commentators keep mentally erasing us; perhaps we mess up their pretty theory. I'm less sure about foreign markets, but in the American midlist, SF seems a pretty level playing field between men and women writers. There are lots of women editors in the genre, as well.

But even in fantasy, the very top best-sellers do seem to be disproportionately male. I've heard it theorized that it's because more women will buy and read books by male writers with male protagonists, but fewer men will buy and read books by women writers with female protagonists. Women writers with male protagonists seem to get a partial free pass.

I get to meet my own fan-base at conventions and book signings and on-line. They seem to be pretty evenly divided between men and women, and with ages ranging all over the map, from eleven to eighty and sometimes up, with a diverse array of views on practically everything. A lot of folks report reading my books in families, passing them between siblings and generations both. They're a flatteringly bright bunch, on the whole. This seems to suggest my books don't exclude readers by gender.

LSC: This same question crops up among mystery readers—can a woman write believably from a man's viewpoint? The reverse seems to be less of an issue.

LMB: Ditto for romance. The reverse is often an issue in SF, though. I think the real answer is, "Some writers can, some can't." Men and women aren't that different from each other, in most areas of life. I think the proper question is, how on earth do writers avoid insight into the opposite gender? Guys are all around us, all the time. We live with them—I had a father, grandfathers, brothers, a husband, a son, male colleagues, bosses, fellow students—we read books written by and about them ... Nowadays, we read on-line posts by them, in perhaps more startling variety than one's immediate family might offer, or so I would hope. Swapped around, the same is true for male observers. I think some people must screen out this data, as if knowing, or at least, admitting to knowing, was somehow a violation of their own gender identity. I was on a convention panel once with a male writer who was complaining—actually, covertly bragging—that he couldn't write female characters very well, the not-so-hidden subtext being that he was so ineluctably masculine, the terrible effort at getting his mind around this alien female viewpoint was just beyond him. (As though it were a subject impossible to research!) I didn't think he was ineluctably masculine. I just thought he was a lazy writer.

LSC: And you're a good writer. At least you've won lots of awards—which doesn't, however, mean the same thing.

LMB: Reading is an active and elusive experience. Every reader, reading exactly the same text, will have a slightly different reading experience depending on what s/he projects into the words s/he sees, what strings of meaning and association those words call up in his/her (always) private mind. One can never, therefore, talk about the quality of a book separately from the quality of the mind that is creating it by reading it, in the only place books live, in the secret mind. The real reason discussions of the quality of literature get emotionally hot very rapidly is that they inescapably entail a covert judgment being passed on the private and invisible mind of another human being. You can get into trouble by mistaking *your* reading experience for *the* reading experience, as though anyone who ran their eyes over the same words brought the same mind to it.

I'm not one of those control-freak writers who feel that everybody has to read the book precisely as I intended. I know perfectly well they're going to take this text and turn it into something in their heads that is at most fifty percent my contribution. When I do get feedback, it's kind of interesting to see the different things they'll do with it. They startle me sometimes.

Broadly, there seem to be to be two kinds of great books, and a lot of linguistic confusion engendered because people keep trying to conflate the two categories: books which are great because they are greatly loved, by many readers over time or perhaps only by a few, but no less passionately for that; and books that are historically important because they change the way other books are written. Not infrequently, a book may be both (*Don Quixote*, anyone?), but students of literature tend to concentrate on the second sort, and I think they are right to do so.

In general, it takes a deal of time to see if a book or writer will have the latter sort of impact. And sometimes books that pass the test with flying colors, such as the works of Arthur Conan Doyle or Georgette Heyer, still get excluded from consideration, but in that case one suspects that the excluders are merely, shall we say politely, inadequately informed, and may be disregarded.

Therefore, due to the inherently subjective nature of reading, awards are not won by the writer, as in a race—they are given, as gifts, by other people to the writer. To attempt to control something one cannot, in fact, ever control—the actions of others—is a short route to madness. Writers can control what they write. Full stop. Everything that happens after is some class of unintended consequence or chaotic emergent property.

That said, the validation of winning awards is enormously gratifying. Winning one's first major award does a lot to make a new writer more visible (wasted if one does not then produce a follow-up book in short order), and winning the second helps prove that the first wasn't a fluke. After that it becomes a matter of diminishing returns, in terms of the practical consequences or, as it were, economic utility of the things. These are not as magnificent as the average fan imagines; an award is good for generating a few thousand more domestic paperback sales and for garnering foreign sales if one isn't getting such already; but the foreign SF markets are tiny. (Which they make up partly in numbers, if you can collect the whole set.) Over time, awards help but do not guarantee works to stay in print or get reprinted.

I discovered when I won my first Nebula back in the late Eighties that while I might put blank pages under that classy paperweight at night, there would be no words magically appearing on them in the morning. Writing the next book is the same slog, only now with heightened expectations. "Each one better than all the others" seems to be the demand.

LSC: Was there any one award which meant more to you than any other?

LMB: Probably the most important was the first, the Nebula for *Falling Free*, which made folks sit up and take notice. I was very pleased when *Barrayar* won its Hugo, because I didn't think it could win back-to-back with *The Vor Game* like that, and it was the book closer to my heart. The Hugo for *Paladin of Souls* was great, first, because I am hugely fond of its heroine Ista, and second because it finally stopped people driving me crazy by saying brightly, "Just one more and you'll match Heinlein!" It's not a race, drat it.

I have no idea why some of my books draw awards and other don't, except that the ones I spent the least time worrying about other people's response to—that I wrote for myself—seem to do the best of all.

LSC: Why are some books closer to your heart?

LMB: Whenever a writer who has produced more than one volume is asked to name their favorite, it is almost the routine to respond with some mumble about choosing among your books being like choosing among one's children, each has its strengths and weaknesses, you really can't say. This is actually a lie. Not all books are created equal, and for the special ones, you begin to know it sometimes even before the work is finished, but always by the time you slam that last line home and shriek, "Done! Done!," and fall head-down across your keyboard like the runner from Marathon.

Some books reach higher, dig deeper, take more terrifying chances. And you know it, when you've done it; you can't do something like that and not know it. You then spend the next two years sweating through the publication process, those first reviews, the first sales figures, waiting and hoping that you haven't deluded yourself—because you most certainly can delude yourself—waiting for that validation and biting your tongue against any words you might be compelled to eat later.

LSC: Speaking of validation, on the "photos" section of the Dendarii site, you are captured with your amazing necklace of award tie tacks. You mention looking at them in the box and thinking "thirteen tie tacks and no neckties. Deconstruct the subtext of this one, grrls."

LMB: Mike Resnick has a wonderful sort of "South American Colonel" look when valiantly wearing all his rocket pins at Worldcons, but that's just not in my style. I tried sticking them all on my name badge, which worked for a while, but I was running out of room. So I took my box of award nomination pins to Elise Matthesen, a Twin Cities crafter of art jewelry and a good reader, who understands both her art and my audience, with some vague notion of a charm bracelet or necklace. But she had much better ideas.

The goofy glory of the final necklace design is all Elise's doing, partly driven by technical considerations such as not attempting to cut up the pin backs, risking breakage. I'd like to think I do the same thing to genre tropes in my writing, but that's not for me to judge.

LSC: It's for your fans to judge. Is there a difference between your fans, that is, the people who enjoy your work, and Fans with a capital F?

LMB: Not really; fandom fans are a subset of the broader readership, in my experience. I first found fandom, or it found me, in the fall of 1967, just after I'd graduated from high school and was working in the book department of a downtown department store. I met a fellow from the local SF fan club, who invited me to a meeting. (The guys vastly outnumbered the girls, back then.)

I went to a few local conventions, and attended two Worldcons—my first was BayCon in '60-hum-something, '68 or '69. So when I returned to the convention scene in the mid-Eighties as a wanna-be pro, it was a fairly socially comfortable milieu for me. I understand some writers who first encounter fandom after they are published are a little baffled how to go on there, as it doesn't really fit expected commercial, literary, or academic models of writer-reader relationships, though it partakes of all of them. But most writers seem to learn pretty quickly. Note, fandom is not a unified body so much as an alliance of varied special interests; you have to locate your own kindred spirits in the array.

I have the fondest memories of sitting around the hotel bar in St. Petersburg, Russia, when I went to an SF conference there, discussing our mutual favorite old SF novelists with the full-blooded Tartar computer programmer from Kazakhstan. This stuff gets around.

LSC: Which brings us to the subject of fan fiction, and through that, to the Internet.

LMB: What the Internet has done to fan fiction has been fascinating. Fan fiction has completely exploded. What has stunned me and blown all my prior theories of fan fiction out of the water was the number and variety of things that have fanfic written about them. I would never in my wildest dreams have expected there to be fifty fan fictions based on *1984* on one site, and even *Flatland* had some. Say what? Pat Wrede has a theory that the Arthurian Cycle was actually medieval fan fiction, and the more she points out parallels the more you realize she's right! People took their favorite characters and wrote expanded stories about them. They didn't have the Internet, but they did their best.

The Internet has made the idea of fan fiction accessible to a whole bunch of people who have never heard of fandom, run across the mimeographed magazines, or otherwise discovered the genre. So you had things like 35,000 *Lord of the Rings* stories, and over 125,000 *Harry Potter* stories on that same site where I found the ones based on *1984*. (More by now, no doubt.) Many of them are dire, but even the bad ones have this weird fascination at first. And once in a great while, there's a brilliant one that could only be fanfic, as part of its brilliance comes from a sort of embedded commentary on the original text.

During the year leading up to and away from my mother's death—she passed away in 2003 at the age of 91—I discovered and read a huge amount of on-line fanfic (not on my work, I should add). Besides the sheer novelty and fascination of seeing what a form I'd first discovered thirty-five years ago was now mutating into, it was about the only thing I could stand to read—it felt like fiction for which I was in no way responsible, I suppose, at a time when my real-life responsibilities had no possible happy outcome, but still had to be met and endured. Anyway, reading in slices down and across fandoms, with all the other variables held constant, I could actually see the way each reader-writer's head was processing the primary text differently, according to their measure. And having watched the process of how different psychological concerns hijack the texts in the petri dishes of fanfic has also altered my awareness of how the exact same processes work, better disguised, in profic.

LSC: What do you think of fan fiction based on your own work?

LMB: I find it very flattering, like fan mail but in different media. It tells me my work touched someone on a very deep level, for it to evoke that kind of energy in return. It's art in response to art: some folks sew costumes, some write or sing songs, some draw or paint pictures. Some write fanfic.

For a while there was a theory that if you did not defend your copyright from these things you would lose it, but I think reality has changed so much that theory is never coming back. You can't stuff the genie back in the bottle. That's a relief, because I understand what kind of game those people are playing. Writers who don't like fanfic may not understand the psychology of reading for pleasure, or may fear their own work could be distorted in readers' heads by the adulteration, which is I think true but inescapable; all original texts are altered in the first place by the mere act of different minds reading them. I think there's more power to be had by figuring out the flow and going with it. It's a huge, fascinating new phenomenon and I think it's going to go some interesting places. Nevertheless, I daren't read fic on my own work, because I get idea and style leaks—I pick up voice like lint—and I'm afraid of losing track of where an idea might have come from.

LSC: What has the Internet done for you personally?

LMB: It has given me a window on the world, and is in process of eating my life, or at any rate, most of the waking time in it. I'm only just beginning to learn to use its resources. Usenet chat groups have been a laboratory of human behavior and blogs are a kind of networking out, tentacles reaching into all corners of society, so people who have otherwise been completely isolated are finding each other. My fan e-mail has been fabulous, but makes up for being easier to answer than snail mail by being more copious. I love being in easy e-mail touch with my agent, my editors, my friends and my children.

The main thing the Internet has done for my writing, I'm afraid, is slow it down. And it's severely cut into my reading time, unless you count reading off the screen.

LSC: Conversely, what have you done for the Internet?

LMB: I have a Website, The Bujold Nexus at www. dendarii.com, entirely fan run, which has proved to be a wonderful resource for all my PR needs. It came as manna from e-heaven. I was guest writer at a science fiction convention in London in 1995 and a British fan named Michael Bernardi came up to me and asked, "Do you have a Website?" to which I replied, "What's a Website?" At the time I didn't even have a modem. So computer-professional Mike, bless him, put one together for me, and has filled it with wonderful things and all sorts of useful links. So now when reporters or anyone else wants to know, "Who is this Lois/Louis/Louise...um, how do you pronounce that last name?" without having to read a pile o' books, I can just direct them to The Bujold Nexus.

LSC: And there's the on-line publishing of your most recent novels' first chapters at the Baen Website.

LMB: I adore the advent of on-line sample chapters, not least because they allow my books to sell on the basis of their words instead of their packaging. "The first sample is free...." It allows people to browse on-line and make an informed buying choice. Every bit of increased exposure helps. People can't choose what they don't know about.

There are the e-books available from Fictionwise, too. As a new market, e-sales don't have to beat their way through the system of middlemen to get shelf space, and they're available to fans all over the world. That's cool. Most fascinating to me have been the recent sales of my audiobooks as MP3s over the Net—ninety percent or more of my current Blackstone audiobook sales are as downloads through its partner Audible.com.

LSC: For most of your career, "the work" meant the Vorkosigan novels. And yet recently you've moved on. Or at least away.

LMB: One of the reasons I had for leaving the Vorkosigan universe for the Chalion books—or at least leaving Miles, who is rather agnostic when he isn't in a foxhole—was that I wanted to do a fairly serious exploration of grown-up religion in a fantasy context. Miles's universe doubtless includes all the beliefs of ours plus a lot of new ones invented since. People are like that. Nonetheless, when I wanted to explore religious themes more directly, I needed a new universe and new characters.

I have been bemused by a certain kind of fantasy that treats religion and magic in a mechanical fashion—"Throw another virgin on the altar, boys, the power level in the thaumaturgistat is getting low!" People running about shooting lightning bolts from their fingers as though they were mystical Uzis, that sort of thing.

A lot of the ways genre fantasy treats religion seemed to me to be both superficial and unsympathetic. I wanted to look at both the positive ways religions function as social institutions, ways for people to organize themselves to get the everyday work of a civilized society done, and at serious mysticism. The real questions real religions grapple with don't have easy answers. A well-built fantasy world's religion ought, I thought, to reflect that complex reality.

The more recent *Sharing Knife* books, on which I've spent the past three years at this writing, have more to do with exploring genre-blending and series structures, being my first really long, closely connected, epic-sized tale—a tetralogy, it seems. They are also about bringing it all home, on more than one level.

LSC: Have you found any difficulties in switching genres?

LMB: A lot of my role models for writing were ambi-dextrous between fantasy and SF—Poul Anderson, C. J. Cherryh, L. Sprague de Camp, Roger Zelazny, the list goes on and on. I've always considered it normal to write both. The actual mechanics of putting a narrative together—scene selection, characterization, pacing, viewpoint, transitions, plotting, and so on—are the same for both. The two genres have slightly different lists of things to which they pay close attention. Fantasy tends, on the whole, to be more language and style conscious, and reaches, at its most intense, for some sort of experience of the numinous. SF rewards the exploration of ideas, and reaches for a kind of intellectual oh-wow oh-cool moment when the reader's understanding of the world seems to increase, and which may be the SFnal equivalent of the numinous.

Editor Teresa Nielsen Hayden had this little dissertation about writers as otters. You can't train an otter, she says, because when you reward it, instead of saying "Let's do that again!" it says "Oh, let's do something else that's even cooler!" This is the writer's approach. They want to surprise you, and if too many people have the same idea it begins to seem not so surprising anymore. "It does not appeal to my Inner Otter!" Drives editors nuts, because they're trying to train their writers. They want something within the range of marketability.

LSC: You have to go through the editors, the publishers, and the marketers to reach the reader. But then, you've done so.

LMB: I've always tried to write the kind of book I most loved to read: character-centered adventure. My own literary favorites include, among many others, Dorothy Sayers, Arthur Conan Doyle, Alexandre Dumas, and of course C. S. Forester. All of these writers created not works of art, but, on some level, works of life. Theirs are creations who climb up off the page into the readers' minds and live there long after the book is shut. Readers return to such books again and again, not to find out what happened—for a single reading would suffice for any book if plot and idea were all—but because those characters have become their friends, and there is no limit to the number of times you want to be with your friends again.

I have been, therefore, vastly pleased with the number of readers who have written to tell me that my stories have stood their friend in time of need: the mother of a handicapped child; a blind man who lived in rural Kentucky, and "read" the books on audio tape; a woman who reread them all over a weekend and went back to solve a problem at work that had seemed intractable; a soldier serving in a difficult post in the Middle East; a young woman who took them with her to reread during the week of aftershocks of the California earthquake, when she was camping in her backyard, unable to return to her damaged house; a woman fighting depression and an array of medical problems, who felt well enough after a reread to get up and continue coping with her life.

One reader wrote to let me know that my books had informed his thinking, when he grappled with the task of composing a statement for his national church council on what its position was to be viz cloning and other looming biotechnologies.

And then the writer gets one of those letters, as I

suspect most writers do—paraphrased from memory—
"Dear Ms. Bujold, I want to thank you for the very
great joy your work gave my husband during the last
six months of his life..."

Joy to the dying? Where does that fall on any
intellectual grid of "literary merit"?

And then you realize that we're all dying, here.
And so.

I admit, though, my all-time favorite fan letter was
from a woman in Canada. She wrote to tell me she
had been reading *Shards of Honor*, and, not wanting
to put it down, took the book along to read while
standing in line at the bank. She is not, she added,
normally very scatterbrained or oblivious, but she does
like to focus on what she reads. Eventually, she got
to the teller to do the necessary banking. The teller
said she could not give her change, as the robber had
taken all her money.

"What robber?" my reader asked.

"The one who just held us up at gunpoint," the
teller explained. It turned out that while she had been
engrossed in reading, a masked gunman had come
in, robbed the bank, and made his escape, and she
never noticed a thing.

My reader wrote me, "All I can say is, it must
have been a very quiet robbery. The security guard
at the door asked if I could describe the thief for the
police. Embarrassed, I said no, I didn't think I could."

LSC: This story was told to me at a mystery
convention—I was pleased to discover that it wasn't
the equivalent of an urban legend, but quite true.
Talk about escaping into a book!

LMB: Years ago I read an interview with a forensic pathologist who said he had never gone into a bad crime scene, where he had to clean the blood off the walls and whatnot, in any place where there were a lot of books. It occurs to me that because books give us escape even though we may be physically trapped wherever we are, they give us a "time out" space. People who don't have this have to stay in the pressure cooker as the pressure goes higher and higher, until they finally explode into violence expressed either externally or internally in stress illnesses. Books give readers a place to go. This is good for your health and potentially good for the health of the people around you as well. In that sense, I think reading can be a form of self-medication.

Both historical fantasy and futuristic science fiction have the appeal of being very far away from here, that escapist element. Of course the more you read about history, the less you want to go live there, but it still has that romanticism—not in the sense of sexual romance but in the sense of exotic places. "Escapist" is one of those terms that get used with a sneer, but I'm getting to be more and more of the opinion that it has a value in its own right that isn't being properly appreciated.

That said, if there is any meaning at all in any work of fiction that can be transposed back to real daily life, it lies in the characters' lives and moral dilemmas. "All great deeds have been accomplished out of imperfection," as one of my characters remarks. The human condition is a mess and always has been, and visions of perfecting it are a snare and a delusion, but we can all grab for great moments—for one floating instant, to do better than we think we can. Heroes are just people who are lucky or determined enough to match the moment—and at least once, to get it right when it matters.

LSC: So now, after this long strange (and one hopes, ongoing) journey, that's what it's all about?

LMB: If writers have a duty, it is to think as clearly as we can; to reexamine all our assumptions repeatedly on both micro and macro scales. Happily, this also will yield us better fiction. A novel is a slice out of the writer's worldview. The slice in turn, if it is coherent, generates as an emergent property a comment on living as human beings, which is the book's theme. We experience theme, even if we cannot articulate it openly, as an exhilarating sense of meaning to the book. The book has succeeded in creating meaning inside the head of another person. And in my worldview, that's what art is for.

LSC: Thank you. For every word.

# Publishing, Writing, and Authoring: Three Different Things

## Lois McMaster Bujold

You may imagine that a bunch of writers discuss High Art when they get together, but I'm sorry to say they more usually bitch about the publishing business. (The less obvious reason for this is that no writer can talk about his/her own work in front of another writer with the emotional intensity they really feel; it just doesn't work, socially.)

The business as it is presently constituted consists of three parts: publisher, distribution system, and bookstores, followed at a remove by readers. A publisher's actual main customers are therefore not the readers, but the book chains and the big distributors who in turn supply small bookstores and libraries. Present conditions have the publishers trying to push ten gallons of books into a five-gallon pipeline (the distribution system) into a three-gallon bucket (the bookstores). Something has to give, and it does.

One way to get More Stuff through is to speed it up, which is why books whip on and off the shelves with such velocity (category romance novels are given, count 'em, thirty *days* on the market before being replaced by the next batch). What this means is, the speed of book turnover has grown to be faster than the speed of word of mouth, a slowish process formerly vital to a new book or author. All but the very first readers to buy a book thus have no way to send economic feedback messages back through the system saying, "More, please." The late reader's vote is not counted; the reader who borrows instead of buying casts no vote at all.

The selling of any book traditionally falls into two periods. The first phase takes place months before the book is published, out of sight of any reader, when the publishers send their sales people out to take orders from their real customers, the aforementioned middlemen. I was bewildered when I first heard of a large ad budget being spent on a book when I never saw sign of an ad in any newspaper or even bookstore. Turns out that money was being spent advertising to distributors of various ilks. Publishers have turned, in something like despair, to attempts to *buy* room for their books in that narrow pipeline; hence such things as paid placement at the front of a bookstore, front page treatment in book chain newsletters, various complex incentives for high volume, etc. (I won't even get into the horrors of the book returns system.) The sales force works like mad to pitch the *packaging* of their books to a harried crew of buyers who, given the volume of books to pass through their hands, cannot possibly read the actual texts.

Only after those orders are collected is the size of the print run chosen. So to a great degree, the level of success any book can obtain is set before anyone reads it. If orders are low, the book will never have a chance to find readers through store placement, or ever get near any best-seller list. It's like a glass ceiling; breaking through it seems almost impossible. If a book—or rather, its packaging and the sales numbers of previous books by that author—fails to pass muster at the stuffing-in end of the pipeline, no reader (or very few) will ever learn of its existence in order to ask for it. Reader input is limited to an expensive and wasteful negative—readers can (and do) reject books they do see, but they have no way of asking for books they don't see.

Such was the hair-tearing state of the business up to the middle of the Nineties. Then along came the Internet. And publishers' Websites such as Baen's Bar. And Amazon.com, with shelves that never get too full to hold More Stuff. And, most critically—word of mouth got hyperdrive through chat groups and e-mail. Word of mouth got faster, even, than the system's book-removal rhythm.

And suddenly, publishers had an economical way of getting the word out to the excluded people in this process, the actual book readers, of their books' existences—totally jumping over the unfortunate book-blocking nature of the distribution system. Instead of trying to push books through the pipeline, this intelligence network potentially allowed a thousand or ten thousand actual readers to line up on the other end and *pull* the books through—the books they wanted, not the ones some desperately overworked distribution exec imagined would sell. It was briefly very exciting and hopeful—until the Internet filled up. Still, those new lines of communication are solidly established now.

It is at this point still unclear to me what the Internet will do in the long run to publishing. It's certainly a boom time for readers: more books are simultaneously available in more formats, more readily accessible, than ever before in history. MP3 download-ing of audiobooks over the Internet is a new market that looks very promising. So far, e-books seem to be falling into a supplemental niche just like audio books. Tree books are mortgage money; e-books are (still) pizza money, although as the generation comes up for whom reading off a screen is the default norm, and as reading devices improve, I expect to see more e-books sold, or at least downloaded. But I'm not sure how much this will help the economics of individual living writers, as given the infinite shelf space in such e-book stores as www.fictionwise.com (who are adding upward of a couple of *hundred* new titles a *week*), writers finds their books competing for reader attention not just with one season's releases, but with a century's worth of offerings. The glut has been shifted from the publishers' laps to those of the readers. Time in which to read is still only issued 24/7, a hard limit. You do the math.

That said, people still want to write, for reasons that have little to do with publishing economics. I have concluded by experiment that teaching writing is not my strength—teaching is a different, complex, and underrated skill—but I get asked how-to questions anyway. My writing methods have a lot of intuitive elements that I can't even analyze, let alone articulate and transfer, so all my tips tend to cluster around problems I've had to solve for myself, which may or may not be the same problems a learner is having. I suspect one could trace most writers' own problem spots just by the advice they give. With that warning, here's a bag of things I've learned or observed along the way.

If you want writing time in your day, you have to take it—no one will give it to you. Often, you can only take it from your own alternate activities; writers' lives tend to get rather stripped-down for that reason. Nowadays, I have more control over my own time, and the limiting factor isn't writing time per se, but the speed with which I generate and refine my ideas. When I was most pressed for time, in my younger days, having a separate place to go work, out of the house—in my case the library, because it was free and quiet—helped focus my energies. Two of my writer friends, back when they both had day jobs, used to have regular lunch dates where they would meet in a coffee shop and write like mad for the first forty-five minutes, eat in fifteen, and go back to work. One, I know, still works in short bursts, just as I still use my outlining system that was originally designed to make my actual people-free first-draft writing time intensively productive, because it was so limited.

Other than a limitless imagination, a fiction writer should possess self-discipline. Writing is great fun, but it's not all fun; if you can't steel yourself to plow through the un-fun parts, you'll never finish anything worth the writing. This quality includes both drive, and relentless self-correction—a continuous search for how to Do It Better, from whatever sources one can find.

We pause now for my "Writer's Block—Your Friend" spiel. There's something in my back-brain which puts on the brakes when I try to do the wrong thing in my book, put in something that the book isn't supposed to be, take a wrong turn. I just go blank. The words won't be forced. It takes a while to sort out if this is what's going on, or if it's just normal distractibility, but when I do get it correctly identified, the only thing to do is go back and revisualize the story itself. Noodling around on the sentence-revision level isn't the cure.

I've come to think theme is an emergent property of a book, and so it really isn't right to talk about a book's theme before the text is complete. But I think what's happening with this kind of block is that the wrong thing I was trying to do wouldn't have fit that complex emergent meaning that doesn't exist yet, but is trying to become. This sense of story, which I often can't even see or name at that point, is the invisible template against which I ultimately test each choice—of action, of viewpoint, whatever. When it finally fits, it all clicks in and I'm off and running again. This process is far more visceral than it is analytical.

Remember that scene from the movie *Roger Rabbit*, where Roger whips his hand out of the handcuff in which it has been stuck, and the human asks in outrage, "Could you always do that?" and Roger replies, "No! Only when it was funny!" It might seem, in something as apparently generic as an action-adventure novel, that almost any action would do. It doesn't. Only when it fits the theme. Then it's the right one. Then it's unstoppable.

And then there are the writer's blocks that come

from simply not knowing what happens next. Some days the ideas flow, some days they have to be laboriously pieced together. Sometimes the attempt at piecing-together jostles the real answer loose. I attack both from the logic-side, scribbling outline after outline, and the long-walk relaxed-visualization-side, and while neither alone is enough, the combination synergizes. Which is just a fancy way of saying, "I think about it a lot, day and night."

In making up a new world, a writer has to be conscious of where language comes from, especially if trying to transport the reader into a different time and place than their everyday normal twenty-first century. (Pardon me while I walk around and admire that phrase. For most of my life, "the twenty-first century" was shorthand for "the future"; now I'm living in it. Time travel the hard way . . . shouldn't we spare a few more moments for marveling?) A writer needs to be a little bit conscious of the sources of words, too. I found in writing books in the *Chalion* and *Sharing Knife* series particularly, where the setting is, while not historical, at any rate preindustrial, I had to be constantly watching my vocabulary for anachronisms. I couldn't refer to objects that wouldn't have been invented in those worlds; all my metaphors had to be checked to make sure that they would work in this new context. I puzzled a bit over borderline words like "sanguine" and "choleric," which have their roots in an obsolete theory of physiology that never existed in Chalion, but have since acquired general meanings; I decided to leave them in lest I be stripped of vocabulary altogether.

The inverse of screening wrong words out is putting right ones in. Neologisms in fantasy and science fiction present an ongoing challenge. A certain number of new words are needed for new concepts, a certain number to give atmosphere, but if there are too many the reader may get vocabulary overload. Was that last polysyllable a noun or a verb, a person, a place, or a thing? When as a reader I get saturated like that, the words just fuzz out into meaningless white noise, which is probably not the effect the writer intended.

A large vocabulary and a sense of where words come from, their roots and histories, help keep the writer from going astray. It can take time and a lot of reading to develop this kind of ear, but any newbie can use a dictionary. A quick dictionary check of any made-up word to be sure one hasn't accidentally duplicated a term already taken will help prevent, say, inadvertently naming one's major fantasy character after an airplane part. (True story. Not one of mine, happily.) Checking that one hasn't used some absurd word in a foreign language can be harder, although an Internet search may help here. Ursula Le Guin's essay "From Elfland to Poughkeepsie," although it applies only to a partial range of story types, is recommended reading to sensitize one to the issues.

When you finish book one, don't just sit down and wait for it to sell; start on book two. Novel publishers want writers who have proven that they are capable of doing continuing work, and at a steady rate, not one-book-wonders. And your second book, or your third, or fourth, may actually be the one that breaks the barriers for you. If you're lucky, as I was, you'll be able to clean out your manuscript drawer then and there (remember, publishers want more than one book, at least until your books tank and then they don't want any). Also, writing the second or later books may teach you more about writing, and more about how to improve your early work, than getting caught in an endless loop of revising the same material and rehashing the same problems.

Right revising is a most excellent thing. Perpetual revising that eats new work is not.

My best advice to aspiring writers is to write what you are passionate about, rather than trying to write "to the market." After all, if you try to write what you think others will like, and its flops, it will have been an absolute waste of your time; worse, if it succeeds, people will want you to write more of the same, not what your heart is set upon. If you love your work, there is more of a chance that others will too, and you are more likely to produce your best—which will create its own market, the mad gods of luck and publishing willing.

So, this ambles roundaboutly over to the next set of hard tasks, not terribly closely related: marketing one's tale.

I landed my first novel sale to Baen without an agent, but I wouldn't recommend this course of action to a new writer. I did it the hard way—wrote seven published books and won my first Nebula. *Then* I found my agent. On the bright side, she is a very good one.

Besides checking books on writing and Net-based sources, which have grown far more abundant these days (if varied in utility), if a new writer is looking for an agent it certainly can't hurt to attend the larger science fiction conventions, such as Worldcon or especially World Fantasy Convention, where a high concentration of agents and editors appear, and better still, appear on panels, where you can actually ask them your questions. Beyond that, it's just the usual slog of query letters and partials-and-outlines, as described in the many how-to books. If you have a published friend, you can sometimes get an introduction to their agent, but beware that you're putting your friend's professional reputation on the line when you do this. Your offering had better justify it.

Keep in mind, agents are not, normally, writing instructors. (Some agents do critique their clients' work, some don't. Mine mostly doesn't. It's not her job. Wrestling with French tax forms, or Bulgarian pirates, or publishers' accounting departments, or corporate-speak contracts, that's her job.)

Since the mid-Eighties when I broke in, the slush piles have grown bigger and the number of publishers who will even look at unagented submissions has grown smaller. Baen is one of the few publishers who still read slush (unsolicited novel manuscripts), but even they can only "start" perhaps one or two new writers a year. It's worth it to try every channel, but if you can land an agent who likes your work, so much the better. While no agent can sell a book that wouldn't sell on its own, once you have an offer, you'll want an agent anyway to do things like retain subrights, be sure your contract is reasonable, and market foreign sales.

Most agents do not handle short work even for their established clients, so of course new writers who can work at both lengths should send off their short tales to the magazines themselves. There isn't much to negotiate or change in most magazine contracts (though you should be sure you have a proper reversion clause), and a short story sale looks good in one's cover letter when offering a novel. No, it is not necessary to write or sell short stories before tackling novels; different writers have different natural lengths, and it's not a bad idea to play to one's strengths in the beginning.

Much depends on whether one writes better at short or long lengths. Many (not all) writers have a length that comes most readily to them. Both my friend Pat Wrede and I tend to be natural novelists. Our good ideas come in novel-sizes. Her first five sales were novels, before she ever figured out how to construct a salable short story. A lot of famous writers seem to be natural short-form writers. One is most likely to sell whatever one writes best. (Duh.) The odds are about the same, i.e., ghastly. (The mantras "They have to buy something," "Odds are for other people," and "There's always room at the top" are useful when contemplating this. Also "If s/he can do it, so can I." At least when "it" is properly understood as "the bloody hard work.") The short story market is shrinking at present, and many more people complete, and therefore submit, short work than long, so it's very competitive. On the other hand, the turn-around time for new novel submissions has become unconscionably long, literally years sometimes, and one can't simultaneously submit works of fiction. Any professional sale is a good thing, and will look good in the cover letter—selling either a novel or short work to an editor's respected colleague establishes your professional status, and the editor is likely to give your next submission, of whatever length, a closer glance.

There is a lot of on-line help out there these days

that did not exist when I was breaking in. The Science Fiction and Fantasy Writers of America has a valuable Website—the page at www.sfwa.org/writing is a gold mine. I suggest starting with Patricia Wrede's "Worldbuilding Questions" and Tappan King's "The Saga of Myrtle the Manuscript," and going on till you come to the end. Newsgroups such as rec.arts. sf.composition are on-line hangouts for both new writers and some helpful old pros, and hundreds of on-line critique groups of varying value have sprung up. E-mail has freed writing groups from geography. The SF publishing news magazine *Locus* is probably the best resource for publishing, bookselling, and convention news, as well as having extensive review columns and excellent interviews with writers. Not to mention photos of both famous and important behind-the-scenes faces—I was able to recognize my new publisher in an elevator crush at the '86 Atlanta Worldcon because I'd seen his photo in *Locus*.

Which brings us to reviews. Good reviews are always heartening, bad ones depressing. Curiously, a few bad ones manage to be far more excoriating than the ten or twenty good ones are uplifting. There's a psychological study in there somewhere, I'm sure. Ignore the bad, enjoy the good, and don't take either sort too seriously.

The most popular novels have both a good story and a good set of characters, accessible to a broad range of readers, not just to a tiny elite. (Though I will cheerfully maintain that elites deserve their reads, too, "elite" and "bestseller" don't usually occur in the same sentence for an obvious logical reason.) Books with legs usually need to be books that sell themselves, that people will recommend to each other; clever or expensive publicity can boost a book up onto bestseller lists for a moment, but only the story itself can keep it there for any length of time. There is also the question of cracking that critical mass, of getting enough people recommending it to each other (or arguing about it) that other readers become curious just because they've heard about this thing six times in two weeks in several completely different conversations, and start to actually remember it well enough to go look for it.

Some of a writer's necessary work lies midway between art and commerce, as in learning how to deal with editors and agents and contracts and business etiquette (many writers have no business background, and unfortunately it shows). Paranoia is certainly one of the pitfalls that up-and-coming writers need to avoid. No editor is trying to steal your work, really. It is perhaps also wise to avoid buying too blindly into the "whine and cheese" fests some writers indulge in. Dissing one's publisher, agent, or other professional colleague in public is as unappetizing to listen to as someone dissing their ex-spouse, and can lead the uninitiated newbie into mistaking as adversarial, parts of the publication process that are, in fact, best accomplished in a cooperative spirit. It's a good idea for any writer, though, to become aware of what level of sales constitutes success for one's chosen genre, so as to avoid either inflated expectations or selling oneself short. "How far is up?" can be a confusing question to answer.

I've discovered as my career advances that "take the money and run" is not an option for a responsible writer. By the time one's latest book arrives on bookstore shelves, a lot of other folks have bet their own time, money, and reputation on its success, only starting with its purchasing editor and publisher. The book needs to succeed for them, as well. So I've discovered that some degree of financial independence doesn't actually free me from needing to compete, after all, and that I still care.

Which brings me to authoring. Which is another whole job, demanding yet another skill-set.

While in normal speech "author" and "writer" are used interchangeably, I've found it handy to hijack the terms in order to make a useful distinction. Using the two synonyms gives me a way to talk about two separate aspects of a writing career: the actual sweat and uncertainty and frustration and joy of writing, which no one sees (and which would be very boring to watch); and the promotion, which is where the author gets out in public, but which has nothing to do with writing and can sometimes, for the shy or low-energy writer, be actively detrimental to creativity. The promotional/"author" side involves things like interviews, book tours, convention or speaking engagements, Net-based promotion, writing *about* one's writing (as I'm doing here), answering fan mail, and the like.

The people who imagine that writing is a glamorous profession tend to be looking at the "author" side of things; reasonably enough, since that's the most visible, and when a writer is out in public like that, he or she is usually trying to look as attractive as possible, in hopes of luring readers to their prose. At home we are much grubbier.

There are moments when one is "only" an author,

books tours for example. I certainly get no writing done on book tours. All my attention is taken up with not missing planes, trying not to get sick from the travel stress, trying to pay close attention to a rapid succession of people, and never, ever losing my cool with a reader, even if it's the thirtieth time I've been asked the same question that week. After about the third stop I can get pretty tired of listening to myself. And I develop nightmares about airports.

It takes me two to four weeks to recover enough from such a tour to pick up my thread of thought and begin writing again. About the same for an international trip. So they are very expensive in terms of lost writing time. But then, book tours can feed the writer part of my brain just through being intense experiences—getting out and glimpsing new places and meeting folks and listening to the stories they tell me, not to mention sometimes staying in fascinating hotels that would normally be quite beyond my budget.

After I'd been on a few book tours, I really began to wonder about their economic utility for my publishers, not just their huge time and energy costs for me. It's exhilarating when a mob of readers turn out for a stop, and booksellers are always cool folks to chat with, but surely anyone who'd come to an author's signing would have bought the book anyway...? Book tours alone can't increase sales that much, though they may cluster them in early weeks in an effort to game the system of best-seller lists. It all harks back, I finally realized, to those middlemen again. I theorize that having a tour signals a book as receiving a major push from its publisher, just as raised gold foil lettering once did, and so the wholesalers presumably order more copies nationwide. Either that, or it's pure cargo-cult thinking, or a trap like the returns system; a few people tried tours, sales went up, everyone got into the act, and now no one dares be the first to stop. As they said in *Shakespeare in Love*, one of my favorite films about writing: "No one knows. It's a mystery."

I've been asked whether I think high-profile author blurbs are important to the sales of books. In my experience, readers are largely indifferent to blurbs. The place they seem to be important is, again, during the pre-selling phase, just like the gold lettering and book tours. Like sausages and the law, it is perhaps unsettling to know too much about how books are made—or at least, sold.

One less baffling perk of being an "author" is the authorial meal with an editor. These have various subtle social functions that took me a while to figure out. They are not, as I had somehow expected in dithering anticipation of my first official editorial meal—a breakfast at the '86 Atlanta Worldcon with my then-new publisher Jim Baen—to work out the details of book contracts. Those are done by telephone, with lots of long, thoughtful pauses between calls. What these meals are for is to make the next phone call easier. When you've never met face-to-face, the lack of visual cues over the phone, and the presence of unrestrained writerly imagination, can create confusion and misunderstanding. When you can picture the real person, with their actual tics and tones and grimaces and grins, those phone calls somehow go more smoothly ever after. Still, it's a bit startling in the convention green room to witness the fannish cry of "We're hungry—let's go find a restaurant" transmute into the authorial version of, "We're hungry—let's go find an editor!"

The other charm of editorial dining, of course, is the chance to venture into upscale restaurants that neither writer nor editor, in our scruffy at-home personas and income levels, would ever get within whiffing distance of. An editorial dinner was the first time I ever had a waiter come around between courses and rake the tablecloth free of detritus (the area around my plate always seems to have lots) with one of those cute little brass scrapers. At such a dinner with my friend Lillian's editor at a convention hotel restaurant in Dallas, we were all charmed and boggled when we were each brought, between courses to clear our palates between courses, a small scoop of sorbet—sitting on half a lime—sitting in an individual sculptured ice swan about a foot high with a tiny white Christmas light in the base. I swear we hadn't even ordered lighted swans; they just swanned in, as if naturally.

That wasn't quite as surreal, however, as the editorial dinner at Chicon V in Chicago, when Jim and editor Toni Weisskopf took Elizabeth Moon and me out to some tower of power reached only by marble-lined elevators. The vegetable course, a mounded puree of what I dimly remember as featuring mainly turnips, arrived—decorated with a microscopically thin layer of gold foil about five inches square. As a science fiction writer, I take it as my duty to try any food once, a dubious rule that once led me to eat a wichetty grub, but that's another story. Elizabeth, however, was quietly horrified by the gold, and carefully ate around it and under it, cautiously excavating with her spoon. "Elizabeth!" I murmured in maternal reproval. "You're not eating your gold!" We let her have her dessert anyway.

I've been asked what has surprised me most about writing and the writing business. Actually, I live in a state of perpetual surprise. "My God! The Bulgarians paid me after all! I signed that contract three years ago!" "Good heavens! The Dutch sub-agent has disappeared with all the receipts!" "*Publishers Weekly* gave me a starred review!" "My first quarter's estimated taxes are higher than my first quarter's income!" "The fans put/didn't put *that* one on the Hugo ballot?!" "They're putting *that* cover on my book? Eep!" "They're putting *that* cover on my book? Hallelujah!" "They went to six figures?! Oh!...well...*how* much past?" "Somebody e-mailed me from Kazakhstan/Alice Springs/Finland/South Africa/Portugal/Pakistan/Croatia?" "What's '*The New York Times* Extended list'?" "A fan who is dying from cancer wants to see my book early?" "The fan I sent the story to last month passed away yesterday." "I've been stuck on this same damned plot point for 2/3/4/5/6 weeks!" "Pirated in Greece? I didn't even know they read SF in Greece!" "My brother/mother/cousin actually read my latest novel!" "How many days ago did you mail it overnight express?" "Korean rights?" "I can't figure out what the devil happens in Chapter 4." "The Russian fans are holding a Bujold convention in Moscow!" "The new minor character, who I hadn't even imagined last week, just hijacked Chapter 4 and is closing in rapidly on 5 and 6. Will my putative hero ever get another sentence in edgewise?" "We got a blurb from *her*? Wow!" "Perth?" "Spain?" "London?...England?" "St. Petersburg? You mean the one in Russia?" "Where is Zagreb?" "New Zealand?"

All real examples. If a week goes by without a surprise, these days, I get pettish. From fried wichetty grubs to gold-plated turnips, when you're a writer you never know what's going to appear on your plate next. It keeps a woman alert, it does.

• • • • •

# A Conversation with
# Toni Weisskopf

## JOHN HELFERS

Toni Weisskopf has been working closely with Lois almost from the very beginning, when she was establishing the Vorkosigan Saga. As the current Editor-in-Chief at Baen Books, she has been instrumental in bringing out another Miles novel, as well as editing practically all of the books in the series. I asked her to share what it has been like working with Lois, and here is what she had to say.

*How did Lois get discovered by Baen?*

This was actually before my time at Baen, but legend has it that the three novel manuscripts *The Warrior's Apprentice*, *Shards of Honor*, and *Ethan of Athos* had made the rounds of all the older, established publishers, and that they had either been rejected or languished unappreciated, before they came to Baen Books, which had just shipped its first books in 1984.

Jim took one look at *The Warrior's Apprentice* and called Lois up to ask her if she had more. She did, two more novels, and Jim bought all three on the spot.

*Did anyone see her potential during that early time?*

Jim Baen certainly did. They were the first books he told me to read when I was hired at Baen as an editorial assistant. I was so jaded (straight out of college and already jaded!) that I didn't believe new SF authors could bring anything fresh to the table. Jim and Lois proved me wrong, gloriously wrong.

*What do you remember best about the first time you read one of Lois's manuscripts?*

The first time I spoke to Lois after reading her books, I offered to have her baby. Luckily, she declined. They made a tremendous impact on me. I started with *The Warrior's Apprentice* and never looked back. I got the same sort of feeling reading her works as I had gotten from classic Heinlein: a renewed faith in humanity and a desire to explore and do good in the universe. Great feeling.

*Did Lois have a clear idea of what she wanted to accomplish with the Miles novels at the time, or did the series evolve in scope as the books were written?*

That one you'll have to ask Lois directly, but I do know there was some give-and-take between Jim and Lois about the nature and direction of the series. Jim, of course, wanted more like *The Warrior's Apprentice*, with the military concerns that were so close to his interests—and pocketbook. It was the clear front-runner for sales for a long time.

*Please describe the typical editorial process with one of Lois's books.*

She writes, I read. It seems to me Lois really doesn't require a lot of editorial input. There have been occasions, as with any writer, that a particular point will need talking out, and I'm happy to be able to provide an interested ear for that process. Sometimes a stray comment, like mentioning I thought *A Civil Campaign* needed more of a science fictional feel, will be answered in odd ways, like, say, butter bugs.

*How has Lois's writing changed over the years that you've been working with her?*

She's always been an accomplished, smooth writer.

*Do you feel there are any publishing decisions that you made that have helped Lois's books achieve their success? If so, what?*

I think Jim's stubbornness and obstinacy helped build the audience for the books. Baen from the very beginning has been good about keeping backlist titles of series in print, and that was essential to the Vorkosigan Saga, especially since they weren't written in chronological order.

Jim also went against the common wisdom and published those first three books within the space of a year, and I think that jump-started the series and the awareness of Bujold within the SF community. It might have cost Lois a Campbell Award, since she didn't have the traditional career path of a Campbell winner and it looked liked she'd been writing for a long time!

On a more minor note, I think putting the Vorkosigan Saga Timeline in the back of the books has been helpful—I'd asked my colleague Hank Davis to put it together for me originally just so I could keep the books straight in my own mind, but I think it's helped a lot of readers sort the series out.

*What are your favorite books in the Miles series, and why?*

My favorites are the *Shards of Honor* and *Barrayar* combo published under one roof as *Cordelia's Honor*. One of my favorite scenes is in *Barrayar*, when Cordelia comes back from "shopping" in the city and rolls the head of the pretender onto the conference table in the midst of military men. In fact, I have a shopping bag from Siegling's (from Steve Salaba's authorized line of Vorkosigan memorabilia) in honor of that scene; I use it as my range bag and carry my ammo and ear protection in it!

*Who are your favorite characters, and why?*

I have a soft spot for Ivan, but don't tell anyone.... I like Cordelia, obviously. And I like Taura, the werewolf girl. As for why—I guess because they are all honorable people doing the best they can in situations that are not "normal" for them.

*What do you think readers see in the Miles series that keeps bringing them back to the series?*

There's the charm, the wit, the nice touch of invention. The intricate plotting, the real characters—and the reality is, at bottom, the key. Lois creates real people, behaving in ways you can believe in—intelligent people act intelligently, venal people are venal, and the Cetagandans have loooong plans. It all feels right. Lois has talked about the writer/reader collaboration—for that to click, there has to be enough meat for the reader to chew on. Lois gives filet mignon.

*What do you look for each time a new Miles novel lands on your desk?*

A free evening to read and a comfy chair! I admit, it's hard to complain about the press of work when "work" is sitting back and reading a Vorkosigan Saga book!

*As the series editor, what would you like to see explored in future Miles books?*

As a reader, of course I want to see Ivan settle down with a nice girl just like his mom and live happily ever after. As a series editor, I'm afraid Ivan is due for some adventures before Lois will let him settle down, if she even does let him settle down. But getting away from the personalities—which is hard; Lois makes her characters come alive for her readers so that we *can* talk about them like people we know, because we *do* know them—I think the series can grow thematically if Lois wants it to. The previous books have explored what cultures do to individuals. It might be interesting to see what individuals do to cultures. We've seen some of that with Cordelia's fairly subtle influence on Barrayar, but to me the big question is what will Miles do when serious problems shake the Barrayaran way of life he's worked so hard to protect, his Winston Churchill moment.

*What kind of challenges did you face bringing this series from its early years to today's success? Were there any specific issues that come to mind?*

It's been hard to market these books so that all of those whom they will appeal to will find it. In the early years if a chain store passed on a book, it would take years to build an author or series back up with that chain, even if you could prove they were losing sales. These are not easy books to put covers on, too, and the cover is your primary advertisement about the content of the book, especially before an author has built up a reputation. The Vorkosigan Saga is about heroism—but how can you portray a short guy with bone problems heroically? How do you *paint* charisma? The books are about family and loyalty and honor—great to read about, hard to portray in concrete images. They contain epic love stories—but how to put that on a cover without alienating the people who are first attracted to the interesting world-building and scientific extrapolation, which are also integral? Probably we needed to put three or four covers on each printing of each volume in the saga!

*What goals do you have for the future Miles novels?*
I think there's a tremendous, broad market for Lois's work, equal to that of the great SF of the 1980s which regularly hit the *NY Times* best-seller lists without media tie-ins. She has all the appeal of McCaffrey *and* Heinlein and I'd like to get her books into as many readers' hands as possible.

*Do you have any advice for aspiring writers that would like to follow in Lois's footsteps?*
A young writer could scarcely do better than to follow Lois's career path. She wrote several short stories and sent them around before and during the

writing of her first novels. She didn't rush to send out the novels before they were ready for a general audience. She didn't rush to accept any old agent, but by the time her career was at a point to actually benefit monetarily from an agent she was able to get one of the top agents in the field. She took and takes her writing seriously. She respects her fans and her readers and responds to them with grace and care.

And she's constantly refreshing her brain—researching all different sorts of things, from metallurgy to medieval history—which diverse inputs she can then draw on in her fiction. Keep expanding your horizons—good advice for anyone who doesn't want to get mentally flabby, not just writers.

*Aspects of the Vorkosiverse*

# Romance in the Vorkosiverse

## MARY JO PUTNEY

I'm a romance writer, so it's no surprise that I discovered the Vorkosigans through an online romance discussion group. Several fans of romantic SFF kept recommending this Bujold person. When I inquired where to start, I was told that *Shards of Honor* was a strong romance as well as first in the series.

*Shards* should have been classified as a "gateway drug." Once I read the story of Captain Cordelia Naismith and Aral Vorkosigan, the Butcher of Komarr, I was doomed. Since then, I've read and reread every novel Lois McMaster Bujold has ever written. (And checking facts for this essay kept hooking me into still more rereading!)

The Vorkosiverse is a feast of relationships, not just romances. I love how cousins Miles and Ivan interact like evil brothers who nonetheless trust each other unconditionally. The way marriages mature and change. The way the boy emperor, Gregor, grows into his insanely demanding role. Cordelia, Aral, Gregor, Mark—there are so many marvelous characters who are defined as much by their relationships as by their actions.

The Vorkosigan books aren't genre romances, where the developing relationship is at the heart of the story. Yet the series is romance in the literary sense: a vast and sweeping tale of high adventure. The story of Miles Vorkosigan is a classic bildungsroman, the chronicle of a young man learning about life as he grows to manhood.

And, like most young men, Miles has a natural interest in the female half of the species. (We won't get into Betan herms here.) His passion for Elena Bothari, with whom he was raised, is unrequited, but there will be other women in his future.

Terrific women, too. As a female reader, one of my pleasures in the books is how strong the female characters are. Perhaps this isn't surprising, given that the author is female, but there are never enough great fictional women to take them for granted.

Miles's lovers are always accomplished and interesting. A favorite moment of mine is when clone brother Mark, whose actions have gotten Miles killed, is confronted by the ferocious Amazons that were his clone brother's former girlfriends.

Elli Quinn, whose face was burned off in battle, is given a new face courtesy of the Dendarii Free Mercenary Fleet, and grows into his second-in-command and eventual successor. A "drunkard's dream" of a girlfriend, Quinn is funny, smart, sexy, and a warrior to reckon with.

Sergeant Taura is equally dangerous—bred as a disposable super-warrior, she can terrify with a smile, but inside she's a lonely girl who has never known affection, much less love. Granted, when an eight-foot-tall teenager with fangs and claws wants sex as a price for her cooperation, a man might suffer world-class performance anxiety, but Miles is up to the challenge. Indeed, he and Taura develop a lasting bond they both cherish.

Though Miles tends to be monogamous, sometimes circumstances bring on diversity. His occasional liaisons with Taura when they're far from the Dendarii overlap his long affair with Quinn. And during his amnesia after cryo-revival, there was that fling with Rowan Durona, his accomplished and attractive doctor. Very healing.

Miles isn't the only one who gets to fall in love. When Bujold first takes us to Barrayar, it's a brutal world where women have little status and life is run along hierarchical and militaristic lines. One of the pleasures of the series is watching how Barrayar changes after Cordelia arrives and Aral becomes the Regent. Their rock-solid marriage, based on mutual trust and respect, lays the foundations for a more civilized society.

For that reason, several romances have a feminist and radical subtext. When Cordelia settles in Barrayar, the military is strictly for men, and a girl with warrior aspirations is shut out. Ludmilla Droushnakovi, known as Drou, is the tall, blond, athletic daughter of a non-com. She can't join the imperial forces, but at least she's trained to fight while serving as a bodyguard to Princess Kareen.

Drou is attracted to Lieutenant Koudelka, Aral's war-injured secretary, and vice versa, but the romance almost founders over the issue of a woman's strength. When Kou attempts to confess to Aral that he raped Drou, Aral summons Cordelia and Drou. Drou almost breaks her confused lover in half while proving her point that he couldn't have laid a hand on her if she hadn't been willing.

It takes Cordelia in terrifying Betan matchmaker mode to sort out their misunderstandings and send them toward their happy ending. When Drou and Kou marry at the Imperial residence, Aral comments that every class of Barrayaran society is represented on the guest list. It is a sign of the changes ahead. Drou and Kou go on to produce a gaggle of handsome blond daughters who will have romances of their own.

Elena Bothari is another Barrayaran woman frustrated by her native world's sexism. The romance of Elena and Baz Jezek is only sketched in, but I've always assumed that part of their bond is that they're both Barrayarans who can't go home again. She won't and he *can't*, but they have each other and a shared culture.

Miles is shocked when he realizes that Lord Vorkosigan has no sex life. Quinn and Taura and Rowan Durona are the lovers of Miles Naismith. The little admiral of the Dendarii fleet has sucked up all the passion and fun available to Miles's identities.

When a disastrous lie forces Miles to leave his mercenary fleet and rediscover what it means to be Barrayan, that includes finding a mate who will fit into his new future. He and Elli Quinn do their best to persuade each other to a different path, but Quinn won't settle on Barrayar and Miles won't abandon his homeworld. In the end, they settle for parting as friends. Which is a fine ending to a love affair, actually.

Inevitably, the love of Miles's life, the widowed Ekaterin Vorsoisson, is Vor. Like Miles, she has faced struggles in life that have seasoned and matured her.

She is a "woman [who] went down and down, like a well to the middle of the world."

Though no warrior, Ekaterin doesn't lack courage, and she shares Miles's Vor values right down to the cellular level. To be Vor is to serve, even if the cost might be one's own life. To be Vor also means living by a code of honor. Miles is shocked when an angry Lieutenant Vorberg accuses him of abandoning Illyan, head of Imperial Security, who has been asking for Miles as his mind slowly shatters. Miles immediately answers the call, even if that means bringing down the fearsome walls of ImpSec itself. Both he and Vorberg understand that it matters to "make Vor real."

Hyperactive overachiever that he is, Miles almost loses Ekaterin by failing to understand her need to make him a gift of her talents. She, too, has her honor. As always, Miles learns the hard way, but he learns. Just as his military skills include the ability to bring out the best in those around him (a trait inherited from both parents), he is able to bring out the best in Ekaterin. And she is wise enough to cherish all that is special about Miles, while being entirely aware of his many and colorful shortcomings.

The essence of good romance is to show how two people suit each other. What is unique about each individual, and about their relationship to each other? What does he love about her, what does she love about him? Bujold shows such things with impeccable accuracy. By the time Ekaterin proposes to Miles in front of the entire Council of Counts, there is no doubt that these two people are made for each other.

Another Vorkosiverse romance that feels utterly right is that of Emperor Gregor. Gregor's cool, razor-insightful style defines him brilliantly. He serves the Imperium as he was born and bred to do. Yet when he falls in love, the object of his affection isn't a tall, slim Vor maiden "whose family tree crosses [his] sixteen times in the last six generations," but Doctor Laisa Toscane, a luscious and intelligent Komarran heiress. (What female reader can't appreciate the fact that the round girl gets the guy?)

It's a powerful moment when Gregor, whose life has been lived for Barrayar, tells Miles that Laisa is the one thing that he absolutely wants for himself. Miles gives Gregor permission to grab her with both hands and "don't let the bastards" take her away. Gregor deserves no less than a woman as lovable and loving as Laisa.

There are romances in virtually all of the books, because romance makes a great subplot and also they're fun. But the real Saturnalia of romance is *A Civil Campaign*. While the centerpiece is Miles's courtship of Ekaterin, the Koudelka girls fall for an amazing range of men.

In *Memory*, Delia Koudelka secured Komarran Duv Galeni, who had yearned for Laisa Toscane, but didn't move fast enough. As Miles observed after that book's final crisis, it would take four large and foolhardy men with hand tractors to pry Delia off Galeni's arm. Galeni clung to her just as hard. This one wouldn't be allowed to get away.

In *A Civil Campaign*, Martya sets her sights on the mad Escobaran scientist Enrique Borgos, who needs a managing woman to take care of his interests while he spends fourteen-hour days in his lab. Martya is fully qualified to manage a man, and she won't mind spending all the money his inventions will make, either.

Olivia Koudelka pairs off with the most unusual Lord Dono Vorrutyer. Though perhaps the quietest of the Koudelka girls, she was trained by her mother and is quite capable of taking down three thugs when they attack her beloved—two with a stun gun and one by bashing his head into a concrete pillar. The Koudelka girls are as formidable as they are blond.

But the romance that proves the Vorkosiverse is circular is that of clone brother Mark Vorkosigan and Kareen, the youngest Koudelka daughter. When terrorized by Miles's "hellish harem" in *Mirror Dance*, Mark had thought wildly that he wanted a nice small, soft, meek blonde. Kareen isn't meek, but she's blond and soft and compassionate, and she loves the dark and twisty complexities of Mark's tormented soul.

Her parents are less enthused, given the massive amount of baggage Mark carries. Once again Cordelia goes into Betan matchmaker mode to convince Drou and Kou that Mark and Kareen deserve a chance to see if they suit.

Thirty years have passed, and it is no longer necessary for young people to claim their sexuality in "a mad secret scramble in the dark, full of confusion, pain, and fear." That was a time Drou remembers without affection. Barrayar is a better place now, and even Kareen's protective Da eventually agrees to give love a chance.

The last romance that I'm really waiting for is Ivan's. What clever lady is going to see beyond his carefully cultivated façade of the cheerful dolt to the strong, honorable man below?

While I'm waiting, I'll reread the whole Vorkosigan series. Again.

* * * * *

# Biology in the Vorkosiverse and Today

## TORA K. SMULDERS-SRINIVASAN, PH.D.

"All true wealth is biological."
—Aral Vorkosigan in *Mirror Dance*

Lois McMaster Bujold's science fiction series that takes place in the "Vorkosiverse" is excellent for many reasons. One of them is Bujold's exceptional grasp of biology, including her ability to imagine and depict future biological technologies and their social implications.

Though she began writing the series more than twenty years ago, the sound basis for the biology in her Vorkosiverse books makes the future biological technologies in them still relevant today. Even more satisfying to a biologist, these technologies do not become the bad guy, as is common for science fiction stories such as *Frankenstein* and *Jurassic Park*. The good and evil both come not from the technology, biological or otherwise, but from within the characters.

126

Bujold does not thrust these biological technologies on her readers as extraneous frills, but rather the technologies are an intricate part of the plot, the setting, or even the characterization in her stories. In one scene, after an assassination attempt against them by poisonous gas fails, Cordelia Vorkosigan tells her husband Aral not to worry, that all they need to procreate is "...two somatic cells and a replicator. Your little finger and my big toe, if that's all they can scrape off the walls after the next bomb..." (*Barrayar*). That quote alone implies a whole area of advanced reproductive technology: the ability to clone somatic cells and differentiate them into viable eggs and sperm, outside of the body; as well as the ability to grow the fertilized egg into a baby.

Unfortunately for Cordelia and Aral, the antidote to the poison is very damaging to their unborn son. Cordelia manages to organize some advanced galactic technology on their backwater world and the son, Miles, survives, though the repercussions, physical and psychological, last throughout his entire life (*Barrayar*).

In *Ethan of Athos*, the world on which the story begins is comprised of only males. Again, advanced reproductive technology allows the entire population of Athos to be maintained by Reproductive Centers where the sperm of potential fathers is collected and used to fertilize eggs from ovarian cultures that have lasted over two hundred years.

The Vorkosiverse also has other advanced biological technologies, such as cryonics (being brought back from death after being specially frozen) and the eidetic memory biochip implanted in Simon Illyan's head that ends up being the target of sabotage, the consequences of which are very far-reaching (*Mirror Dance, Shards of Honor, Memory*). Not to be forgotten are the live cat blanket that purrs, likes to half-strangle one in sleep, and is associated with a murder plot (*Brothers in Arms, Winterfair Gifts*); the genetically beautified (and metabolically modified) butter bugs (*A Civil Campaign*); and a kitten tree in *Cetaganda*.

The kitten tree is not even the most impressive of the Cetagandans' biological innovations, as they are a multi-planetary civilization run by master gene manipulators. Though this list of biological technologies that exist in the Vorkosiverse is far from complete, this article will focus on four of the main technologies whose influence is felt throughout the Vorkosiverse series.

A prominent feature of the Vorkosiverse is the uterine replicator technology. The uterine replicator is a piece of technology that frees women from pregnancy and allows men to have babies without women around. This piece of high-tech scientific equipment is used by Bujold in a wide variety of ways.

A particular uterine replicator is the most important object in the universe in one of her books (*Barrayar*); a slew of them cause an entire series of catastrophic events in another (*Diplomatic Immunity*); and the technology itself is the basis of life for the inhabitants of an entire planet in yet a third (*Ethan of Athos*), and those are just a few examples.

In some areas of the Vorkosiverse, there is a choice between a traditional pregnancy (called a "body birth") and a uterine replicator. If a couple wishes to have a baby by uterine replicator, the sperm from the father fertilizes the egg from the mother *in vitro* (in the lab) to create a zygote. After a few cell divisions, the zygote becomes a blastula. In a female, this is the point the embryo would become implanted into the uterus. Instead, the blastula created by *in vitro* manipulation is implanted into a uterine replicator. The embryo then grows into a baby in the uterine replicator and is "decanted" rather than birthed at the end of the·process. The replicator must be monitored and maintained (addition of nutrients, elimination of wastes, etc.) throughout the *ex vivo* pregnancy, but is completely independent of the mother's body. Naturally, this kind of technology could have huge repercussions on society and even the direction of further human evolution. Bujold has depicted some of these fascinating possible outcomes and worlds for us.

How close is this kind of technology to what is done today? Recent research into in vitro fertilization (IVF) has allowed the discovery of many of the factors essential for the initial stages of embryonic development, and research into helping premature babies survive has allowed babies born after as few as twenty-four weeks of gestation to live. The gap between a few days and twenty-four weeks must be overcome before a baby can be produced completely outside the mother. However, researchers have recently been experimenting with improving IVF rates by co-culturing the fertilized human eggs with endometrial cells from the lining of the womb before transferring the blastocysts to the mothers.

In other experiments, the same group has produced tiny artificial wombs by growing these endometrial cells in a collagen matrix, which allows the cells to form a plug with a 3-D structure. They have even added fertilized eggs to these uterus-like plugs of cells and found that the early-stage embryos implanted themselves within the plugs at about six days post-fertilization just as they would in a womb. Implantation is a very essential step in growing a baby, so this area of research may very well lead to fully functional artificial wombs within the next fifty years.

Another group of scientists examined the possibility of creating an artificial placenta to keep mid- to late-stage goat fetuses alive. They attached catheters to the umbilical blood vessels, exchanged nutrient-enriched blood with the blood of the fetuses while they were held in a tank of artificial amniotic fluid, and managed to keep a few alive to full term. For various reasons, these experiments have not been continued, but the research does sketch out a path for future exploration.

Though there have been some exciting advances in the area of reproductive technology, today's technology has not yet reached the level of the Vorkosiverse uterine replicators. As Bujold explored this topic more than twenty years ago, it is impressive that the uterine replicator technology is not now outdated, but rather a cutting-edge topic of research.

A second major feature of the Vorkosiverse is the cloning technology, which includes creating specific body parts or whole humans. Cloning to create tissues or body parts or even organs from the genetic material from a single cell is called therapeutic cloning. Bujold explores this kind of cloning in the Vorkosiverse: characters get their hearts replaced with new ones grown from their own cells (*Mirror Dance*), reconstructive surgery can replace a face better than new (*The Warrior's Apprentice; Ethan of Athos*), and new body parts can even be grown that can then convert a female to a fully-functioning male (*A Civil Campaign*).

Reproductive cloning, or cloning whole humans from a single cell, is usually the immediate thought when cloning is mentioned. Bujold addresses this type of cloning head-on: her main protagonist, Miles Vorkosigan, is cloned by his family's enemies. That clone first becomes part of the picture in *Brothers in Arms*, but his role as a main character continues throughout many of the books in the series.

In *Mirror Dance*, Miles's clone, known as Mark, not only is one of the main characters, but is a viewpoint character for much of the story. Not coincidentally, the storyline for *Mirror Dance* involves many other clones as well, including an entire family of doctors created by cloning, the Duronas. Cloning means taking all the genetic material (the nucleus with its chromosomes/DNA) from one cell and creating a new tissue/organ or a whole new organism from that genetic material. While some science-fictional depictions of clones have the resultant organisms being completely identical in mind as well as in body, Bujold's clones are appropriately individual even though they share the same genetic material.

In reality, a clone is no more than an identical twin born at a different time. Identical twins also share the same genetic material, but most people who have met identical twins will know that they do not really look completely identical and that they are not mental duplicates of each other. Thus in Bujold's work, the clone Mark's personality is accordingly as much shaped by his experiences as is Miles's.

In science-fictional contexts, a clone also has a

tendency to appear in almost no time at all, which would really be impossible to accomplish. In the Vorkosiverse, Mark was not born yesterday; he is appropriately only five or six years younger than Miles and was growing and being trained for years. Avoiding other science-fictional clichés, the clone also does not become Miles's evil twin.

Bujold has also explored some of the ethical and societal effects of this technology: one of the main plotlines in *Mirror Dance* involves a clone-farming operation that provides young healthy new bodies to wealthy elderly clients, utilizing a technique known as brain transplantation. Unsurprisingly, this is not looked upon as an ethical option, but as an illegal blot on society. In addition, different planets in the Vorkosiverse have different legal guidelines for dealing with clones: on Beta a clone is a legal sibling and on other planets a clone may be a legal child. All in all, Bujold does an impressive job of depicting a universe where this technology of cloning parts or people is extant.

What about current-day technology? Does the cloning of Dolly the sheep mean people can be cloned now? Cloning of humans is, understandably, a controversial subject. Reproductive cloning of humans, essentially creating a whole new person from the genetic material from one cell of a person, has been ruled illegal in many countries. Cloning of animals, on the other hand, has been taking place for as many as fifty years. However, the cloning of Dolly the sheep in 1996 was a huge advance in cloning technology—it was the first time a mammalian clone from an adult cell was successful (the adult cell was an udder cell, hence the sheep was named for Dolly Parton).

Since then, cloning of other mammals has been announced on a regular basis: goats, cows, mice, pigs, cats, dogs, horses, and rabbits. Though there have been no successful adult clones of non-human primates, macaque monkey embryos have been created by cloning, which implies that adult clones may yet be achievable. A report or two claim to have demonstrated successful human cloning, but those reports have never been substantiated. Because cloning is possible in many mammalian species and early stages have been demonstrated in non-human primates, the technology to clone humans is a distinct possibility for the near future.

Nevertheless, at the current level of technology, not only is cloning very expensive, but the resultant cloned animals are riddled with defects. To start with, there are on average only one or two offspring that survive out of a hundred, and those clones that do stay alive past birth have problems such as high rates of infection, tumor growth, poor health, and early death. The cause of these problems appears to be faulty reprogramming of the DNA of an adult cell to that of a developing new organism, but there may be other problems as well.

At the current state of technology, then, it would be irresponsible and unethical to attempt to clone humans, which is reflected in the law in most countries. However, as more is discovered about the technique and the ability to modify the DNA more directly is developed, cloning humans may become a more viable option.

Therapeutic cloning is somewhat less controversial, though any use of human tissue is highly regulated in most countries. If a tissue or organ can be created from a person's own genetic material by therapeutic cloning, that means it can be transplanted into that person without being rejected as are tissues or organs from other people. As stated earlier, macaque monkey clones have been created to develop as far as embryos and those embryos have been used to create primate embryonic stem cell lines. This may be one step on the way to creating primate clones, but it is also a step for therapeutic cloning.

If researchers can apply the techniques used in creating the primate-cloned-embryos for human cells, human therapeutic cloning may allow the production of individualized human embryonic stem cell lines in the same way. Also necessary for human therapeutic cloning is the ability to mold the embryonic stem cells into tissue, organs, and parts. Some of that research is taking place as this is written, but is mostly at early stages.

Reproductive cloning of humans, however, will hopefully not be attempted until the technology is hugely improved and shown to be much safer in animals. Even then, if it is scientifically possible to clone whole humans, we, like the inhabitants of the Vorkosiverse, will have to address the ethical and legal issues as to whether reproductive cloning should happen, and if so, what the legal status of the clones produced will be. Again, Bujold has managed to incorporate biological technologies that are still very current topics of research today.

A third feature of the Vorkosiverse that plays a leading role in many of the stories is the almost unimaginable ease with which genes and entire genomes are manipulated to create new types of humans and other organisms. Bujold imagines an entire race of humans (quaddies) optimized to live in a zero-gravity environment by having an adjusted metabolism and replacing their legs with arms. The quaddies arose by use of genetic manipulation and use of the then-new uterine replicators (*Falling Free*).

*Falling Free* is mostly concerned with the origin of the quaddies, but the quaddies are revisited in a story that takes place a few hundred years later, contemporaneous with Miles, and they have thrived and populated a number of space habitats (*Diplomatic Immunity*).

In *Diplomatic Immunity*, much of the action takes place in the quaddies' part of the galaxy, and many of the characters are quaddies. At that time, the technology also exists to aid quaddie/human couples in having children of either the human or quaddie type—or any other mix, for that matter (*Diplomatic Immunity*).

Fully functional hermaphrodites were created on Beta, one of the planets in the Vorkosiverse, but were a short-lived experiment (*The Warrior's Apprentice*). It never caught on as a preferred way of life, but one of the main characters in many of the books is a herm (*The Warrior's Apprentice*, *Mirror Dance*).

Yet another planet in the Vorkosiverse, Cetaganda, rules its entire multi-planetary system based on the manipulation of genomes (*Cetaganda*). The highest echelons of the society (the haut) are in charge of the Cetagandan genomes. The children of the haut are carefully genetically crafted by the women of the Star Crèche, placed in their uterine replicators, and distributed once a year to the rest of the haut, a very precious cargo to be delivered to the Cetagandan planets (*Diplomatic Immunity*). Thus, those who control the genomes in the Cetagandan society have the most power—and the struggle to control that power exists at the highest levels, as Miles discovers in *Cetaganda*.

Though the Cetagandans have these awesome powers of genetic manipulation, they must also experiment. They do so by testing new gene combinations in a class of genderless servants called ba who cannot reproduce. *Diplomatic Immunity*'s plot not only concerns uterine replicators, but also hinges on one of these servants.

However, not all the genetic manipulation in the Vorkosiverse is on such a population-wide scale. A main character in *Diplomatic Immunity* is engineered to live underwater, which includes frog-like webbed hands and feet and a set of gills to go along with his lungs.

In *Ethan of Athos*, a very top-secret Cetagandan gene-manipulation experiment goes wild, and another top-secret gene-manipulation experiment to produce super-soldiers does the same in "Labyrinth." Though the victim of experimentation in *Ethan of Athos* does not appear again, the created super-soldier first seen in "Labyrinth" has a very interesting relationship with Miles, remains one of the major and most memorable characters in the Vorkosiverse, and becomes one of the two main characters in "Winterfair Gifts." Thus, wholescale genetic manipulation is a key factor in the Vorkosiverse.

Is it possible to manipulate genes and genomes in the same way today? On the one hand, people have been manipulating genes by agricultural methods and animal husbandry for thousands of years, and, for a hundred years now, scientists have been mutating, altering, and adding individual genes to lab model organisms which include plants, bacteria, yeast, worms, fruit flies, mice, and human cells. On the other hand, the kind of genetic manipulation implied by the substitution of limbs, a fully functioning hermaphrodite, and the rest described in the previous paragraphs is completely beyond what is attainable today. The comprehensive knowledge of what genes need to be manipulated to make those kinds of changes simply does not exist.

Scientists are mostly discovering the function of genes one by one, though all of the genome sequencing projects proliferating within the last five or so years since the completion of the human genome have added immensely to the knowledge of what sequences exist and how those sequences combine to form genes. The complete genomes also can be studied to discover how they relate to each other evolutionarily, which may shed light on the genes' functions. Yet, there are many genes for which we do not know the function.

An additional complication is that, even if the function of a gene is known, each gene affects many other genes and characteristics. Beyond that, any particular trait (such as skin color) is determined by many genes working together, but skin color may be only part of what any one of those genes does.

Genes also work differently depending on which other genes are being expressed along with them: in different stages of development, in different tissues, and in different organisms. Or a particular gene may execute exactly the same molecular function in another organism, but that same function in the second organism causes something else to happen at the next higher level of complexity. As a result, deducing what all the genes do and how they do it is an amazingly complex endeavor that may or may not ever be achieved by humans.

Scientists today can cut out particular pieces of DNA (a whole gene, parts of one, etc.), insert them into other places in the same organism (depending on which ones) or other organisms (depending again), delete genes in certain organisms, mutate genes in certain organisms, make artificial chromosomes and insert them into certain organisms, etc. Accordingly, some of the technical tools to make the kinds of genetic manipulations essential to create quaddies or herms may be currently feasible; nonetheless, the knowledge of how to manipulate genes to achieve those ends is lacking. The Vorkosiverse ability to genetically manipulate may then not be reached for many more years.

The fourth and final feature of the Vorkosiverse discussed here is the vital cryonics technology. Bujold postulates a technology with which people can be brought back to life from a death. But only if the death happens in a certain way, and particular equipment and expertise are nearby and can be brought to bear quickly enough. Cryonics technology is used quite often for the Dendarii Mercenaries (a mercenary group that Miles leads on and off throughout the books) and is mentioned in passing many times (*The Warrior's Apprentice*, *Brothers in Arms*).

However, at one point, the cryonics technique becomes much more important, as it impinges very closely on Miles Vorkosigan himself (*Mirror Dance*). The consequences of this particular use reverberate through to the following book as well (*Memory*).

For the cryonics technology to work, the person must be drained of blood, filled with cryo-fluid within four minutes of death, and then frozen in a cryo-chamber. The cryo-revival involves careful thawing and complete healing of the original injuries, which could include the cloning and growth of organs. The patients often end up with amnesia, which may or may not resolve. In the Vorkosiverse, doctors specialize in cryonics, and ethical questions arise when all the cryo-chambers are already in use and yet another person dies. Bujold has again explored a fascinating technology as well as some of the ethical debates that follow from its use.

Is cryonics simply a science-fictional invention or is there current-day scientific research that supports it as a future advance? Some frogs freeze in the winter, then revive in the summer, and appear to do so by having extraordinarily high urea levels, which serves as an "anti-freeze." They are not the only organisms to survive freezing: the nematodes (worms) used as a model organism by many researchers are regularly frozen to be stored in liquid nitrogen and thawed for reuse. Organs from mammals, including the brain, have been frozen and brought back to some levels of function.

In addition, pigs have been taken down to very low temperatures (10 degrees Celsius core temperature for 60 minutes) using a method that sounds very similar to Bujold's description of cryonic techniques: the blood is drained quickly and replaced with a cold cryo-protectant fluid. After they were reanimated, the pigs were tested for brain function by learning and memory assessments, and they performed equivalently to pigs that had not been cryonically frozen and revived.

Along the lines of reproductive technology mentioned earlier, there have been advances in the freezing of sperm, eggs, and embryos for later fertilization/gestation. A group of well-respected scientists have even signed an open letter (www.imminst.org/cryonics_letter/) that supports cryonics as "a legitimate science-based endeavor that seeks to preserve human beings, especially the human brain, by the best technology available." They emphasize that this is a credible hope for future technological developments rather than a current possibility. Thus, cryonics could be a very real possibility for the future, and some have estimated it happening within the next thirty to fifty years.

Lois McMaster Bujold's Vorkosiverse is an imaginary universe, yet its advanced biological technology still allows us to picture it as a future that we could see following from where we are today. The solid biological principles it is based on have stood the test of time for over twenty years. In my view, they are likely to be relevant and possible for at least twenty more.

Actually, as all four of the main technologies covered in detail here are currently progressing along the lines of Bujold's projections, the technologies may become everyday realities in exactly the way Bujold has described. The realization of many "futuristic" biological technologies may be closer than previously thought.

I hope that excellent science fiction authors like Lois McMaster Bujold will continue to write about and explore the ethics of such technologies so that readers and society as a whole will think about how to handle them when they arrive.

• • • • •

# "What's the Worst Thing I Can Do to This Character?": Technology of the Vorkosiverse

## ED BURKHEAD

Lois loves her characters. As she says, when you are writing character-based books, each character tries to take over the story. Oh, but the things she does to her characters...

Some of Lois's best character tortures are biological, but she supports and tortures her characters awfully well with other technologies, too.

Interstellar flight in the series is through jump ships, using mapped, fixed wormholes from star to star. Finding wormholes is dangerous survey work and wormholes may not take you to somewhere useful. Usually, there are several wormhole jumps and solar system traverses to move from one useful system to the next along a route. Interstellar travel can take days and even months depending on the distance, connections, and speed of the ship.

The opening of *Shards of Honor* is based on discovery of a route enabling the Barrayaran invasion and conquest of Escobar. Barrayar has found and mapped and is stocking supplies on a planet midway along the invasion route. Independently finding that planet from another entry, Cordelia Naismith's Betan Astronomical Survey ship begins surveying the planet for its potential, since science and research are the dominant products of Beta Colony. From Barrayar's point of view, allowing the Betans to report back could compromise the route and the invasion.

Many of the military technologies are established in the first dozen pages as Cordelia finds her survey camp torched and "nothing short of a plasma arc could have melted the fabric of their tents." Within minutes, she finds Lieutenant Rosemont dead, shot by a nerve disruptor. Moments after that, at a rustle in the grass, Cordelia snaps her stun gun to the aim.

We've been introduced to three of the main weapons used throughout the series. And the very civilized Cordelia Naismith, captain of a peaceful, exploratory Betan Astronomical Survey ship and pretty strongly anti-military-stupidity, is involved in the opening shots of a war.

Not all the technologies are military, certainly. Cordelia is wearing her short-range wrist comm, and the scientific party has assorted instruments and tough, durable equipment. Cordelia pulls out of a drawer a long-range communicator, powerful enough to contact her ship now pulling away from the planet.

Making its escape, the fast Betan ship can easily stay away from the slow Barrayaran warship. The means of propulsion are never mentioned throughout the series.

Normal space accelerations are high, in the dozens of gravities range, with acceleration compensated by the ships' artificial gravity system.

Spaceships never land and shuttles are used which can land without problems with exhaust or blast effects, apparently supported by an anti-gravity effect.

Once the invasion of Escobar starts, technology comes into play in the plot twists. Beta Colony has a defense against the major Barrayaran ship-to-ship weapon, the plasma arc—the plasma mirror reflects the plasma-arc beam back to the sender. Beta Colony helps its neighbor Escobar by providing this technology.

A bit of side plot involves Escobar's female military people raped in Barrayaran captivity. Using uterine replicators, Escobar gives the raped prisoners' fetuses back to Barrayar.

In *Barrayar*, technology is the thumbscrew used to torture Cordelia and Aral Vorkosigan.

Modern Barrayar may have jump ships, energy weapons, comconsoles and more, but the technological revolution is still new as Barrayar comes out of the Time of Isolation. Parts of even the capital city are still the old slums. The former city center, with narrow lanes and alleys and run-down buildings, has no electricity—old technology that is used well in the story.

Since Aral Vorkosigan is the regent for the child emperor, an attempt on his life is made with a "class four sonic grenade, probably air tube launched ... Unless the thrower was suicidal."

In the next attempt, poison gas is used. Though failing to kill Aral, the gas poisons him, Cordelia, and their unborn child, who suffers permanent bone-destroying damage from the poison's *antidote*.

But now the thumbscrew is turned again. The child *might* be saved if he could be given heroic treatments which would poison and kill Cordelia. Enter the uterine replicators given to backward Barrayar by the Escobarans at the end of their war. If the fetus, Miles, can be transferred to the uterine replicator, heroic measures *could* be tried.

That's good till the next crisis.

Civil war breaks out as an opportunistic count sees a chance to make himself Emperor. In the fighting, we see the use of aircars (lightflyers) and scanners which can find people. Separating the animals from the people through a forest canopy is a lot harder, allowing General Piotr Vorkosigan, Cordelia, the child emperor Gregor, and Bothari to escape on the high technology of the Time of Isolation—horses.

The backcountry of Vorkosigan's district, the Dendarii Mountains, runs on old technology—no electricity, modern vehicles extremely rare, outhouses and wood-burning fireplaces.

Then comes one of the implications of having your baby in a uterine replicator—the unborn baby can be kidnapped and held for ransom. The unborn baby is in a technological device not understood by the kidnappers and needs heroic medical treatment to reverse the poison gas cure's damage. The kidnappers could never manage the treatment even if they knew of it!

Cordelia takes action, using car, truck, monorail, sewers, and the high technology of an actual sword to drive the dynamic final quarter of the book.

By the beginning of *The Warrior's Apprentice*, Miles, at seventeen, has already undergone "an inquisition's worth" of medical treatment to his ruined bones. He can walk, even run and do most physical activities, if he's very careful of his bones. He's short, at "just-under-five-foot," and distinctly hunchbacked. He looks like a mutie on a mutation-hating world.

Miles is the child of one of the youngest ship captains and admirals of Barrayar, who was then chosen as regent for the child emperor and later made prime minister of Barrayar. His astrogator mother was captain of a ship of the Betan Astronomical Survey, exploring and mapping wormholes and exploring new worlds. The least members of her crew were the cream of Beta Colony's intelligent and scientific elite. Miles is not dumb.

Miles fails the physical entrance test to the Barrayaran military academy, but, being Miles, he goes off to find *something* to do.

On Beta Colony, Miles buys a junkyard-ready starship, serviceable but old and not economical. Jumpship pilots use neural interfaces to control their ships, particularly during the jump. The pilot of Miles's obsolete ship has the neural interface for the obsolete drive system and has been medically down-checked for a new interface. If he's ever to fly a jump again (which he thinks is "better than a woman—better than food or drink or sleep or breath"), he has to go with the ship.

Miles finds his cargo and supplies via the comconsole in a process quite similar to using the World Wide Web—noteworthy since the story was written a half-decade before the invention of the World Wide Web and a decade before most of us noticed it.

The logistics of paying and supplying a mercenary fleet become important. When receiving the fleet's pay

Miles has a "fantasy of glittering diadems, gold coins, and ropes of pearls. Alas that such gaudy baubles were treasures no more. Crystallized viral microcircuits, data packs, DNA splices, bank drafts on major planetary agricultural and mining futures; such was the tepid wealth men schemed upon in these degenerate days."

On planets, most financial transactions are done with credit cards and electronic transfers; however, paper money is still used as currency on most planets.

The range and intermixing of technologies is a key part of "The Mountains of Mourning" as Miles investigates an infant murder in the backcountry hills of the Dendarii Mountains.

As deputy for his father, the district count, Miles meets the locals on their own terms by riding horseback into the mountains rather than using a lightflyer. The village speaker has a small, battery-powered radio to pick up news from the outside and that's about all the modern technology in Silvy Vale. Miles's armsman, Pym, uses a hand-scanner to search the brush for threats when Miles seems threatened.

It comes down to convincing the locals that Miles *can't* make a mistake on identifying the true murderer because he's going to use the modern technology of fast-penta, an effective truth drug.

*The Vor Game* technologies are similar to those in *The Warrior's Apprentice*. The action takes place on spaceships and space stations that are gearing up for war. When this resolves into the Cetagandan invasion of Vervain and the Hegan Hub, we see the only major space battle shown in the Vorkosigan Saga as Miles's Dendarii Mercenaries join in the defense of the Hegan Hub's jump point.

Since the development of the plasma mirror the plasma beam is less effective and several ships need to gang up on one to overwhelm the plasma mirror defense. The few ships with the short-range gravitic imploder lance try to find chances to use it. Another navy with longer-range gravitic imploder lances is much more effective.

One of the few uses of major automation in the series is the tactical computer. As Miles sits idly in the tactics room, he's reminded of the academy jape *"Rule 1: Only overrule the tactical computer if you know something it doesn't. Rule 2: The tac comp always knows more than you do."*

The main technologies in "Labyrinth" tend to be biological. Prototype 9, for instance, is a wholly engineered human. Nine is a constructed warrior human and a sixteen-year-old girl, albeit eight feet tall with fangs and claws. Other characters include Nicole, the quaddie (four arms, no legs), and Bel Thorne, a Betan hermaphrodite.

On the side is House Ryoval, purveyor of depravity in a bordello using bioconstructed and surgically altered slaves. Not somewhere you'd want to be taken captive—yet Nine, the girl, has been sold to Ryoval.

At one point, the Dendarii find themselves barreling along in a float truck, over the trees at a paltry 260 kilometers an hour, all the speed that crate would do.

On a space station, we see Nicole, the quaddie, in something like her natural environment as she floats in a null-gee bubble. In null-gee, she can play her two-sided hammer dulcimer using all four hands at once, with virtuoso skill. Quaddies use a cup-shaped anti-gravity float chair when they visit planets and one-gee space habitats. They control it with their lower hands, leaving their upper hands and arms free.

The plot in *Cetaganda* keys on computer technology. Lois lets the surprisingly decent Cetagandans suffer the utter folly of having a single point of failure of their most important resource.

The Cetagandans are masters of chemistry and especially genetics. The ghem compete with genetic wizardry on plants and animals. The haut only work with human genetics. They gene-engineer their race as they work for something higher than human and it looks like they're making progress. *All* haut children are engineered from the single master gene bank.

In the Emperor's Celestial Garden's Star Crèche is a frozen genetic sample of every haut who has ever lived—in randomized order. There are hundreds of thousands of samples. But there is only one master-index Key with no backups. "It is a matter of... control," said haut Rian Degtiar, Handmaiden of the Star Crèche.

The previous Empress decided that the haut race was getting stagnant and new competition and expansion was needed. So she ordered the gene bank to be duplicated and distributed to the governors of the eight Cetagandan planets to make eight new, competing centers of expansion. But the one, master, Great Key is not yet duplicated and distributed. Instead, it is stolen.

The Celestial Gardens, home to the Emperor and the haut, is permanently covered by a force dome six kilometers across requiring an entire power plant to maintain it. The haut-women's float chairs use force bubbles for safety and privacy, as the haut-women are never seen by those unworthy. Even a penthouse roof-top garden has its own force dome and the Empress's cremation is contained inside a force bubble.

Little things that show up include marvelous per-fumes, technically enabled art and sensitized asterzine, the fabric that can be formable, dyeable, and totally inert until it comes in contact with the liquid catalyst, at which point it explodes.

*Ethan of Athos* begins on Athos, an all-male planet which gets away from the sin of women's influence over men by using the uterine replicator and cultured ovarian tissues. But a couple of hundred years after the colony's founding, the ovarian tissue cultures are dying of old age.

An attempt to buy ovarian tissue cultures on the market has returned junk tissues, the real ones never having been sent or having been stolen along the way. Ethan Urquhart, a senior reproductive doctor, is sent out into the galaxy to buy new ovarian cultures. Kline Station is the first stop on the route from Athos to the rest of the galaxy.

Dendarii Commander Elli Quinn follows Cetagan-dan agents from Jackson's Whole to Kline Station in pursuit of something biological but she doesn't know what. The Cetagandans are pursuing tissues that are a result of a decades-long research project to develop spies who are telepathic. Losing the cultures might lead their enemies to develop telepathic spies. They think the valuable samples have been sent to Athos, so they capture and question Ethan.

Tiny electronic bugs and tracers are used by the spies in the story, including Quinn. The Cetagandans use fast-penta and other interrogation drugs. One produces high firing rates of sensory nerves and another, applied to the skin, produces agony but leaves no marks.

Kline Station is in an otherwise empty solar system with six wormholes. The station is a transshipment and trading center with over a hundred thousand permanent residents and sometimes a quarter that many transients.

Safety is paramount. Quinn quips that some places have religions, we have safety drills. The biocontrol cops have immense power to make break-in searches and decontaminations as they see fit.

Oxygen comes from aquatic plant life in tanks, which grows, requiring something to eat the excess growth lest it overrun the tanks. Newts eat the plants and something must be done with the newts. Among other uses are fried newt legs, cream of newt soup, newt creole, newts 'n' chips, bucket of newts, newt nuggets, ad infinitum.

Everything is recycled, from water to the bodies of the stationers who've died (though bodies are broken down to the molecular level and fed to plants). Some organic materials are broken down to a lesser degree and fed to food products growing in vats. All meats (except newts) are vat-grown tissues with no (ugh!) live animals to be killed.

*"How could I have died and gone to Hell without noticing the transition?"* is the perfect opening line of "The Borders of Infinity," describing the Cetagandans' torture chamber for the Marilacan prisoners of war.

Rather than building walls, roofs, and floors and posting armed guards, the Cetagandans simply generate a force sphere, showing above ground as an opalescent force dome, perfectly circular, a half-kilometer wide.

With the force dome, the Cetagandans meet the treaty requirement in the cruelest way. *So many square meters a person*—make the dome just big enough. *No solitary confinement*—everyone is together with no privacy of any kind. *No dark periods longer than 12 hours*—no dark periods at all, just the same light, twenty-four hours a day forever. *No beatings*—with no guards in contact with the prisoners the guards can't beat the prisoners. *No rapes by the guards*—no contact with the guards handles that, but since the captors don't enforce any rules, if a prisoner rapes or beats another, too bad. *No forced labor*—no labor or work or occupation of any kind—nothing to do, forever.

Even the rule requiring *access to medical personnel* can work as torture if you confine the medically qualified prisoners with all the others, but don't give them *any* equipment or supplies.

Food is delivered when the Cetagandans bulge one side of the force dome. When the bulge disappears there is a small stack containing exactly one ration bar for every prisoner.

Arrayed against the Cetagandan technology is Miles, who starts out naked, and two spies among the Cetagandans, Elli and Elena, who have some means of burst-transmitting data to the Dendarii fleet.

Then, there's the final problem technology—the mechanics of the combat drop shuttle's ramp. With the recessed slot for the ramp *inside* the door, if the ramp gets damaged and jammed, the door can't close and that's not good for a combat shuttle taking off for space under combat conditions with pursuit.

As Miles arrives for his first visit to Earth, in *Brothers in Arms*, he can contemplate taking a submarine

tour of "Lake Los Angeles" or visiting New York
behind the famous dikes. London, his destination, has
either settled or the ocean has risen—it is protected
from the Thames and the ocean tides by a huge set
of tall dikes.

While Miles is stuck in the Barrayaran embassy on
Earth, he "gets" to attend ambassadorial receptions.
One reception, with planetary representatives who
speak no English, suffers because the keyed translator
earbugs are misdelivered somewhere else in London,
leaving them all just smiling and pantomiming. Alas, the
replacements arrive *before* the interminable speeches.

Miles encounters body laser mapping and computer-
controlled garment creation. An expensive store in the
mall gives him a chance to buy a cultured "live" fur
that seeks warmth and purrs. It's blended from the very
finest assortment of *Felis domesticus* genes. It doesn't
eat, shed, or need a litter box and is powered via an
electromagnetic net at the cellular level, which passively
gathers energy from the environment. If it seems to
run down, the salesman points out, just put it in the
microwave for a few minutes on the lowest setting, but
"Cultured Furs cannot be responsible, however, for the
results if the owner accidentally sets it on high." It makes
an excellent blanket, spread, or throw rug.

In an assassination attempt to kill Admiral Naismith,
the lift lorry at the spaceport shows that even a lift
truck can rise up high enough to be entirely over one
little admiral before its lift is shut off.

The Earth-side cell of Komarran terrorists gives
Miles his first experience of being interrogated with
fast-penta and he provides results unique to his warped
biochemistry.

The action dissolves to a game of kill the clone in the dikes of London's Thames River. The dikes provide an unpopulated site for a game of stunner tag—though some of the players are cheating by using nerve disruptors. Moving up and down, inside and outside of the enormous structure, Miles puts to good use a powered rappelling harness with the ability to lift two or three people.

The best exploration of technology in *Mirror Dance* comes from the death of Miles and his re-"birth." But, before Miles can die, there's the fighting.

Mark impersonates Miles and steals the *Ariel*. Then he takes Bel Thorne and the Green Squad of commandos, led by Taura, down to the surface of Jackson's Whole to raid House Bharaputra's clone-raising facility.

The technologies in the fight aren't new or surprising to the series. The drop team wears half-armor as is common in normal temperatures and atmospheric pressures—space armor isn't needed. The half-armor starts with a full body and head cloth-suit containing nerve-disruptor shield net. Next comes torso armor that would stop anything from deadly needler-spines up to small hand-missiles. Over that goes a combat fabric uniform, with equipment belts and weapons. The backpack contains a one-man-sized plasma arc mirror field. Topping it off is the combat helmet, and since Mark is able to wear Admiral Naismith's equipment, he has plenty of command and control electronics.

Mark, Bel, and the team get delayed and surrounded, then trapped on the ground when their only drop shuttle is destroyed by a thermal grenade in the cockpit. All they can do is huddle with the valuable clone children around them.

Miles to the rescue! Wearing as much borrowed equipment as he can get that came close to fitting, Miles leads another drop team to the rescue.

A Bharaputran guard shoots Miles in the chest with a needle grenade. Since Miles's borrowed equipment doesn't include the torso armor, the fatal shot blows out his heart, lungs, and organs.

In this case, the future combat medics come with a portable cryo-chamber. Miles's throat is cut, his blood is drained and replaced with cryo-fluid, and he's put in the float cryo-chamber and frozen. Then, as the combat worsens, a medic takes Miles's portable cryo-chamber to the fully automated shipping department and ships him to an address on Jackson's Whole where he should be safe. Miles makes it to a cryo-revival facility, where they grow new organs for him and rebuild him.

A risk of returning to Jackson's Whole is that on their last visit, Miles and Taura destroyed Ryoval's tissue bank, used to construct genetic monsters as treats in his depraved bordello's dungeons.

When Baron Ryoval captures Mark, he is ready to spend years torturing him, thinking he's Miles, or using him for practice if he's actually the clone. Ryoval uses beatings, force feedings, and humiliation using violent aphrodisiacs and degradation—photographed from all angles by hovering (anti-gravity) holovid cameras.

Ryoval also skins Mark alive, not with knives but with a chemical spray that melts his skin off, leaving his raw tissues and pain nerve endings exposed to any touch—he can't sit, he can't lie down, he just stands, shifting from foot to foot till his legs give way.

The final item of technology is Ryoval's key to all

his doors, archives, files, and his entire empire—in (what could be better?) a secret decoder ring.

At the beginning of *Memory*, Miles has been mustered out of the Imperial Service due to a case of seizures he picked up in the process of his death and cryo-revival.

The technology explored in the plot is Simon Illyan's eidetic memory chip, which has helped him be such an effective administrator and a terror to subordinates, whose errors are never forgotten. The "chip" is actually a complex sandwich of organic and inorganic components placed between the hemispheres of Illyan's brain. It has a fiendishly ornate data-retrieval net and data storage with an autolearning-style system which installed itself after insertion. It has thousands and thousands of neuronic leads.

Now that complex device is breaking down, "turning to snot inside his head" as one of the medical staff puts it. Illyan is losing track of time, and memories from years before pop into his head as if real and current. Since the breakdown of the chip is unstoppable and irreversible, Miles, who is now the 800-pound Imperial Auditor, orders the chip removed and autopsied.

The thing that killed Illyan's eidetic memory chip is a bioengineered apoptotic prokaryote or, as the scientist says, "A little bug that eats things." It barely qualifies as a life-form but it does eat, it manufactures an enzyme that will destroy the protein matrix in Illyan's chip, and it reproduces itself—up to a point—then self-destructs.

The prokaryote started as a legitimate medical product but was modified to be specific for Illyan's chip. By the molecular evidence it looks like Jacksonian, rather than Cetagandan, work. Miles investigates Imperial Security, from the top floor down to the basement.

He finds that the building is almost as tight as a spaceship, with air filters and cleaners capable of handling poison gases. Locked in the basement evidence room, Miles finds the prokaryote on the shelf, evidence left over from a Komarran terrorist cell broken up some time back—and two vials are missing from the box.

It looks like an inside job with evidence left in the computer system showing that Miles himself probably stole the missing vials.

As Miles is now in charge of the investigation and knows he didn't enter the evidence vault, he knows that the secure computer system was diddled. A technical team is set to freezing and analyzing that system to determine who diddled it, and that traces back to another person Miles trusts, Duv Galeni.

Miles determines who the real culprit is but proving it takes technology and psychology. The technology comes from a spray that fluoresces in the presence of the prokaryote.

In the novel *Komarr*, technology makes life possible on Komarr, a marginal world. There's atmosphere but it's not suitable for humans due to the low oxygen content and cold temperatures—the people live in sealed domes.

With hope for the future, the Komarrans long ago built the enormous soletta array of orbital mirrors to reflect more sunlight down on their chilled world. It's the collision damage to the soletta array that brings Miles to Komarr. A freighter has slammed edge-on into the array, destroying three of the seven hexagonally arranged mirrors. The central seventh mirror is dulled.

Miles, as a newly appointed Imperial Auditor, goes to Komarr to see what effects the soletta disaster will have on the project.

Though the soletta mirrors only increase the insolation by a percentage, it's a critical percentage to foster plant growth in the ecology outside the domes. Even inside the domes, extra lights need to be rigged for the dome's ornamental plants because of the disaster. No plants are purely ornamental on a closed, dome world; they provide much of the breathable oxygen.

Increasing the planetary oxygen percentage is part of Komarran's Terraforming project, as they use plant growth and even peat bogs to break the carbon from the excess carbon dioxide and sequester the carbon long-term.

Besides the soletta mirrors, the Terraforming project also warms Komarr with waste heat power plants. There's no need to conserve energy in the cities—all energy produces waste heat that warms the world.

The soletta accident was caused by a branch of the Komarran resistance which was formed around an N-space (wormhole interstellar drive) mathematician who thinks he's discovered a way to destabilize a wormhole and close it permanently.

Already, two of their people were killed in the soletta accident. Their large test prototype, a single, funnel-corkscrew Necklin rod, was mounted on the soletta array and pointed at an unused wormhole. When an ore freighter crossed the beam, it was, somehow, sucked into the transmitter on the soletta array, damaging the array.

To the remaining conspirators, working without the test's instrument readings, the accident looks like just a fluke of traffic. The full-size device might well work.

If it works as planned and the wormhole permanently collapses, Barrayar will be cut off from galactic civilization, since it has only one wormhole to the outside, the one through Komarr—a new Time of Isolation will begin that may last hundreds or thousands of years or longer.

A trivial side technology is a necklace with a small globe of Barrayar accurate down to the one-meter scale.

*A Civil Campaign* begins back on Barrayar. Two technologically inspired issues involving inheritance of countships are important to the story.

Count René Vorbretten just had an unpleasant encounter with technology when he and his countess went for gene analysis, preparatory to starting their first baby in a uterine replicator. The analysis showed that René's grandfather, the seventh count of the line, was not descended from the sixth count, but from a Cetagandan invader and the sixth count's wife.

A family branch with an untainted bloodline sued in the Council of Counts for the fraudulent inheritance to be voided and the countship to be passed to the senior male in their line.

In another case, Count Vorrutyer died suddenly and his sister, Lady Donna Vorrutyer, filed a motion of impediment with the Council of Counts to block the automatic inheritance of a hated cousin Richars. Then, Lady Donna disappeared on her way to Beta Colony. Speculation is rife on what she'll bring back, an unknown brother or a clone of her late brother, the count. The surprise comes when she returns *as* the brother of the late count, having had a Betan sex-change operation.

Beta Colony's technical supremacy means that the

sex change from Lady Donna to Lord Dono is fully functional with cloned and force-grown parts. In particular, the testicles (the part necessary for inheritance) are her DNA with the Y chromosome taken from her late brother (incidentally made genetic-defect-free in the process).

Now, Lord Dono wants to inherit the district countship from "his" brother, claiming status as the closest "male" relative.

The final technological issue is the side story of Mark, who returns to Barrayar for the summer and the Emperor's wedding with eight thousand incredibly ugly bugs and their creator.

The bugs are simply the carriers of a "carefully-orchestrated array of symbiotic bacteria" which take the ingested food and produce "bug butter," the perfect food, completely nutritionally balanced. But the "butter bugs" are repulsive.

Because the bug's ugliness is a marketing problem, Ekaterin is hired to create a "glorious" bug. Once the bug's creator modifies the bugs' genetics to make them breed true in the new appearance, a lot of the sales resistance melts away.

Body modifications, a space habitat, and bioweapons are the starring technologies in *Diplomatic Immunity*, as the belated honeymoon of Miles and Ekaterin gets interrupted to solve a crisis in a remote corner of the wormhole nexus.

Four-armed, free-fall-adapted quaddies have made their home in a remote, planetless solar system. A Komarran trade fleet with Barrayaran military escort has become enmeshed with the quaddies when an officer disappears. Several liters of the officer's blood (confirmed by DNA analysis) are found on the deck in an empty ship loading bay.

Another character is a human-amphibian who survives an attack from a Cetagandan bioweapon.

A Cetagandan ba has "kidnapped" a thousand haut children, yet to be born and still in their uterine replicators. The ba is fleeing pursuit desperately and is willing to use the haut bioweapons on as many people as necessary to escape. The ba's main weapon is an engineered organism that reproduces in the blood of the victim and builds reservoirs of chemicals. When a critical mass is reached, the chemicals are released and combine. So much heat is produced the victim melts into a puddle over a few hours.

"Winterfair Gifts," the wedding story of Miles and Ekaterin, manages to stay firmly within the normal home environment of Vorkosigan House and Vorbarr Sultana. The Jacksonian neurotoxin and ImpSec's forensics lab are the only exotic technologies used— along with Sergeant Taura's bioengineered, enhanced vision, which saves the day.

Listed last though it takes place two hundred years before *Shards of Honor*, *Falling Free* has no Vorkosigans—it's about the origin of the quaddies.

Before the development of artificial gravity, space workers may only spend limited time in zero-gee. Their bones weaken and their bodies degrade. To eliminate this extra expense, GalacTech has bioengineered a stable race of four-armed humans who are biologically adapted to free fall.

Just as the oldest group is ready for their first job, artificial gravity technology is announced. GalacTech wants to cut their losses by stranding the zero-gee adapted race on the planetary surface, but the quaddies decide to flee.

The habitat is modular and the quaddies disassemble it even though it takes tiny explosives to break the decades-long vacuum welding of the clamps holding it in the old configuration.

The solar panels are folded and the modules are reconfigured to fit the tubular volume that will fit inside a "super-jumper." The super-jumper is a ship capable of traveling through the wormholes between stars. It has four arms arching back along the cargo. Two are for normal space engines. The other two house the Necklin rods to generate the fields allowing the ship to drop out of normal space into the wormhole.

Laser soldering guns have the safeties removed to make real guns for the hijacking of the super-jumper.

An accident damages a vortex mirror which reflects the field at the end of the Necklin rod, ruining the entire ship. The titanium vortex mirror is made in a complex shape to angstrom tolerances.

Leo Graff, the engineering instructor, has read about the crude method used to make trial units—explosive forming. All of the habitat's titanium is melted using laser units and then zero-gee splat-cooled into almost the right shape to make the metal blank for the final forming. Using the identical mirror from the other Necklin rod arm, they make a meters-thick mold out of ice. The large titanium blank is explosively molded to it using a common chemical mixed with gasoline. The resultant shaped blank is made angstrom-perfect with a final laser polish.

❖    ❖    ❖

Lois writes stories about people, their interactions, their problems, and their heart-tearing striving to overcome their faults. Her Vorkosigan stories are the best of science fiction, as she uses science and technology as the environment and often the cause or solution to the truly human problems of her characters. And besides, she likes to torment the living daylights out of her victims.

. . . . .

*Appreciations*

. . . . .

. . . . .

# Through Darkest Adolescence with Lois McMaster Bujold, or Thank You, but I Already Have a Life

## LILLIAN STEWART CARL

It was simple clerical chance that assigned Lois and me to Section 7-2 at Hastings Junior High School in Upper Arlington, Ohio—a suburb of Columbus.

Perhaps we were attracted to each other because we had both already achieved our adult heights—the breathtaking altitudes of 5'5" and 5'7" respectively—and compared to the other seventh graders felt as though we were dragging our knuckles on the linoleum floors.

At first I was in awe of Lois. She had attained little-girl apotheosis: she owned a pony, alas soon to be outgrown. At the riding school just down the road from her home she acquired the equine knowledge that would lead in time to Fat Ninny and the other trusty steeds of Vorkosigan Surleau. The first award I saw Lois win was a blue ribbon and silver bowl in a riding competition. When the judge called her number, she sat disbelieving for a long moment, then reached around to pull the number off the back of her shirt and make sure it was really hers.

The most important things we had in common, though, were a love of reading, vivid imaginations, and the compulsion to write. While I'd been reading history and mythology for years, tastes that I passed on to Lois, I'd never before encountered the strange new worlds of Lois's favorite, science fiction.

These were the years after the Cuban Missile Crisis, the last spasm of the Wonder Bread Fifties, when imagination was suspect. Our parents were shocked speechless by the haircuts of the Beatles, a dance called the Twist, and women wearing pantsuits. (Although Lois's mother did break down and sew her some pantsuits during her college years, supposing they were better than miniskirts.) Except for *The Twilight Zone*, which Lois would sneak downstairs after her bedtime to watch, televised SF consisted of *My Favorite Martian* and *Bewitched*.

Fans, to us, were the girls who read movie magazines and were gaga over Doctor Kildare and Little Joe Cartwright.

Lois read, and passed on to me, Poul Anderson, A. E. van Vogt, Zenna Henderson, James Schmitz, Cordwainer Smith, Ray Bradbury, and Robert Heinlein (we thought *Stranger in a Strange Land* was racy, and were unduly impressed by this first exposure to "adult" content in SF). Conan Doyle and C. S. Forester we discovered together. And Tolkien's *Lord of the Rings* remains to this day one of our all-time favorite books.

We went to movies, from *Lilies of the Field* to *Battle of the Bulge*, from *Wild in the Streets* (anyone remember that?) to *Goldfinger* to *Lawrence of Arabia*—the latter implanting the image of the brooding hero permanently in our literary vocabularies. We followed Peter O'Toole from *Lawrence* to *Becket*, a story that much later influenced one of my own novels.

We wrote, turning out bits and pieces of poetry, fractions of stories, assuring ourselves that this was "practice" for "later on"—although just what "later on" was going to be, we were never able to articulate.

Lois did contribute to the school literary magazine, narrative poems that would have done Ogden Nash proud. One included the line "curses vitriolic," which ended up in the magazine as "curses nitriolic" because the typist couldn't read the copy and didn't know what vitriol was anyway.

I wish I could remember what Lois *rhymed* with "curses vitriolic."

We had an excellent history teacher, who not only confirmed our fascination with antiquity—the future being the trajectory of the past—but accepted with quizzical grace our habit of taking notes on one piece of paper and simultaneously writing a story on another. (This skill came in handy years later, when we found ourselves writing novels and minding children at the same time.)

Lois and I sat at the same desk during different periods in his class, and left penciled notes to each other on the wall—usually initials of the characters of the moment, including one named, presciently, "Riker." I was sitting at that desk when our principal announced the assassination of President Kennedy.

We duly moved on to the rarefied air of high school. Television produced *The Man from U.N.C.L.E.* and

Illya Kuryakin, an example of the sidekick being more interesting than the hero. (It's no accident that the head of Imperial Security on Barrayar is named Illyan.)

A Baskin-Robbins opened halfway between our houses. Some fantasies may be fueled by alcohol, but ours depended upon butterfat.

Still we wrote, isolated in dweebliness—my gosh, we read books that *weren't assigned!* Our heroes weren't the cheerleaders and the captain of the football team but English teachers. We each had one who not only critiqued whatever we wrote, in class or out, but unlike every other adult we knew never found anything suspect in our writings' fantastical content.

Fans, to us, were girls screaming at a Beatles concert, or men shouting at a football game.

Then, one fall, I returned home from a vacation to find Lois enthusing over a new television program, one that linked naturally into her years of reading science fiction.

I watched *Star Trek.* I fell for it too. Spock made intelligence classy. He was so cool, so—unattainable. Unlike Kirk, who was incessantly Available. And there were women on the *Enterprise.* They wore miniskirts and said, "Hailing frequencies open," and "Captain, I'm scared," but they were female nonetheless.

Every Thursday evening during our senior year found us sitting in front of Lois's television (she had the color set) watching *Star Trek.* We suborned other friends into joining us. We rigged up Lois's father's reel-to-reel tape recorder and recorded each episode—audio only, the concept of the VCR being science fiction itself.

The tape would pick up the sound of the telephone ringing in the background, chairs scooting, popcorn crunching. And during the previews to the episode "This Side of Paradise," it recorded half a dozen female squeals as Spock actually (be still, my teenage hormones) *smiled!*

I wish we still had the tape which immortalized her mother's voice saying, "You girls are going to be so embarrassed when you grow up and remember how you acted over this program."

For a time our writing explored the *Star Trek* universe. Then, finding ourselves choked by working in someone else's cosmos, we moved above and beyond and into a multigenerational future history that absorbed our attention for several years. Among other things, we allied our version of the Klingons with the Federation long before *Next Generation* did.

Our graduation from high school took place on a Thursday night, forcing us to miss the episode "Shore Leave." Strangely, our families refused to attend the ceremonies without us. The younger sister of a friend was deputized to do the taping and fill in the video portion with gestures and expressions.

The next fall I went away to college, in a town that had only two television stations, neither of which showed *Star Trek*. Lois transcribed the episode "Amok Time," including the stage directions ("bowl of soup flies across passageway"), and sent it to me. My roommate sniffed and said I was psychologically abnormal. But another friend gave me a poster of Spock.

Meanwhile, back in Columbus, Lois had struck gold in the SF section of a bookstore: a young man who invited her to come to a *science fiction fan club.*

We were no longer alone.

By the time I returned for the summer, Lois was a well-established member of COSFS, the Central Ohio

Science Fiction Society. The only female member, at least until I arrived. Whether our mothers ever knew this is mercifully unrecorded. We ourselves were blithely unaware of the implications. When *2001* opened, the group attended en masse. Lois and I wore cotton dresses and sandals over bare legs. The other girl in the party, someone's date, came dressed primly in a party dress and heels.

Oh well, so we were still dragging our knuckles.

There were enough members interested in writing that COSFS extended a pseudopod, a writing workshop meeting at the house of member Lloyd Kropp, a graduate student in English at Ohio State. (Lloyd, too, went on to become a pro writer.)

One of the stories Lois wrote during this time concerned a hermaphrodite, no doubt a symbolic ancestor of Bel Thorne.

One warm, dark evening no one had anything to read, so we went for a walk around Lloyd's neighborhood. Since his only flashlight wasn't functioning, he and his wife provided us with candles. Looking like a procession of monks who'd lost their way through the cloisters, we strolled along a railroad track, tried out the equipment at a park, and at last found ourselves on a street corner waiting for the traffic light to change. A police car pulled up beside us. The eyes of the officers inside opened so wide they reflected the candle flames. Demurely we crossed the street and returned to Lloyd's house, not breaking into laughter until we were inside.

Some members of the group, heavily into intellectual pursuits such as *Also Sprach Zarathustra*, were dubious about our enthusiasm for *Star Trek*. Others took it in stride. Until the day that Lois and I, like Garland and

Rooney declaring, "Let's put on a show!," announced that we were going to try our hands at one of those things called a "fanzine." One dedicated solely to *Star Trek*.

The others members of COSFS informed us gently that there was no such thing as an all-fiction 'zine. Neither was there any such thing as a media-dedicated 'zine. So what? we replied with the zeal of the innocent. We're going to do it anyway!

Lois and I ended up writing almost the entire 'zine ourselves. Embarrassed, we made up pseudonyms for a few pieces—including stanzas lifted from Shakespeare's "Venus and Adonis" which could be applied to Spock. ("Art thou obdurate, flinty, hard as steel, Nay more than flint, for stone at rain relenteth...") Illustrations came mostly from Janie Bowers, the aforementioned younger sister, and from Ron Miller, now a pro artist. Intent on doing it up right, we paid to have *all* the illos electronically etched. More shaking of heads among the COSFS members.

We typed every word ourselves, on long sheets of waxy purplish paper, and, since neither of us were skilled typists, became intimately acquainted with correction fluid, or "corflu."

Bribed by chocolate chip cookies, COSFS member John Ayotte agreed to run off our 'zines on his basement mimeograph machine. Janie's cartoon cover had too many dark areas, and stuck inkily to the whirling drum, but John, bless him, donated his own thicker paper for the covers. And so *StarDate* was born.

There we were, seeing our words in black and white type for the first time. Daring to air our psyches before the world. We were giddy, and not only from the fumes of the corflu.

Lois and I gathered up the precious piles of *Star-Date* and headed down to Cincinnati for Midwestcon, our first convention, squabbling all the way over how much to charge for our baby. Fifty cents? A dollar?

Midwestcon passed in a blur. Rooms full of (mostly male) people talked at the tops of their voices. A man showed old Flash Gordon movies in a subterranean chamber of the motel. There was a banquet at an all-you-can-eat restaurant just up the way. I suppose someone gave a speech, but all I can remember is the quantities of food put away by an enormous individual rumored to be a bodyguard.

The guest of honor, Fritz Leiber, held court by the pool, but we weren't brave enough to approach him. It had still not sunk in to our feeble brains that we, too, even as women, could become Professional Writers.

I don't remember whether it was at Midwestcon, earlier, or later that we discovered the existence of another Trek 'zine, the delightful *Spockanalia*. Our impulse hadn't been an aberration after all—Trek 'zines were appearing all over the country. The media 'zine became a fundamental of fandom, until, decades later, most fan writing moved onto the Internet.

Within months of *StarDate*'s appearance my family moved away from Ohio. Our 'zine was doomed to be a one-shot; the name was later picked up by someone else. Lois went to her first Worldcon, in California, without me. But she sent me a present, a chalk-on-velour portrait of Engineer Scott. The package arrived on my doorstep borne by a very amused postman—all over the wrapping paper Lois had written exhortations to Handle with Care. "Oh yes," my mother told him with a patient sigh, "that's from my daughter's little friend."

We survived adolescence, only to confront adulthood. But we still had science fiction. And we still wrote.

One evening, as my infant son—who was born on a Friday the thirteenth—crawled over our feet, Lois told me of a story she'd been toying with: a Klingon officer and a redheaded Federation scientist (the latest in a long line of redheaded heroines) are stranded together on a planet resembling the African plains which Lois had recently toured....

The years passed. Lois, too, gave birth to a son on a Friday the thirteenth. Then, one summer, soon after I'd made my first professional sale—proving that it was, amazingly, possible—she arrived at my house with the manuscript of her first novel. We sat until the wee hours of the morning crossing its *t*'s and dotting its *i*'s. Like a medieval alchemist she'd taken her germ of an idea, mixed in Ignatius Loyola, Winston Churchill, and Dumas's musketeer Athos (as portrayed by Oliver Reed in the 1972 movie), and decanted Aral Vorkosigan.

He and Cordelia Naismith trudged off across that alien plain and never looked back.

All four of our children have been nourished on *Star Trek*, *Star Wars*, *Dungeons & Dragons*, the occasional con, and, of course, books. Lots of books. My crawling infant is now married and the father of two, and murmuring of going to graduate school to study Creative Writing, while Lois's daughter is becoming an artist in metals. Lois and I each have tucked away one moldy old copy of *StarDate*.

And sometimes, small but distinct on the horizon, we can still glimpse Excalibur, the One Ring, or the *Enterprise*.

* * * * *

# *Foreword to* Falling Free

JAMES A. MCMASTER

*Falling Free* is a futuristic tale of a faraway world, populated mainly by people, even if some have some superficial changes in their bodies. *Falling Free* is also a brief look into welding engineering, a not-so-well-known engineering discipline that is the science of joining materials, primarily metals. Welding engineering, at least as taught at Ohio State University in the mid-1960s, was a combination of electrical engineering, mechanical and civil engineering, metallurgy, coupled with some courses taught inside the department that looked at the unique and sometimes transient aspects of these engineering disciplines on a weld or a welded structure.

*Falling Free* is one of the few novels that the American Welding Society has ever offered for sale. There is even a copy in the library of the Edison Welding Institute in Columbus.

*Falling Free* is dedicated to our father, "Dad," Doctor Robert C. McMaster. He was a student, a teacher, a researcher, a writer, a speaker, and a performer. As I read the book, I looked for and found many of his characteristics in Leo Graf. He had the same dedication to and belief in his ability to use engineering to solve social problems. He had the same sense of ultimate duty to integrity, truth, and honesty. He had the same disdain for people who would use technology to achieve other than ethical and responsible goals. He shared Leo's disdain for management and accountants who, it often seemed to Dad, killed good ideas before they could really be tested. He had the same narrower view of the world, but one which in its simplicity was perhaps more accurate and certainly more provable.

Many of the characteristics of Leo I would attribute to our father. For example, in the classroom where he is teaching the quaddies and the repeated radiograph of the good weld baffles the quaddies, who just can't comprehend the possibility that anyone could do anything dishonest. I can also relate to the loudly delivered "TURN THE POWER OFF" as a quaddie was about to send a stream of electrons off into space. That was how Dad would remind a student of any particular safety precaution that it appeared he was about to violate in one of the many laboratory classes to which we were regularly subjected in our five years at school.

The expression "Those who can, do, those who can't, teach" was one heard around the school and often applied to undergraduate students encountered throughout the university. I don't know if the addition of "Those who can't teach go into administration" was a *Loisism* or had a different source.

❖     ❖     ❖

The Welding Engineering Department at Ohio State was an unpolished gem—something that seemed lost on the college administration. It was unique in the country, being the only school accredited to grant a degree in welding engineering. Our class was only thirteen people, the one before just six, making ours the largest ever. OSU was the only school in the country that graduated WE students. I was never sure if that meant that the welding engineering was something no one else wanted so there were no clones, or if it really was the best of the best, but industry paid the highest average starting salary to our graduates of any school at OSU.

I took the five-year Welding Engineering course. I took a number of classes from my father. He was the best and most enthusiastic teacher under whom I ever had the opportunity to study. The first day of the first class is indelibly embedded in my memory—he came in, introduced himself, rubbed his hands together (he was too polite to spit on them first), and said "Let's go to work." And we did.

The Welding Engineering Department was always underfunded. One of the classes that was taught by my father and in which I participated dealt with resistance welding, a high-current welding process where power supply was of great importance. Everyone has seen the automobile advertisements with the robotic welding machines where a hundred copper electrodes all converge on a car body at once and set off a shower of sparks. Dad pointed out that metal expulsion as evidenced by the sparks usually resulted in a sub-standard weld, something apparently lost on the advertising types who probably thought the drama was a good thing.

I suspect that some of the disdain for "Administrators" came from Dad's sometime disdain for their activities. He would work hard to get research money only to see most of it siphoned off as "overhead," or maybe get some expensive piece of welding or inspection equipment donated, only to have the administration withhold the funds needed to connect it for service.

One of the first assignments was for each of us to choose one of the clunky old resistance welding machines—my choice was a World War II surplus "Capacitor Discharge Welder." Anyway, we were supposed to trace the power for our particular equipment back to its source, an exercise that sent many enterprising students into the many tunnels that carried steam and utility piping and electrical distribution buses throughout the university. In my case, my machine needed some special thyrotron tubes—this was a high-amperage switching device that does the same thing as a transistor, except it was a vacuum tube with a pool of mercury in the bottom. The signal current caused the mercury to evaporate, and that in turn was the conductor for a rush of several thousand amperes to the machine. There were no spares, and they cost a couple of hundred dollars each. We found a couple in the Electrical Engineering Department and boosted them after an evening class. They had more dust on their boxes than a forgotten bottle of wine in an underused cellar. I don't know if they were ever missed, but they gave the machine about an hour of life before the next component failure proved fatal.

One annoying distraction was the heat-treating laboratory, just outside the lecture room door—and also just outside my father's office. Back in those days, in the Welding Engineering Department, we learned about metallurgy and the heat treatment of carbon steel by making a chisel out of steel bar. First, you heated the end to a glowing red, then brought it out to forge on an anvil. Visualize something out of Dante with a dozen students pounding with five-pound hammers—maybe the origin of the expression "the Hammers of Hell."

The X-ray room had thick concrete walls, except for a sheet metal roll-up door. There were signs on the outside of the door telling people of the X-ray hazard, which would suggest that they not linger there. Parking at the university was a problem. Dad used to park his car in front of that door with a sign that said "Car here for radiation protection" that solved his parking problem and seemed to be sufficient to keep the campus cops away. Once at the end of an operating session when the car was not there, the door was opened and there were a couple of neckers pretty far along in their activities. I always wondered if they had any four-armed kids as a result.

Roy McCauley, department chairman in the 1960s, was known to put on lead-lined gloves, run in and pick up the Cobalt Gamma radiation source, move it to where it was needed for an exposure, and then run behind the shields. Such was the dedication of this small group of professionals.

Robert McMaster was known as "Doc" around the Welding Engineering Department. I assume this came from his Ph.D., earned from California Institute of Technology just before WWII. He was always a student, taught the value of it by his own grandmother. His dedication to education and hard work is truly what pulled our family from the relatively menial jobs held by our grandparents into a life that was at least at the high end of the great American middle class.

He used to give pop quizzes and would count each answer as one point on his mathematical scale of numbers from 0 to n. He even did a "Sneak Midterm" test one day. Even though I lived at home, our intelligence on these activities was not very good.

His grading system solved the dilemma of how to grade his own son without appearing to favor (or not). It was so based on hard numbers that it was beyond dispute—except once, when the final quarterly grades were given. There was a group of grade totals that started in the mid-nineties and dropped down to about 87, then there was this gap with the next score being about 80. The usual A to B cut would have been made at that point, but instead it was done at 88, leaving me and one hapless fellow 87-total student without effective recourse.

For the most part, our days at Ohio State were pretty dull, but some history of import was happening right in front of us. Few people know that the origin of the "Campus Riot," something that became quite common at the height of the unpopular Vietnam War, was actually a student reaction to the Faculty Council decision to not let the Ohio State football team go to the Rose Bowl. I can still remember one of my high school classmates—well, maybe he was a year ahead—leading the chant "Give me an R, Give me an I, Give me an O...." It was several more years before these things turned really ugly and culminated in the tragedy at Kent State University.

❖      ❖      ❖

Welding cannot be long separated from nondestructive testing. Nondestructive testing, or NDT, encompasses a number of methodologies for determining that a part or component is sound without actually destroying the part by testing it to destruction. Radiography, or the use of X-rays or gamma rays to look inside a part, is one of the best-known examples. NDT mimics our own senses. But it has the ability to go beyond the abilities of our senses by extending their range.

I don't know where nondestructive testing came in as such a serious pursuit, except that it is a topic that goes hand in hand with welding. I do remember him, maybe in about 1948 or 1949, talking about nondestructive testing. Somehow, and because his favorite topics were high-pressure arcs and nondestructive testing, that led him to Welding Engineering.

All NDT involves a probing medium and a detector. You see with your eyes, hear with your ears, smell with your nose, feel with your fingers and other body parts, and taste with your tongue. Think of it as using your own five—or, for some, maybe six—senses. When you walk into a room, you "see" using visible spectrum radiation, you "hear" using a range of acoustic vibrations sound, you "smell" trace amounts of chemical present in the air, you feel heat or "touch" to determine the textures of a surface, you "taste" to determine the salinity or sweetness of things.

One of his class and lecture demonstrations was to show how carefully a coin slot in a vending machine tested your nickel before it would give up a bottle of Coke or whatever prize you sought from the machine. He would drop a nickel into the slot and in a brief second it clicked and clanked through the mechanism to fall into the collection tray. But then he went back and looked at each step in detail. First, the coin had to be the right diameter and thickness just to get it into the slot. But then it rolled down a ramp past a magnet that ether speeded or slowed the coin depending on its magnetic characteristics. Its mass determined how fast it might be going at the end of the ramp, and the coin had to make a leap at just the right velocity from the end of the ramp into a narrow space in the middle that didn't lead it back to the reject bin. And then he would say, "Do you think they trust you for your nickel yet?" and go on to explain that the nickel then hit an anvil such that if it was just the right hardness would bounce it to the acceptable bin. He always loved to go on to explore how in places where there was a lot of underutilized brainpower, like at an undergraduate engineering school, how much ingenuity and effort might be applied to slip something other than a nickel past the inspection regime. He would also point out that the nickel often received much more inspection than was applied to critical engineering structures where the results of a failure could go way beyond a nickel.

NDT also uses visible spectrum. The "Mark One Eyeball" is still one of the most powerful inspection tools in the arsenal. But NDT then goes beyond using other wavelengths of radiation: infrared and ultraviolet radiation, X-rays, and gamma rays, and beyond.

Nondestructive testing is moving from application to engineering structures into our everyday lives through application in the medical field.

One of our dad's unrealized dreams was the possibility

of using several NDT methods simultaneously to probe into the unknown, and then combining those responses and comparing them to our experience. In a way, maybe that is the ultimate sixth sense that we sometimes seem to have—the unconscious use of several of our senses at one time, perhaps in very subtle ways, coupled with our experience to recognize a danger or a situation that is not so clear when we just use one or two of our senses. How else does one "sense" the presence of another person in a dark and quiet room?

The welding and nondestructive testing technology described in *Falling Free* is pretty accurate. Most of the devices described have a basis in real life (I'm not so sure about the Necklin rods). For example, the plasma arc, which Lois has as a formidable hand weapon is to a welding engineer a heat source for welding. Same with the electron beam. Back in the late 1950s, electron beam welding was a new and novel process. One of the OSU students, J. Whittier Slemmons, built one using junk in the early days of the process.

Lois consulted with Wally Voreck, a friend of my family who has spent a lifetime in the explosives field—some military and some industrial. Wally was also a voracious reader of science fiction and was pleased to read the book in an early form and to have a chance to offer suggestions to make the descriptions more authentic. I think it was he who suggested the explosive forming of something for *Falling Free*.

My own career has largely been devoted to titanium metal. I suppose that was the source for the choice of titanium for the mirror in the book. Titanium is just a metal with a fancy name, but it has of late come to signify something important enough that even credit cards scramble to usurp the name.

One maxim of our dad was the idea that whatever you would do, you should do it better than anyone else. He illustrated this at his Ohio State University office by displaying for many years, taped to the wire-reinforced door, a cartoon of a guy with an enormous ball of string and a caption "Whatever you do, do it to the best of your ability." Lois has gone on to fulfill that axiom in her writing.

We were taught, apparently by example, to take responsibility for our own actions and to behave in what I perceive to be a reasonably moral way. Sort of a proletarian form of noblesse oblige. Lois reflects this in *Falling Free* in the whole exposure of the innocent quaddies to the less innocent characteristics of man, illustrated particularly by the example of one radiograph that was presented over and over again as proof of the quality of many welds, and Leo's appalled reaction to this. I could see precisely the same reaction from our dad—and maybe it was a real case based on some work he did on the Alaska Pipeline.

Dad always claimed that his father sat him down one day in early life and asked him what he wanted to be. He responded, "An electrical engineer," thinking that he could drive the big electric locomotives that were just coming to the rails near Pittsburgh. His father's menial jobs provided little chance of affording a higher education. He won scholarships first to Carnegie, then Case, and finally Caltech based on incredibly good grades (those genes and that drive never got passed to any of us). He did study electrical engineering and the nature and effects of lightning, which I suppose was the source for his interest in arcs and welding. During the war and after at Battelle Institute, I know he worked with some early inspection of drill pipe in west Texas and torpedo drive systems in the Chesapeake Bay. We remember the stories of errant torpedoes that either toppled the observation barge, sending everyone on board in with the jellyfish, or went to the beach, causing a rapid retreat of the sunbathers in its path.

Dad was an inventor with a very wide range of interest. He held nineteen patents covering a wide range of disciplines. Some of these ideas have become very important in the lives of the modern world. He holds the basic patent on xeroradiography, the application of the Xerox (halide) patents to X-ray rather than visible light like today's copy machines. This has evolved into the medical imaging equipment used to detect breast cancer. He also holds the basic patents on the first television X-ray system, a device that he made possible by the introduction of a low-density beryllium window in place of glass that would block the weak X-ray signals, and precursor to the X-ray machines used in real-time medical imaging and luggage inspection at airports. Every time you go to a dentist using the new direct film-to-digital system, you are touched by his work.

For a time throughout the 1950s, Dad was the "TV Weatherman" to most of Central Ohio. This was truly during the infancy of television. Ours at the time was a six-inch black-and-white Hallicrafters with a row of channel-selector buttons across the bottom. Dad had taken a weather course at Caltech from Irving Krick—one of the key people in the decision to go into Normandy on June 6, 1944—so he came to the program with more real background than the weather readers of today. Like most else he did, he used the five-minute show to teach everyone in Ohio about weather. The shows always started with the same somewhat startled "Well, hi there."

## People Whose Names May Have Been the Inspiration

For those who studied Welding Engineering at Ohio State University in the early 1960s, the names of at least some of the *Falling Free* characters are familiar.

Leo's family name may have come from Professor Karl Graf, who became chairman of the Welding Engineering Department a few years after McCauley left.

The real-life name source for "Leo" may have been the first black student in Welding Engineering, Leo Wilcox, who was a few years ahead of me. We all met him in the mid-1950s at the annual Welding Engineering Department picnics.

"Claire" may have been inspired by Clarence Jackson, a family friend as well as a professor in the Welding Engineering Department. Clarence specialized in submerged arc welding and had learned the trade the hard way. Getting him on the staff proved to be a real exercise for the silver-tongued McCauley, since the university looked down its collective nose at anyone who had not actually graduated from college, and to have such a person as a professor, even in the mostly forgotten Welding Engineering Department, was a real leap of faith for the school.

Another professor was Bill Green. I don't think he got mention by name, but maybe Silver was just a better and certainly sexier sounding substitute name.

Doctor Minchenko may have been based on Hildegard Minchenko, who was a researcher of Russian origin who worked on a sonic power project that Dad had developed and obtained funding for. For the few of us at the school at the time, this project was remembered because the frequency chosen for the 10-hp high-energy transducers was 10 kHz, right in the middle of the range of human hearing. Many a class discussion was given by yelling over the incessant screaming of the horns operating just outside the lecture room door.

## Finally: Lois

Lois and I spent the first half of the summer of 1965 hitchhiking in Europe—then a relatively safe activity, and one which had a built-in filter to be sure you encountered interesting people along the way, but still a stretch for our parents to accept. I had never thought that she would find the experience any different than I. I was after small towns and rural scenery, figuring that I would see the cities later in life from a more comfortable point of view.

There were a few memorable occasions. After our first overseas flight, we arrived in London very tired. We left Heathrow heading for Stratford, because that was something we had all heard of in England. Our first night was spent in a park in a town west of London. We remember the bobby who helped us into the city park and to a park bench for a bed, and then promised to look in on us from time to time overnight.

We went to a Shakespeare play in Stratford the next day. I fell asleep, but Lois was enthralled by it all, seeing Shakespeare as it was meant to be for the first time. Staying in youth hostels was a wonderful experience. They ranged from rude sheds to ancient castles. One near Inverness had statuary in all the halls and was more like a museum.

In Ostende, we joined a group of young men for an overnight in a loft over a pub. I was impressed that Lois was able to remove her bra right in front of the crowd, but completely under her shirt. I never have figured out how that was done.

You met young people from all over the world doing the same thing. It was automatic that they were interesting, particularly the ones from Australia and New Zealand, places that seemed so far away to us. What a sad thing it is that people have become so untrustworthy as to make this remarkable diplomatic activity a danger and that it never grew the same way in the U.S. One wonders how much different the world would be if more people had had this cross-cultural exposure in their youth.

The rides were something interesting as well. The most comfortable was a Rolls-Royce Silver Cloud driven by a Member of Parliament. He pointed out the straight sections of road built by the German prisoners of war in World War II and the telephone poles along both sides to discourage their use as landing fields. And then there was the back of a truckload of American onions on the ride over the "Devil's Elbow" in Scotland—we were given a few samples and added them to our stew for supper, and it probably took a week to air the hostel out afterward. We were picked up by a just-wedded couple in Belgium in a Citroen—the one with the corrugated steel sides that wobbles along the road. I think they just wanted to tell someone.

Some of the scenery probably has helped Lois in her descriptions. I'm sure the lake in *Spirit Ring* is modeled after Lake Como. Baocia's bony soil looks like some of Scotland, although colored by her later visits to Spain under plusher circumstances. The castles described may have been in part from this trip.

Lois joined my older brother—an accomplished sailplane pilot who occasionally finds time for work or other life activities—and me long before we had any sense of where babies came from. I think she had the usual experience of the youngest of siblings and I suppose we can blame ourselves that she was something of an introvert in her early years. Somehow that turned out okay as it led her to the Trekkie counterculture that, combined with a large collection of science fiction novels in Dad's library, may have had a small part in sending her down the path she has taken.

Lois used to drag home the most motley-looking collection of characters—I think they were fellow Trekkies, or at minimum early incarnations of hippies, the counterculture norm of behavior for those who wanted to be different, but they all looked the same to me. Some of these folks have gone on in the science fiction field. Lillian Stewart Carl was a frequent visitor to our house, and is a successful fantasy writer and remains a close friend of Lois to this day. Her dad was also a professor at the university, in Agricultural Engineering. Ron Miller has gone on to a career of illustrating science fiction novels. In the early days he did beautiful renditions of Martian, Lunar, and other far-world landscapes that looked like the stuff Wernher von Braun and Willy Ley dreamed of.

I don't think Lois liked having babies. I think she may have been okay with the first part, but the production stage and then the years of launch activities may have taken a toll. At least that is what I assume was the source for the "uterine replicator" that plays a minor role in *Falling Free* but is more significant in the Vorkosigan series. However, if nothing else, the child-rearing experience allowed her to write the scene of feeding Andy with great realism.

Lois was a perpetual student and we often wondered if she would ever do something—anything. I don't think she ever did finish a degree, but that doesn't seem to have fazed her much. She lived in relative poverty for years.

She paid her dues for years before *Shards of Honor* was published and even after until her Vorkosigan series began to draw a following. On the other hand, if she had not had this experience of poverty and the time it provided, she might never have written the first several novels that were completed before she sold the first.

I have read all her novels and have become a fan. They make pretty good gifts for overseas trips. Lois got twenty copies of *Falling Free* in Japanese from Japan, which she then signed, and which I carted back to

Japan in my luggage to support visits to a number of fabricating shops and metal suppliers. It's sometimes handy to have a famous author in the family.

The cover of my paperback copy of *Falling Free* finally fell off as I reread it for the fourth time to help with this writing. However, I personally like her fantasy series best, *The Spirit Ring*, *The Curse of Chalion*, and last year's *Paladin of Souls*. Based on reading the first chapter, I look forward to *The Hallowed Hunt*, which should be out later this year. I have read *Chalion* seven times now and am rereading *Paladin* and keep enjoying them more each time as an added bit of subplot becomes a little more clear to me. Her recognition is deserved.

—James A. McMaster
Huletts Landing, New York
2004

· · · · ·

# *Foreword to* Shards of Honor

## JAMES BRYANT

*Shards of Honor*, written in 1983 and published three years later, is Lois McMaster Bujold's first novel. It is also the first story of her Vorkosigan series, a collection of fifteen books set in the same Universe, most of them involving Miles Vorkosigan or his parents. She has also written a number of short stories, one historical fantasy novel set in an alternate Italy, and two fantasy series, the "Five Gods" Universe, with three of a planned five novels published, and the "Sharing Knife" Universe, of which the full set of four novels has been written, but as of mid-2007, only two have been published. Her work has garnered three Nebula Awards and five Hugos, three of them for Best Novel—more in that category than any other author except Robert A. Heinlein.

Despite these achievements it is surprising how little known she is outside the world of SF. When the birth of Dolly (the cloned sheep) was announced, the media consulted the Great and the Good on the issues of human cloning—but no one consulted Lois, who had considered the human problems of such cloning in half a dozen books, and had reached more humane and useful conclusions than most of those who were quoted. To mention but one: The result of the cloning process is a baby who must be reared and nurtured for at least a decade, more probably two, before becoming a productive member of society. The costs, economic and human, of this rearing are rarely considered by those prophesying cloned armies of slaves or soldiers. ("They call it women's work." [*Ethan of Athos* Chapter 5])

She is a superb writer, with a wicked facility for emphasizing points by clever choice of phrase. She has said that a book as a work of art is not the printed text but the engagement between the ideas of the author and the perceptions of the reader. It is the author's place to facilitate that engagement and Lois does. She may make us work to appreciate her allusions, but she is never deliberately obscure.

To those familiar with her works it is evident that *SoH* is an early one; the background to her Universe is still comparatively sketchy. But she already has all her skills of insight, compassion, characterization, a sly and subtle wit which comes back and bites you three sentences down the page (never read an LMB story while eating or drinking), and an ability (which she ascribes to "an unreconstructed inner thirteen-year-old") to create plots which excite by leading the reader's expectations one way and then delivering an entirely unexpected dénouement. In *Barrayar* Cordelia reflects that as a stranger to the planet of Barrayar one must "Check your assumptions—in fact, check your assumptions at the door." (*Barrayar* Chapter 5) Lois's readers should do so, too. (*Barrayar* [1991] is the direct sequel to *SoH*, and the second half of the story arc [Lois's term for an entity comprising two or more separate novels] which she has described as "The Price of Becoming a Parent.")

Lois is well read in many areas, including, of course, SF, and, as the daughter of an engineer and herself a sometime medical technician, does not confuse the unrealized with the unscientific. Her works contain echoes of Austen, Heinlein, Heyer, Russell (Eric Frank), Shakespeare, Tolstoy, and many, many others.

Her skill in characterization is impressive. Even her minor characters grow as the stories progress, and we can feel the emotions and motivations of all of them, even walk-on "prop-box" characters like spaceport officials and hero-worshipping starship pilots. (I loved the response of Cordelia's CO to the psychiatrist's comment that "A middle-aged career officer is hardly the stuff of romance." [*SoH* Chapter 13]) Her major characters, heroes and villains, are three-dimensional— none is all good or all bad—and here again we need to be careful of our assumptions.

Throughout her SF Lois uses the "tight third person" point of view (POV) where, although the text is written in the third person, the reader sees and knows what the POV character sees and knows—almost like a first-person account—which does not necessarily correspond to objective reality. In *Shards of Honor* we are confined to Cordelia's POV, but in later works she uses more—there are five in *A Civil Campaign*—and it is further evidence of her skill that the personality of each POV character illuminates the narrative.

But one of her greatest attributes is her empathy. She makes us feel for all her characters, even the villains. In fact it is this empathy, manifest in Cordelia, the heroine and POV character, which gives us the title of the book. She and Aral Vorkosigan both seek to do what is right rather than simply follow rules; she calls the quality "grace of God," he calls it "honor," and it drives them both to very hard choices. It is Cordelia's honor, manifested in burying the dead and helping the injured despite practical imperatives to do otherwise, which first attracts Aral in the first few pages of the book and the first few minutes of their acquaintance. *Cordelia's Honor* is actually the title of an omnibus volume containing *Shards of Honor* and *Barrayar*.

Lois's practical policy, that the best way to advance a plot is to work out the worst possible thing that can happen to her characters—and do it to them—gives ample scope for the exercise of empathy!

This particular combination of qualities attracts SF readers who are practical, widely read idealists. The Internet mailing list devoted to her works is erudite, compassionate, courteous, and wide-ranging in the topics discussed and (non-Bujold) books recommended—and contains members of all ages and many nationalities. (Lois's works have been translated into about twenty languages.) If you have access to the Internet you can find more about Lois herself and this mailing list at www.dendarii.com.

C. S. Lewis and J. R. R. Tolkien have both said that they wrote children's stories because that was the proper medium for a particular thing that they had to write.

Lewis further pointed out that only bad children's stories were read by children exclusively. Nevertheless many adult readers eschew all such works. Lois writes science fiction and fantasy, and so her talents are concealed from the many readers who similarly "don't read that sort of thing." We cannot avoid classifying literature into genres, but we should recognize that a single work can be classified in a number of different ways. *Shards of Honor* is science fiction. It is also a romance, a military adventure, a political novel, and a study of the morality of war. All her works cross genres in this way—all her novels are SF and fantasy but she has written romances, military adventures, espionage thrillers, mysteries, and a comedy of biology and manners. I should love to see her write a Western set on Barrayar—or Sergyar.

If I had to sum up *Shards of Honor* in a sentence I would recall a conversation between two minor characters at the very end of the book. In the aftermath of battle they are recovering frozen corpses, of both sides, from space, for burial. "Is it true," asks the pilot, "you guys call them corpse-sicles?" "Some do," the medtech replies. "I don't. I call them people." This is a book for people.

—James M. Bryant
Midsomer Norton—England
August 1999
(amended October 2007)

•  •  •  •  •

# "More Than the Sum of His Parts": Foreword to The Warrior's Apprentice

## Douglas Muir

An angry young man perches at the top of a wall.
Should he climb carefully down, or save a few seconds
by jumping? He makes his decision, he jumps... and
we're off on a high-speed adventure that will take us
through space battles and murder plots, unrequited love
and bloody death, laugh-out-loud fun and hair-raising
horror, and finally to the private audience chamber
of the Emperor of Barrayar.

It's not giving too much away to say that Miles
Vorkosigan has a great fall. Unlike Humpty Dumpty,
Miles's problem is that he can't stop putting himself
together again. Smuggler, would-be soldier, unrequited
lover, con artist, space commander, entrepreneur...
Miles Vorkosigan, you'll soon find, is a young man
of parts. And his story is just as complex as he is,
for *The Warrior's Apprentice* is at least three books
folded into one.

Running up the middle of the book, as it were, is the central plotline, a story of high adventure and a young man's coming of age under several different sorts of fire. There are combats and ambushes, plots and pursuits, and a final twist that loops the story around to—almost—where it started. It's a ripping yarn, a classic example of the genre that was once known as "space opera" and now seems to be called "Military SF," and by itself it's a perfectly good reason to buy and read this book.

But there's so much more. Twining around this central plot, like vines up a tree or the twin serpents around a caduceus, are two other stories—one a comedy, and one a tragedy.

People tend to talk about Lois's complex and believable characters or her richly detailed worlds. Well, they are terrific characters and the world is so deep and so plausible that people have gotten lost in it. Lots of other people have already written essays on these things, and I just think it's really nifty the way she puts her plots together, the skeleton working smoothly under the skin. If you're one of those people who are just bored to tears by reading about plot structure, please, skip to the section marks. Or you could even go right ahead to the book—it's a very good book, and my feelings won't be hurt a bit. I might even talk about symbols, too, so don't say you haven't been warned.

The comedy lies in the story, as old as Aristophanes, of the little white lie that grows out of control, the plot that accelerates until the plotter is desperately scrambling to keep up with it. It's about good intentions gone wildly awry, salesmanship run out to its logical conclusion, and the dangers of picking up strays.

And it's funny—funny in all sorts of ways, from dry irony to wild slapstick. This book made me laugh out loud, unexpectedly, at least half a dozen times. The scene where Miles varies his financial structure, for instance. Or his inspection of Captain Auson's ship, and its outcome: "My Lord—those are the *old* regulations—" from Bothari.

Or the cultural misunderstandings between Betans and Barrayarans. I don't know which is funnier: the scene in the junkyard—"But that would kill him!"—or the repayment of Miles's financing: "Y'know, there's something backwards about this," from Ivan, as they tie their creditor up and then stuff bundles of money into his clothing.

Or just the little throwaway lines:

"'I always knew,' Miles lied cheerfully. 'From the first time I met you. It's in the blood, you know.'"

"You can't eat an exhibit!"

"Who wouldn't? Who do you think you are? Lord Vorkosigan?"

"—even if he is at a convenient height for it."

And finally, there's the quiet smile that comes from subverting the conventions of the genre. A space opera/MilSF hero should be tall and ruggedly handsome (or tall and curvaceously gorgeous) and physically hypercompetent; s/he should have a plucky sidekick and a trusty blaster, should go charging valiantly into battle, and should be the center of attention and admiration, especially from the opposite sex. Miles is short and funny-looking, he's generally unarmed except for an old knife, his sidekick is anything but plucky, he's in danger of collapsing before charging into battle, and as for the opposite sex . . . well, you'll see. *The*

*Warrior's Apprentice* isn't a satire—it's a real science fiction adventure story, not a parody of one—but if you listen carefully, you can hear the sound of genre clichés being picked up, flipped over, and shaken hard to see what falls out.

Now, combining a picaresque space opera with a comic romp would be accomplishment enough for any author. However, Bujold goes for the hat trick. There's a third story being told here, and it's a grim, gothic tale of violence and violation, of innocence lost and old secrets coming back to bite. Be warned: there's death in this book, and pain, and bad things happening to characters that you've come to care about. While it's by no means a grisly or explicitly violent story, there are scenes here that are creepy, and disturbing, and that may haunt you for a long time afterward.

Comedy, it is said, ends best when it ends with a marriage or a voyage; tragedy, with a death and perhaps a redemption. *The Warrior's Apprentice* has all these things, though not necessarily in that order, and at the book's end you may be surprised to find that the seemingly disparate plot threads have come together. The tragedy plays out as it inevitably must, the comic elements are resolved, and the wild adventure loops around to an end. Just as the fragmented plotlines come together, so too—perhaps—do the fractured pieces of Miles Vorkosigan. I don't want to give too much away, but pay close attention to the book's final scene. Like the first, it involves a test, a difficult colleague, and the ascent and descent of a wall . . . but with a difference. Lois Bujold, you will find, does little by accident.

No discussion of Bujold would be complete without at least mentioning her quiet but effective use of recurring symbols. (I warned you I was going to talk about symbols, didn't I? Oh, come on, we're almost finished.) I'll just mention one, and then you can have the fun of trying to catch some of the others. Keep an eye out for old Piotr's knife, a tool that is put to a startling variety of uses, from the horrific to the comic. Sign of authority, implement of torture, means of escape...the knife hints at the complexity of old Piotr himself, and of the role that Miles is trying to grow into.

Well, all right, just one more: the title. Of course it's a sly reference to *The Sorcerer's Apprentice*, the foolish young man who conjures up an army of brooms and buckets and then finds that they've multiplied beyond his control. But there's at least one level of meaning beyond that. As you read, pause now and then to think about it. Who is the warrior's apprentice? There's more than one warrior here, after all, and more than one apprenticeship being served.

Okay. Those of you who left when we started talking about plots and suchlike can come back now.

*The Warrior's Apprentice* is, depending on how you count, either the second or the third novel of Lois McMaster Bujold's celebrated Vorkosigan cycle. Before you ask, no, it's not one of those dreadful one-chapter-in-an-endless-saga things. There are threads leading into and out of the story, but the book is complete in itself, and you needn't have read anything else to enjoy it. It's the first book to deal with Miles (the earlier ones are about his parents) and so an excellent beginning point if you haven't read any of the Vorkosigan stories before.

I suspect that, once you've finished this book, you'll probably want to read the others. Be happy: there are a dozen or so, they're all good, and Lois is likely to write even more. They're books that sketch out a big, roomy universe filled with, well, richly detailed worlds and complex and believable characters. They have nice complicated plot structures, too, for those of us who like that sort of thing.

Right. Off you go, and hold on to your hat.

—Douglas Muir
June 2001

· · · · ·

# *Foreword to* Ethan of Athos

## Marna Nightingale

(2007 note: I am grateful to Suford Lewis of NESFA Press for asking me to write this introduction in 2003 and for her stalwart support while I did so, to Lillian Stewart Carl for giving me the opportunity to revisit and revise it for this new volume, and to Lois McMaster Bujold for providing occasion for both.)

Those of us who are loud, joyous, unabashed lovers and partisans of science fiction—that is to say, nearly everybody reading these words—have learned to greet the remark that a book or a writer "transcends the genre" with narrowed eyes and brusque demands to be told exactly what the speaker means by *that*. Our response is remarkably similar to the one which used to baffle and sometimes hurt the well-meaning souls who once roamed the earth telling especially bright or competent women that they thought "just like men." We've learned to see the dismissal beneath some "compliments"—to ask, what's wrong with being a science fiction writer? What's wrong with being a woman?

The analogy I am drawing—between gender and genre—is not accidental, and it's not casual. The words are almost the same for a reason—*genre* is the French word for kind or type, and our word *gender* comes from the same root: a genre book is a *certain kind* of book. A genre writer is a *certain kind* of writer. A gendered person is a *particular type* of person—and there's nothing wrong with that. Genre *is* important, though not all-important—it's the bones under the flesh, the underlying structure.

*Ethan of Athos* could not be what it is, could not ask the questions it asks in the way it asks them, and be anything but a science-fiction novel, a supremely good one: herein are fascinating new technologies, space adventure, and mystery. Here are richly textured cultures at once alien and recognizable, endlessly surprising and at the same time inevitably and always products of their particular intersection of basic axioms and advanced technology. *Ethan of Athos* has suspense and trouble, people shooting at each other, and people in love with each other. It's got spaceships and space stations. It's got genetically engineered superhumans, heroes, villains, nice normal folks just trying to get through the day. It's got a wonderfully twisty plot, as Bujold books always do. It's even got a Mad Scientist (and a few who are just really annoyed).

(This is as good a time as any for a few public service announcements. First of all, if you're wondering whether you came in halfway through, you should know that *Ethan of Athos* is, as are all of the fourteen books of the Vorkosigan Saga, intentionally freestanding—in theory, you *can* read just one—though in practice, there are no known cases of this occurring. Secondly, this foreword therefore contains no series synopsis or anything like that. If you want to, you can skip the rest of it and dive straight into the book, maybe drop by here again after if you care to. I promised to get up here and juggle, but you're under no obligation to hang around and watch. Lastly, you may wish to know that there is a mailing list for fans of Lois' work, which you can find out about by going to www.dendarii.com. This may come in handy once you've finished reading every single bit of Bujold published to date and need some understanding people to keep you good company until the next book comes out.)

Where was I? Right. If *genre* is the bones of a story, the fundamental understanding of *gender* which a story reveals might be described as a look at the skin that covers the flesh of our common humanity. I would be grievously underrating the potential capacities of men to say that *Ethan of Athos* could only have been written by a woman, but it *is* fair to say that it could only have been written by someone who has a deep knowledge of and respect for that half of the human experience—the skills and the collective knowledge—which we have until recently regarded as the almost-exclusive province of women.

The question of gender in science fiction has had a long but curiously tame history, remarkably similar to the treatment of gender in that other would-be-time-traveler's delight, historical fiction: everything else about a novel's setting may be rich and strange and suited to the time in which the novel is set, but the gender roles portrayed generally fall safely within at least the broad limits of what is acceptable to the time in which the author is living—at least by the end of the book. Exceptions exist, but they are rare enough to be memorable: *Herland*. *The Left Hand of Darkness*. *The Gate to Women's Country*. The Darkover books. And *Ethan of Athos*.

With the exception of *The Left Hand of Darkness*, which concerns itself primarily with beings who are both men and women, and the partial exception of *The Gate to Women's Country*, however, even in writing which seriously discusses gender roles in science fiction we're generally talking about women's roles, and for good reason—women's roles have been a social preoccupation and source of anxiety in the West for as long as there have been novels. Still, there it is again, that assumption that women are the troublesome—and troubled—gender, the gender that needs to "transcend their type" if we're ever going to get anywhere.

These days most science fiction—in lockstep with most of Western society—at least takes it for granted that women *can* transcend "their type," that women's options should and will be expanded, but that expansion is to come in very specific directions, toward greater access to "men's stuff." Problematic female characters, now, are not the ones who try to be more like men, but the ones who do not.

And the men? Well, there they are, doing pretty much what fictitious men have usually done (and wanted to do), and actual men have generally done and at least pretended to enjoy, conquering new worlds, getting into fights, working at the office, running the country, or the planet, seducing women, all that. Sometimes we might get a world where war and competition have been abolished, or farmed out somehow, but those are dystopic tales, and if the question is even raised, the effect on the male role is not to change it, but to transfer it—the warriors, whoever they are, become the new *real* men, the ones to be reckoned with, while the "original" men become something else, something less, at least until they see the error of their ways.

In these new takes on gender roles, it's not just the potential for male change which is largely ignored; all that messy "womanstuff" is generally left behind, too—some way is found to get the meals cooked and the children raised, the clothes made, washed and ironed, the relationships maintained, and so forth— some machine will be built or some inferior race or underclass will be there, economically created or conquered, or maybe cloned. Possibly the underclass will be made up of those problematic women who just can't, or won't, learn to play a man's game by the men's rules. It's a simple enough bit of handwaving, and after all, it's really not very important, right?

(2007: I think the generalizations of the foregoing three paragraphs were far too simplistic even in 2003, when I wrote this; *mea culpa*. As of four years later, they seem downright quaint; gender bending, gender blending, and reimagining masculinity is where it's at, culturally and SFnally—and we're all richer for it.)

But of course it's not quite that simple, and it *is* that important. While there is no shortage of women, freed by technological and cultural change from confinement to "women's work," doing the things that we traditionally think of as masculinely adventurous and powerful in Bujold's fiction, she never neglects the other side of the coin. When women are no longer biologically bound to childbearing, and to the home-based service role that this bio-logic seems invariably to create, men are no longer biologically bound to "not childbearing," nor to the "men's work" that we consider appropriate for those appointed to the supporting role in human evolution.

When reproduction and parenting and love are no longer inexorably linked to either gender or sex, the possible consequences for gender relations, sexuality, love, and partnership are almost limitless. In *Ethan of Athos*, Lois sets out to explore two basic, but much-neglected, aspects of the gender-role question as it relates to SF—what happens to men's roles, and to women's work, when technology sets them free of biological sex?

(Remembering the title of a certain high-school class in which, as a suburban substitute for a more solemn Initiation Into Womanhood, we were taught the "mysteries of womanhood"—mostly menstruation, meatloaf, mending, IUDs, and ironing—I want to say that this book belongs to an entirely new genre: Domestic Science Fiction—but that would be reductionist as well as, frankly, kind of lame. I do want to say, however, that it is partly as a result of reading Bujold that I have reconsidered my disdain both for the title of the course, which at the time I considered pretentious, and for the curriculum, which I considered deeply inferior to Shop, where one was given access to power tools.)

One of the central and most fascinating pieces of technology in Lois's writing is the uterine replicator.

This seemingly innocuous piece of equipment, which had its beginnings as a bit of convenient handwaving in *Shards of Honor*, has gone on to become one of the greatest agents of social change in the Nexus (the series of star systems which provide the context for *Ethan of Athos*, as well as for the Vorkosigan adventures) on each planet according to its cultural assumptions. In *Ethan of Athos* we see Lois's early consideration of the impact that the uterine replicator will have on gender roles, still sketchy in spots, but full of hints as to the directions she will later take—in particular, we get a sense of the genre (and gender) conventions she proposes to play the best sort of merry hell with.

The most obvious form that this consideration takes is the social structure of Athos, a planet with no women and a great many children. There is also the evolving understanding and partnership between Elli Quinn and Ethan Urquhart—the woman who wants to be a mercenary fleet commander, and the man who wants to go home, settle down, and raise a bunch of kids. There is the very proper Athosian Ethan's progress from terror at the mere *thought* of a woman to understanding and acceptance of the human women—the mothers, in a sense—whose ovarian cultures helped build his world, to real friendship with Elli. There is Elli's sideways look at the paths she has rejected, and her own coming to terms with them. Biology is not destiny in a Bujold story; *destiny* is destiny, and when it comes for you it looks at what's in your heart, not what's in your pants.

So we have the bones of genre, and the skin of gender, but what of the flesh, our common humanity? (And it is, always, a question of humanity—Lois has commented a number of times that she deliberately chose not to have aliens in the Nexus; the aliens, she says, are *us*.)

We are thinking creatures and tool-using mammals, we are usually (2007: not always—*meâ culpa* again) either men or women, but beyond the first and underneath the second, we are members of the human race. (Another word for *race*, from the same root as *genre* and *gender*, is *genus*; to speak of ourselves as "members of the human race" is to make yet another series of statements—about the kind or type of being we think we are, and about who we do and do not think counts as a member.)

Because this is science fiction, Bujold considers the question of humanity through the mechanism of technological change; because this is a book about gender and sex, the particular focus is reproductive technology. And because this is a book about how we create, become, remain, designate, and treat members of the human race, Lois's use of the advantages and perils of biotech's capacity to give us almost total control over the creation, prevention, and form of human life never degenerates into the easy and cheap answers so common in science fiction and in our own society.

Bujold never makes technology the villain, destroying our humanity, nor does she cast it as the hero—which is why, at this reprinting, *Ethan of Athos* is one of that rarest of science fiction stories: a story which instead of becoming dated as time has passed and the breakthroughs it discusses have come nearer to or reached fruition in the real world—in 1986, the year *Ethan* was published, ovum donation was experimental; now (2007) it is commonplace—has become *more* relevant, *more* timely, because it relies for its power on eternal, increasingly urgent human questions instead of on rapidly changing technological answers.

The question is a basic theme of science fiction, given a quarter turn—when she asks, in *Ethan of Athos* and elsewhere, how far we can go in redesigning ourselves before we cease to be human, the question is not only, or even primarily, for the products of replicator gestation and precision genetic design. The question is for those already alive: the progenitors, the choosers, the parents.

As we follow the adventures of Terrence Cee we see what his creators and their technology have made of him—and what they have made of themselves in the process. As we watch Ethan chase frantically around the galaxy to retrieve his—and all of Athos's—future offspring, or as Elli Quinn considers her options, we see how their choices about parenting change them forever. And just to make sure we haven't mislaid the point under all the futuristic machinery, Ecotech Helda and her absent son are there to remind us that our worst nightmares about biotech are probably no worse than the things we've been doing to our children for centuries.

Lois has commented that her early works have mostly, often unbeknownst to her, turned out to at least touch on "the price of parenthood" on the way to wherever else they were going—most overtly in *Ethan* and *Barrayar*, most painfully in "Aftermaths," which chilling little tale you may find at the end of *Shards of Honor*. I'd add to that that she has one of the most clear-eyed views of the sins of the fathers—and mothers—I've ever encountered. (2007: In the original version of this foreword that read "to be about the price of parenthood," a misquote and a terrible oversimplification that I am pleased to have the chance to correct.)

Whatever tools we may have at our disposal when we set out to create and raise children, the issue most central to our success or failure remains the same—are we using our things to make people, or are we trying to make people into things? The crucial difference is in us, not in our offspring: what is important about the notion of a "superhuman" versus the notion of a "subhuman" is not the difference but the similarity—to label a person as either is to label them not-quite-human, and that makes it terrifyingly easy for us to think of them as a thing.

This is not a question only for parents; not everyone, after all, experiences or desires parenthood, but we all have a stake in humanity nonetheless, and some degree of influence thereof, and so in Bujold's fiction; whenever we have power over others, we have a responsibility to them as well, and not even our most private decisions about who and what we are going to be exist in a vacuum. And so what is most intriguing, and in the end most important, about Terrence Cee is not what his progenitors designed and intended him to be—a genetically advanced, fanatically loyal super-spy—but the person he himself decides to become.

Being human, it turns out, is simple, though not easy: you become a human when you choose to be human—and *keep* choosing it, over and over. And so Terrence Cee both fulfills and overturns another science-fiction trope: he is the genetically engineered ultimate weapon who becomes something far beyond his creators' wildest dreams.

As do we all, sooner or later, for better or worse—for better *and* worse, generally. Because under and above it all, animating the bones, skin, and flesh of any creation—a novel or a human being or anything—is one more thing, the most important thing: the unique spark of life that properly belongs to any creation—and, of course, there is a phrase from the same root as *genre, gender,* and *genus* for that as well—*sui generis,* one of a kind, the only of its type. The aspect of a story that no analysis can capture; the part that turns A Great Book into A Life-Changing Story. The piece of a human being that neither nature nor nurture can account for. The inexplicable, unlooked-for capacity within us that makes us the species that commits atrocities and makes miracles happen; that can inspire a woman named Lois to create an Ethan, provincial, frightened, out of his depth—and able to respond to someone as completely outside of his experience as Elli Quinn with respect, and to all the promise and peril of a Terrence Cee by seeing him, and naming him, as exactly what he is: "You are my brother, of course."

Of course.

—Marna Nightingale
May 2003 (September 2007)

. . . . . .

# The Fans

. . . . .

# Come for the Bujold, Stay for the Beer[1]: Science Fiction Writers as Occasions of Fandom

## Marna Nightingale

This is what I know about Bujold fandom: not as much as I thought I did before I started to write about it, despite having been a listee—a member of the official Lois McMaster Bujold Discussion List,[2] hereafter "the List"—since 1999.

Admittedly, the List is not Bujold fandom. All the lists and fora that exist for people to meet to discuss Lois's work are not, among them, Bujold fandom. At most, they're places where Bujold fandom tends to occur. (Home, Aral Vorkosigan observes, is not a place. Home is people.) Nevertheless, it's nice to have

---

1  The role of beer in fandom has been much exaggerated; I'm just very fond of alliteration.

2  See www.dendarii.com for details and for the list archives.

a roof over your head, and Bujold fandom hangs out in some very nice places, of which the List, founded in 1994 by Michael Bernardi and graciously hosted by Melanie Dymond Harper, is the largest, the oldest, and arguably the oddest.

It complicates attempts at description that a mailing list, like a fandom, is a living thing, with a past and a future as well as a present, and virtual structures age and change very much like real structures do. Things break. Things get repaired. Walls fall down, or get moved around; you build an extension or two, you redo the wiring—the inhabitants adapt, more or less, to the new space. Meanwhile, things keep happening out in the larger world, and what happens in the larger world doesn't stay there. The boundaries get blurry. People meet, become friends, fall out, move in together, marry, give birth, die, leave.

The Bujold list isn't the place it was when I came to it; whether it's better or worse is not for me to say—it's different. It'll be different again by the time this article sees print. So "Bujold fandom," or even the List, isn't a thing that I can pin down and describe in a few thousand words, even if I were what I can never be, and don't want to be, an objective observer.

On the other hand, I promised Lillian I'd write an article about Bujold fandom. It has occasionally been suggested that I ought to learn to think before I speak. . . .

So this will have to be an article about what Bujold fandom looks like to me, here and now,[3] as someone who has been an active, vocal, passionately engaged

3  July–December 2007.

member of it for nearly a decade. (I feel as though I'd like to write an article dedicated to explaining why each and every one of you ought to come and join us, but the fact is that if you're reading this you're probably already a Bujold fan, and if you aren't you should *stop* reading this and go read *Cordelia's Honor*, because then you will be. No, seriously. We'll wait. Then come and find us on the list, or on Baen's Bar, or just poke about on Google until you find a group that appeals to you—Bujold fans are fairly easy to find, and generally friendly.)

So. Here and now, I am writing this article, which is I suppose a form of participating in Bujold fandom, and the way I got—and found out about—the job strikes me as as good a place as any to begin. Always begin at the end; it saves time.

I was on my way from London to Bath, through a flood, when my e-mail caught up with me. Lillian Stewart Carl needed someone to write an article about Bujold fandom for *The Vorkosigan Companion*, Lois thought I might be both suitable[4] and interested, she e-mailed fellow-listee James Bryant, because she knew I was on my way to his house, and he, knowing that I was checking e-mail off and on, forwarded the message to me.

I was on my way to his house in the first place because of Lois. Because one of the things about being a member of the List is that you can go to a place you've never been before and someone will pick you up at the bus terminal (airport, train station), feed you, house you, and throw a party, which between

4  I have no idea. But I am very grateful.

three and sixty of your closest friends will attend. You may have to ask most of them which friend they are, mind you, but you'll almost certainly have an excellent time. (If James Bryant is involved, you will not only have an excellent time, you are likely to be given curry. Incredibly good curry, prepared under all sorts of odd circumstances—he made curry for thirty or so in a hotel-room kitchenette, once—is a specialty of his.) So there I was, in a country I'd never been to before, going to the house of a listee, to meet up with other listees, most of whom I'd never met face-to-face before—which made them what listee Dorian Gray, who was there, calls "axe murderers." It was a splendid gathering of axe murderers, by the way.

Since 1999, this has been the sort of thing that happens to me on a fairly regular basis. Not the part where I get asked to write about Bujold fandom, the other part. The part with the parties and the really good food: for some reason, Bujold fandom seems to have an unusually high concentration of extremely good cooks.[5] Also the part involving being offered sofas by—or offering them to—people I've never actually seen in person before. (Which has been known to involve the part where I end up burbling on to Immigration Officials about why they need to read some Bujold, and giving them the mailing list URL. Note to international travelers: "We're fellow members of a literary discussion group" is just as true as and works *much* better than "I met him/her/them on the Internet." Axe murderers, again.)

5  A not-quite random sampling of listee recipes may be found at www.rojizodesign.com/makosti/.

I am assured that it's not just me: my girlfriend—whom I met on the Bujold list—called me a few years back, at midnight, to tell me that she was stranded in New York City, her train had been late, she'd missed her connection, she was short of cash, were there any listees nearby? She had a place to stay in fifteen minutes. This sort of thing happens on the List.

The funny bit was, the person I got hold of wasn't even an *active* listee. That happens all the time, too; we're not exactly the Mailing List California, but we don't necessarily consider a failure to post or remain subscribed, even should said failure last for several years, evidence that a person has actually, you know, *left*. I mean, it's not that we'll stalk you, but if you find yourself in hospital, or Iraq, or somewhere, there may be phone calls and cards and parcels of books and things from people you haven't talked to in years....

(The books! Talk about the books!)

Right, the books. It's all about The Books. Except when it isn't. Then it's about gender relations, kosher cooking, cats, weird links, and who's going to which cons or throwing the next party.[6] At which we will talk about the books. Probably.

It can be, or at least, it can seem—on checking the List over the last few days I find we are on topic about half the time; so perhaps it's just that we talk twice as much as normal people—harder than is at all sensible, on a list full of people who love the Vorkosigan books—and the Vorkosigans—as much as

---

6  And footnotes. I don't know why; we just really like footnotes. They add verisimilitude to an otherwise bald and unconvincing narrative, or something.

we do, to get a conversation going about the books. Just about any time, you can get a conversation going about why there's all this off-topicness, though. There are several theories, ranging from "it's all been said" to "it's too difficult, what with some people getting ARCs[7] and others having to wait for library copies," though "you people are the weirdest bunch of so-called fans I've ever seen" has its defenders as well.

There are offshoot lists for the discussion of Bujold from both the Lord Peter and the Dunnett lists (LordV and MostlyBujold, respectively), and it is rumored that there is much discussion of the Vorkosigan books to be found on those. This, and the fact that both lists were founded to deal with the tendency of Bujold threads to slip in among the Lord Peter and Lymond discussions, gives rise to yet another theory, which is "Bujold fans, as a class, will tend to talk about anything except what we are meant to talk about." (It occurs to me that we could have saved a certain amount of trouble on-list a few years back by making mention of U.S. politics in all posts mandatory.[8])

Whatever the explanation is, it's not a lack of love for Lois's writing. We have, indeed, been known both individually and collectively to do some extremely mad things to get hold of Lois's works. (She sent a manuscript copy of *Diplomatic Immunity* to two listees on the occasion of their wedding, which was at least a year before publication date. To prevent a spate of

7 Advance Reader Copies. They used to be for the exclusive use of reviewers, but now there is eBay.

8 For complex reasons, we don't discuss U.S. politics on the list anymore. At all.

impulsive marriage proposals I ought to note that a) we already tried that—that, not the original marriage, was the mad behavior to which I was referring—and b) that manuscript distribution is rare, entirely at Lois's whim, and not to be got by bribes, begging, or backflips, so this is unlikely to happen again; it was the first, and as far as I know so far the only, wedding to come about because of the list.)

Rather madder was what happened when "Winterfair Gifts" was, for complex publisher-related reasons, released in Croatian a year before it came out in English. Quite a few of us bought it in Croatian. Then we translated it ourselves: rather, a Croatian listee (Vlatka Petrovic) translated it, Bo Johannson and Robert Parks edited it, I proofread it—on the bus from D.C. to New Orleans, as I recall—Robert typeset it, and everyone who had bought a Croatian copy got an English copy. I still have mine; it's a really good translation, actually. (And was responsible for at least one new convert to Lois's writing: a gentleman on the bus who started by reading over my shoulder and ended by snaffling pages from me as fast as I could get them done.) It all seemed a completely reasonable course of action at the time. . . .

And then there's our crack team of ARC-spotters, who patrol eBay while sane people sleep, and the people who deal with the logistics involved in dividing five or so ARCs by one planet's worth of eager readers, not to mention the mailing costs . . . And yet, we do it. So I think we can definitely conclude that whatever fuels our inability to stay on-topic, it's not a lack of interest in the books.

I suspect that some of the explanation lies in the

books themselves, and in the broad range of people and situations they speak to; it is possible to conclude, by careful reading of Lois's books (a practice I recommend with some fervor, every chance I get; if you are ever buttonholed in the SF aisle of a bookstore by a wild-eyed[9] Canadian who wants to press a copy of *Cordelia's Honor* or *The Curse of Chalion* into your hand, it's probably me), that either everything is on-topic, or nothing is. Lois once described her fans as "a flatteringly bright bunch," and I'd add to that that we tend to be an engaged bunch: not only do we collectively know a lot of stuff, we tend to care. A lot. And can explain why, sometimes at truly incredible length.

So, things can get heated, on-topic and off-, from time to time and as occasion serves—that Lois's books speak to such a wide range of people, and say such wildly different things to each reader, is, I think, a sign of her quality as a writer. It also makes for some—interesting—conversations among Bujold fans. Perennial on-topic favorites include "Beta Colony: Socialist Utopia, Stalinist Dystopia, or Kind of Scary but Better Than Barrayar?," "Ivan Vorpatril: How Can You Help Loving That Man? (Give Several Examples of How, Please)," "Uterine Replicators: Best Tech Ever or Unnatural, Wrong, and Just Plain Way Too Risky?," and "He Was Bisexual, Now He's Monogamous: How Aral Vorkosigan's Love Life Changed a Planet (Several Times)." Despite the fact that it seems unlikely at this time that any of Lois's books will be filmed, there is also the ever-popular (or much-feared) Casting Thread.

---

9  If it's a fairly sane-looking Canadian, it's probably one of the other ones.

In the midst of it all there's Lois. Not "in the middle," exactly; Lois is, by some alchemy, the exact trick of which escapes me, as much a listee as any of us, without being self-effacing or falsely humble. I mean, she has this day[10] job which has been known to come up on-list and which frequently requires her to lurk until she's finished a book, but it doesn't stop her being Lois, or from chatting about subtle points in the books, unsubtle misbehaviors practiced by her cats, what else she's reading, or current events—or, indeed, from posting truly brain-breakingly strange links on occasion. If her presence has an effect on the operation of her fandom, if Bujold fandom is because of her in any way different from other fandoms, and I think it is, it's subtle; it is, perhaps, a little difficult to deliberately behave more badly than you absolutely have to in front of the woman who invented Cordelia Vorkosigan—and Alys Vorpatril.

Or, just possibly, it is a bit easier for a Bujold fan to be a little better, a little more open to points of view they once considered completely deranged, than they thought they were—because of the woman who invented Mark Vorkosigan and Konstantin Bothari, whether she is around or not.

(Talking of Mark, shortly after *Mirror Dance* came out I had occasion to point Lois out at a convention to a new, young, male fan of hers. "She wrote *Mirror Dance*?" he said, in tones of deep shock. "She looks like somebody's mother!"

"Well, she is," I said rather dryly, and managed to wait until he was out of sight to laugh. It was several

---

10  At least, some of it seems to happen while the sun is up.

years before I dared tell Lois this story; as I recall she laughed quite a lot, herself.)

The list refers to new Bujold readers as "converts"; it's a running joke, funnier than it ought to be because of Lois's stunning improbability as a cult leader. On consideration, like most good jokes, it hides a grain of truth. To read Bujold—to read her with the kind of passion and fascination her works seem to inspire— is to see the world a little differently, forever after. She'll tell you that her characters' approaches to the difficulties of ordinary—or extraordinary—life are a case of "professional driver; closed course," and not necessarily to be attempted if you don't have the author on your side, and it's good advice.

The Vorkosigan series is fiction for a reason, and suborning, scamming, intimidating, and beheading people who get in your way should not be expected to produce excellent results when attempted as real-life forms of conflict resolution. Nevertheless, Lois has a great deal to say about how, and why, to be human, and while you're enjoying the twisty plots and the cracking dialogue and the entrancing characters, some of it will tend to slide under your skin. Lois and her characters get into your conversation, then into your mind, and eventually into your human, imperfect heart, and as any reader of the books knows, where her characters go, things tend to change, and, usually, to get better.

This suggests a definition of "Bujold fandom" I can get behind, actually: Lois once defined a genre as "a body of works in close conversation (or heated argumentation) with one another," and I think, if pressed, I might define a fandom as "a collection of individuals in close conversation—or heated argumentation, or both at the same time—with a body of works *and* with each other." On the surface we don't necessarily have a lot in common, but we do have the fact that we are all drawn to the kinds of stories Lois writes, and we have all, I think, been changed a little or a lot by spending time with her books, whether reading them alone or discussing them in a group.

In *A Civil Campaign*, Ekaterin muses on whether or not you can judge a person—Miles, in her particular case—by the quality of the company they attract and enjoy, and concludes that you can. Put it on my tombstone, someday, then—*she was a Bujold Fan, and enjoyed it very much*—and I shall be well content.

. . . . .

# The Vorkosiverse Itself

. . . . .

. . . . .

# A Pronunciation Guide to the Vorkosigan Universe

## SUFORD LEWIS

The author says that we may pronounce the names as we please, but many readers wish to know how *she* pronounces them. Without getting too finicky, this is to give an indication of the syllables which are more emphasized and the approximate values of the vowels and consonants of most of the names used in the Vorkosigan universe of Lois McMaster Bujold. Brief identifications will include the work in which the person or place principally appears, if it appears little outside of that work.

This is not a complete guide to the pronunciation of all the names in Bujold's Vorkosigan universe. It contains . . . what it contains, with an attempt to cover all major characters and the minor ones whose pronunciation might be tricky. Names of persons are in alphabetic order by last name. When we have only one name for a person, it is in order just as we know it without there being a set of "unknown last name" entries somewhere, which also solves the problem of not always being able to tell whether it was the first name or last name that we knew. At least the author consistently uses European name order—given name first and family name last—so we don't have to cope with, for instance, whether Ky Tung belongs with the Tungs or the Kys.

Place and organization names are listed mixed in with the people. Even less attempt has been made to be complete. The Black Escarpment, for instance, is not listed since it is unlikely to be a pronunciation problem. Jackson's Whole House names are listed under their House names rather than all being collected under "House."

## Pronunciation Key

aa — a in as, cat

ah — a in arm, father, alleluia

aw — a in awe, dawn, caught

ay — a in bay, sake

eh — e in bend

ee — e in week

ih — i in it

ai — i in sight, like

oy — oy in boy

oh — o in go, oat

oo — o in choose, ruse

uh — u in sun, done

c — either k or s will be used except for ch

g — hard g as in good

j — soft g as in germ

zh — s in vision, second g in garage

Diphthongs (besides ai, ay, and oy) will be indicated by vowels separated by an underline; for instance, ai could be equivalently written as ah_ee. Many subtle differences are ignored: the "th" in thin is not distinguished from the "th" in then, the precise pronunciation of the "u" in survey is simplified to its less continental cousin "uh," and the rolled "r" is ignored. The swallowed vowel, as the "e" in "other" or the "o" in "carton," is simply left out. Purists beware.

Syllables are somewhat arbitrarily determined, more for convenience in indicating the vowels and stresses and to avoid the confusion of overloading many consonants onto a single syllable, than for exact indication of which syllable they would be pronounced with if one said the word syllable by syllable. So feel free to let the consonants indicated at the end of a syllable migrate to the beginning of the next and vice versa. Usually the difficulty about pronouncing an unfamiliar word is to choose among alternatives, and indicating which of the possible pronunciations the author prefers is the intent here. Stressed syllables are indicated by capital letters. If there is a secondary stress in a name it is indicated by small capitals, for instance: BAA-ruh-POO-truh. There are many multi-syllable names with no indication of a secondary stress, when the rest of the syllables are all pretty much equal. Again, the pursuit of minutiae has been eschewed. Ship's names are in *italics*.

# Key to Abbreviations for Works

B — *Barrayar*
BA — *Brothers in Arms*
BI — "The Borders of Infinity"
C — *Cetaganda*
CC — *A Civil Campaign*
DD — "Dreamweaver's Dilemma"
DI — *Diplomatic Immunity*
EA — *Ethan of Athos*
FF — *Falling Free*
K — *Komarr*
L — "Labyrinth"
M — *Memory*
MD — *Mirror Dance*
MM — "The Mountains of Mourning"
SH — *Shards of Honor*
VG — The *Vor Game*
WA — The *Warrior's Apprentice*
WG — "Winterfair Gifts"

Agba — AAG-bah — Quaddie in charge of work teams getting clamps open during the disassembly of Cay Habitat. (FF)

Ahn — AAN — Lieutenant, meteorology officer at Lazkowski Base. (VG)

Aime Pass — AI-mee PAAS — Pass through the Dendarii Mountains taken by Gregor, Cordelia, and Piotr during Vordarian's Pretendership. (B)

Anafi, Ser — aa-NAA-fee, SUHR — Agent of Rialto
    Sharemarket Agency that lent Tien Vorsoisson
    money he invested in a Komarran trade fleet. (K)

Apmad — AAP-maad — Vice President, GalacTech
    Operations. (FF)

Arata, Tav — ah-RAA-tah, TAAV — Captain, Kline
    Station Security, friend of Elli Quinn. (EA)

Arozzi — aa-ROH-zee — Komarr Terraforming
    Project, Serifosa Branch, engineer substituting
    for Radovas managing the Waste Heat section,
    also involved in Radovas's and Soudha's other
    project. (K)

Aslund — AAS-luhnd — A system off the Hegen
    Hub that is wary of Barrayar. (VG)

Athos — AA-thohs — Planet within two-month
    sub-light voyage of Kline Station settled by a
    religious sect that banned women from the
    planet. (EA)

Auson — AW-sn — Captain of the *Ariel* in the
    Oseran Mercenaries, captain of the *Triumph*
    in the Dendarii Mercenaries. (WA)

Avakli — ah-VAH-klee — Doctor, rear admiral,
    biocyberneticist researching Simon's illness. (M)

ba — BAH — Caste of sexless aides and servitors
    to the haut of the Celestial Garden. (C)

Baneri — BAH-nee-ree — Marilacan leader, killed
    at the siege of Fallow Core. (BI)

Bannerji, George — BAA-nr-gee, JORG — Captain, GalacTech Company Security, Shuttleport Three, Rodeo, accidentally shot Tony during the attempted escape. (FF)

Barrayar — BEHR-ah-yahr — System off the Hegen Hub through Pol and Komarr, its wormhole connection to the rest of human space closed just after it was colonized, leading to several centuries of isolation and regression. (All except FF)

Baruch, Cynthia Jane — baa-RUHK, SIHN-thee-ya JAYN — Doctor, geneticist who built the original ovarian cultures for Athos, and put herself into her work. (EA)

Beatrice — BEE-uh-trihs — Marilacan lieutenant, tall, redhead, lost in the escape from Dagoola IV. (BI)

Beauchene Life Center — BOH-shayn LAIF SEHN-tr — Medical facility on Escobar specializing in cryo-revival. (MD)

Benar, Fehun — bay-NAHR, FAY-huhn — Commander of an orbiting Felician ore refinery and a friend of Major Daum. (WA)

Benin, Dag — BEH-nihn, DAAG — Ghem-colonel in charge of the investigation of Ba Lura's death. (C, CC)

Beta Colony — BAY-tah KAH-luh-nee — Second extra-solar colony, first successful one, founded from the U.S. before the advent of wormhole technology. (DD, FF, SH, WA, CC)

Bharaputra, Vasa Luigi — BAA-ruh-POO-truh,
    VAA-suh loo-EE-jee — Baron, head of House
    Bharaputra on Jackson's Whole, maker and
    seller of clones (and his own customer). (BA)

Bianca — bee-AHN-kah — Doctor and psychiatrist,
    he married into a pharmaceutical company
    and wants more control. (DD)

Bollan Design — BOH-lahn dee-ZAIN — Small engi-
    neering firm specializing in odd and experimental
    Necklin field generators and custom repairs
    especially of obsolete jump ship rods. (K)

Boni, Tersa — BOH-nee, TR-zah — Medtech,
    Escobaran, in Personnel Retrieval and
    Identification for nine years, made sure it was
    done right for her daughter. (SH)

Bonn — BAWN — Barrayaran engineering lieuten-
    ant at Laskowski Base, ordered to have his
    men clean up a fetaine spill. (VG)

Bonsanklar — BOHN-saang-KLAHR — Large seaside
    resort in Vorkosigan District. (B)

Borgos, Enrique — BOHR-gohs, ehn-REE-kay —
    Escobaran, doctor of entomology rescued with
    his bugs and lab equipment by Mark from his
    creditors on Escobar. (CC)

Bothari, Konstantin — boh-THAH-ree,
    KOHN-stehn-tihn — Armsman to (in order):
    Aral Vorkosigan, Ges Vorrutyer, Aral Vorkosigan,
    Piotr Vorkosigan, Cordelia Naismith Vorkosigan,

and Miles Vorkosigan; absolutely loyal to the
Vorkosigans and absolutely deadly, but not
absolutely sane. (SH, B, WA)

Bothari-Jesek, Elena — _____-JEH-sehk,
ay-LAY-nuh — daughter of Konstantin Bothari,
childhood friend of Miles, Ivan, and Gregor,
apprentice to Commodore Tung and captain in
the Dendarii Free Mercenary Fleet, married
to Bazil Jesek, later retired as a merchant captain. (All except EA, DI, FF, SH)

Brownell — brah_oo-NEHL — Betan Port Security
officer attempting to arrest Arde Mayhew. (WA)

Brun — BRUHN — Captain in the Imperial forces,
Security commander in Barrayaran trade fleet
escort. (DI)

Calhoun, Tav — kaal-HOON, TAAV — Owner of
the *RG 132* who accepts a deed of Vorkosigan
land as security on payment for it. (WA)

Canaba, Hugh — kah-NAH-bah, HYUU — Doctor,
geneticist working for Bharaputra Labs, target
of clandestine pickup from Jackson's Whole by
the Dendarii Mercenaries. (L)

Cappell — kah-PEHL — Mathematician in the Waste
Heat Management section of the Komarr
Terraforming Project, Serifosa Branch. (K)

Cavilo — kaa-VEE-loh — Commander of Randall's
Rangers, promoted herself by assassination disguised as accident. (VG)

Cay, Daryl — KAY, DAA-rihl — Vice President, R&D, biological, and major stockholder of GalacTech, a geneticist, he had a vision for humans in zero gravity. (FF)

Cecil — SEH-sl — Major in personnel at the Academy, personally involved in deciding every cadet's first assignment. (VG)

Cee, Terrence — SEE, TEHR-ehns — L-X-10 Terran-C, experimental result of Faz Jahar's genetics project on Cetaganda. (EA)

Cetaganda — SEE-tuh-GAAN-duh — Empire of eight planetary systems plus "allied worlds." Tried and failed to conquer Barrayar, Vervain, and Marilac. (C, DI)

Chalopin — CHAA-loh-pn — GalacTech Shuttleport Three Administrator, Rodeo, she is annoyed with Van Atta for bypassing her authority in handling his escaping quaddies. (FF)

Chenko — CHEHNG-koh — Doctor, neurologist on Miles's team at ImpMil diagnosing his seizures. (M)

Chodak, Clive — CHOH-daak, KLAIV — Dendarii sergeant, key to saving Miles and getting Gregor home. (VG)

Clogston, Chris — KLOHG-stn, KRIHS — Captain, Senior Fleet Surgeon, has to take up forensics and a nasty nanotech-engineered virus on the fly. (DI)

Corbeau, Dmitri — kohr-BOH, d-MEE-tree —
     Ensign in the Barrayaran Imperial forces, he
     fell in love with Garnet Five on Graf Station,
     touching off a chain of circumstances resulting
     in a diplomatic crisis. (DI)

Couer — KOO-her — Commodore, one of the few
     surviving senior officers in the invasion of Escobar;
     he helped Vorkosigan with cleanup. (SH)

Croye — KROY — Imperial Security lieutenant at
     Barrayaran Embassy on Beta Colony, in charge
     of watching Miles while he is there. (WA)

Csurik, Harra — SHUH-rihk, HAA-ruh — Hiked
     to Vorkosigan Surleau to speak her complaint
     when her village speaker would do nothing
     about her murdered baby. (MM)

Csurik, Lem — _____, LEHM — Accused of his
     daughter's murder, but unwilling to convict the
     true killer by his words. (MM)

Csurik, Raina — _____, RAY-nuh — The murdered
     daughter of Lem and Harra. (MM)

D'Emorie — deh-EHM-oh-ree — Imperial Security
     major of Solstice, engineering analyst investi-
     gating the Waste Heat Management's experi-
     mental station. (K)

D'Guise — d-GEEZ — Doctor, cryonicist at Imperial
     Military hospital diagnosing Miles's seizures. (M)

Dagoola IV — duh-GOO-lah FOHR — Location of

Cetagandan prison camp for Marilacan prisoners of war. (BI)

Dal, Harman — DAHL, HAHR-mn — Cover identity
for ghem-Colonel Millisor on Kline Station. (EA)

Darobey — DAH-roh-bay — One of the mutineers
under Radnov. (SH)

Daum, Carle — DAA_OOM, KAHR-leh — Felician
major that hired Miles and the *RG 132* to
take "agricultural supplies" to Felice. (WA)

Dea — DEE — Doctor and lieutenant, assistant to
the Regent of Barrayar's physican, also competent
as a large animal veterinarian. (MM)

Degtiar, Rian — DEHG-tee-AHR, RAI-ahn —
Cetagandan haut-lady, Handmaiden of the Star
Crèche, serious geneticist and member of the
inmost ruling circle. (C)

Dendarii — dehn-DEH-ree-ee — Mountain range
on Barrayar; also the name borne by a galactic mercenary troop led by Admiral Miles
Naismith. (All except SH)

Deslaurier — dehs-LAW-rih-r — Ensign and Fleet
legal officer in lieu of a senior officer on
death leave, Barrayaran trade fleet escort. (DI)

Desroches — day-ROH-shay — Doctor and Chief
of Staff at the Sevarin Replication Center on
Athos. Doctor Ethan Urquhart's immediate
superior. (EA)

Destang — des-STAHNG — Commodore, Chief of
Security for Sector II, hopes to retire before
Miles shows up in his area again. (BA)

Diaz, Carlos — dee-AAZ, KAAR-lohs — Private eye
who lost his license and is looking for a new
source of income, aka Rudolph Kinsey. (DD)

Droushnakovi, Ludmilla — DROOSH-nuh-ĸAW-vee,
luhd-MIH-luh — Bodyguard to Princess
Kareen and her son, Gregor, later married to
Captain Koudelka. (B)

Dub — DUHB — Imperial armsman encountered by
Miles after his unscheduled landing at Vorhartung
Castle, did not believe who Miles was. (WA)

DuBauer, Chalmys — doo-BAA_OO-r, CHAAL-mihs —
Pilot in pre-wormhole jump days between
Earth and Beta Colony. (DD)

Dubauer, Ker — doo-BAA_OO-r, KR — Assumed
name of *Idris* passenger seeming to be a
Betan hermaphrodite, actually a renegade
Cetegandan ba. (DI)

Durona Group — doo-ROH-nuh GROOP —
Medical research group allied to House Fell,
founded by Lilly Durona and composed of her
clones. (MD)

Durrance — duh-RAANTZ — Captain, GalacTech
freight shuttle commander, Ti's supervisor, who
spreads gossip of Beta Colony's invention of
artificial gravity. (FF)

Dyan — DAI-aan — House on Jackson's Whole, taken over by House Ryoval. (DI)

Escobar — EHS-koh-BAHR — A high-tech world, located near to Beta Colony and Sergyar in the Wormhole Nexus. (SH)

Esterhazy — EHS-tr-HAH-zee — Vorkosigan arms-man, good with horses, aids Bothari, Cordelia, and Gregor to escape Vordarian's squads. (B)

Eta Ceta — AY-tuh SEE-tuh — Capital world of the Cetagandan Empire. (C)

Farr, Andro — FAHR, AAN-droh — Komarran, a friend of Marie Trogir, worried about her and about what to do with her cats. (K)

Felice — fay-LEES — Nation on Tau Verde IV, warring with Pelias. (WA)

Fell — FEHL — House and criminal syndicate on Jackson's Whole, specializing in arms deals. (L, MD)

Ferrell, Falco — FEH-rehl, FAAL-koh — Escobaran Pilot Officer, assigned to personnel retrieval after the war with Barrayar. (SH)

Fetaine — feh-TAYN — Gas terror weapon, causes genetic damage to its victims. (VG)

Firka — FUHR-kuh — One of Gras-Grace's fellow smugglers, business manager of their enter-prise. (DI)

Fors — FOHRZ — Sergeant, GalacTech Security, he led an unsuccessful team of three attempting to recover a stolen shuttle on Rodeo. (FF)

Foscol, Lena — FOHS-kohl, LEE-nah — Accountant for the Komarr Terraforming Project, Serifosa Branch, a most meticulous thief. (K)

Galen, Ser — GAY-ln, SUHR — Dedicated Komarran rebel, his sister Rebecca was killed in the Solstice Massacre. (BA)

Galeni, Duv — geh-LEHN-ee, DUHV — Born David Galen, son of Ser Galen, captain in the Barrayaran Imperial Military. Security chief of Barrayaran embassy on Earth, later head of Komarr Affairs, Imperial Security. (BA, CC, M, WG)

Gamad — GAH-mahd — Felician Lieutenant who became enamored of his own importance upon succeeding Major Daum. (WA)

ghem — GEHM — The lower of the two Cetagandan castes of nobility. (C)

Giaja, Fletchir — gee-AH-jah, FLEH-chr — Emperor of Cetaganda. (C)

Giaja, Slyke — _____, SLAI-kee — Satrap Governor of Xi Ceta and half brother of the current emperor. (C)

Gibbs — GIHBZ — Colonel, ImpSec, Solstice, financial analyst called in to examine the books of the Komarr Terraforming Project at Serifosa. (K)

Goff — GAWF — One of four thugs hired to assault Lord Dono Vorrutyer on Barrayar. (CC)

Gompf, Laurie — GAWM-pf, LOH-ree — GalacTech's Hazardous Waste Management Officer, George Bannerji required a proper work order signed by her to fire on the D-620. (FF)

Gonzales, Helmut — gohn-ZAH-lehs, HEHL-muht — Feelie-dream distributor who has contracted for a sequel from Anias Ruey. (DD)

Graf, Leo — GRAAF, LEE-oh — Welding engineer and expert in nondestructive testing, eighteen-year veteran of GalacTech, leads the quaddies to freedom. (FF)

Greenlaw — GREEN-law — Union of Free Habitats' Senior Sealer for Downsider Relations, equivalent to a minister plenipotentiary reporting to the very top level of their government. (DI)

Grishnov — GRIHSH-nawv — Minister of Political Education, he thought he might become the real power in the Barrayaran Empire; his ministry was one of Ezar's experiments in centralization that failed. (B)

Gulik, Ti — GOO-lihk, TAI — Lieutenant, GalacTech freight shuttle pilot drafted to pilot the quaddies' superjumper. (FF)

Gupta, Russo — GUHP-tah, ROO-soh — aka "Guppy." A genetically engineered amphibious human attempting to make a semi-honest living as an engineer on a smuggling ship when the crew was double-crossed and murdered in a deal only Guppy survived. (DI)

Gustioz, Oscar — GOOS-tee-OHZ, AHS-kr — Escobaran parole officer tasked with retrieving Doctor Borgos from Barrayar. (CC)

Halify — HAA-lih-fee — Able young Felician general who hired Miles to stop the war with the Pelians. (WA)

Haroche, Lucas — hah-ROHSH, LOO-kuhs — General and Head of Domestic Affairs, Imperial Security, sabotaged Simon Illyan's memory chip to take his job. (M)

Hassadar — HAA-suh-DAHR — New capital of Vorkosigan District after the destruction of Vorkosigan Vashnoi in the Cetagandan War. (CC, MM)

haut — HOHT — The higher of the two Cetagandan castes of nobility. (C, DI)

Hegen Hub — HEH-gn HUHB — Nexus of four wormholes connecting Pol, Vervain, Jackson's Whole with five wormholes, and Komarr with six wormholes, an important trade and political crossroads. (VG)

Helda, F. — HEHL-dah — Biocontrol Warden for Sector Four on Kline Station. Her son emigrated to Athos, making her hate the males-only planet. (EA)

Henri — HEHN-ree — Doctor and first Barrayaran
uterine replicator specialist, beaten to death
by Vordarian's men seeking Miles. (B)

Hewlett — HEE_OO-leht — Jacksonian pilot, one
of Gras-Grace's smuggler crew. (DI)

Husavi — hoo-SAH-vee — Group Commander,
Komarran commander of Station Security on
the Barrayaran jump-point station at Komarr. (K)

Hysopi, Karla — hai-SOH-pee, KAAR-lah — Widow,
caretaker of Elena Bothari. (B)

*Idris* — IH-drihs — Komarran trade ship held at
Graf Station. (DI)

Illyan, Simon — EEL-yn, SAI-mn — Captain in
Barrayaran military, implanted with a memory
chip in his brain to ensure perfect and verifi-
able recall. Becomes Chief of Security afterward. (All except DI)

Jackson's Whole — JAAK-snz HOHL — System off
the Hegen Hub run by the greater and lesser
houses, each headed by a baron under the
principle that "the Deal is the Deal." (BA, EA)

Jahar, Faz — jah-HAHR, FAAZ — Cetagandan
geneticist, obsessed with finding the genes for
telepathy. (EA)

Janine — jah-NEEN — J-9-X Ceta-G, experimental
telepathy subject and companion to Terrence
Cee, killed during escape from Cetaganda. (EA)

Jankowski — jaang-KOW-skee — Vorkosigan armsman, one of the three allotted to Miles while
he is at Vorkosigan House. (M)

Jankowski, Denys — _____, DEH-ns — Son of
Armsman Jankowski. (CC)

Janos — YAA-nohs — Son of Ethan's father's designated alternate parent who Ethan wished
would be his designated alternate parent,
moved to Outlands on Athos. (EA)

Jesek, Bazil — JEH-sehk, BAA-zl — Deserted from
the Barrayaran military, sworn as armsman
by Miles, fell in love with and married Elena
Bothari, commodore and fleet engineer in the
Dendarii Mercenaries until his resignation. (WA)

Jole — JOHL — Lieutenant, aide to Aral
Vorkosigan. (VG)

Joris — JOH-rs — Vorrutyer armsman, driver, loyal
to Dono. (CC)

Kanzian — KAAN-zee_uhn — Admiral in the
Barrayaran military, allied with Aral during the
Vordarian Pretendership, a top military strate-
gist. (B)

Karal, Serg — KAA-rl, SRG — Speaker for Silvy
Vale, a veteran and a traveled man. (MM)

Kety, Ilsum — KEH-tee, IHL-suhm — Satrap
Governor of Sigma Ceta, impatient, manipula-
tive. (C)

Kline Station — KLAIN STAA-shuhn — Three-
hundred-year-old station orbiting a faint star in
a nexus of six wormholes, a thriving crossroads
with one hundred thousand citizens, already a
hundred years old when Athos was founded. (EA)

Klyeuvi, Amor — klai-OO-vee, AY-mohr — "Kly
the Mail," retired major, served Piotr in the
Cetagandan War, then eighteen years as the
Imperial Mail in the hills, he aids Cordelia
and Gregor in escaping Vordarian's squads. (B)

Komarr — koh-MAHR — Important wormhole
nexus, living off its trade routes; controlled
by Barrayar, as its only outlet to the rest of
human inhabited space. (CC, K, M, SH)

Korabik, Gottyan — koh-RAH-bihk, GOHT-yahn —
Eager for promotion, joined Radnov's mutiny;
got his captaincy in the expedition against
Escobar, died soon after. (SH)

Kosti — KAWS-tee — Corporal, gate guard at
Vorkosigan House provided by ImpSec. (CC)

Kostolitz — KOHS-toh-lihtz — Unhappily paired
with Miles for the academy entrance physical
tests, later befriended. (WA)

Koudelka, Clement — koo-DEHL-kuh, KLEH-mnt —
Suffered nerve disruptor damage in Radnov's
attempted takeover of the Sergyar expedition, became secretary to the Regent, married Droushnakovi, has four daughters: Delia,
Olivia, Martya, and Kareen. (B, CC, SH, WA)

Koudelka, Delia — _____, DEE-lee_uh — Eldest
　　Koudelka daughter, involved with Commodore
　　Duv Galeni. (CC, M, MD, WG)

Koudelka, Kareen — _____, kah-REEN —
　　Youngest Koudelka daughter, returning home
　　after a year studying at Beta Colony with
　　Mark Vorkosigan, finds it hard to return to
　　Barrayar. (CC, MD)

Koudelka, Martya — _____, MAHR-tee_uh — One
　　of the middle Koudelka daughters, interested
　　in Doctor Borgos. (CC)

Koudelka, Olivia — _____, uh-LIH-vee_uh — One
　　of the middle Koudelka daughters, attracted to
　　Lord Dono Vorrutyer. (CC)

Kshatryia — KSHAH-tree-uh — Culture whose mili-
　　tary includes imperial mercenaries they rent to
　　anyone. (WA)

Kyril Island — KIH-rihl AI-lnd — Location of
　　Lazkowski Base, a Barrayaran infantry winter
　　training camp. (VG)

Lazkowski Base — laas-KOW-skee BAYS —
　　Barrayaran infantry winter training camp on
　　Kyril Island, also called "Camp Permafrost." (VG)

Leutwyn — LOOT-wihn — Adjudicator called in on
　　Graf Station to judge if warrants could be issued
　　for arrest and fast-penta interrogation, arrived
　　in time to witness the arrival of Russo Gupta
　　and sanction his arrest and interrogation. (DI)

Lura — LOO-ruh — Ba, loyal servant of the Haut Lizbet Degtiar, the Dowager Empress, its involvement in the copying of the Star Crèche cost it its life. (C)

Malka — MAAL-kuh — One of four thugs hired to assault Lord Dono on Barrayar. (CC)

Marilac — MAA-rih-laak — Invaded by the Cetagandans. Barrayar aided them for five years until the Cetagandans left. (BI)

Mayhew, Arde — MAY-hee_oo, AHR-dee — Jump pilot who allowed Cordelia to stow away on his ship from Beta Colony, rescued by Miles when his ship was about to be scrapped. (WA)

Maz, Mia — MAHZ, MEE-uh — Vervani embassy Assistant Chief of Protocol specializing in women's etiquette, she accepts Ambassador Vorob'yev's marriage proposal. (C)

Mehta — MEH-tah — Doctor, captain in Betan Security, and a devious psychoanalyst. (SH)

Metzov, Stanis — MEHT-zawv, STAA-nihs — General commanding Laskowski Base, an old line veteran, after his resignation, he left Barrayar and joined Randall's Rangers. (VG)

Millisor, Luyst — MIH-lih-sohr, LOIST — Ghem-colonel in charge of security on Faz Jahar's genetics project, determined to dispose of the last experimental results. (EA)

Minchenko, Ivy — mihn-CHEHNG-koh, AI-vee —
Musician, historian-performer, second-best
musician on her planet. (FF)

Minchenko, Warren — _____, WAH-rn — Doctor,
chief medical officer, Cay Habitat, worked
from the beginning on the thirty-five-year-long
project to create the quaddies. (FF)

Molino — moh-LEE-noh — Senior Cargomaster of
the Komarran trade fleet. (DI)

Muno — MOO-noh — Sergeant, assistant to Parole
Officer Gustioz. (CC)

Murka — MUHR-kuh — Dendarii lieutenant,
beheaded by plasma fire on Dagoola IV. (BI)

Naismith, Cordelia — NAY-smihht, kohr-DEE-lee_uh —
Betan Astronomical Survey, captain of the *Rene
Magritte*, stopped the mutiny on Aral's ship,
married Aral and became Countess Vorkosigan,
ended the Vordarian Pretendership while rescuing her son. (All except FF)

Naismith, Elizabeth — _____, eh-LIHZ-uh-BEHTH —
Replicator repair tech on Beta Colony,
Cordelia's mother. (EA, WA, CC)

Naru — NAH-roo, — Ghem-general, commander of
Cetagandan Imperial Security and ghem-Colonel Benin's commanding officer. (C)

Navarr, Pel — nah-VAHR, PEHL — Haut-lady, consort of Eta Ceta, ally of Rian Degtiar, receives

the kidnapped Star Crèche shipment to Rho Ceta, and performs the duties of the murdered consort of Rho Ceta. (C, DI)

Necklin field — NEHK-lihn FEE_IHLD — Five-space field necessary for wormhole jump travel, generated by the Necklin Drive. (All)

Negri — NEH-gree — Captain, head of Imperial Security under Emperor Ezar Vorbarra, died saving Gregor from Vordarian's men during the coup attempt. (SH, B)

Nevatta, Grace — neh-VAH-tah, GRAYS — "Gras-Grace," captain of a small smuggling ship trying to make a living, she is the brains of the operation. She has an alternate ID as Polian Louise Latour. (DI)

Nicol — nih-KOHL — Harp and hammer dulcimer player with the Minchenko Ballet orchestra after roaming outside Quaddiespace. Bel Thorne lives with her. (L, DI)

Norwood — NOHR-wd — Lieutenant, medtech who shipped Miles's cryo-chamber away from Bharaputra Labs. (MD)

Nout — NAA_OOT — Dendarii put in charge of the worthless Felician millifennig payment for delivery of Daum's cargo. (WA)

Nu, Livia — NOO, LIH-vee-uh — Cover identity for Commander Cavilo. (VG)

Okita — oh-KEE-tah — Sergeant, one of ghem-Colonel Millisor's men, killed by Ellie Quinn. (EA)

Oliver — AH-lih-vr — Marilacan Commando Sergeant, first recruit to Miles's new Marilac resistance. (BI)

Olshansky — ohl-SHAHN-skee — Colonel, Head of Sergyaran Affairs, newly appointed. (M)

Orient Station — OH-ree-ehnt STAY-shuhn — Barrayaran Security HQ for Sector IV. (BA)

Oser — OH-sr — Admiral of the Oseran Mercenaries, killed during the Vervain conflict. (WA)

Overholt — OH-vr-hohlt — Sergeant in Imperial Security, Miles's bodyguard on his assignment in the Hegen Hub. (VG)

Parnell — pahr-NEHL — Pilot Officer of the decoy vessel captained by Captain Cordelia Naismith. (SH)

Pelias — PEHL-ee-uhs — Nation on Tau Verde IV warring with Felice. (WA)

Pol — POHL — System linking Komarr to the Hegen Hub. (VG)

Pramod — PRAA-mawd — Quaddie welding tech, another top student of Leo Graf. (FF)

Ptarmigan — TAHR-mih-gn — Dendarii lieutenant noted for aggressive shuttle piloting. (L)

Pym — PIHM — Vorkosigan armsman. (CC, MD, MM, WG)

Quinn, Elli — KWIHN, EH-lee — Commander,
Dendarii Free Mercenary Fleet, originally from
Kline Station. (All except FF, MM, SH, B)

Quintillan — KWIHN-tihl-aan — Minister of the
Interior, promising Barrayaran bureaucrat lost
to an untimely accident. (B)

Radnov — RAAD-nawv — Barrayaran lieutenant,
Political Officer on the *General Vorkraft*, tried
and failed to assassinate Aral Vorkosigan. (SH)

Radovas, Barto — RAA-doh-vahs, BAHR-toh —
Engineer with a doctorate in math from
Solstice University killed while testing worm-
hole-closing device. (K)

Rathgens — RAATH-jehnz — General, Imperial
Security chief on Komarr. (K)

Rau — RAH_OH — Ghem-captain, minion of
ghem-Colonel Millisor. (EA)

*Rene Magritte* — reh-NAY mah-GREET — Sixty-
person vessel of the Betan Astronomical
Survey. (SH)

Rigby — RIHG-bee — Group-Patroller, Komarran
civilian police force, Serifosa Dome Security. (K)

Riva — REE-vuh — Doctor, five-space mathematical
physics expert from Solstice University. (K)

Roic — ROYK — Vorkosigan armsman, former
policeman in Hassadar, feels intimidated

by the military backgrounds of most other armsmen. (CC, DI, WG)

Rond, Este — RAWND, EHS-tee — Satrap Governor of Rho Ceta, the Cetagandan territory closest to Barrayar. (C)

Rotha, Victor — ROH-thah, VIHK-tohr — Arms dealer cover identity for Ensign Lord Miles Vorkosigan in Hegen Hub. (VG)

*Rudra* — ROO-druh — Komarran trade ship held at Graf Station. (DI)

Ruey, Anias — RAY or RUH_EH, uh-NAI-uhs — A struggling artist and author of the feelie-dream *Triad*. (DD)

Ruibal — ROO_EE-bl — Doctor, a neurologist, head of the medical team handling Simon Illyan's "illness." (M)

Ryoval, Ry — RAI-uh-vahl, RY — Baron, head of House Ryoval, purveyor of flesh, genetic collector, and paranoid loner. (MD)

Sahlin — SAH-ln — Felician captain who takes Daum's cargo down to Tau Verde IV. (WA)

Sencele, Mount — sehn-SEHL, MAH_OONT — Site of the third day of the entrance exams for admission to the Barrayaran Imperial Academy, where the cadets must run a hundred kilometers. (WA)

Sens — SEHNZ — One of the mutineers under
Radnov. (SH)

Sergyar — SRG-yahr — Barrayar's wormhole neighbor and colony planet. (CC, SH, DI)

Serifosa Dome — SEH-rih-FOH-sah DOHM — One
of the sealed arcologies on Komarr, capital of
Serifosa Sector. (K)

Setti — SEH-tee — Minion of ghem-Colonel
Millisor, killed on Kline Station. (EA)

Sevarin — SEH-vah-rihn — Large city on Athos,
location of the Sevarin Replication Center,
where Doctor Urquhart works. (EA)

Siembieda, Ryan — saim-BAI-dah, RAI-uhn —
Dendarii tech sergeant killed on Mahata
Solaris. Revived on Earth, he wondered what
had happened and is filled in by Miles. (BA)

Siggy — SIH-gee — Quaddie airsystems maintenance tech, part of Silver's organization to
obtain forbidden books and vids. (FF)

Silica — SIH-lih-kah — Underground city on Beta
Colony with a notable zoo. (WA)

Silvy Vale — SIHL-vee VAYL — Small village in
the Dendarii Mountains, progressing with help
from the Vorkosigans. (M, MM)

Skellytum — SKEH-lee-tuhm — Cylindrical plant
up to five meters tall, brown with upward-
growing tendrils, native to Barrayar. (K)

Smolyani — s-mohl-YAH-nee — Lieutenant in
    Imperial Security, captain of the courier
    *Kestrel* sent to find Miles to negotiate a solu-
    tion to problems at Graf Station. (DI)

Soletta Array — soh-LEH-tah ah-RAY — Hexagonal
    array of seven insolation mirrors built by the
    Komarrans three centuries ago to aid in terra-
    forming their world. Four mirrors were dam-
    aged or destroyed in an accident. (K)

Solian — SOH-lee-n — Lieutenant, Barrayaran secu-
    rity liaison officer to the Toscane-owned ship
    *Idris* of the Komarran trade fleet, killed by
    renegade Cetegandan ba. (DI)

Solstice Dome — SOHL-stihs DOHM — A sealed
    arcology on Komarr and the planetary capital. (K)

Soltoxin — sohl-TAHK-sihn — Gas weapon that
    attacks the lungs. The antidote is a teratogen
    that affects fetal bone development, severely
    injuring Miles before birth. (B)

Soudha — SOO-duh — An engineer with a degree in
    five-space technology, Head of Waste Heat
    Management for Serifosa branch of the Komarr
    Terraforming Project. He tries to close the
    wormhole to Barrayar to free his planet. (K)

Sphaleros — s-FAA-lr-ohs — Ground Captain
    ImpSec, sent to transport Nikki and various
    others to confer with Gregor. (CC)

Stauber, Georish — STAA_OO-br, JEE_OH-rihsh —

Baron of House Fell, half brother of Baron Ryoval, and Lily Durona. (L, MD)

Stuben — STOO-behn — Betan lieutenant, second-in-command of the *Rene Magritte*. (SH)

Suegar — SOO-gahr — Marilacan prisoner with a prophetic text on Dagoola IV. (BI)

Szabo — ZAH-boh — Chief Vorrutyer armsman with a special care for the succession of Count Pierre. (CC)

Tabbi — TAH-bee — Quaddie who figured out a way to open vacuum-welded clamps by using slurry explosive. (FF)

Tafas — TAA-fahs — One of the Radnov's mutineers, he helped Cordelia stop them. (SH)

Tanery Base — TAA-neh-ree BAYS — Barrayaran military shuttleport, Aral's base of operations during the Vordarian Pretendership. (B)

Tarpan, Lucan — TAHR-paan LUH-kn — From Jackson's Whole with ties to House Bharaputra, tries to have Ekaterin assassinated to cover his escape. (WG)

Tau, Varadar — TAH_OH, VAAR-ah-dahr — Bandit leader whose tax-collecting accountants were the first counts of Barrayar. (B)

Tau Verde IV — TAH_OH VAYR-dee FOHR — Location of Felice and Pelias. (WA)

Taura — TAH-rah — Ninth (and only survivor) of ten experimental supersoldiers made on Jackson's Whole, rescued/recruited by Miles for the Dendarii. (L, MD, WG)

Teki — TEH-kee — Kline Station hydroponics specialist and cousin of Ellie Quinn. (EA)

Teris Three — TEH-rihs THREE — Third-shift supervisor for Graf Station Security. (DI)

Tesslev — TEHS-lehv — Best guerrilla lieutenant General Piotr ever had, killed during the Cetegandan War. (WA)

Thorne, Bel — THOHRN, BEHL — Officer on the *Ariel* in the Oseran Mercenaries, captain of the *Ariel* in the Dendarii Mercenaries, forced to retire from the Dendarii for its role in the clone rescue raid, ended up in Quaddiespace as Assistant Portmaster on Graf Station, and wants to be a Union of Free Habitats citizen. (All except B, FF, SH)

Toscane, Laisa — TAHS-kayn, LAI-sah — Ph.D. in business theory and on Barrayar to lobby for Komarran shipping interests. Ends up marrying Emperor Gregor. (CC, M)

Touchev — TOO-chehv — Sergeant in the Imperial forces, squad leader of the Security team sent to retrieve Ensign Corbeau when the Barrayaran escort fleet went to alert status. (DI)

Tremont, Guy — treh-MAWNT, GEE — Marilacan
colonel and a brilliant commander, he was
betrayed at Fallow Core, died on Dagoola IV.
(BI)

Tris — TRIHS — Marilacan, field-promoted to lieutenant. She and her disciplined corps are
the core of Miles's organization of the prisoners
and of the new Marilac resistance. (BI)

Trogir, Marie — troh-GEER, mah-REE —
Engineering technician in the Waste Heat
Management group, working for Radovas.
She died in the test of the wormhole-closing
device. (K)

Tung, Ky — TUHNG, KAI — Captain-owner of
the *Triumph* in the Oseran Mercenaries, commodore and chief of staff in the Dendarii
Mercenaries until his retirement. (BA, BI,
MD, VG, WA)

Tuomonen — too_oh-MOH-nehn — Captain,
head of ImpSec for Serifosa, married to a
Komarran, helps Miles investigate the Soletta
Station accident. (K)

Ungari — uhng-GAA-ree — Captain in Imperial
Security, assigned to make a military evalu-
ation of the Hegen Hub situation and given
Miles as a resource. (VG)

Urquhart, Ethan — R-kwahrt, EE-thn —
Doctor and Chief of Reproductive Biology
at the Sevarin Replication Center, sent to

replace the ovarian cultures bought from
Jackson's Whole. (EA)

Ushakov — OO-shah-kawv — Colonel in Barrayaran
    Imperial Security, commander of Major
    Zamori, Captain Ivan Vorpatril, and Lieutenant
    Alexi Vormoncrief, among others. (CC)

Vaagen — VAH-gn — Doctor and biochemist on
    Barrayar, expert in combat medicine, granted
    a research empire by Cordelia when he saves
    Miles's life. (B)

Valentine — VAA-ln-TAIN — Admiral, one of the
    seven sitting Imperial Auditors when Simon
    suffered his memory chip sabotage. (M)

Van — VAAN — Pilot Officer on a commer-
    cial liner, on the board of the pilot's union,
    acquainted with Arde Mayhew. (WA)

Van Atta, Bruce — Vaan AA-tah, BROOS — Head
    of the Cay Project after the death of Doctor
    Cay, sees his job as making the project profit-
    able. After interpreting his orders to termi-
    nate the quaddies, he tries to stop them from
    escaping. (FF)

Vandeville — VAAN-d-veel — Town on Barrayar's
    South Continent where Ekaterin grew up. (K)

Venier, Ser — veh-NEER, SEHR — Administrative
    assistant to Tien Vorsoisson, a slight, nervous,
    rabbity Komarran. (K)

Venn — VEHN — Crew Chief of Graf Station Security, offended by the armed violence of Barrayarans in military alert mode. (DI)

Vervain — vr-VAIN — System linking the Hegen Hub to the Cetagandan Empire, attempting to remain neutral vis-à-vis Cetaganda. (VG)

Vervani — vr-VAAN-ee — An inhabitant of Vervain.

Villanova, Liz — VIH-lah-NOH-vah, LIHZ — aka "Mama Nilla," a popular crèche mother to the younger quaddies. (FF)

Virga, Valeria — VUHR-gah, vah-LEH-ree_ah — Author of romantic novels Silver is fond of, possibly a committee. (FF)

Visconti, Elena — vihs-KAWN-tee, ay-LAY-nuh — Escobaran trooper captured in the early stages of the Barrayaran invasion of Escobar, tortured by Serg and Vorrutyer, rescued to the best of his ability by Bothari, she kills him in front of their daughter, Elena. (All except FF and SH)

Vorbarr Sultana — vohr-BAHR suhl-TAH-nah — Capital of Barrayar and also of the Vorbarra District. (B, CC, M, MD, SH, WG)

Vorbarra, Dorca — vohr-BAA-ruh, DOHR-kuh — "The Just," Emperor of Barrayar, after an age of chaos was unifying the counts under his rule when Barrayar was rediscovered by the rest of galactic humanity. He presided over

the first defeat of the Cetagandans. (All except
EA and FF)

Vorbarra, Ezar — _____, EE-zahr — Emperor of
Barrayar, experimented with more centralized
government, managed the transition from the
rule of men to the rule of law. (SH)

Vorbarra, Gregor — _____, GREH-gohr —
Emperor of Barrayar, Miles's foster brother
and friend. (All except EA, FF, and SH)

Vorbarra, Serg — _____, SRG — Prince, he is
Ezar's deviant son and heir; killed in battle
with Escobar at the Emperor's order. (SH)

Vorbarra, Xav — _____, ZAAV — Prince, second
son of Emperor Dorca, diplomat, married a
Betan. (B)

Vorbarra, Yuri — _____, YOO-ree — "Mad
Emperor Yuri." His massacre attempting to
kill all of his relatives made him too many
enemies. (SH)

Vorbataille — vohr-bah-TAI-l — Lord with connections and a space yacht, used as a pawn in a
hijacking. (WG)

Vorberg — VOHR-brg — Lieutenant, ImpSec
courier rescued from hijackers in Admiral
Naismith's last adventure. (M)

Vorbohn — vohr-BOHN — Count, commander of
the Vorbarr Sultana municipal guard. (CC)

Vorbretten, René — vohr-BREH-tn, reh-NAY — Count, brilliant, talented, and one-quarter Cetagandan, center of a controversy on the inheritance of countship. (CC)

Vorbretten, Sigur — _____, SEE-guhr — Descended from René's great-uncle without any Cetagandan interlopers, claims René's countship. (CC)

Vordarian — vohr-DAYR-ee_uhn — Family whose colors are maroon and gold. (B)

Vordarian, Vidal — _____, vih-DAHL — Commodore, count, archconservative and isolationist, had political differences with Aral Vorkosigan, desired Princess Kareen, and tried to take the throne by force. Killed by Bothari at Cordelia's command. (B)

Vordrozda — vohr-DROHZH-duh — Barrayaran count attempting to influence young Emperor Gregor by accusing Miles of treason. His plan fails when Miles returns to defend himself. (WA)

Vorfolse — VOHR-fohls — Count whose vote Miles's alliance seeks for the Vorrutyer and Vorbretten cases. (CC)

Vorgarin — vohr-GAH-rihn — Count, one of Alys Vorpatril's circle. (CC)

Vorgier — vohr-GEER — Captain in Imperial Security and the head of Barrayaran jump-point station at Komarr, he's ready to go in against the terrorists, all guns blazing. (K)

Vorgorov, Cassia — VOHR-GOH-rawv, KAA-see-uh — Lady and acquaintance of Ivan, she is engaged to Lord William Vortashpula. (CC)

Vorgustafson, Van — vohr-GUH-stahf-sn, VAAN — Lord, Imperial Auditor, retired industrialist and noted philanthropist. (M)

Vorhalas — vohr-HAA-lahs — Count, father of Carl and Evon, conservative, Aral Vorkosigan's longest-standing enemy. (WA)

Vorhalas, Carl — _____, KAHRL — A young hothead, killed a man in a drunken duel, executed for it. (B)

Vorhalas, Evon — _____, EE-vahn — Lieutenant, attempted to assassinate Aral Vorkosigan to avenge his brother's death, caught and condemned, freed to fight by Vordarian, doomed by Vordarian's failure. (B)

Vorhalas, Rulf — _____, RUHLF — The younger brother of Count Vorhalas, admiral in the Escobar Invasion fleet, killed in the invasion. (SH)

Vorharopulos — vohr-haa-ROH-puh-loos — Family whose colors are chartreuse and silver. (CC)

Vorhartung Castle — vohr-HAHR-tuhng KAA-sl — Meeting place of the Council of Counts. (B, CC, WA)

Vorhovis — vohr-HOH-vihs — Imperial Auditor, Gregor's top man, a soldier and diplomat, lean, cool, and sophisticated. (M)

Vorinnis — vohr-IHN-ihs — Count, head of the military
  faction and one of Alys Vorpatril's circle. (CC)

Vorkalloner, Aristede — vohr-KAA-ln-r, AA-rihs-TEED —
  Lieutenant commander on the *General Vorkraft*
  under Aral Vorkosigan, and commander on
  Gottyan's vessel in the expedition against
  Escobar. Killed in action. (SH)

Vorkosigan Surleau — vohr-KOH-sih-gn, suhr-LOH —
  Estate of the Vorkosigans on the Long Lake,
  once a castle destroyed in the Cetagandan
  Wars; later a house converted from the old
  barracks. (B, CC, SH, M, MD, MM, WF)

Vorkosigan Vashnoi — _____ VAASH-noy — Old
  capital of the Vorkosigan District, became a
  blue-glowing crater in the Cetagandan Wars.
  (B, CC, M, WA)

Vorkosigan, Aral — _____, AA-rl — Conqueror of
  Komarr, architect of the Barrayaran withdrawal
  from Escobar, admiral, regent, count, prime
  minister, worthy successor to his father, General
  Count Piotr Vorkosigan. (All except EA and FF)

Vorkosigan, Mark Pierre — _____, MAHRK
  pee_EHR — Clone brother to Miles, he is six
  years younger and did not have his own name
  before Miles told him what it was as his parents' second son and insisted it was his. (BA,
  CC, MD, WG)

Vorkosigan, Miles Naismith — _____, MAI_UHLZ
  NAY-smihth — Stunted and deformed by an

assassination attempt on his father, wants
nothing more than to be a worthy successor to
him. Invented and became Admiral Naismith
trying to be of service. (All except FF and SH)

Vorkosigan, Piotr Pierre — _____, pee_OH-tr
pee_EHR — General, count, chief architect of
both Barrayaran victories in the Cetagandan
Wars, and Ezar's succession in Mad Yuri's War,
died in bed—the first Count Vorkosigan to do
so—at ninety-two. (B, MM, WA)

Vorkosigan, Selig — _____, SEH-lihg — General,
count, possible original owner of Miles's seal
dagger, inherited from his grandfather. (K)

Vorlaisner — vohr-LAYS-nr — One of the seven
Imperial Auditors serving when Simon was
stricken. (M)

Vorlakial — vohr-LAI-kee-uhl — A military strategist
Aral Vorkosigan rates as superior to himself.
Killed under mysterious circumstances. (SH)

Vorloupulous — vohr-LOO-puh-loos — Count who
sought to evade Dorca's law limiting the number of armsmen a count could have. (WA)

Vormoncrief, Alexi — vohr-MAHN-kreef,
aa-LEHK-see — Lieutenant in the Barrayaran
military and the nephew of Count Boriz, a
meddlesome young man who didn't react well
when Ekaterin refused his offer of marriage.
(CC)

Vormoncrief, Boriz — _____, BOH-rihz — Barrayaran
count suing the Council of Counts on behalf
of his son-in-law, Sigur Vorbretten. (CC)

Vormuir, Thomas — vohr-MEE_UHR, TAA-ms —
Count who has a great ambition to be a father
to 122 illegitimate daughters. (CC)

Vormurtos — vohr-MUHR-tohs — Lord, and sup-
porter of Richars' cause, prone to inebriation.
(CC)

Vorob'yev — vohr-OHB-yehv — Ambassador, head
of Barrayaran Embassy on Eta Ceta. (C)

Vorparadijs — vohr-PAH-rah-dees — General in
the Barrayaran military and Imperial Auditor
appointed by Ezar, one of the seven Imperial
Auditors serving when Simon was stricken. (M)

Vorpatril, Alys — vohr-PAA-trihl, AA-lihs — Lady, a
woman of impeccable taste, many friends, and
subtle influence, good friend to Simon Illyan.
(B, CC, WG)

Vorpatril, Eugin — _____, YOO-jihn — Admiral of
the Barrayaran escort of the Komarran trade
fleet impounded at Graf Station; his flagship is
the *Prince Xav*. (DI)

Vorpatril, Falco — _____, FAAL-koh — Count, he
is Ivan's cousin several times removed. (CC)

Vorpatril, Ivan — _____, AI-vn — Miles's second
cousin and heir, closest coeval relative and

friend since childhood. A dedicated lady's man. (B, BA, C, M, MD, WA, WG)

Vorpatril, Padma — _____, PAHD-mah — only descendant of Prince Xav besides Aral to survive Yuri's assassination squads. (SH)

Vorpinski — vohr-PIHN-skee — Count, one of Alys Vorpatril's circle. (CC)

Vorreedi — vohr-REE-dee — Colonel in Imperial Security and Chief of Protocol of Barrayaran Embassy on Eta Ceta IV, also head of Intelligence department there. (C)

Vorrutyer, Byerly — vohr-ROOT-yr, BAI-r-lee — Assiduous town clown. (CC)

Vorrutyer, Dono — _____, DOH-noh — Lord, formerly Lady Donna, part of her scheme to prevent Richars from succeeding to the countship. (CC)

Vorrutyer, Ges — _____, GEHS — Admiral in Barrayaran military and co-commander with Prince Serg of the Barrayaran invasion fleet launched against Escobar. Killed by Bothari before the battle. (SH)

Vorrutyer, Richars — _____, RIH-chahrs — Successor to Pierre that no one looks forward to, unprovably involved in other suspicious deaths. (CC)

Vorsmythe — vohr-SMAITH — Count, one of Alys Vorpatril's circle. (CC)

Vorsoisson — vohr-SWAH-sawn — Officer in the South
    Continent district government, best friend of
    Sasha Vorvayne, has a son, Etienne, about ten
    years older than his friend's daughter. (K, CC)

Vorsoisson, Ekaterin Nile Vorvayne — _____,
    ee-KAY-tr-ihn NAI_UHL vohr-VAYN — Lady,
    married to Etienne Vorsoisson at age twenty,
    has a son, Nikolai. Her uncle is Imperial
    Auditor Professor Vorthys. (K, CC, WG, DI)

Vorsoisson, Etienne — _____, eht-YEHN —
    Administrator of the Serifosa branch of the
    Komarr Terraforming Project, a minor bureau-
    crat of no particular talent, thinks everything
    is accomplished by doing and calling in favors,
    has no use for the concept of merit. Dies try-
    ing to save his own skin at the Serifosa exper-
    iment station. (K)

Vorsoisson, Nikolai — _____, NIH-koh-lai — The
    nine-year-old son of Ekaterin and Tien, has
    inherited the Vorsoisson family genetic condi-
    tion, Vorzohn's Distrophy. (K, CC)

Vorsoisson, Vassily — _____, VAA-sih-lee —
    Etienne's third cousin, guardian of Nikki after
    Tien's death. (CC)

Vortaine — vohr-TAYN — Count, rather elderly,
    Ivan's heir, one of Alys Vorpatril's circle. (WA)

Vortala — vohr-TAA-luh — Ezar's prime minister
    and Aral's when he is regent. (B)

Vortalon — vohr-TAA-ln — Captain, vid series jump-pilot hero, sidekick of Prince Xav, tracked down and killed those responsible for his father's death. (CC)

Vortashpula, William — vohr-TAASH-puh-luh, WIHL-ee_uhm — Lord, acquaintance of Ivan, engaged to Lady Cassia Vorgorov. (CC)

Vorthalia — vohr-THAH-lee_uh — "The Bold," also "The Loyal," legendary hero of Barrayar also a historical person. (WA, K)

Vorthys, Georg — VOHR-tais, JOHRJ — Professor of Engineering at the Imperial University at Vorbarr Sultana, an Imperial Auditor specializing in diagnosis of engineering failures and sabotage sent to Komarr to investigate the Soletta Array accident. (CC, K, WG)

Vortrifrani — vohr-trih-FRAA-nee — Count, head of the isolationist faction. (M)

Vortugalov — vohr-TOO-gah-lawv — Count, head of the Russian language faction. (B)

Vorvane — vohr-VAYN — Lord, Minister for Heavy Industries. (MD)

Vorvayne, Edie — vohr-VAYN, EE-dee — Daughter of Hugo and Rosalie, a preteen, she has two elder brothers. (CC)

Vorvayne, Hugo — _____, HYOO-goh — Holds a post in the Imperial Bureau of Mines in the northern regional HQ in Vordarian's District, Ekaterin's elder brother. (CC)

Vorvayne, Sasha — _____, SAH-shuh — Officer in the South Continent district government, eager for his daughter, Ekaterin, to marry his friend's son, especially as he was remarrying. (K)

Vorvayne, Violie — _____, VAI-oh-lee — Second wife of Sasha Vorvayne, stepmother to Ekaterin. (K)

Vorventa — Vohr-VEHN-tuh — Lord, "The Twice Hung," during the Time of Isolation, tried after he was dead, an unusual legal precedent on Barrayar. (K)

Vorville — vohr-VEEL — Count, head of the French language faction, one of Alys Vorpatril's circle. (CC)

Vorvolk, Henri — VOHR-vohk, ahn-REE — Count, one of the few counts Gregor's age, friend of Gregor, and an official in Accounting, watching over expenses. (WA)

Vorvolynkin — vohr-voh-LIHN-kn — Count, one of Alys Vorpatril's circle. (CC)

Vorzohn's Distrophy — VOHR-zhohnz DIHS-troh-fee — Genetic condition and adult-onset neurological disorder that begins in slight tremula, progresses to mental collapse and death, treatable by complex and expensive means, curable by gene therapy. (K)

Watts — WAHTZ — Boss or supervisor of Graf
     Station Downsider Relations, a job that
     includes the duties of Portmaster. (DI)

Weddell, Vaughan — WEH-dehl, VAWN — Hugh
     Canaba's new identity on Barrayar. He is a
     genetic researcher at the Imperial Science
     Institute just outside Vorbarr Sultana, brought
     in to assist on Simon's case by Miles. (L, M)

Wyzak — WAI-zaak — Chief, Life Support Systems,
     Cay Habitat. (FF)

Xian — zai-AHN — Marilacan general, had sworn
     to return to Fallow Core but was killed before
     he could do so. (BI)

Yegorov — YEH-goh-rawv — Barrayaran lieutenant
     on the *Prince Serg*, attempts to advise Admiral
     Naismith on etiquette when meeting Aral
     Vorkosigan. (VG)

Yei, Sondra — YAY, SOHN-drah — Doctor, head of
     psychology and training for the Cay Project,
     she takes a spanner to Bruce Van Atta's head
     when he attempts to kill the quaddies. (FF)

Yenaro — yeh-NAH-roh — Cetegandan grandson
     of ghem-General Yenaro, the last of five lead-
     ers of the Barrayar invasion, wishes to be an
     imperial perfumer. (C)

Yuell — YOO-ehl — Doctor, math professor, col-
     league of Doctor Riva. (K)

Zamori — zaa-MOH-ree — A major working in the Imperial Military, found excuses to call on the Vorthys residence to see Ekaterin. (CC)

Zara — ZAA-rah — Quaddie pusher pilot, her skill got the strike team docked with the D-620 superjumper. (F)

• • • • • •

# An Old Earther's Guide to the Vorkosigan Universe

### DENISE LITTLE

## Worlds of the Imperium

The Barrayaran Imperium consists of three planets, a number of space installations, and roughly fifty million people scattered across its various components.

## Barrayar

Barrayar is the homeworld of the three-planet Barrayaran Imperium. Barrayar was originally founded as an Earth Colony long ago, by what are known in Barrayaran history books as the Fifty Thousand Firsters. These settlers descended from several Earth cultures, with the result that Barrayar's official languages today are various dialects of English, French, Russian, and Greek.

But what should have been an orderly colonization and terraforming job for these settlers soon turned into a voyage back into the Dark Ages. The interstellar wormhole through which they had transited from Earth vanished just as mysteriously as it had appeared. The colony cascaded back into a near-Stone Age without the aid of support ships from their home planet. Most of the technology of advanced civilization vanished on Barrayar.

And so the colony was lost to galactic civilization for several hundred years, a period known as the Time of Isolation. The colonization of Barrayar—unlike those of Beta Colony or Escobar—degraded into a ragged fight for survival, as the world descended into chaos.

But humans are stubborn, and the settlers managed to hang on and multiply despite hostile native flora and the constant threat of mutations cropping up among the descendants of the original settlers. A new civilization was born. A feudal aristocracy developed among the contentious settlers as factions among them fought for power over their world. The warring elite were eventually united and merged into a real unitary government by Dorca Vorbarra. His central government restored a rough and ready order planet-wide, though one that strongly favored its elites.

Ruthless customs, including infanticide, sprang up among the population to keep human mutations at bay and the colony healthy and growing. As the population grew, the canny use of all the planet's resources—native and Earth-derived—helped the colony thrive, though hardly in the ways foreseen by the initial settlement plans. Among the many problems tackled by the early colonists was how to aggressively make Barrayar hospitable to Earth-descended agriculture and animal husbandry before they all starved to death. They succeeded, but much of the original planetary ecology was irrevocably lost in the areas so cultivated.

During this Time of Isolation from galactic civilization, the basic political structure on Barrayar settled down into a single government headed by a hereditary Emperor, supported by an equally hereditary aristocracy known as the Vor. The word Vor implies an obligation of duty and service to the Emperor. The Vor were originally the planet's warrior caste.

More than a hundred years prior to the present galactic civilization, Barrayar was once again rediscovered by the larger human community. The planet rapidly absorbed newly available galactic technology, but the habits acquired during the Time of Isolation died hard. To this day, the planet remains an archaic society in the eyes of galactics, who view it as both fascinating and primitive. But its unique issues also give rise to unique virtues.

The opening of the planet to the galaxy had consequences far beyond the importation of lightflyers and computers and the exportation of a reputation as a backwater. The Cetagandans invaded Barrayar through a wormhole near Barrayar's closest neighbors, the planet Komarr, in an attempt to claim Barrayar as a colony. The Barrayarans responded in a way that the astonished Cetagandans never anticipated. Led by Ezar Vorbarra and General Piotr Vorkosigan, the Barrayaran resistance retreated to the mountains and fought back viciously, relentlessly, and successfully. It took twenty years, and the deaths of five million Barrayarans, but the Cetagandans were eventually driven off the planet.

They left an odd gift behind. Because of the necessity of utilizing every bit of their native talent to survive in the wider galaxy, the traditional Vor privileges of Imperial service were no longer reserved for the Vor alone. The war opened up the Imperium to the idea of service based on merit, rather than bloodlines. The Imperial academies were opened to non-Vor applicants based on aptitude, and the society eventually became more level, with the military serving as an egalitarian force on Barrayar. But it is still forbidden for non-Vor to privately own deadly weapons, including a wide range of swords, though many citizens gain access to such weapons through Imperial training and government service.

At the apex of Barrayar's hereditary Vor aristocracy are the counts. The term "count" derives from the job's origin in the people—accountants—who procured taxes for the Emperor from the local populace, amassed it into organized offerings, counted it, and delivered it to the proper Imperial authorities. The North Continent is divided into sixty districts, each run by its own count. The counts give their loyalty to the Emperor though a ceremony of fealty, which includes a placing of their hands between the Emperor's, and a voiced repetition of oaths. (This style of vocal affirmation—spoken vows serving as binding words of honor—is something that pervades Barrayaran society.) The fealty ceremony is renewed with the installation of each new Emperor.

The counts serve in a legislative Council, which has a great and glorious history, along with a number of highly archaic traditions, and its share of insane adventures—including the famous affirmation of a horse named Midnight as a count's legal heir. In modern

Barrayar the Council of Counts is a rather mixed body of progressives, conservatives, geniuses, and idiots. But, having grown into being along with the planet, this form of government provides a workable, if occasionally erratic and confusing, arm of the Imperium. Signs of modern progress in local government are evident everywhere on the planet, thanks mainly to a law passed during Aral Vokosigan's Regency government, which allows ordinary citizens to move from Count's District to Count's District without restriction. On Barrayar, the planet's people in effect vote with their feet for the best forms of local government.

After a number of bloody insurrections, including everything from quick and dirty wars over the distribution of the horse manure from the Imperial Stable to the rebellion of counts against the insane Emperor Yuri Vorbarra, private armies have been abolished on Barrayar. All military service is through the Imperium, with the single exception of the counts' armsmen. Each count is allowed to maintain a private, oath-sworn force of twenty loyal men for personal protection.

The Barrayaran planetary day is 26.7 hours long, and Barrayaran ships keep Imperial, rather than Old Earth, time cycles. The planet has two moons, a temperate climate with four distinct seasons (as on Earth, winter, spring, summer, and fall), and a topography that is very Earth-like, including large oceans. There are two main continents and a number of islands. The North Continent was settled by the original colonists, and is the main population center of the planet, although the South Continent, which is the personal property of the Emperor, has been opened to settlement for some years and is expanding in population quickly.

Barrayar's mythology is varied. Military and cultural heroes from the planet's recent and distant past are celebrated, along with a number of carryovers from Old Earth culture, including Russian fairy tales and Greek mythology. The main holidays celebrated on Barrayar are the Emperor's Birthday, Midsummer Review, and Winterfair, where the coming of Father Frost is eagerly awaited by all Barrayaran children. The planet's society is still very much a male hierarchy, with inheritance laws based on primogeniture, and the military and Imperial Security academies are still closed to women. The Army and its domestic arm, Imperial Security, or ImpSec, are still all-male organizations. Women are making strides toward more rights, but they have a very large amount of ground to cover before true equality is achieved. Currently their power base is gained through manipulating the men around them, for better or worse. But with increasing levels of education and pressures from other galactic civilizations, great change is inevitable in the long term.

## Komarr

Komarr is a planet with a single main reason for its settlement, namely a rich supply of wormhole jump-points in its immediate vicinity. By charging a hefty tariff on all goods passed through those jump points, the various merchant families who formed the ruling oligarchy on Komarr amassed both riches and power. The planet is essentially a galactic parasite, surviving and thriving on the taxes placed on interstellar trade.

The planet may have economic riches, but it is an inhospitable place. Human habitation is possible only in domed cities. An array of solar mirrors to increase the natural light sources and a planet-wide terraforming project are scheduled to make Komarr habitable by humans outside the domes in the very long term, but all current expeditions outside are only possible with the use of some form of serious breathing apparatus.

The Komarrans grew up as an independent colony, but when they gave access to Cetaganda for an invasion of Barrayar, they sealed their fate to become part of the Imperium. Under the leadership of Aral Vorkosigan, Barrayar invaded and conquered Komarr. Given its lack of habitable land for any resistance to retreat to, and its vulnerability to attacks that might shatter the domes, the conquest of Komarr was quick, though not as bloodless as Vorkosigan had envisioned when setting up the invasion. During the war, two hundred members of the planet's ruling families, gathered under a flag of truce to negotiate the surrender, were killed by a political officer acting without orders from above. Despite murdering the responsible officer with his bare hands, Vorkosigan was never able to convince the Komarrans that the political officer's action wasn't planned, leaving some segments of the planet ripe for seeking revenge against Barrayar. Vorkosigan became known throughout the galaxy as "the Butcher of Komarr." But galactic aid was not forthcoming to the Komarrans from neighboring states, because Barrayar immediately reduced the tariff on interstellar goods passing through Komarr from twenty-five percent to fifteen percent. This made galactics favor keeping Komarr in Barrayaran hands.

Currently the planet seems to be adapting well to Barrayaran rule. The Imperium is fast-tracking suitable Komarrans into positions of power, and Emperor Gregor Vorbarra recently married a Komarran, Laisa Toscane. As a wedding gift to the planet, he arranged for a much-expanded solar mirror array, speeding up the terraforming project by several orders of magnitude.

## Sergyar

Barrayar discovered a wormhole jump that led to the planet Sergyar, and claimed the planet as its own. Named for Emperor Ezar's son, Crown Prince Serg, the planet is earthlike and beautiful, and since it had no native species possessing higher intelligence, it was ideal for opening up to human settlement. But Barrayar's main reason for settling Sergyar in the beginning was to use it as a staging point for an invasion of Escobar. The invasion failed miserably, in part because of aid to Escobar from Beta Colony, and Prince Serg and a number of high-ranking Barrayaran military officers died in that attempt. After a peace treaty with Escobar was worked out, the planet was retasked to more peaceful purposes, and is currently a rapidly expanding human settlement. Government of the colony is handled by an Imperially appointed viceroy. Early difficulties that impeded settlement, including a terrible worm plague that hideously bloated its victims, have been overcome, and the colony is on track to become a vibrant and valuable member of the Imperium.

# Other Political Entities in the Wormhole Nexus (In rough order of importance to the Vorkosigan universe)

## Cetaganda

The Cetagandan Empire consists of eight developed worlds and a number of allied and puppet dependencies, many of them forcibly acquired. Cetaganda is ruled by a genetically engineered emperor, and the Imperial government consists of a two-tiered aristocracy. At the head of the Imperial power structure is the haut class and at the head of the haut class is the emperor—currently Emperor Fletchir Gaija. The Emperor serves as the only point of meeting between the affairs of the haut and the affairs of the second tier of the aristocracy—the ghem.

The haut consider themselves to be a post-human breed, the result of several centuries of genetic engineering that they have carried out upon their population. They have a vaguely attenuated elf-like look, and their physical beauty is revered throughout the galaxy. Haut women are so beautiful, in fact, that they are rarely seen in public, traveling in float chairs surrounded by opaque force screens as they move through the landscape, and exiting their protective chairs only in safe and restricted confines familiar to them. The sight of a haut woman has been known to induce instantaneous emotional slavery in typical human men.

The haut do not believe that their genetic experimentation has reached its apex yet. The work of improving the genome is undertaken by the Star Crèche—which is run by the haut consorts of the various planetary governors and headed by the emperor's mother or the mother of his heir. Each year, the result of their genetic work is sent out to the Cetagandan worlds in the form of a shipment of developing haut embryos in uterine replicators. These children-to-be are taken in by their respective genetic constellations when they reach their home planets, where they will be raised and educated to take their place among the planets' ruling elite. The haut own nothing individually, despite their luxurious lives spent in isolation in the incredibly beautiful enclaves inhabited exclusively by the haut and their genderless ba servitors. All property is held in trust by the government, and awarded to the haut caste based on breeding, merit, status in the haut hierarchy, and ceremonial needs.

The ba are asexual genetic siblings to the haut, and are created by haut geneticists to test out new genetic additions to the haut bloodlines. The ba are engineered to be servile and loyal, but a few incidents in which they have behaved with startling initiative and ingenuity have raised some questions among the haut as to the degree to which their genetic control has been effective.

The haut control their empire though a secret and reputedly devastating collection of bioengineered weapons. The few examples of haut genetic weaponry that have been used throughout the galaxy have been so terrifying that it is widely believed that the reputation of haut for maintaining a strong arsenal has been, if anything, underestimated.

The haut look inward at what they are becoming, while the ghem are the outward face of the Cetagandans. The ghem women, in imitation of the haut, also work in genetic engineering, but they concentrate on non-human material. The ghem men concentrate on politics and conquest, and favor a very aggressive brand of territorial expansion. Their most recent adventures have been universally disastrous for the last century (Barrayar, Vervain, Marilac, etc.). It is widely hoped throughout the galaxy that the Cetagandans are embarking on a newly peaceful period in which they concentrate on improving their own empire, instead of aggressively invading their neighbors.

The ghem are kept under control by the haut through a system of rewards and restraints. Haut women who have fallen from grace are awarded to successful ghem men as trophy wives. Ghem who achieve great things have their genetic material taken up by the Star Crèche for inclusion into the haut genome. Ghem who fail are ruthlessly dealt with, sometimes by difficult and messy "suicides" that can include multiple stab wounds in the back, though more elegant forms of elimination are preferred.

# Planets of the Cetagandan Empire

## *Eta Ceta IV*

The central world in the Cetagandan Imperium, and the home of the Imperial Gardens, where the planetary government and the Star Crèche are situated.

## *Tau Ceta*

Located in Sector II.

## Rho Ceta

The nearest Cetagandan world to the Komarran wormhole jump point.

## Dagoola IV

A Cetagandan prison planet, which, while run in exact accordance with galactic treaties, is as fiendish and Darwinian a place as ever conceived by the minds of humans.

# Other Civilizations of the Wormhole Nexus

## Beta Colony

Beta Colony is a technologically advanced planet with superb schools, a very high standard of living, and a very advanced approach to personal liberty, sexual orientation, and lifestyle choices. The planet is essentially a desert, with little surface water other than flat saline lakes, and the vast majority of human habitation located underground. Rebreathers and nose filters are required for humans to survive on the Betan surface, along with personal heat shields during the hotter months. Betan politics are based on a planetary-wide constitutional democracy. Logic and scientific exploration are central to the Betan way of life, just as oaths and honor are central to Barrayarans.

Sexual behavior is wildly free on Beta Colony, but at the price of reproduction being strictly controlled. This is a legacy of the planet's unique colonization by sub-light generation ships. To bear a child on Beta, a couple must undergo extensive training in parenting, apply for a child permit, and arrange for the health and welfare of the offspring in advance of its arrival. The first permit (actually, the first two half-permits) are free; more may be purchased on a secondary market, where the price varies, or are sometimes rewarded for merit. While a woman or herm may still undertake an old-fashioned risky body birth, and some do, most responsible parents choose *in vitro* fertilization with the zygote being carefully examined and treated for any genetic flaws before it is placed in a uterine replicator for its next nine months. Sexual preferences among the three genders (male, female, and hermaphrodite) are indicated by earring designs worn by all sexually active Betans, with a design to accurately indicate adult sexual status and the wearer's preferred variations, with gradations ranging in every stage from "not interested at all" to "involved in an exclusive relationship" to "will screw anything willing to allow it." Contraceptive implants are required by law, and may only be removed temporarily with government approval for reasons involving health or officially sanctioned reproduction.

Among the galactic tourist spots on Beta Colony is the Betan Orb of Unearthly Delights, where every kind of human sexual behavior ever observed is practiced with enthusiasm, and even accompanied by psychological counseling as needed.

Poverty is unknown on Beta Colony, and every citizen is guaranteed access to information, education, health care, and occupation.

## Marilac

Given its conveniently placed wormhole access to other planets, Marilac was a prosperous and advanced world. But it was invaded and conquered by Cetaganda. The planetary resistance was rounded up and sent to the Cetagandan prison planet Dagoola IV, and the conquest seemed complete. But a daring massive prison break arranged by the Dendarii Free Mercenary Fleet brought all the planet's rebels back into play at once. Eventually Cetaganda withdrew from Marilac, and left it to once again govern itself.

## Escobar

A technologically advanced neighbor of Beta Colony, Escobar was settled by colonists who were, judging by its resulting Latin culture, most probably from Brazil, Spain, and Italy.

## Jackson's Whole

Originally founded as an interstellar base by libertine space pirates, Jackson's Whole has since evolved into a planet run by a nongovernmental structure of 116 viciously competing Great Houses, countless Minor Houses, and a desperate population of ordinary citizens trying to stay out of the way of politics—which are generally widely terminal on Jackson's Whole. Only the Deal is sacred on the planet—and Jacksonians are expert dealers. The Great Houses have amassed power through traditional criminal enterprises, including slavery, illegal genetic manipulation of living organisms, clone slavery—including implantation of human brains into unwilling clone body donors—weapons dealing, and so on. Scientific research facilities, even if criminal, are top-notch, and do a large trade in galactic one-off contracts for poisons, assassinations, drugs, bioweapons, and other lucrative industries. Anything in the galaxy can be bought, traded for, or stolen on Jackson's Whole.

## Pol

An advanced planet that serves as a wormhole link from Komarr to the Hegen Hub. It is part of the Hegen Hub Alliance along with Aslund, Vervain, and Barrayar.

## Illyrica

It is a planet on the fringes of wormhole nexus famous for its interstellar shipbuilding.

## The Hegen Hub

A nexus system bare of habitable planets but rich in wormholes with a collection of adjoining worlds. The Hub serves as a galactic trading post and transportation hub.

## Vervain

A technologically advanced and comfortable Earth-like planet adjoining the Hegen Hub, it was invaded by the Cetagandans, and only saved from conquest by the actions of the Dendarii Free Mercenary Fleet and the Barrayaran space fleet under the leadership of Aral Vorkosigan. It is part of the Hegen Hub Alliance along with Aslund, Barrayar, and Pol.

## Old Earth

The original home of humans and the beginning point for all human interstellar expansion, Earth has become a sleepy galactic backwater due to the few usable wormholes in its sector of space. It still remains of some importance due to religious and cultural tourism, and all major galactic political entities maintain embassies on the planet. Its population of nine billion is still handicapped by a divisive number of competing governments, as opposed to a single planetary government structure that is commonly practiced elsewhere throughout the galaxy. The planet has managed to maintain a large number of its cultural pilgrimage sites despite global warming and a major rise in ocean levels, thanks to intricate engineering and a vast series of water-controlling coastal dikes.

## Union of Free Habitats (Quaddiespace)

Located on the edge of Sector V, Quaddiespace has been in existence for more than two centuries. It was originally founded as a haven for quaddies—a class of humans genetically altered for zero-gravity environments by the addition of two more arms where their legs used to be, and claimed as slaves by the corporation that genetically engineered them. After anti-gravity technology in a large part rendered the quaddies redundant, the quaddies escaped to freedom by commandeering a D-620 super jump ship and heading out to the far edge of human colonization to found their own civilization.

They staked their claim on a double ring of asteroids and expanded through it to form a population group over a million strong. With a bottom-up government organized around the principle of work groups, and a work ethic that cannot be matched in the galaxy, the quaddies have done well for themselves. Graf Station, with a population of fifty thousand, is the oldest settlement, and the original asteroid and jump ship are preserved there as a museum. The population does include some legged humans, and areas with artificial gravity include Graf Station, Metropolitan, Sanctuary, Michenko, and Union Station. The quaddies conduct their interstellar trade through these outposts.

## Kline Station

A three-hundred-year-old space station orbiting a planetless dark star, Kline Station serves six nearby jump points and the interstellar traffic that flows through them.

## Athos

Athos is a predominantly agricultural planet settled and governed by a monastic order. All human residents of Athos are male. Reproduction is carefully controlled by the government, and is practiced through uterine replicators, using ovaries harvested from off-planet women and the sperm of the planet's males who have been selected as worthy parents. Fear of women is endemic in the society, and few men from Athos travel through the wormhole nexus other than for necessary spaceflights to restock the planet's egg banks and for galactic trade. Even access to information and literature from outside Athos is restricted on the planet, except for necessary scientific journals and other research material.

## Frost IV

A colonized world destroyed in recent history due to a major tectonic disaster. The planet is frequently used by the illicit on Jackson's Whole and elsewhere as a convenience for forging new identities. Given that all Frost IV's official records were lost in the planetary disaster, it is very simple to assign an untraceable identity from Frost IV to someone seeking a new life, assuming that they are old enough to have lived through the disaster.

## Aslund

One of the Hegen Hub worlds, it is part of the Hegen Hub Alliance.

## Nuovo Brasil

Mentioned in the Vorkosigan Saga, but no detail about it is provided.

## Mahata Solaris

Miles Vorkosigan passed through this planet's local space in his guise as Admiral Naismith while fleeing

Cetagandan assassins shortly after the breakout from
Dagoola IV.

## Lairuba

A world settled by Muslims. The ruler is a hereditary
head of state with both political and religious power.
He is known as the Baba.

## Zoave Twilight

A nearby neighbor of Marilac, with a rich neighborhood of wormhole jump points that provide cross-
routes throughout the nexus.

## Kshatriya

A distant planet famed as the source of mercenaries
hired for interstellar conflicts.

## Tau Verde IV

This planet system was the site where Miles Vorkosigan began his mercenary career and his work as an
interstellar troubleshooter. Here he found his destiny
when he joined up with the Oseran Mercenaries,
which he eventually converted into the Dendarii Free
Mercenary Fleet. The Dendarii still serve as a secret
arm of Barrayaran Imperial Security.

• • • • •

# The Vorkosigan Saga
# Novel Summaries

## JOHN HELFERS

Editor's Note: Instead of the traditional method of listing the books and novellas in their first published order, we have chosen to arrange them in chronological order as events unfold in the Vorkosigan universe.

## "Dreamweaver's Dilemma"
## First published in
## *Dreamweaver's Dilemma*, 1996

Approximately six hundred years before Miles Vorkosigan's birth, Anias Ruey, a "feelie-dream" composer, uses a device called a dream synthesizer to create artificial dreams that people can experience as if they were actually dreaming themselves, a sort of virtual reality. She is late providing a sequel to her most successful feelie-dream, a romance called *Triad*, mostly because the idea bores her, and takes a new commission from a mysterious man named Rudolph Kinsey, who makes her uneasy, but the price he offers is too good to pass up. To recharge herself, she travels to the secluded home of her friend Chalmys DuBauer, a spaceship pilot who spent more than a century traveling between Earth and its first off-planet habitat, Beta Colony, and who was rendered obsolete by the technological developments made during that time. She completes the commission, a dark and violent scenario, and gives it to Rudolph in exchange for a bonded check. Before he leaves, he requests a brief feelie-dream for his aunt. When Anias goes to set up her dream synthesizer, she finds it has been sabotaged, and would have killed her if she had used it. Suspecting that Kinsey had tried to kill her, she lures him to DuBauer's Ohio home, which is surrounded by a forest full of lethal creatures. After taking him out to the woods and threatening to leave him there, DuBauer learns that Kinsey's real name is Carlos Diaz, and that he was hired as a middleman by a man he knows as Doctor Bianca to get the feelie-dream made. Anias realizes that, if used on a sleeping person without their knowledge, the disturbing vision could drive them to suicide. With the help of Lieutenant Mendez, who had been investigating the synthesizer accident, she confronts Doctor Bianca and recovers the master cassette for the feelie-dream, returning the payment in the process, and thwarting a would-be murderer.

## *Falling Free* (1988)
## Winner of the 1988
## Nebula Award for Best Novel

Leo Graf, an efficient, by-the-book engineer for GalacTech, a galaxy-wide corporation, is sent to the mysterious Cay Project Habitat on a space station orbiting the planet Rodeo. Upon arrival, he learns he will be training a group of genetically engineered humans who have a second pair of arms instead of legs, for increased agility in freefall, as well as other modifications to adapt them to living permanently in space. GalacTech's plan is to train them and hire them out as deep-space labor to other companies. The project is run by Bruce Van Atta, a former subordinate of Leo's who moved into management, who is also the epitome of the soulless, profit-minded, middle-management corporate executive. After getting used to his trainees' appearance, Leo begins teaching space engineering, and over the next few months finds the "quaddies," as they are nicknamed, intelligent, quick to learn, and very capable. However, that intelligence is also creating problems. Treated as property by the corporation, the quaddies have begun forming attachments to each other, especially during the breeding process. This leads to a near-disaster when Tony and Claire, who have a baby, are told that they won't be allowed to stay together, and try to escape the station and flee the system. Van Atta alerts planetside security, and an overzealous security guard shoots Tony, foiling their escape. After the incident, Leo learns that if the Cay Project fails, the quaddies would

be sterilized and left on Rodeo, suffering under the
planet's gravity every day, until they died. Not long
after the incident, his worst fears come true. When
Beta Colony announces the development of a prototype artificial gravity system, the quaddies become
expendable, and Van Atta is ordered to scuttle the
project, dump them all on Rodeo, and get out as
soon as possible. Knowing he cannot abandon the
quaddies to the fate the corporation is planning for
them, Leo comes up with a desperate plan—he'll
enlist them to hijack the entire space station, disassemble it, and move it through the nearby wormhole
to deep space, where the quaddies can live free.
He enlists several quaddies as ringleaders and rigs a
simulated accident to evacuate the human personnel
off the station. However, there are several obstacles
hindering their escape. Tony is stuck in the hospital
on Rodeo, and must be rescued. An accident breaks
a critical component of the jump mechanism, forcing
a jury-rigged replacement in space. Not to mention
the thousand-and-one other things that need to be
done to make the station as self-sufficient as possible.
And all the while, Leo knows Van Atta will be coming
after them to take back what was his, even if only
to see it destroyed. Working frantically, Leo and his
cobbled-together crew manage the nearly impossible,
and get the space station through the wormhole, and
into space controlled by a friendly government—and
find freedom for the quaddies, for the first time in
their young lives.

## Shards of Honor (1986)

On what should have been a routine surveying mission, Commander Cordelia Naismith of the Betan Astronomical Survey Department returns to her base camp to find it in ruins, with evidence of a hostile force having driven off the rest of her team. She contacts her lieutenant, who has escaped to their ship in orbit, and learns the camp was attacked by Barrayarans, a militaristic culture currently plotting to launch a war through the newly discovered wormhole. After ordering the lieutenant to break orbit to avoid capture and to let Beta Colony know what has happened, Cordelia, along with her survey partner Ensign Dubauer, are taken by surprise by a Barrayaran soldier, later identified as Sergeant Bothari, who shoots Dubauer with a nerve disruptor and knocks Cordelia unconscious. She awakens to find herself a prisoner of Aral Vorkosigan, known as "The Butcher of Komarr" for supposed previous wartime atrocities. Bargaining for Dubauer's life—although injured by the disruptor blast, he is still alive, but severely impaired—she agrees to go with Aral as his prisoner to a cache of equipment and weapons. Along the way, Cordelia realizes Aral had been left for dead here in a mutiny by his men. They set out for the cache, fending off assorted wildlife and getting to know each other along the way. Cordelia realizes that Aral is not a coldhearted killer, but a man with deep principles and honor who does what he feels he must for his homeland. After reaching the cache, Aral regains control of the men loyal to him, including Bothari, and ends the mutiny, although two ringleaders escape capture on the planet. He takes Cordelia back to his ship, where he proposes a most surprising idea—marriage. Cordelia asks to think about it, but before she can give an answer, learns some of her ship's crew have boarded the Barrayaran ship to rescue her, bringing some of the mutineers back with them. Before she can do anything, the mutineers commandeer the engineering room, demanding the surrender of the bridge officers, or they will turn life-support off. Cordelia sneaks down and stuns the ringleaders with the help of a former turncoat who switches sides again. She then frees her crew and they steal a shuttle to escape. Several months later, Cordelia is in charge of creating a diversion to let Betan cargo ships travel to Escobar through the Barrayaran blockade, using a holographic image of a capital ship as her bait. It works, but she and her crew are captured, and she comes very close to being tortured and raped by Admiral Ges Vorrutyer, who first orders Sergeant Bothari to do it. He refuses, claiming she is Vorkosigan's prisoner. Vorrutyer is about to force himself on her when Bothari kills the admiral. Discovered by Aral, Cordelia and the psychologically disintegrating Bothari are hidden in his quarters while Aral and his personal security officer, Simon Illyan, deal with the aftermath of the murder. Prince Serg Vorbarra comes aboard to let Aral know he's going to lead the Barrayaran fleet against the Escobarans. Aral protests, but he knows better, or worse—the Escobarans will counterattack at the right time, and although he hates the sacrifice of so many Barrayaran soldiers, he has no say in the matter. When the Escobarans do counterattack, they use a new weapon brought by Cordelia's convoy called a plasma field mirror, which turns an attacking ship's blast back upon itself. The resulting carnage destroys the ship that Prince Serg was on, along with much of the attacking fleet. Cordelia is told that Aral had extracted the information about the weapon from her while she was under sedation, but apparently didn't let the rest of the command staff, or Prince Serg, know about it. She later realizes that Aral actually had prior intelligence on the plasma mirrors, but was ordered not to reveal his knowledge so the Emperor of Barrayar could be rid of Prince Serg, a venal, deviant sadist—and his own son. Cordelia is transferred to a prisoner-of-war camp to be held for a future exchange, where the rest of the prisoners think she killed Admiral Vorrutyer, making her a hero, the last thing she wanted. Back on Beta Colony, she is feted as such, and the stress of keeping secret what she knows and living up to the propaganda her own government has created about her brings Cordelia to the breaking point. When military representatives believe that she has been programmed to be a spy for Barrayar, she escapes and travels there, where she takes Aral up on his proposal of marriage. Afterward, they take care of unfinished business, including seventeen uterine replicators that were bestowed upon the withdrawing forces by Escobar, containing fetuses formerly engendered upon female Escobaran prisoners by Barrayarans. Sergeant Bothari's daughter, Elena, the product of a rape he was ordered to do by Vorrutyer, is born from one, and he vows to raise her as best as he can. Aral and Cordelia are summoned to an audience with the dying Emperor Ezar, where Aral is made Regent of Barrayar, to assist in keeping the planet safe for when

Ezar's grandson and heir, Gregor, currently five years old, takes the throne. In an epilogue, an Escobaran Personnel Retrieval Team moves through the former battlefield in space, recovering bodies and cleaning up the leftover debris, and a mother says good-bye to her daughter for the last time.

## *Barrayar* (1991)
## Winner of the Hugo and Locus Awards for Best Novel

The day after Aral Vorkosigan is named Regent by Emperor Ezar Vorbarra, Cordelia and he travel to the Imperial Residence to meet the heir to the throne, Gregor, and his mother, Princess Kareen. The meeting goes well, with Cordelia being given one of the princess's personal guards, Ludmilla Droushnakova, as her bodyguard. Life settles into a routine, with Aral up to his neck in administrating the affairs of the Empire, and Cordelia attempting to navigate the confusing intricacies of Barrayaran social life. One bright spot in their lives is Cordelia's pregnancy, which has drawn her closer to Aral's father, Piotr. When Aral goes before the Council of Counts to be approved as Regent, Cordelia meets Evon Vorhalas under unpleasant circumstances when his brother insults Aral's secretary, Clement Koudelka. Aral is approved with little difficulty. Emperor Ezar dies a week later, and the job of running the Empire until Gregor comes of age begins in earnest. Cordelia gets her first idea that it might be dangerous when someone shoots a grenade at Aral's armored groundcar, narrowly missing it. She also learns of the long list of people and groups that might want to kill the Regent of Barrayar. At a celebration of the Emperor's Birthday, Cordelia meets Count Vidal Vordarian, who tries unsuccessfully to shock her by telling her that Aral is bisexual. Cordelia counters by obliquely threatening him, and has Simon Illyan keep closer tabs on him as well. She also has her own issues in running the household, dealing with Sergeant Bothari beginning to remember his time served under Admiral Vorrutyer, Koudelka depressed and suicidal over his physical handicap, Droushnakova in love with Kou, but him oblivious of her, and Aral having to make decisions that will slowly destroy him, such as ordering the execution of Evon Vorhalas's younger brother for dueling, which is strictly prohibited under Barrayaran law. In revenge, Evon attacks Aral with a soltoxin grenade that severely damages Cordelia's unborn child. The embryo is saved by transferring it to a uterine replicator and giving it experimental calcium treatments. This course of action, however, divides Cordelia and Piotr, who is aghast at the idea of a deformed heir to the Vorkosigan family being born. Piotr even tries to order the doctors in charge of the project to destroy the child that will be Miles Vorkosigan, but fails. He threatens to cut Aral and Cordelia out of his estate, but that doesn't faze them. His tirade is interrupted by a mortally wounded Captain Negri crash-landing on the country-house lawn with Gregor. Before he dies, Negri tells them Count Vordarian has launched a coup to take the throne. Cordelia takes Gregor into hiding, guided by Piotr into the mountains, where she uses a clever ruse to draw away the Imperial men looking for them. In time she is reunited with Aral, and they face the potential civil war together, up to the point when Vordarian declares himself Regent. But when Doctor Vaagen escapes and says that Vordarian has confiscated Miles's uterine replicator, Cordelia launches a secret rescue mission to recover it using Bothari, Droushnakova, and Koudelka when he stumbles on them leaving. The group is sidetracked by encountering the Vorpatrils, Aral's kin, hiding in the slums where they're planning to strike from, who are discovered by Vordarian's security. Padma is killed but the group rescues Alys, who goes into labor, forcing them to deliver the child immediately. Even with larger issues looming over them, Cordelia patches things up between Koudelka and Droushnakova, then sends Kou with Alys and her newborn son Ivan to escort her out of the city while they continue into the Emperor's Residence. They find what Cordelia thinks is the replicator, but it is a fake, set as a trap. Caught by Residence guards, Cordelia, Bothari, and Drou are captured and taken before Vordarian. But when Cordelia produces evidence that Gregor is alive, not dead as Vordarian told Kareen, the princess tries to kill him, but is killed in the ensuing firefight. Taking Vordarian hostage, Bothari has Cordelia set the Residence on fire, then she orders him to behead the pretender. Taking the real replicator, the three escape the Residence through the secret tunnels underneath, presenting Vordarian's head to Aral and the rest of the loyal counts. The coup collapses, and Miles is born, although it's obvious he will have his own difficulties. Koudelka and Droushnakova get married, and the book ends with an epilogue five years later, with a precocious Miles already getting into trouble, and winning Piotr over in spite of himself.

## The Warrior's Apprentice (1986)

Miles Naismith Vorkosigan, son of Aral and Cordelia Vorkosigan, is seventeen years old, and at loose ends. His brittle bones forced him out of the military academy entrance exams after he broke both legs while trying to complete an obstacle course. Feeling guilty over breaking his grandfather's heart by washing out, and believing he inadvertently hastened Piotr's death, Miles takes Elena Bothari, on whom he has a crush, to Beta Colony to visit his grandmother Naismith. In reality, he is taking her to research her mother's side of the family, since her taciturn father hasn't told her very much about her relatives. At Beta Colony, Miles helps a down-on-his-luck pilot named Arde Mayhew, and also finds a Barrayaran deserter named Baz Jesek hiding out in a recycling station. Taking them both on as sworn armsmen, Miles quickly gets in over his head. Forced to take a quick shipping job to pay off the outstanding lien on Arde's ship, which Miles now owns, he finds one that would pay off everything, with even a bit of profit left over. However, the job is a risky weapons-smuggling run to the nation of Felice, on Tau Verde IV, currently in the middle of a planetary war. Camouflaging the weapons to resemble farm equipment, the freighter is stopped by mercenaries working for the enemy Pelians. When they decide to take Elena as their hostage instead of the usual jump pilot, Miles captures them, then takes over their ship as well, leaving him with two spacecraft. Miles convinces the soldiers of fortune to join his Dendarii Mercenaries, an outfit that exists only in his mind. From there, they take over an ore refinery after they discover that their employer's in-system contact has been captured. More mercenaries join the nascent Dendarii group, among them a woman named Elena Visconti, whom Miles recognizes as Elena Bothari's mother. However, his plan for reuniting the family goes horribly wrong when the elder Elena kills Bothari in front of her daughter. That, along with the strain of putting together a working mercenary group completely on the fly, pushes Miles to the breaking point physically and mentally. He confesses his love to Elena, but she turns him down, citing the impossibility of their different castes on Barrayar, and besides, she is already falling for Baz Jesek. After coming up with a plan to break the blockade by setting the Pelians and their mercenary employees at each other's throats by hijacking payrolls, Miles ends up in the infirmary with a bleeding ulcer just before they are about to embark on their most hazardous mission yet. With Elena in charge, working alongside a hired space captain named Ky Tung, also formerly of the enemy mercenaries, they take the payroll. Miles finds out about this when he awakens after his emergency surgery, and also finds his cousin Ivan Vorpatril sitting next to his infirmary bed. Ivan had been ordered to find Miles, as rumors of his raising a mercenary army—expressly forbidden on Barrayar—have caused enemies of his father to attempt to accuse Miles of treason. Ivan was to have been killed in a jump accident, but when he missed his ship, he stuck to his original mission, and found Miles at Tau

Verde IV. Miles figures out the plan, but before he can get back home, he is contacted by Admiral Oser, the leader of the mercenaries hired by the Pelians, who wants to join the Dendarii. After working out the details of his rapidly expanding mercenary army, and a quick stop to drop mercenary Elli Quinn off at Beta Colony for reconstructive facial surgery, he gets back to Barrayar just in time to expose the plot against his father, and see the conspirators arrested. Miles gently nudges Emperor Gregor Vorbarra to bring the Dendarii Free Mercenary Fleet under the control of Barrayaran Internal Security, and then, as "punishment" for his escapades, Miles is sent to the Imperial Service Academy for officer training.

## "The Mountains of Mourning" (1989) Winner of the Hugo and Nebula Awards for Best Novella

A ragged, wild-eyed woman named Harra Csurik comes to Vorkosigan Surleau, demanding to see the count for justice for her murdered baby, Raina. After hearing her story, Miles decides to take her in to see his father as a lark. After breakfast, however, Aral sends Miles to the small village of Silvy Vale to find out if the woman's husband did kill her baby, which had been born with a harelip, something the backwoods people often take for a sign of mutancy. After a two-day horseback ride into the Dendarii Mountains, Miles, his armsman Pym, and an Imperial military surgeon, Doctor Dea, arrive at the backwoods hamlet. Cutting through feeble resistance by the village's Speaker,

Serg Karal, Miles begins his investigation in earnest, exhuming the baby's body, and having Dea perform an autopsy, which reveals the child was killed by having its neck broken. They take a look at the couple's cabin, and Miles has Harra recount her actions the day she found her baby dead. He sends the Speaker to bring Lem Csurik in for questioning under fast-penta, to determine his guilt or innocence. The men return, and say he's fled. That night, the village honors Miles with a feast and music, and he meets both mothers-in-law, Csurik's, who protests her son's innocence, and Harra's mother, Ma Mattulich, who is a dark, angry woman, and who refers to Miles as "mutie lord." There are two attempted assaults that night; first on Miles's Service-issue tent, which he had let the Speaker's children sleep in, and which is fortunately fireproof, and later on his horse, Fat Ninny, which could have killed the animal if they hadn't chased off the attacker. Early the next morning, Miles sees Lem, who has come out of the mountains to clear his name, but he insists on not naming any one else in the incident, although he clearly knows more than he's saying. Miles agrees, and has the doctor fast-penta him for the interrogation, which proves his innocence. Miles now knows who killed the child, and summons the suspects and witnesses. He clears up the matter of the burning torch thrown on the tent, finding out it was Dono Csurik, Lem's younger brother, trying to scare Miles. Miles leaves his punishment up to the family. He has Doctor Dea fast-penta Ma Mattulich, who reveals not only that she killed Raina, suspecting she was a mutant, but had killed two of her other deformed children, born twenty years earlier. Faced with handing down a proper sentence, but not really wanting to order her execution, Miles sentences her to death, but stays her execution indefinitely. Instead, he strips her of all legal rights, remanding her to her daughter's care for the rest of her life. He also offers Harra and Lem the chance to attend teacher's school and work in Hassadar, and promises to get comm units to the village, along with a lowlander to teach the children until Harra and Lem return. Miles rides away from the village with a deeper understanding of not only himself, but also the people whom he must serve as Count Vorkosigan, and he swears to make good on his promises to them.

## *The Vor Game* (1990)
## Winner of the Hugo Award for Best Novel

Having graduated from Barrayaran Imperial Academy, Miles is ready to begin his first assignment as an ensign, but is disappointed when he is stationed to be Meteorological Officer at the remote Lazkowski Base on bleak Kyril Island. Before he leaves, he learns that if he can keep his nose clean for six months there, he will be assigned to the *Prince Serg*, the newest dreadnought in the Barrayaran space navy. Miles ships out to Camp Permafrost, as the base is colloquially known, and finds his superior officer a drunk, the base commander a humorless martinet, and the rest of the camp treating him with the usual mixture of disdain and insubordination. After nearly being killed when a practical joke almost drowns him in mud, Miles settles down to the job at hand. He solves a brief mystery of a dead cadet found in the sewers, and thinks he's about to get through his tour unimpeded when what starts as a routine accident turns into a near-mutiny. When ordered to clean up a fetaine spill, the cadets refuse to go near the virulent poison, leading the base commander to threaten them all with being shot if they don't obey. Miles joins his lieutenant in resisting the order, resulting in their arrest, and him being shipped back to the capital, Vorbarr Sultana. Miles offers to resign in exchange for the charges being dropped against the other men. After being held more or less incommunicado for a few months, with visits only from his mother and Emperor Gregor himself, Miles is instead brought out of involuntary confinement and given an assignment to dust off his Admiral Naismith persona and investigate the sudden heavy military activity on the various planets surrounding the Hegen Hub, a system with four wormhole jump points that is a nexus linking routes to several planets. Miles also learns that the Dendarii Free Mercenary Fleet has been hired by one of the sides. Posing as an arms dealer, Miles is recognized by one of his former mercenaries, nearly blowing his cover. Meeting with the man later, Miles finds out Admiral Oser has taken back command of the Dendarii, demoting Baz Jesek and Ky Tung, but keeping them on staff. Still playing the weapons dealer, Miles has another meeting with a potential buyer, only to find his target has been replaced by a blond woman named Livia Nu, who is interested in the single-person nerve disruptor shield net he's selling, and also in seducing Miles, which he resists, thinking it might be an assassination attempt. Later, however, there is a charge of murder against

Miles's cover identity, forcing him and his superior officer to flee from the Pol Six station to Jackson's Whole jump-point station, where Miles is found and captured by hired thugs executing a bid arrest by a person named Cavilo. Miles is thrown in the local jail, where he is astonished to meet Emperor Gregor, who has fled the stifling realm of politics and planetary rule and is off on his own. Switching identification with engineers press-ganged into building Aslund's new space station, Miles and Gregor get aboard, partly to escape prison, and also to learn what's really happening in the region. However, Miles gets captured by the Dendarii first, and brought before Admiral Oser, who is none too pleased to see him, and who responds to Miles's suggestion of allying again by ordering him thrown out the nearest airlock. Saved by Elena, Miles contacts Ky Tung for help smuggling Gregor off the station to safety. Unfortunately, the shuttle pilot is a double agent, and delivers Miles and Gregor into the hands of the mysterious Cavilo, who, it turns out, is also Livia Nu. She is the leader of Randall's Rangers, a mercenary outfit hired by Vervain for protection. Cavilo is clever, ruthless, sociopathic, casually homicidal, and makes new friends quickly, her latest being Stanis Metzov, the former Lazkowski Base commander whose career Miles helped end on Barrayar. She sends Miles on a mission to subvert the Dendarii from within, thereby allowing her mercenaries to raid Vervain in the chaos of allowing an invading Cetagandan fleet through the wormhole to "rescue" Vervain from the mercenaries, and seal an alliance with the planet, ensuring that Empire more direct access to the Hegen Hub—and getting closer to Barrayar too. However, Gregor in the mix changes everything, and Miles figures Cavilo will now reach even higher—for an empress's crown, gained by marrying Gregor. Miles retakes the Dendarii, frees Gregor from Cavilo's grasp, and sends his outmatched fleet to hold off the Cetagandan invasion force until reinforcements arrive. They do, in the form of the dreadnought *Prince Serg* and a Barrayaran fleet. Admiral Oser escapes during the fighting, and is killed when his shuttle is blown out of space. The Cetagandans are routed, and Cavilo, who had escaped from the brig in the confusion, kills Metzov when he tries to kill Miles, and is granted safe passage out of the area. Miles is reunited with his father, and is assigned to be the Barrayaran liaison to the Dendarii Free Mercenary Fleet—as "Admiral Naismith," with an accompanying promotion to lieutenant in the Barrayaran military as well.

## *Cetaganda* (1996)

Lieutenant Lord Miles Vorkosigan and Lieutenant Lord Ivan Vorpatril have been assigned to attend the funeral of the late Cetagandan Empress Lisbet Degtiar, and to observe the Cetagandans in their native habitat. The trip gets off to a surprising start when a strange-looking person bursts into their ship upon landing. Thinking he's an assassin, Miles and Ivan try to subdue him, but he gets away, leaving a nerve disruptor and a short, unusual rod behind. Miles decides not to tell their commanding ImpSec officer about the incident right away, as he wants to figure out why it happened in the first place. They attend a welcoming party that same evening, where Miles meets Lord Yenaro, a Cetagandan lord and perfume maker who has supplied a large, walk-through sculpture for the Marilacan Embassy. Invited inside, Miles suffers an accident when a power field heats his leg braces, causing painful burns. Miles is now even more suspicious that something is going on, and his instincts are confirmed when, during a gift presentation and viewing of the Empress lying in state, a Cetagandan haut-lady named Rian Degtiar contacts him, demanding the return of the strange rod. Miles arranges to meet with her again, then takes his place back in the viewing procession just in time to see the same strange person who had invaded their ship, member of a Cetagandan servant neuter caste known as ba, lying dead behind the funeral dais, its throat slit. Continuing his investigation, Miles discovers the short rod is the Great Key of the Star Crèche, a security device that stores all of the information on the Cetagandan genetic lines kept for reproduction purposes and to maintain the lines of descent for the ghem and haut-lords. Invited to a party at Lord Yenaro's estate, Miles makes contact with Rian again, and returns the Great Key, which is revealed to be a fake. Miles demands to continue his investigation, feeling he was set up for this, with Barrayar to take the fall, provoking an interstellar war with Cetaganda. To make matters worse, he has less than nine days—the mourning period for the Empress, after which a new one will be chosen—to uncover the plot before it happens. Pressing Rian for more information, he learns the Empress had made eight copies of the haut gene bank, feeling that Cetaganda was growing stagnant, and hoping that dispersing the gene bank to the governors of eight satrapy planets would revitalize the Empire. Miles sees the move as insanity, creating eight smaller, aggressive empires out of one large one. He figures out that the ba was played, and was supposed to give Miles the fake key to jump-start the conflict. However, since Miles hadn't reported the incident, and with the ba dead, the person behind the plot, whom Miles christens Lord X, hasn't been able to put it into action yet, except behind the scenes. He goes back to the party to find Ivan there, upset at being seduced by two beautiful ghem-ladies, only to find he couldn't rise to the occasion because he had been slipped an anti-aphrodisiac, confirming Miles's suspicion that Lord Yenaro is involved in the plot. The next day, he is interrogated by Dag Benin, a Cetagandan security colonel, about his unauthorized viewing of the ba's body. That afternoon they attend a poetry reading in the Empress's honor, and at the following reception Rian meets with Miles again, telling him she suspects that one of the governors, Slyke Giaja, is the traitor plotting to create a Barrayar-Cetaganda war. Miles makes plans to board Giaja's ship and search for the real Great Key, and plans to meet Rian's handmaiden at a genetic-engineering exhibition to plan the infiltration. However, Lord Vorreedi, the head of ImpSec security on Cetaganda, accompanies them, so Miles has to ditch him first. They stumble across Lord Yenaro, who almost unknowingly attempts to assassinate them with asterzine, an explosive, malleable chemical that reacts violently with the proper catalyst. Caught, Yenaro tells them that Governor Ilsum Kety is behind the whole scheme. While elated at the news, Miles can't make his meeting with Rian's representative, as Vorreedi sticks with him until they leave. The next day, Vorreedi interrogates Miles first, then Colonel Benin questions Miles and Ivan about what happened since they first landed on Cetaganda. Miles tells a heavily edited version of events, leaving out the Great Key and his meetings with Rian. Invited to a garden party by another haut-lady, both Miles and Ivan attend, and Miles is taken to confer with the Star Crèche—all the haut-consorts of the governors plus Rian—to plan their next move. Off a casual suggestion from Ivan, Miles suggests recalling the copies of the gene pools from each governor's ship, with Rian claiming they are defective. While the haut-ladies put this plan into action, Miles and Ivan attend yet another ceremony, where Ivan is captured by one of Kety's people. The float-bubble with the lady and Ivan inside is captured, and Miles uses it to infiltrate Kety's ship and find the missing consort, whose float-chair was stolen, and the Great Key. Caught by Kety's security, Miles has the contents of the Key downloaded to a transfer station, where it would be picked up by thousands of people; then Pel locks the key inside the float bubble, effectively putting it out of Kety's grasp. As the governor tries to open the field, Colonel Benin, Ivan, and reinforcements arrive to save them and arrest Kety for treason. Miles has a private audience with the Cetagandan Emperor, Rian, and two of the other haut-consorts, to wrap up the matter, and the Emperor awards Miles the Order of Merit, the highest honor on Cetaganda, and has him walk to the cremation of the Empress's body at the Emperor's left hand. Miles is left with clashing thoughts; he did perform his duty to Barrayar, preventing a terrible war, and also assisted Cetaganda, but the award he received would be viewed with suspicion at home, particularly since the events surrounding it could never be brought to light. He ponders his motivations for putting himself into that much danger on the trip back to Barrayar—was it to be a hero, to prove himself to his superiors, or something else entirely?

## *Ethan of Athos* (1986)

Doctor Ethan Urquhart, Chief of Reproductive Medicine, lives and works on the planet Athos, an out-of-the-way world where women are prohibited from living. They reproduce male children by uterine replicator, and face a drastic problem: their stock of ovarian cultures, brought to Athos by its founders more than two centuries earlier, has reached the end of its life span, and the planet needs new material to continue. When a replacement order from Jackson's Whole arrives, Ethan discovers it is filled with nonviable ovaries. At the Population Council meeting afterward, it is decided that a representative from Athos will go off-planet to procure viable stock for the planet. The council also decides that Ethan is the right man for the job. Unceremoniously sent to Kline Station, Ethan encounters the opposite sex for the first time in his life. Elli Quinn, a commander in the Dendarii Free Mercenary Fleet, takes a particular interest in him, saving him from a nasty beating at the hands of several station techs. She escorts him back to his room, where he is immediately kidnapped and harshly interrogated by a Colonel Millisor. Ethan tells everything he knows—which isn't much—and is taken out to be killed by one of Millisor's men. Just before he is about to die, Ethan is saved by Elli, who kills the assassin in the process. Wanting some answers, Ethan helps her dispose of the body, a difficult task, given the space station's efficiency in tracking its resources. Afterward, she and Ethan exchange information, and he learns that the shipment destined for Athos came from House Bharaputra, but that Colonel Millisor and his team have been chasing it for months, killing anyone who gets in their way or is associated with it. After accidentally running into Colonel Millisor again, Ethan escapes by virtue of being disguised as a maintenance engineer. He is then approached by Terrence Cee, the man that Colonel Millisor is really after, and who began this entire mess. Terrence is a telepath, specially bred on Cetaganda for use as a military weapon. Along with another female telepath, Janine, he tried to escape with her and four telepathic children, but everyone else was killed during the flight from Cetaganda, leaving Terrence alone and on the run. He inserted an ovarian culture made from Janine's remains into the shipment, in hopes of somehow bringing her back to life. However, the shipment is still missing, and Terrence doesn't know where it is. Showing up at Terrence's doorstep, Elli tries to get him to join the Dendarii Free Mercenaries. Terrence, however, won't do anything until he is able to probe both Ethan's and Elli's minds, to ascertain that they are who they say they are. After proving their identities, the three try to deduce the possibilities of who might have the missing shipment, but there are simply too many suspects to narrow their search. Quinn then gets a message that a relative of hers, Teki, whom they used earlier to expose one of Millisor's surveillance teams, has gone missing, and they figure he was taken by Millisor for interrogation. Elli calls Biocontrol on Millisor's suite, pretending that the colonel is carrying a nasty STD. They find Teki, and in the ensuing chaos afterward, learn that the head of Biocontrol was the one who intercepted the tissue cultures meant for Athos, in a vain attempt to force her son to come back from the planet. Millisor and his second-in-command are taken to Quarantine, but both escape with the aid of his third man on the station, and capture Ethan, Elli, and Terrence, intending to kill the first two to keep the telepathy project a secret, then take Terrence back to Cetaganda. There seems to be no way out, until Ethan remembers an electronic message device given to him by an unnamed man in a pink suit to deliver to Millisor. Realizing it's a boobytrap, Elli uses it to create a diversion, then shuts off the gravity in the spacedock to try and stop Millisor from killing all of them. Millisor and his henchmen are killed by two men from House Bharaputra, who then capture Elli and try to get back the money they paid her to assassinate Millisor. However, she negotiates a deal with them that costs her only a dislocated elbow. Ethan is about to resume his quest for ovarian cultures, but first convinces Elli to donate one of hers to the Athosian cause. As Ethan is about to leave, Terrence and he locate the lost shipment of original ovarian cultures, and he brings both it and Terrence back to Athos, securing his planet's future, and perhaps a new life for himself as well.

## "Labyrinth" (1989)

Miles goes to Jackson's Whole to pick up a defecting genetic scientist for Barrayar, under cover of buying munitions on the criminal planet. The mission gets off to a rocky start when Bel Thorne insults one of the ruling barons at a party while defending the honor of a quaddie musician. Then the quaddie finds them later, wanting to hire them to smuggle her off-planet. Also, the scientist they're liberating needs several valuable genetic samples that happen to be injected into another of his bioengineered creations, which is held by House Ryoval. He wants Miles to kill the creature and bring back the samples. Miles and his team try to break into the laboratory to retrieve it, but his men are caught and escorted out, leaving Miles behind. He finds a guard and interrogates him under fast-penta, but the man turns out to be the head of security. Captured, Miles is thrown into a basement room where they're keeping the creature. She turns out to be an intelligent, eight-foot-tall, bioengineered super-soldier, whom Miles befriends in an unusual way, even giving her a real name, Taura. During an attempt to escape, Miles stumbles across Ryoval's genetic library, which he destroys. He almost finds his way out, but the guards come for them, planning on trading Miles to Baron Fell in exchange for the quaddie. Out of options, Miles attacks the guards with Taura, Nicol, and Bel, succeeding in escaping in a float-truck. They are about to be forced down by the chasing security forces, but Dendarii reinforcements arrive in a combat shuttle, driving the House Ryoval forces off and evacuating Miles and his group. Taura joins the Dendarii, and Miles and his team, with the scientist safe under their protection, escape from Jackson's Whole by the skin of their teeth, leaving a furious Baron Ryoval behind.

## "The Borders of Infinity" (1989)

The expected invasion of the planet Marilac by the Cetagandan Empire has happened, and Miles Vorkosigan finds himself in a force-field prison camp filled with ten thousand Marilacan soldiers. Beaten and stripped naked within five minutes of his arrival, he nevertheless sets about his mission—to find Colonel Guy Tremont and rescue him to form the nucleus of a new Marilacan guerrilla army. His only ally at first is a man named Suegar, who refers to Miles as "The One" that will save them all, and who just might be mad—or might not be. But Tremont is catatonic and dying, and Miles realizes his mission is now not to save just one man, but to save ten thousand. He slowly gains control of the camp, first by uniting the disparate factions inside, then by transforming the riots for the ration dispersal into an orderly food distribution. His organization of the camp serves a vital secondary purpose as well—to prepare the prisoners for the rescue they don't even know is coming. When the force shield drops due to the Dendarii's attack, Miles now faces the logistical problem of organizing and loading ten thousand people—and finding room for all of them on his ships—before Cetagandan reinforcements arrive. Using the food distribution plan as the blueprint for loading the prisoners, he manages it, although they lose two shuttles, one empty, one full, to a Cetagandan fighter in orbit. Also, Beatrice, one of the leaders Miles had relied on to maintain order in the camp, is lost due to a ramp malfunction on the last shuttle to lift off, which haunts Miles, as he risked his own life to save her, and failed.

## Brothers in Arms (1989)

After the prisoner rescue on Dagoola IV, Miles and the Dendarii head to Earth to rest and repair the fleet, having been chased halfway across the galaxy by the vengeful Cetagandans. Also, they need to get paid by the Barrayaran government for their efforts—and badly, as the Dendarii are literally broke. Still juggling his Admiral Naismith persona alongside Lieutenant Vorkosigan, Miles goes to meet his superior officer, a Komarran named Duv Galeni, at the Barrayaran Embassy. Miles's cousin Ivan is assigned to orient him at the embassy, and soon Miles is doing mind-numbing data analysis and providing escort duty for social events. However, his first task, an afternoon reception, is interrupted by Miles getting an urgent message to save three Dendarii troopers who have busted up a wine shop and are threatening to blow it up, creating a standoff with the local police. Miles heads over and saves his men and the clerk, but not before the shop goes up in flames, earning him a spot on the local news for his bravery in carrying the clerk out through the fire. Taken back to the Dendarii, Miles learns that since the expected payment hasn't arrived from Barrayar yet, the fleet is in real financial trouble, forcing them to take out a short-term loan, using one of their ships as collateral, to cover expenses. Adding to Miles's complications, he gets romantically involved with Elli Quinn, who's had a long-term crush on him. After a dressing-down from Captain Galeni for the wine shop incident, Miles attends another embassy function, where he stumbles on the same reporter that interviewed him earlier, and comes up with the story that Admiral Naismith is his cloned brother. Granted leave to attend to the Dendarii, Miles is nearly killed on the way by hired assassins. After a mutually satisfying liaison with Elli—despite the fact that she turns down his marriage proposal—and coming up with the idea to hire out the Dendarii for any job that needs doing, dangerous or not, Miles returns to the embassy to find that Duv Galeni has disappeared, strengthening his theory that the captain has stolen the Dendarii payment and vanished. While searching Galeni's private personnel file, Miles learns that his father and mother were involved in Komarr's government when Barrayar took over, during Miles's father's time in the military, when he acquired the sobriquet "The Butcher of Komarr." Galeni's aunt was killed in the Solstice Massacre, and his father, who had joined the resistance, was blown up by a home-made bomb. Against Simon Illyan's wishes, Aral had let Duv join ImpSec, which was how he came to be at the embassy on Earth. Meanwhile, Elli has scared up some work—a mysterious party wants the Dendarii to kidnap Lieutenant Vorkosigan from the embassy. Going to a preliminary meeting, Miles is stunned and replaced with an exact duplicate of himself—his wild story to the press has come nightmarishly true. Held

prisoner along with Duv, Miles discovers that Duv's
father, Ser Galen, is very much alive, and has hatched
a plot to insert Miles's double back into Barrayar to
kill Aral and sow political chaos. The clone believes
he is going to take the throne, but Miles, who views
him as his flesh-and-blood brother, dubbing him Mark,
tries to convince him that it will never happen, and
that he should be his own man, not Galeni's puppet.
Just before he can convince Mark, Galen bursts in and
separates them. Miles tries to overpower the guards,
but is stunned, and has a terrible dream combining
the events of the Dagoola prison break with what's
currently happening. About to be stunned and killed
by Galen's guards, Miles and Galeni are rescued by
Elli, who has been staking out the building they've
been held in, searching for Galeni. They all go back
to the Barrayaran Embassy, where they find that Mark
has been arrested on suspicion of putting out the hit
on Admiral Naismith. Going to the police, they find
that Galen has beaten them there and sprung Mark
first. Back at the embassy, Galeni investigates the
suspected corrupt courier officer who had not been
passing along the messages to and from Barrayar as
he was supposed to, and finds he has been subverted.
The officer in charge of the investigation, Commodore
Destang, has brought a clean-up squad to eliminate
Mark and the Komarran rebel cell if possible, and
also gets Miles the payment the Dendarii have been
sorely missing. Through a loophole in procedure,
Galeni gives Miles tacit permission to use the Dendarii
to find Mark and Galen. Heading back to his fleet,
Miles sets his intelligence department on it, planning
to buy Mark from Galen. While he's setting up his

plan, Galen contacts him first—he's kidnapped Ivan, who was escorting a society matron to a flower show, and demands a meeting at the Thames Tidal Barrier. Miles takes Galeni and Elli and goes to meet Galen and Mark, where he makes his pitch: Mark and Ivan in exchange for half a million Imperial marks and Galen's promise to retire from the rebellion. Galen double-crosses them and orders Mark to kill Miles and Galeni. Mark hesitates, and when Galen grabs for his nerve disruptor, Mark shoots him instead. Before they can escape, however, they have to elude not only the Barrayaran hit squad, but a team of Cetagandans that are also after Admiral Naismith, and the local police, who have been called to investigate the disturbance in the area. In the end, Miles, Mark, Ivan, Elli, and Galeni all make it out in one piece. Miles upholds the bargain he made to Mark, giving him the half-million marks in exchange for Mark helping him to free Ivan, and sets Mark free as well. Miles gets one last surprise as the Dendarii receive orders to stop a hostage situation involving Barrayarans—Ky Tung is retiring from the mercenary trade and getting married, leaving the Dendarii with a loss of one of their best commanding officers.

## *Mirror Dance* (1994)
### Winner of the Hugo and Locus Awards for Best Novel

The first Vorkosigan novel to be told from two viewpoints, it begins two years later, with Mark Vorkosigan posing as Miles to take command of the Dendarii

Free Mercenary Fleet. He leads the *Ariel* and a team of commandos to Jackson's Whole to free the clones raised by House Bharaputra for its brain-transplant operations. Although he gets them there, the operation falls apart against fiercer-than-expected resistance, leaving him, the Dendarii, and the clones trapped planetside. Meanwhile, Miles, coming back from an assignment with Elli, learns what happened, and heads to Jackson's Whole to save Mark and his mercenaries. When negotiations with Vasa Luigi, the baron of House Bharaputra, break down, Miles goes down to get his brother and men back himself. It is a fatal decision, as Miles is shot with a needle grenade and killed. He is put into a cryo-chamber for later resuscitation, but Mark and the medic get cut off from the rest of their squad, and Mark gives him directions through an underground tunnel system to escape, then heads back to help the others get out. He makes it back to the rescue shuttle, only to discover on the ship that they don't have Miles's cryo-chamber. They negotiate with Baron Fell for the return of the chamber, but the baron's men cannot locate it either. Mark discovers that before getting killed, the medic had shipped the chamber to an unknown address through an automated cargo dock, leaving Mark and the Dendarii with no way of finding him. Taken back to Barrayar, Mark is introduced to his parents, as well as life on Barrayar, including his role as the potential Vorkosigan heir, should Miles not be recovered. During this time, Aral suffers an arterial aneurism, which incapacitates him. Fully aware of his potential role in House Vorkosigan and on Barrayar, and wanting no part of it, Mark gets permission to review the ImpSec files for Miles's whereabouts, believing him to still be somewhere on Jackson's Whole. When he finds evidence of where his brother's remains were shipped, he gets Cordelia's approval to mount a rescue mission. Meanwhile, Miles begins his slow recovery in the hands of the Durona family, a cloned group of doctors created by House Ryoval, but which escaped to House Fell, and who now serve as the physicians for the upper echelons of the House. Miles's recovery is slow and painful, hampered by the fact that he has lost his memory, but is helped when he falls for one of his doctors, Rowan Durona. Mark, Elli, and Bel Thorne arrive on the planet to recover Miles, but the price is getting the Durona clan off Jackson's Whole, away from the barons completely. Before they can negotiate the Deal, security from House Ryoval break in and kidnap Mark. Miles and Rowan are taken by security from House Bharaputra. Mark is tortured by Baron Ryoval, who thinks he is Miles at first, and Mark's personality splits into five parts during his captivity. Miles and Rowan are held by Baron Luigi, who tries to figure out the best way to profit from the whole mess. With the help of a Durona clone girl who had been rescued by Mark, but who had chosen to return to captivity, Rowan escapes, and so does the clone girl Lilly, before Ryoval's men come for Miles, part of a Deal Baron Luigi had made with the other baron. After repeated torture sessions, Mark kills Baron Ryoval and escapes his hidden compound, which falls apart with the baron's death. Miles is taken there, escapes his guards, and calls for help. Fell, as half brother and next of kin, comes to collect Ryoval's body, and they are all contacted by Mark, who wants a meeting with

Fell to make a Deal. He arranges for Fell to take over House Ryoval, the Duronas to leave Jackson's Whole for good, and a hefty profit, enough to set up the clones with an excellent education, and some money left over for himself as well. Mark and Miles head back to Barrayar and the Winterfair celebration, where Mark keeps a promise he made to Kareen Koudelka at the Emperor's Birthday before he left to save his brother—a dance with her, as Mark Pierre Vorkosigan.

## Memory (1996)

Miles Vorkosigan's life grows even more complicated, beginning with his accidental maiming of the ImpSec courier he and the Dendarii had been sent to rescue, due to the unusual seizures he has been suffering from since his resuscitation from cryo-stasis. Convinced this isn't a permanent problem, Miles leaves the cause of the accident out of his report to Simon Illyan, but gets into a heated argument with Elli Quinn over it, as he hadn't told her about his problem before the mission either. He promotes her to commodore, but their argument leaves them both tense and rattled. Another surprise is the requested resignation of Baz Jesek and Elena Bothari-Jesek, who want to settle down and start a family. They ask to be released from their armsman's oath, which Miles grants. Recalled to Barrayar, Miles spends the weeklong trip with Sergeant Taura, and realizes that she is growing old fast, owing to her accelerated metabolism, and may die in the next couple of years. He is greeted with disastrous news on Barrayar, after cooling his heels at Vorkosigan House and getting the place in order while his parents are away during Aral's appointment as the viceroy of Sergyar. Simon Illyan knows all about Miles's medical condition, and even worse, knows he falsified his mission report to ImpSec. He requests Miles's resignation immediately, leaving him adrift without the Dendarii or his military career to anchor him. After literally being washed out of his depression by Ivan and Duv Galeni, Miles spends the next few weeks soul-searching, including going up to the Dendarii Mountains to visit the village where he had solved Raina Csurik's murder a decade ago. He finds some peace there, and begins to rebuild his life. His attempt to help Duv win the heart of a Komarran heiress, Laisa Toscane, goes disastrously awry when she catches the eye of the Emperor instead, leaving Duv, who was moving too slowly for his own good, brokenhearted. Despite Duv's animosity toward Miles, he comes to him with the next pressing matter—Simon Illyan has been having memory problems, reliving events that happened months or even years ago. With Illyan placed incommunicado in the clinic at ImpSec headquarters, Miles is stonewalled by Simon's replacement, General Lucas Haroche, leading him to request Gregor's intercession. The Emperor makes Miles an Imperial Auditor, one of the Emperor's own high investigators, with broad, undefined powers. The circumstances around Simon's health failure grow more troublesome, as the doctors discover that the eidetic memory chip implanted in his brain is failing. They remove it in a successful operation that leaves Simon more or less intact, but somewhat less than the man he used to be. During his recovery, first at Vorkosigan

House, then at Vorkosigan Surleau, Miles comes to know a different side of the ultra-competent former chief of ImpSec. He also finally gets a diagnosis of his seizures, which have been caused by overproduction of neurotransmitters, which build up in his brain until their release in stressful situations, causing the seizure in a biochemical form of epilepsy. It can be treated, but not cured, with a brain implant. Somewhat leery of the idea, Miles puts it off until his investigation is finished. Returning to Vorbarr Sultana, he brings his new powers into play as he plunges headlong into determining what exactly happened to Simon. The doctors reveal that the damage to the memory chip was intentionally done, and unfortunately, the evidence points to Duv Galeni. Convinced the Komarran is innocent, Miles keeps digging, resulting in an offer by Haroche to reinstate him in the military as a captain, and go on being the liaison with the Dendarii as if nothing had ever happened. Miles sees this offer for the bribe that it is, and realizes Haroche was behind the sabotage of Simon's chip, and the destruction of his career. He figures out a way to not only find the evidence of the plot, but also to catch Haroche red-handed in the act of destroying evidence that would convict him. Haroche is arrested, Galeni is cleared of all charges, and Miles's position as Imperial Auditor is made permanent, with the approval of the other current auditors. Miles is given retirement from the military with the rank of captain by Gregor as a favor to him. Galeni recovers from the ordeal of almost having his career ruined, and picks up with Delia Koudelka, to the chagrin of Ivan, who asked her to marry him too late. The Emperor also announces his official betrothal to Laisa Toscane, and Barrayaran society shifts into high gear for the upcoming wedding, led by Alys Vorpatril, who has also started a romance with Simon, which amuses Miles and horrifies Ivan. Miles has the operation to implant the device to control his seizures, and makes peace with who he is at last. After one final, futile attempt to win Elli's hand in marriage, he promotes her to admiral of the Dendarii Free Mercenary Fleet, to continue in his place, as he heads back to Barrayar to assume his new position as Imperial Auditor.

## *Komarr* (1998)

Miles's first off-planet assignment as Imperial Auditor is to assist another Auditor, Georg Vorthys, with his investigation of what first appears to be the accidental collision of an ore freighter with the soletta mirror array that orbits Komarr, providing vital solar energy to the planet's millennium-long terraforming project. Miles meets Vorthys's niece, Ekaterin Nile Vorvayne Vorsoisson, currently trapped in an unhappy marriage to Etienne (Tien) Vorsoisson, an administrator at the Serifosa Dome. Their initial appraisal of the situation indicates a worse-than-feared scenario—if the array isn't repaired, within the next twenty-four months the terraforming progress made on Komarr will stop, as there will not be enough heat in the atmosphere to keep the environment going. This would seem to indicate that sabotage may have been the goal, but by whom? While Auditor Vorthys dives into the technical engineering aspects of the accident, Miles gets to know Ekaterin and her son, Nikolai. He inadvertently discovers that the boy has Vorzohn's Dystrophy, a hereditary, degenerative disease. Tien, fearing backlash among the sensitive Barrayarans, has kept his knowledge of this a tight secret, even preventing his son from getting the treatment that could cure him until Tien can receive it first. When Ekaterin learns of a mysterious disappearance of an engineering tech in Waste Heat Management, she dismisses it at first. However, when the body of another technician in the same department turns up in the wreckage of the accident, it is not a simple coincidence. Eavesdropping on a conversation between her husband and another administrator, Soudha, Ekaterin believes Tien has been taking bribes, which he then lost by buying shares in a failed Komarran jump-ship expedition, which has left the family deep in debt. This, along with Tien's many other failings, including his inability to understand her sense of honor or how life with him has crippled her, causes Ekaterin to make up her mind to leave him. When she tells him her decision, Tien collects Miles from the Administration Building, where he has been reviewing records, and takes him out to the Waste Heat experiment station, a large building in the middle of nowhere, supposedly constructed to conduct experiments with the terraforming process, but which Tien now tells Miles has been used by Soudha for graft, creating phantom employees to draw payroll, ordering fictitious equipment, and pocketing the difference. Investigating the supposedly empty building, they are surprised to find activity there, as Soudha and other employees of the Waste Heat division are busy loading something large into lift trucks.

Soudha stuns both men and chains them to a railing outside, in the non-breathable atmosphere. Although the conspirators have sent for help to free the men, Tien's breath mask was not full when they left, and he panics and dies of asphyxiation while Miles can do nothing but watch. Miles is rescued by Ekaterin, who must now deal with her husband's death, get Nikolai the treatment he needs before Tien's health benefits run out, leave Komarr to go back to Barrayar, and figure out what to do with the life that has suddenly been given back to her at the expense of her husband's. While assisting with treating Nikolai, Miles realizes he is falling in love with Ekaterin at the worst possible time. Tackling the expanded problem of what the engineers had been ordering and working on at the experiment station, Miles, Vorthys, and other engineers figure out that the group had been working on a wormhole destroyer, and were planning to permanently close the wormhole between Barrayar and Komarr, cutting Barrayar off from the rest of the galaxy forever. However, there is a fifty-fifty chance that the device will actually release the wormhole energy in a destructive wave that would destroy the device and anything nearby, such as a ship—or a space station. At the same time, Ekaterin had been sent up to the jump station to meet her arriving aunt, Helen Vorthys, where they both stumble into one of the plotters, forcing him to capture them and hold them hostage until the device can be utilized. After attempting to foil them once by pulling a fire alarm, Ekaterin manages to get her hands on a remote control for a float cradle holding the device, and smash it, foiling the Komarrans' plan. However, they still have their two hostages, and it takes all of Miles's wits and determination to negotiate their release, and the surrender of the terrorists. Miles has to head back to Barrayar to report, but he is secure in the knowledge that Ekaterin will be following, and he intends to do whatever is necessary to make her his—the first step being to make her even consider another marriage.

## A *Civil Campaign* (1999)
### Winner, Sapphire Award

With Emperor Gregor's wedding fast approaching, Miles, Mark, and others arrive on Barrayar to add their own unpredictable chaos to the social event of their generation. Fresh from preventing either the destruction of a jump station or the collapse of Barrayar's wormhole, Miles returns to Vorkosigan House to prepare for his role as Gregor's Second in the upcoming nuptial ceremony. Head-over-heels about Ekaterin Vorsoisson, who is still in her traditional year of mourning, he plots to stay close to her by offering her a commission to create a garden on a bare spot of ground near Vorkosigan House. Meanwhile, Mark has returned from Beta Colony after a year of university and therapy, and has brought with him Doctor Enrique Borgos, a scientist from Escobar who has created "butter bugs," bioengineered insects that he thinks can be modified to eat Barrayaran pest plants, and which secrete a nutritious paste as a product that they plan to market. Mark's burgeoning relationship with Kareen Koudelka, however, has hit a snag, as she is having a bit of an identity crisis, feeling pressured returning to Barrayar and her family, whom she hasn't told about her relationship with Mark, and also worrying about how she will afford her next year at the Betan university. At the same time, Ivan Vorpatril is having his own problems; besides being drafted to help his mother Alys with any of the thousand and one jobs that need doing in preparation for the Emperor's wedding, he's also feeling the acute shortage of Barrayaran brides, courtesy of the previous generation's mania for male children, to the extent that choosing their babies' sexes has created a serious gender imbalance. Working with Ekaterin almost every day, Miles manages to keep his true feelings from her, but can't keep quiet to anyone else, extracting a promise from Ivan to stay away from her, and telling everyone in earshot about his cunning plan. Miffed, Ivan keeps his promise, but sets another man, Lieutenant Alexi Vormoncrief, to woo her instead, figuring his lack of personality won't make him a serious threat, but will shake up Miles a bit. It does shake Miles, for when he next sees Ekaterin, she is tensely entertaining not one, but three gentlemen, Alexi, a ne'er-do-well named Byerly Vorrutyer, and a Major Zamori. Miles immediately puts his plans for a dinner party into high gear. Meanwhile, Ivan is entangled in even more problems of his own; first, Vormoncrief becomes quite taken with Ekaterin, to the point of proposing marriage, which was not what Ivan had in mind at all. Second, one of his former paramours, Lady Donna Vorrutyer, is contesting her late brother's estate passing to his brother Richars, a cold, cruel man. To stop it, she has gone to Beta Colony and has changed herself into a man—completely. Ivan introduces the new Lord Dono to Gregor, who lets him press his claim to the estate. Meanwhile, Mark, Enrique,

Kareen, and Ekaterin have been choosing sites for their expanding butter bug business. Miles's carefully planned dinner party disintegrates into a shambles, from the unexpected Lord Dono making an appearance, to the use of bug butter as a last-minute ingredient in several dishes, to Enrique engineering the Vorkosigan House crest on the backs of his latest batch of butter bugs—and then accidentally releasing them throughout the household. The evening comes to a sudden and terrible end when Simon Illyan lets the cat out of the bag by asking Ekaterin how Miles's courtship is progressing. Since Miles hadn't even hinted of pressing his suit to her, she feels that he has lied to her about the garden commission, and was just using it to get close to her. Storming out, she runs smack into Aral Vorkosigan, followed by his wife, both of whom have just come back from Sergyar in time to see a distraught young woman fleeing their house, with Miles in desperate pursuit. Crushed, Miles retreats into the house to take advice from his parents, who advise making his true feelings known, and the sooner the better. Mark also had an inadvertent revelation come out at the dinner party which let Kareen's parents know of their relationship, and not in the tamest way either. Forbidden from seeing her, Mark is also not at his best. Ivan is still tied up with wedding preparations, and now has to juggle his involvement with the Lord Dono estate claim, which will be going to the Council of Counts in the next few days. Miles teams Dono with René Vorbretten, another lord who is suffering a challenge to his own right to rule, owing to the discovery that he is one-eighth Cetagandan, as a result of one of his ancestors' actions during the Cetagandan invasion, to work together, and strengthen each other's claims. Meanwhile, the events of the dinner party have spread throughout Vorbarr Sultana, and some of the conservative Vor lords, who have also been talking about what happened on Komarr, are spreading the rumor that Miles killed Tien to get Ekaterin. Threatened by Richars with a murder charge unless Miles votes for his confirmation as count, Miles decides to ensure that Richars doesn't claim the title. Lieutenant Vormoncrief, meanwhile, has been trying to gather support after Ekaterin turned down his marriage proposal, writing a letter to her brother and in-laws warning them that Miles was coming after her, and even interrogating Nikolai about the events on Komarr, causing Miles to arrange for Nikolai to meet with Gregor himself to explain how his father had died. Ekaterin is drawn more and more to Miles, particularly after the elegant and heartfelt letter of apology she received from him after the dinner party. Matters come to a head the night before the vote on both Lord Dono's and Count René's claims to their districts. When hired thugs attempt to neuter Dono—literally—Ivan and Olivia Koudelka foil the plan, and gather enough evidence to present Richars's involvement in the plot to several other conservative counts, who are furious not that he tried, but that the plan failed, and he was publicly implicated. At the same time, Ekaterin's brother and brother-in-law arrive at the Vorthys home, and attempt to take Nikolai with them, protesting that he isn't safe in the capital city. Nikolai calls Gregor for help, resulting in everyone being taken to Vorhartung Castle, where the Council of Counts is in session. Gregor clears up the misunderstanding regarding Miles and lets Ekaterin, Nikolai, and her relatives watch the rest of the proceedings. With several counts switching sides, Lord Đono is confirmed, and Richars is arrested, but not before he tries to goad Ekaterin into renouncing Miles. Stunned by his audacity, Ekaterin asks Miles to marry her instead, undermining Richars's plans completely. By the narrowest of margins, René Vorbretten is also upheld as the count for his district. While this is all going on, parole officers from Escobar come into Vorkosigan House to arrest Enrique on charges of fraud and grand theft, as it seems the butter bugs weren't quite his property, having been confiscated by his investors, and liberated, along with Enrique, by Mark. The two officers face the determined wrath of Kareen and Martya Koudelka, however, who pelt them with tubs of bug butter until they can get Enrique back and lock and barricade the laboratory door from the officers. Miles arrives home to find Enrique about to be hauled off to Escobaran jail, and frees him using another loophole in the Barrayaran bureaucracy maze. With all obstacles cleared, Emperor Gregor's wedding goes off without a hitch, the first commercial butter bug product, maple ambrosia, is a smash hit at the reception, and the recolored butter bugs themselves, styled by Ekaterin and renamed Glorious Bugs, are also a success. After initial reluctance, the Koudelka parents, with help from Countess Vorkosigan, come to an arrangement with Mark and Kareen. Ivan, unfortunately, still hasn't found anyone to settle down with, as one of his last hopes, Olivia Koudelka, is engaged to Lord Dono. And Miles has won the heart of Ekaterin, but now has to leap from the wedding ceremony of his foster brother Gregor into a mission perhaps even more dire—planning his own.

# "Winterfair Gifts"
## Published in *Irresistible Forces*, 2004

In the hectic days leading up to Miles and Ekaterin's wedding, Armsman Roic is still trying to get over his mortal embarrassment at meeting his lord's future bride in less-than-flattering circumstances—wearing nothing but his boots, briefs, and about five pounds of bug butter. That had been courtesy of the scuffle he had gotten into several months earlier, protecting Doctor Borgos from Escobaran bounty hunters. Still feeling guilty over his role in the debacle, he attends to his duties as a stream of important visitors arrive at Vorkosigan House for the upcoming wedding. Among them is the genetically modified Sergeant Taura, whom Roic is assigned to accompany during an appointment to get her properly attired for the ceremony, courtesy of Alys Vorpatril. Despite a minor incident with a child at tea afterward, the day goes well, but Roic's inadvertent disparagement of the genetically modified butter bugs falls harshly upon Taura's ears. Also, the bride has been ill for the several days leading up to the wedding, and Roic isn't sure if it is pre-wedding nerves or something worse. When he spots Taura looking through the wedding gifts late one night, and pocketing an elegant strand of pearls that supposedly had been sent by Admiral Quinn, he tries to intervene, hating to think she might be just a thief after all. But Taura's modified eyesight has spotted something on the pearls, and Roic convinces her to let him take them to Imperial Security for a more detailed examination. Her suspicion proves correct; the necklace is poisoned with a deadly neurotoxin cunningly designed to pass a cursory inspection. Ekaterin's wearing it for only a few minutes when she first tried it on was enough to make her quite ill, and prolonged exposure would have killed her for sure. The culprit behind the plan is revealed to be Lord Vorbataille, a minor noble who had gotten caught up in a Jackson's Whole criminal ring, and had been arrested a few days earlier trying to flee off-planet. Taura and Roic are the heroes of the wedding for foiling the plot, with Taura becoming Ekaterin's Second during the ceremony. After seeing Lord and Lady Vorkosigan off on their honeymoon, Taura and Roic reach a new mutual understanding, one that leads to some romantic fireworks of their very own.

## Diplomatic Immunity (2001)

More than a year after their marriage, Miles and Ekaterin have enjoyed a well-deserved two-month galactic honeymoon, and are returning to Barrayar for the births of their children when an Imperial courier ship brings a message from Emperor Gregor. Miles is assigned to investigate an incident at Graf Station, in the Union of Free Habitats, located in an area known as Quaddiespace. Members of a Barrayaran military escort, guarding a Komarran trade fleet, got into an incident that resulted in the Barrayarans shooting up a local police station to try and free some of their men. Graf Station responded by locking down the entire merchant fleet in the docks, and holding all the passengers until the mess can be sorted out, hence Gregor's request that Miles see to the matter,

as he is the closest to Quaddiespace. Taking Ekaterin
with him, Miles is acutely aware of time ticking away
before the births of their children, gestating in uterine replicators back on Barrayar, and wants to wrap
things up as quickly as possible. However, his initial
impression of the station only reveals more problems.
Although a Barrayaran ensign, Dmitri Corbeau, who
seems to have fallen in love with a quaddie ballet
dancer, was the initial cause of the ruckus, Lieutenant Solian, the Komarran-born Barrayaran security
liaison with the merchant fleet, has gone missing in
the station, leaving only several liters of blood in an
airlock, suggesting something dire has happened to
him. Miles also finds another surprise—Bel Thorne,
the Betan hermaphrodite who resigned its commission
from the Dendarii at Miles's request several years ago
after the second Jackson's Whole mission, is working at Graf Station as Portmaster, and is also on the
Barrayaran Imperial Security payroll as an informer.
Miles investigates the station brawl as well as the
missing security officer, and finds more questions than
answers. Ensign Corbeau is seeking asylum at Graf
Station, which would make him a deserter from the
Barrayaran military, and have serious repercussions
for relations between the two cultures. Even more
unusual, Lieutenant Solian seems to have completely
disappeared. Initial suspects include a strange-looking,
genetically modified man anxious to leave the station,
as well as another Betan hermaphrodite, Ker Dubauer,
who is worried about a cargo of uterine replicators.
After someone tries to kill Miles, Bel, or Ker with a
rivet gun, Miles is inclined to view the new herm as
the real target, until he inspects the Betan's cargo,

and finds it to be human fetuses, not bioengineered animals as Dubauer claimed. He also figures out that Dubauer isn't a hermaphrodite, but is a Cetagandan ba, the neuter class that the haut-ladies practice their genetic engineering on before releasing the changes into their future generations. Before he can find Dubauer again, Bel disappears as well, increasing Miles's suspicion that something bigger is going on. When the strange man who assaulted Bel and its partner, Nicol, is caught by the quaddies at the docks, Miles gets a large part of the story. Dubauer had hired Russo Gupta and his smuggler friends to off-load the replicators from a Cetagandan transport ship, then tried to kill all of them with a virulent biotoxin. Gupta survived, and tracked Dubauer down to try and kill him, but failed. When Miles received word that Dubauer and Bel Thorne accessed the ship where the replicators are being held the night before, he knows where the criminal went, but still has to catch him. Going onto the ship that's carrying the replicators, Miles finds that genetic samples have been taken from the embryos. He also finds Bel Thorne there, ill from what appears to be the same toxin that killed Gupta's companions. Miles locks down the ship, and during the search for Dubauer, infects himself when he stumbles upon a trap left by the ba. Dubauer has also never left the ship, as they discover when the ba seals all of the compartment doors and demands a jump pilot to take it away from Quaddiespace, claiming to have left a bomb on the station somewhere. The volunteer pilot is Ensign Corbeau. Miles must fight the poison coursing through him to stop Dubauer and regain control of the ship, which he does right before passing out.

Ekaterin must race against time to get both Miles
and the recaptured fetuses to Cetaganda in time to
save Miles's life and prevent a war-by-mistake. Miles
awakens on a Cetagandan space station, weak but
cured of the toxin's effects. Haut-lady Pel is there,
and Miles explains the plan as he saw it: Dubauer
had stolen the haut-fetuses to create a new empire,
where it would rule over all as both Empress and
Emperor. To cover its tracks, it had planted empty
Cetagandan replicators in Vorbarr Sultana on Barrayar
to create conflict between the two empires. Having
averted yet another war, Ekaterin, Bel, and Miles
are honored by the Cetagandans, with Miles giving a
sample of his genetic structure to the haut-ladies, so
that in the future, a bit of him might become part
of the Cetagandan whole. For Miles and Ekaterin,
however, that pales next to getting home in time to
watch their children, a son and daughter, be born,
and to see the next generation of Vorkosigans take
their first breaths.

• • • • •

# The Vorkosigan Saga Concordance

## KERRIE HUGHES, JOHN HELFERS, AND ED BURKHEAD

The following abbreviations are used to denote where the defined term appeared in the Vorkosigan Saga novels:

| | |
|---|---|
| B: | *Barrayar* |
| BA: | *Brothers in Arms* |
| BI: | "The Borders of Infinity" |
| C: | *Cetaganda* |
| CC: | *A Civil Campaign* |
| DD: | "Dreamweaver's Dilemma" |
| DI: | *Diplomatic Immunity* |
| EA: | *Ethan of Athos* |
| FF: | *Falling Free* |
| K: | *Komarr* |
| L: | "Labyrinth" |
| M: | *Memory* |
| MD: | *Mirror Dance* |
| MM: | "The Mountains of Mourning" |

SH:    *Shards of Honor*
VG:    *The Vor Game*
WA:    *The Warrior's Apprentice*
WG:    "Winterfair Gifts"

Terms are listed alphabetically, without regard to punctuation.

Although we have tried to make this concordance as complete as possible, please note that Lois's novels cover more than one thousand years of future history. The writers and editors are all too aware that mistakes are inevitable in such a mammoth work. Comments, questions, and suggestions or additions or corrections may be sent to the following address:

> John Helfers
> c/o Baen Publishing Enterprises
> 500 Wait Ave., #6
> Wake Forest, NC 27587

• • **A** • •

Abell:
No first name given. A scholar who produced a turgid general history of Barrayar. Cordelia views a video of his work while she is Aral's prisoner. (SH)

Abromov:
No first name given. A corporal in the Dendarii Free Mercenary Fleet, he delivers the helmet recorder files of every Dendarii soldier involved in the clone rescue missions on Jackson's Whole to the officer conference room on the *Peregrine*. (BA)

Aczith:
No first name given. A historian who details the history of Emperor Dorca Vorbarra the Just, Aral's great-grandfather, who ruled at the end of the Time of Isolation. Cordelia views this video while she is Aral's prisoner, trying to gain insight into Barrayaran politics. (SH)

*Adumbration of Trigonial Strategy in the War of Minos IV, The*:
Title of a set of three military history reading discs Miles purchases on the Jacksonian Consortium jump station to pass the time during his trip home after his Victor Rotha persona is revealed. (VG)

Agba:
One of the welding quaddies Leo trains at the Cay Habitat. He inadvertently almost ruins Leo's plan to

create a new vortex mirror by using slurry explosive to blow off clamps while disassembling the station. (FF)

## Ahn:

No first name given. A lieutenant and meteorological officer in the Barrayaran military, he is stationed at Lazkowski Base. Miles replaces him on his first assignment after graduating from the Imperial Academy. An unshaven drunkard, approximately forty years old, he has been in the military for twenty years, and is about to retire. He has been Kyril station's only weather officer for fifteen years, and is able to accurately forecast the weather by smell alone. He was an accomplice in covering up Stanis Metzov's murder of a Barrayaran guard corporal who was going to turn Metzov in for killing a Komarran rebel during interrogation. (VG)

## Aime Pass:

A pass in the Dendarii Mountains where Piotr takes Cordelia and Gregor to hide from Vordarian's security men. Populated by scattered homesteads, it is also the mail route for Major Klyeuvi. (B)

## Aircar:

A cross between a groundcar and a lightflyer, an aircar combines the best of both vehicles. Using anti-gravity technology for lift, it can carry several people, and move either on the ground or through the air, giving it an extended travel range. Miles, Ivan, and Vorob'yev travel to the Celestial Garden on Cetaganda in one. (C)

## Alex:

No surname given. The Speaker's deputy in Silvy Vale,

he is a hulking young man, big-handed, heavy-browed, thick-necked, and surly. He assists in exhuming Raina Csurik's body for autopsy. (MM)

Alfredi, Marsha:
A lieutenant in the Barrayaran prison camp during the Escobar war, she is the ranking officer there until Cordelia arrives. (SH)

Aljean:
A quaddie zero-gee ballet composer. His most famous work is "The Crossing," about the original quaddies' escape from GalacTech to freedom. (DI)

Allegre, Guy:
A general in the Barrayaran military, he is the Head of Domestic Affairs for Komarr, and Lucas Haroche's counterpart before Lucas is promoted to Simon's position. He accompanies Miles to catch Haroche destroying the evidence that he had infected Simon with the prokaryote organism. After being promoted to acting Chief of Imperial Security, his first act is to arrest Haroche on Miles's order. He is then appointed to the position of Chief of Imperial Security after Miles turns the position down.

After the Komarr investigation, he warns Miles not to speak publicly about the rumors regarding Ekaterin until Imperial Security can learn if there is a security leak regarding the recent events there. Before Miles's wedding, he reports to the wedding party about the poisoned pearls, and lets them know that the people behind the plot have been caught. (CC, M, WG)

Alpha-S-D plasmid-2:
A sexually transmitted disease Elli Quinn mentions as part of her plan to bring biocontrol wardens down on Colonel Millisor at Kline Station. (EA)

Alpha-S-D plasmid-3:
A sexually-transmitted disease Elli Quinn mentions as part of her plan to bring biocontrol wardens down on Colonel Millisor at Kline Station. (EA)

Amor Klyeuvi's nephew:
No name given. He guides Cordelia and Bothari out of the Dendarii Mountains. (B)

Anafi, Ser:
A representative of the Rialto Sharemarket Agency, he contacts Ekaterin Vorsoisson after Etienne's death, trying to collect on her husband's loan, which was lost in an investment in trade fleet shares. He tries to get her to cosign a repayment plan, but Miles thwarts him by putting him in direct contact with Colonel Gibbs as part of the investigation into Etienne's finances. (K)

Anderson, Laureen:
A sergeant and shuttle pilot in the Dendarii Free Mercenary Fleet, she is assigned Miles's mission to infiltrate House Ryoval's biological laboratory. She saves Miles, Taura, and Nicol from the pursuing Ryoval security forces, and helps Taura clean up aboard the *Ariel*. (L)

Andy:
Claire and Tony's baby quaddie, born on the Cay Project Habitat. (FF)

Anti-gravity field:
A null-gee field can be created just about anywhere with the proper equipment, and is often used for sleep and exotic recreation. For those not accustomed to free fall, this can cause drop-nausea. While hosting a quaddie musician, House Fell uses a null-gee bubble to allow her to float while playing her instrument with all four arms. (L)

Anti-gravity freight pallet:
A self-powered lift cart that can move freight, luggage, and other equipment a short distance. Often, the user will ride on the pallet along with the cargo. The pallet eliminates gravity, but not inertia, so the cart and cargo have to be stopped manually. (All)

Anti-gravity lift tubes:
Mechanical elevators have been replaced by anti-gravity lift tubes. The traveler rises or is lowered at a certain speed, depending on the tube's setting. Built-in safety programs provide for controlled lowering in case of power or equipment failure; however, they can be over-ridden, as Mark found out while escaping from Baron Ryoval's laboratory. Emergency handholds/ladders are usually built into the tube walls as a safety backup. (All)

Anti-Vor pro-galactic faction:
One of the splinter political groups on Barrayar, they want a written constitution for the government. (VG)

Apmad:
No first name given. The vice president of GalacTech's Operations Department, she is at the high end of

middle age and dumpy, with short, frizzy gray hair and serious eyes. She is inspecting Rodeo and the Cay Habitat when Claire and Tony try to escape, and oversees the hearing into the incident. She is prejudiced and appalled by the genetic experimentation that created the quaddies. As a young woman, she'd had four or five pregnancies that were all terminated due to genetic defects, then gave up trying to reproduce, got divorced, and went to work for GalacTech. She sends the order to shut the Cay Project down. (FF)

Apoptotic Prokaryote:
A bioengineered life-form, smaller and simpler than a bacterium, used by General Lucas Haroche to contaminate Simon's memory chip. Once ingested, it manufactures an enzyme that breaks down the chip's protein matrix, in effect eating the proteins to reproduce. After reproducing a certain number of times, it is supposed to self-destruct, leaving no physical evidence of its existence. The original lot was found in the Imperial Security Evidence Room in Aisle Five, Shelf Nine, Bin Twenty-Seven, and was mislabeled as a Komarran virus. It was originally supposed to be used on Simon in a plot created by the Komarran terrorist Ser Galen. (M)

Aragones:
No first name given. A senior partner and doctor at the Beauchene Life Center, he is a big, bluff man with bronze skin, a noble nose, and graying hair, who works in a very cluttered office. He briefs Miles and Elli on the Dendarii mercenaries injured during the Marilac operation. (MD)

Arata, Tav:
A security officer at Kline Station, he is a neurasthenic Eurasian with lank black hair, pale skin, and eyes like needles, who says little but listens a lot. His uniform is mostly black, with an orange collar and side stripe. Assigned to cleaning up the mess left by Quinn, he gets a date with her for his troubles, and no explanation about what happened. (EA)

*Ariel*:
An Illyrican-made small warship, swift and powerful for its size, that Miles captures after taking Captain Auson and his boarding party prisoner. After taking over the ore refinery orbiting Tau Verde IV, Miles gives it to Bel Thorne as part of the hermaphrodite's brevet promotion. He uses it for the ordnance and scientist pickup at Jackson's Whole, and also in the prisoner escape on Dagoola IV. Posing as Miles, Mark takes the ship on his ill-fated clone rescue mission on Jackson's Whole. (BI, L, WA)

Armsman:
The social title of a Barrayaran retainer who has sworn the armsman's oath to the liege he serves. (All)

Armsman's oath:
The oath that Miles has Arde Mayhew and Baz Jesek swear to confirm their acceptance of him as their liege lord, serving him faithfully until either death of the armsman or his lord, or until the lord releases the armsman from his oath. This can pose problems, as Arde is a Betan and the first ever to swear the oath, and Baz is a deserter from the Barrayaran military,

and already liege-sworn to Emperor Gregor. Mark also has Elena swear the oath to him before going to rescue Miles, breaking Barrayaran tradition as well, since a female had never sworn the armsman's oath until that moment. (WA, MD)

Armsmen's Shout:
A Barrayaran wedding tradition, where the twenty sworn armsmen of a lord cheer his marriage. Pym leads the one for Miles after he marries Ekaterin. (WG)

Arozzi:
No first name given. Miles interviews him about Radovas's death, as he has taken over the man's duties until a replacement is found, and is hoping to be permanently promoted into the position. He is involved in the plot to destroy the Barrayaran wormhole, and when he encounters Ekaterin on the jump point station, takes her and Madame Vorthys hostage to prevent discovery of the plan before it can be carried out. (K)

Artificial gravity:
Spacecraft and space habitats use artificial gravity for human health and to compensate for acceleration. The technology behind the system is not explained. Initial prototype systems required heavy power use, but by the time of the Vorkosigan Saga, there's no mention of the power cost. Shuttles and small spacecraft do not have artificial gravity systems. (All except FF)

Arvin:
No first name given. A ghem-lady with blond hair

who seduces Ivan at Lord Yenaro's party. She and Lady Benello find Miles and Ivan at the bioestheties exhibition, and take both men over to Lady Veda's exhibit, where Yenaro was unwittingly set up to kill all of them with an asterzine-impregnated carpet. (C)

Aslund:
A cul-de-sac planet like Barrayar, the Hegen Hub is its sole gate to the greater galactic web. They hired the Dendarii Free Mercenary Fleet for protection when the Cetagandans began making preliminary moves to capture the Hegen Hub. After the brief war with Cetaganda, it cements an alliance with Barrayar, Vervain, and Pol. (VG)

Athos:
A cloistered planet with three moons in a remote sector of space that is inhabited solely by men. Even the word "woman" is an obscenity in their culture. Humans have been living there for approximately two centuries, using uterine replicators and ovarian banks to create future male generations. The men live in communes and everyone pitches in to help with maintaining their society, as that is the only way to earn social duty credits toward having a child. They grow facial hair as a symbol of fatherhood after saving enough credits for a reproduction permit. Life for the planet's inhabitants is peaceful, if fairly rigidly controlled by the government. When their genetic lines begin to die out, they send a representative into the galaxy to procure new ones, and foil a major Cetagandan plot as well. (EA)

Aura detector:
Used in crime scene investigations, it detects the after-images of human movement for some time afterward. The auras fade over a number of hours. Miles laments that it is too late to use one during his investigation of the murder at Silvy Vale. (MM)

Auson:
No first name given, he is the captain of the *Ariel* who boards Miles's freighter at Tau Verde to inspect their cargo. A decent soldier, but sloppy after eighteen months of blockade duty. When he tries to take Elena as his hostage, Miles and the rest of his crew capture his boarding party, then take his ship. Auson gets both arms and his nose broken by Elena, then endures a General Ship Inspection by Miles and his crew. He signs the contracts of his men over to Miles, and joins the Dendarii Free Mercenary Fleet. He is promoted to captain of the *Triumph* after the capture of the ore refinery.

   Four years later, he still commands the *Triumph* under Admiral Oser, but has put on a few pounds. Dismayed to find he must follow Miles's orders again during the Vervain conflict, he demands an apology from Ky Tung before agreeing to help protect the wormhole to Vervain. (VG, WA)

"Autumn Leaves":
The multimedia sculpture that Lord Yanaro creates for the Marilacan embassy welcoming party, it is a fountain that resembles a small mountain, complete with footpaths. Colored flakes swirl in the air around the base, making tunnels that change color, signifying

the passing of the seasons. The sculpture is large enough to walk through, and when Miles is led inside by Lord Yenaro, the electromagnetic field powering the sculpture heats up his leg braces enough to burn him, embarrassing him in front of the other guests. (C)

Avakli:
No first name given. A rear admiral in the Barrayaran Imperial Service and a biocyberneticist, he is balding, lean, tall, and intense. He normally does surgery on jump pilots and their implants, and has been called in to consult on Simon's eidetic memory chip failure. (M)

Aziz:
No first name given. One of the injured Dendarii mercenaries at the Beauchene Life Center, he suffered brain damage from the cryogenic preservation process, and has lost his personality and all motor and vocal skills. He will need long-term physical and mental therapy and care to be self-sufficient. During his visit, Miles sets up a trust fund to cover his rehabilitation. (MD)

* * B * *

Ba:
The caste name for the mostly hairless, neuter Cetagandan Imperial slaves. They are of the haut genome, but are not cloned; each one is created individually, as a test subject for potential genetic traits that a haut-lady may wish to introduce into future offspring. Each serves its master for life. (C)

Baba:
A Barrayaran social position held by elderly ladies. They serve as arbitrators between the familes of two people that wish to get married, to ensure that the match is a suitable one for the involved parties. Miles pretends to be one to facilitate Elena Bothari's and Bazik·Jesek's marriage. Aly Vorpartril serves as Emperor Gregor's Baba during his wooing of Laisa Toscane, and Alexi Vormoncrief sends one to ask for Ekaterin's hand, with much less positive results. (CC, WA)

Baba of Lairouba:
The hereditary head of state of the planet Lairouba, he has traveled to Earth to discuss right-of-passage through the Western Orion Arm group of planets. Miles is assigned to diplomatic escort duty for one of his four wives during a reception and dinner in his honor, made difficult due to the translator earbugs not arriving in time for the event. (BA)

Baneri:
No first name or rank given. A Marilacan military officer killed during the siege of Fallow Core. (BI)

Bannerji, George:
A captain, he works for GalacTech company security in Shuttleport Three. Alerted by Van Atta about an unspecified threat, he carries an unauthorized weapon during his search, and shoots Tony out of fear. He is officially reprimanded and suspended for two weeks without pay. He redeems himself by not firing on the

quaddies' escaping jump ship without the properly signed waste disposal order. (FF)

Barca:
An area on Athos that has both junior and senior representatives on the Population Council, one of whom proposes the idea that the Council bring female fetuses to near-term and harvest new genetic material from them to revitalize the ovarian cultures, eliciting a horrified reaction from the rest of the council. (EA)

Barinth:
A city on Tau Verde IV that Major Daum and Fehun are trying to free from the Pelians. (WA)

Barrayar:
One of the major planets in the Vorkosigan Saga. It is a lush, verdant planet with at least two continents, several mountain ranges, and large areas of deciduous forest. Its standard day is 26.7 hours long. Settled several hundred years before Miles's birth, its population suffered a return to near medieval-technology status when its sole wormhole suddenly closed, leading to what the Barrayarans call the Time of Isolation. It is ruled as an Imperial Empire, with an Emperor as its head, and an aristocratic-military class known as the Vor, which spend as much time jockeying for power with each other as they do ruling the planet.

Barrayar was the target of a failed twenty-year conquest attempt by Cetaganda, which led Barrayar's leaders to conquer Komarr, the planet at the outlet of its wormhole route to human-settled space, for protection. It also launched an ill-fated attempt to conquer Escobar, and settled the planet Sergyar, where Aral Vorkosgian and Cordelia first meet. After the Hegen Hub conflict, it enters into an alliance with Aslund, Pol, and Vervain. (All except FF)

**Barrayaran Imperial Embassy:**
A Class III embassy located in London, England, on Earth. Miles takes Quinn there to check in with Imperial Security headquarters and get needed money for the Dendarii Free Mercenary Fleet. As Lieutenant Vorkosigan, he is assigned to data analysis and escort duty as needed by the false orders sent by the subverted courier, meant to keep him in place until Ser Galen can kidnap Miles and install Mark in his place. (BA)

**Barth:**
No first name given. A sergeant at the Barrayaran Embassy on Earth, he escorts Miles and Elli to their first meeting with Captain Galen. Prejudiced against women in the military, he dismisses Elli Quinn as a soldier. While he is escorting Miles to the Dendarii at the spaceport, the two are almost killed by hired assassins, and are saved when Quinn takes out the lift-truck with a rocket launcher. (BA)

**Baruch, Cynthia Jane:**
A doctor hired to create Athos's ovarian cultures, and who used her own genetic material to help start the planet's all-male population. Children created from her genetic material tend to be excellent doctors. Ethan Urquhart is a CJB-8. (EA)

Base doctor:
No name given. He checks Cordelia out after her journey with Gregor through the Dendarii Mountains, and suggests an exercise program for her, which Cordelia finds grimly ironic. (B)

Base One:
Where Cordelia's survey team had established camp on Sergyar while they were surveying it. It was attacked by the Barrayarans and most of the tents and equipment were destroyed. (SH)

Batman:
A Barrayaran term for a personal servant or valet. For Vor lords, this person is usually an armsman. (All except FF)

Battle armor:
A self-powered, environmentally sealed, personal armor suit that can be used in space or on the surface of planets with no atmosphere. The suit increases the user's strength proportionately, and provides complete protection against stunners and nerve disruptors, most poisons and biological agents, and some protection against plasma arcs and radioactivity. It contains a communications suite and tactical computer, enabling the wearer to be in constant communication with the rest of their unit. Battle armor can also be slaved to a central control computer, enabling the suit to be controlled by an outside person in the event of the wearer's injury or death. (WA, M, MD)

Beaded lizard:
An animal native to Tau Ceti, weighing about fifty
kilograms. Miles resists purchasing one for Elena on
Beta Colony. (WA)

Beatrice:
No last name given. A tall redhead, she is the leader
among the estimated five hundred women at the
prison camp on Dagoola IV who have formed an alliance to resist rape and abuse. She is instrumental in
reorganizing the camp and Miles becomes very fond
of her. He wants her to be one of the new leaders in
the re-formed Marilacan Army, but she dies by falling
out of the shuttle hatch while trying to free its stuck
loading ramp. (BI)

Beauchene Life Center:
An Escobaran cryotherapy facility, headed by Doctor
Aragones and Administrator Margara, that treats several
injured Dendarii mercenaries after the Marilac operation. Medic Norwood trained in cryogenics there, which
is also where he met one of the Duronas, enabling
him to send her Miles's body after he is killed on
Jackson's Whole. (MD)

Benar, Fehun:
A Felician colonel supposedly in charge of the ore
refinery orbiting Tau Verde IV. He has a wife named
Miram. Captured and psychologically broken by the
Pelians, he was forced to record messages to lure
Felician ships to dock at the refinery to be captured.
He is recovered after the refinery is taken by the
Dendarii, but is catatonic from the torture. (WA)

Benar, Miram:
Fehun Benar's wife. Major Daum asks about her during his conversation with Benar. (WA)

Benello:
No first name given. A ghem-lady with red hair who seduces Ivan at Lord Yenaro's party. The sister of Lady Veda, she and Lady Arvin find Miles and Ivan at the bioestheties exhibition, and escort both men over to Lady Veda's exhibit, where Yenaro was unwittingly set up to kill all of them with asterzine-impregnated carpet. (C)

Beni Ra orbital factory:
A project that Leo Graf worked on for GalacTech, where he found micro-cracks in the reactor coolant lines, saving at least three thousand lives. (FF)

Benin, Dag:
A ghem-colonel in Cetagandan Imperial Security assigned to internal affairs at the Celestial Gardens, he is charged with investigating the death of the Ba Lura. Of middle stature, he wears the dark red dress uniform of the Imperial Security in the Celestial Garden, and full Imperial pattern face paint, base white with black curves and red accents. Miles manipulates him into solving much of the conspiracy, and Benin figures out his superior, Naru, set him up to declare the Ba Lura's murder a suicide rather than actually investigating it. When Ivan tells him Miles has gone to Ilsum Kety's ship, Benin leads security forces there to arrest Kety. The Emperor rewards his service by promoting him to ghem-general.

Several years later, he escorts the haut Pel Navarr to Emperor Gregor's wedding. He also passes along to Miles Emperor Fletchir Giaja's personal condolences on the death of Admiral Naismith, letting Miles know that the Cetagandans know about his alter ego and identity. Benin also tells Miles that the Emperor trusts that Admiral Naismith will stay deceased. When Miles replies that he trusts the admiral will never have to be resurrected again, Benin promises to convey his reply to the Emperor exactly as spoken. (C, CC)

Bernaux:
No first name given. The silver-haired ambassador of the Marilacan embassy, he greets Vorob'yev, Miles, and Ivan at the welcoming party. (C)

Beta Colony:
The first successful space colony, it is located on a hot, barren planet with all of the population living underground. It is known throughout the galaxy for its permissive social attitude, which culminated in the creation of a hermaphrodite class of people. Known for its excellent technology and industrial base, it develops and sells products and services throughout the galaxy. Chalmys DuBauer spent much of his artificially lengthened life span traveling between it and Earth, and Anias Ruey is contemplating making a feelie-dream using it as a background. Cordelia Naismith turns her back on her home when the Betan government tries to use her as a propaganda tool against Barrayar. Miles Vorkosigan finds Arde Mayhew and Baz Jesek there, and takes Elli Quinn back to the colony for reconstructive facial surgery. Mark Vorkosigan and

Kareen Koudelka attend school and therapy there. (DD, FF, SH, WA, CC)

Betan Embassy:
Located on Orient IV. Leo learns the Betans demonstrated an artificial gravity device there, rendering the quaddies obsolete before they can finish their training. (FF)

Betan Expeditionary Force:
An all-purpose exploration unit that is made up of the top scientific minds on Beta Colony. Its primary mission is to explore newly discovered planets and regions of space. Cordelia Naismith is a captain in the organization when she meets Aral on the survey planet that will later be named Sergyar, and observes the preparations for the invasion of Escobar. Her survey team is driven off the planet, but instead of warning Beta Colony about Barrayar's plans, they rescue her from the *General Vorkraft* instead. A documentary, *The Thin Blue Line*, recounts the Force's heroism in helping to repel the Barrayaran invasion, which disgusts Elena Bothari when she watches it nineteen years later. Doctor Enrique Borgos is tremendously impressed when he learns that Cordelia was a member of the Force. (CC, SH, VG)

*Betan Journal of Reproductive Medicine, The*:
A magazine Ethan Urquhart reads after its approval by the Athos Board of Censors, wherein he finds an article called "On an Improvement in Permeability of Exchange Membranes in the Uterine Replicator," by Kara Burton M.D., Ph.D., and Elizabeth Naismith,

M.S. Bioengineering (Cordelia's mother). Their pictures are in the magazine, and Ethan sees a photo of a woman for the first time in his life. (EA)

Betan Mental Health Board:
Mentioned by Arde Mayhew as people he cannot take hostage. (WA)

Betan rejuvenation treatment:
A rumor with unknown provenance about Admiral Naismith that claims he has undergone a mysterious life-extending treatment at Beta Colony. Baron Fell is extremely interested in finding out more about it, and Miles uses his interest as a bargaining tool at first, but eventually tells him that no such treatment exists. (L)

Bharaputra, Lotus Durona:
Lilly Durona's second daughter, she left her clone family and married Baron Bharaputra. She is Eurasian, with white hair streaked with black wound up in elaborate braids around her head, dark eyes, a high-bridged nose, and thin, ivory skin softening with tiny wrinkles. The dark-haired girl Lilly, rescued and then lost in the clone group when she rejoined Baron Bharaputra, is the transplant body Lotus intends to inhabit once the girl has reached the proper age. Lotus is now in her sixties, and ready to undergo the procedure, but is thwarted when Miles convinces young Lilly to escape the Baron's House and join her true family. (MD)

Bharaputra, Vasa Luigi:
The baron of House Bharaputra on Jackson's Whole,

he appears to be forty years old, but has been in a clone body for the past twenty years. He has a strong-boned face, with olive skin and dark hair pulled back and held in a gold ring. Miles first encounters him during his first mission to Jackson's Whole to steal his genetic scientist Hugh Canaba.

Miles tries to negotiate with him for the return of Mark, Bel Thorne, and Green Squad after the clone rescue attempt, but ends up trying to break them out himself when the talks break down. The baron is captured by Yellow Squad during that mission, and is released in exchange for the Dendarii's passage out of the Jackson's Whole system. He captures Rowen Durona and Miles after he is resuscitated at the Durona Clinic, and lets Rowan go, not realizing that she and the young clone Lilly have traded places, and sells Miles to Baron Ryoval. (L, MD)

Bianca:
No first name given. A doctor and executive in the Portobello Pharmaceutical Company, he holds degrees in chemistry and psychology, and runs the product development section. Forty, tan and fit, with slightly graying hair, he is married to granddaughter of the company's founder, and lives in a big, beautiful house in Rio de Janeiro. He hires Carlos Diaz to act as his surrogate to hire Anias Ruey to make a disturbing, violent feelie-dream that he plans to use to get his wife to commit suicide so he can inherit her portion of their business. After figuring out his plot, Anias brings the police in, and forces him to give the feelie-dream back to her. (DD)

Bianca, Mrs.:
A woman in her late thirties, she is thin and tense, with dark hair, arrogant eyes, and a feelie-dream implant. She owns sixty percent of her grandfather's company, Portobello Pharmaceutical Company. Married to Doctor Bianca, she is the unknowing target of a plot to kill her by her husband using a feelie-dream to drive her to commit suicide. (DD)

Bier-gift:
A Cetagandan practice of offering gifts to be burned on the funeral bier of a person in their honor. For the Dowager Empress Lisbet Degtiar, Miles presents a sword carried by Dorca Vorbarra in the First Cetagandan War. All of the bier-gifts are placed around the body, and everything is incinerated using plasma-fire. (C)

Bioengineered parasites:
An assassination weapon developed by the Cetagandan Star Crèche, it can be introduced to a victim by various means, including skin contact. The parasites are sometimes protected by micro-encapsulation that can be set to dissolve under specific conditions, including at a predetermined body temperature. Once ingested, they multiply, then switch to producing two chemicals in different vesicles inside their membranes. The vesicles engorge until an increase in the victim's body temperature bursts them, and the chemicals mix, producing a violently exothermic reaction—killing the parasite, damaging the surrounding tissues, and stimulating more nearby parasites to detonate, becoming microscopic bombs. Deceased victims look like they have melted, dissolving into puddles of flesh and bones.

The Cetagandans have the only known antidote for this weapon. A delaying treatment is to cool the body in an ice-water bath and filter the organisms from the victim's blood. However, since they also hide inside tissues, this is not a cure, as energy is continuously drained from the body to create new parasites until death results. The only known person to survive infection without treatment is Russo Gupta. Both Miles and Bel Thorne are infected during the investigation at Graf Station, and are cured by the haut-women of the Star Crèche, although both suffer permanent physical damage. (DI)

Black Escarpment:
Part of a mountain range located deep in Barrayar's Southern Continent, it is where Miles trained in winter maneuvers during his time at the Imperial Academy. (VG, CC)

Black Gang:
The name Mark gives to his various sub-personalities that emerge during his torture by Baron Ryoval, and which stay with him afterward. (MD, CC)

Bleakman, Greg:
Gregor Vorbarra's alias while he is absent without leave from Barrayar. (VG)

Bloody Century:
A term the Barrayarans use to refer to the time of endless fighting on Barrayar before Dorca Vorbarra united all the Vor under his banner. (B)

Blue cheese dressing:
One of the two provisions at Base One that weren't destroyed in the Barrayaran attack. Cordelia, Aral, and Dubauer survive on it during their trip to the supply cache. (SH)

Bobbi:
A quaddie from Gang B on Cay Habitat. (FF)

Body pod:
Also known as a bod pod, it is a cheap, one-size-fits-all emergency survival module in the form of a mostly spherical balloon. A person can quickly enter and seal the pod, then the automatic system will inflate and maintain the internal environment until the inhabitant can be rescued. (All)

Bollan Design:
A Komarran jump-ship powerplant design firm contracted by Soudha to make five experimental Necklin field generators. The chief engineer of the project quit the company to help with the wormhole destruction plot, and is arrested on the jump station with the other collaborators. (K)

Bone replacement:
A medical operation in which weakened or permanently damaged bones are reinforced or replaced by plastic versions. The existing bone marrow is transferred to the new matrix in the artificial bones. Miles undergoes several operations over his lifetime to replace his skeleton with artificial bones. (BA, VG)

Bone, Vicky:
A lieutenant in the Dendarii Free Mercenary Fleet, she is the outfit's head accountant, and is a precise, middle-aged, heavyset woman. When the payment for the Marilac operation doesn't arrive from Barrayar, she receives permission from Miles to get creative with the finances, including setting up a short-term loan against the *Triumph* itself. She also creates the untraceable half-million-Imperial-mark credit chit for Miles to use to try to buy off Galen, which he gives to Mark instead. (BA)

Boni, Sylva:
A deceased Escobaran ensign found in the aftermath of the final battle between Barrayar and Escobar by Falco Ferrell and Tersa Boni. She was Tersa's twenty-year-old daughter, and the reason the medtech asked to be assigned to retrieval duty in that sector. (SH)

Boni, Tersa:
A medtech of the Escobaran Personnel Retrieval and Identification ship, she performs body recovery after the Barrayar-Escobar war, and locates the body of her daughter, Sylva, who was killed in battle. (SH)

Bonn:
No first name given. A lieutenant of Engineering in the Barrayaran military, he is Miles's immediate superior at Lazkowski Base. A slight man in his late twenties with a craggy face, pocked, sallow skin, calculating brown eyes, and competent hands. He oversees the recovery of Miles's scat-cat after his encounter with the mud. Disobeying General Metzov's order to make

his men to clean up the fetaine spill, Bonn joins his team when they are ordered to strip down to bare skin. He is arrested with Miles and the rest of the disobeying technicians, but the charges against him and the other men are dropped at Miles's request. (VG)

Bonsanklar:
An ocean resort town on Barrayar for the upper class, where Aral's mother used to take him every summer when he was a boy. After their marriage, Cordelia and Aral are about to visit it when Prime Minister Vortala takes them to see the Emperor regarding Aral's appointment as Regent of Barrayar. (SH)

Borgos, Enrique:
A biochemist and genetic entomologist from Escobar whom Mark brings to Vorkosigan House, he is the creator of the butter bugs. After bailing him out of a legal situation on Escobar involving creditors that had taken his breeding stock and equipment, Mark partners with him to develop the insects and their products for use on Barrayar. Enrique admires smart women, feeling they are wasted on Barrayar, and becomes enamored of Ekaterin, Cordelia, and then Martya.

A bit hopeless in social situations, he accidentally reveals that Mark and Kareen had visited the Orb of Unearthly Delights on Beta Colony, to the consternation of Commodore Koudelka. He also tries to ingratiate himself with Miles by genetically engineering the seal of House Vorkosigan on the backs of a group of butter bugs, but inadvertently releases them throughout the house. Eventually bail officers from Escobar show up to arrest him, resulting in the bug butter battle. Miles makes sure that the doctor is not deported. At Miles's wedding, he is taken aside and quietly frisked to be sure that he doesn't have any surprise insect gifts. (CC, WG)

Bothari, Konstantin:
A sergeant in the Barrayaran military, he is a two-meter-tall, broad-shouldered man with a face like an axe blade. His mother, Marusia, was a midwife, abortionist, and prostitute, and she used to sell him to her clients as well. He ran away at age twelve and then ran with gangs till he was sixteen, when he lied about his age so he could join the service.

A paranoid schizophrenic, Bothari is loyal to Aral Vorkosigan and respects him, although he doesn't necessarily like him. He is manipulated and tortured by Admiral Ges Vorrutyer, but kills the admiral when he orders Bothari to rape Cordelia. He cares for Elena Visconti when she is a prisoner of war, and takes responsibility for their daughter, Elena, who was a product of that time. After his discharge from the military, Aral makes him an armsman for House Vorkosigan, and he eventually remembers what had happened during his time serving Admiral Vorrutyer, getting through the healing process with Cordelia's help. During Vordarian's attempted coup, he is first assigned to protect Cordelia and Gregor during their time in the Dendarii Mountains, and later accompanies her into Vorbarr Sultana to rescue Miles, beheading Vidal Vordarian with Koudelka's swordstick at Cordelia's order.

When Miles is still an infant, he saves him from being killed by Piotr Vorkosigan. After Miles washes out of the Imperial Academy, the now gray-haired Bothari is assigned to be Miles's bodyguard. He accompanies

Miles and Elena on their trip to Beta Colony, and on the smuggling run to Tau Verde IV. He shows Miles how brutal a military interrogation can be when he tears out a jump pilot's implant, inadvertently killing the man. He is killed by Elena Visconti in front of their daughter. His remains are buried on Barrayar, at the foot of the plot where Cordelia will be buried. (B, SH, WA)

Bothari-Jesek, Cordelia:
The first child of Elena Bothari-Jesek and Baz Jesek, named after Cordelia Vorkosigan. Elena and Baz bring her with them while visiting Barrayar for Miles's wedding. (WG)

Bothari-Jesek, Elena:
The rape child of Sergeant Bothari and Elena Visconti, she was one of the uterine replicator children taken to Barrayar by Aral and Cordelia, and grows up alongside Miles Vorkosigan. She is six feet tall, slim, vibrant, and beautiful, with an elegant, aquiline profile, long, dark, straight hair, which she cuts short later on, and dark eyes. Raised by Bothari, she did not know the truth about her parents' relationship.

During Miles's trip to Beta Colony and Tau Verde IV, she comes into her own as a mercenary commander, winning a pitched battle to capture the last needed payroll to end the Pelian blockade of the planet. She also learns about Bothari and Elena Visconti when Elena kills her father in front of her. She falls in love with Baz Jesek, turning Miles down when he confesses his love for her. After Miles grants them permission to wed, he appoints Elena executive officer of the Dendarii Free Mercenary Fleet.

She saves Miles's life twice during the Hegen Hub conflict, once after Admiral Oser orders him spaced, and again when Stanis Metzov first tries to kill him. She captures Cavilo and her squad after they are separated from Gregor on the *Ariel*. During the prisoner rescue at Dagoola IV, she infiltrates the Cetagandan forces, posing as part of the prisoner observation teams. After the Marilac mission, Miles sends her to Tau Ceti's Barrayaran Embassy to find out what happened to the overdue payment. She brings Commodore Destang back along with the Dendarii's money.

Elena becomes the commanding officer of the *Peregrine*, and after Miles is killed, she takes charge of getting Mark to Barrayar. At first she despises Mark, blaming him for getting Miles killed, but after coming to understand and accept him, she becomes sworn to him as an armswoman to rescue Miles. On Barrayar, Elena burns a death-offering for her father, and when the Dendarii escort the Duronas to Escobar, she visits with her mother as well.

Along with Baz, she resigns from the Dendarii to start a family and pursue a more peaceful career. She asks to be released from her oath as liege-sworn vassal to Miles, which he grants. She returns to Barrayar to attend Miles's wedding and have his parents meet her first child, a daughter she named Cordelia. (B, BA, BI, M, MD, SH, VG, WA, WG)

Boy:
No name given. About ten years old, he brings Kly's horse back to where Cordelia, Gregor, and Bothari are hiding in the Dendarii Mountains during Vordarian's coup attempt. Kly tells Cordelia that Vordarian's men

used fast-penta on the boy for interrogation, but all he knew was that the mailman needed his horse. (B)

Brain transplant:
A risky, illegal operation performed by House Bharaputra on Jackson's Whole, in which an elderly person's brain is transplanted into a new, cloned body, enabling them to double or triple their life span. (L, MD)

Breath mask:
A portable breathing unit enabling a person to survive in an atmosphere that lacks oxygen, it contains enough air to last fourteen to sixteen hours. Everyone who travels to Komarr is required to view breath-mask video training. Etienne Vorsoisson dies when he fails to check his mask before taking Miles to the experiment station outside the Serifosa Dome on Komarr. (K)

Brillberries:
A seedy, red berry that grows on Barrayar, occasionally on vines that overhang ravines. Harra had gone to pick brillberries the day her baby was killed. (MM)

Brother's War:
A historical event mentioned by Doctor Yei when comparing the different emphases in the quaddies' education to Leo Graf. (FF)

Brownell:
No first name given. A female security officer on Beta Colony who tries to arrest Arde Mayhew before Miles's intervention. (WA)

Brun:
No first name given. A captain in the Barrayaran
military, he is the Fleet Security Commander on the
*Prince Xav*. A lean, tense man, he was in charge of
the patrol that shot up the police precinct on Graf
Station. He is prejudiced against Komarrans, and thinks
Lieutenant Solian deserted his post. (DI)

Bubble-car:
A public transportation system on Komarr. Bubble-cars
are like individual monorail cars that travel along a
tube-track to their destination. Recently the system
has been suffering more traffic jams on certain routes,
leading to disagreement in the government over various
solutions. Miles and Ekaterin take one of the cars on
their shopping trip to the Shuttleport Locks district
in the Serifosa Dome. (K)

Buffa:
No first name given. One of Aral Vorkosigan's faithful
lieutenants in the Barrayaran military, he oversees the
interrogation of Dubauer before Aral stops it. (SH)

Bug butter:
The digested and processed substance regurgitated by
the butter bugs after they have eaten raw vegetable
matter. It is white and curd-like, bland without adding
additional flavors or spices, but rich in nutrients and
vitamins, and able to be stored at room temperature.
Ma Kosti and Kareen Koudelka use it as ingredients
in several dishes at Miles's dinner party without his
knowledge, creating ice cream and a garlic spread.

Their first hit creation is maple ambrosia, created by blending the butter with maple mead from the Dendarii Mountains, which they serve at the Emperor's wedding reception. (CC)

Burton, Kara:
A Betan doctor, she is the co-author of the article "On an Improvement in Permeability of Exchange Membranes in the Uterine Replicator," in the issue of *The Betan Journal of Reproductive Medicine* read by Ethan Urquhart. (EA)

Butter bug:
A hideous-looking, bioengineered insect with six legs, a dull-brown carapace, vestigal wings, and a large, pale white abdomen. They have a hive mentality, with a queen that is attended by sterile workers. They eat vegetation, digesting it in their abdomens using special microbes, then regurgitate an edible substance called bug butter. They are reengineered to be more attractive and appealing by Ekaterin Vorsoisson, Mark Vorkosigan, Enrique Borgos, and Kareen Koudelka. (CC)

Butter bug queen:
The reproductive center of a butter bug hive, the queen is much larger than the workers, and can grow larger than a man's hand. Sterile until given the proper hormones, but until she has started reproducing, a queen is fast and agile, as proven by the one that escapes the laboratory in Vorkosigan House, which is eventually caught by Armsman Jankowski's daughter. (CC)

• • C • •

C6-WG:
The shuttle that was supposed to take Miles to Aslund, but instead puts him in a space pod and ejects him near the *Ariel*. (VG)

Calhoun, Tav:
The man bidding against Arde Mayhew for the *RG 132*, he is a heavy man in a green sarong. Although he wins the auction for the freighter, he accepts Miles's offer of a promissory note against some of his land holdings on Barrayar, not knowing the acreage is radioactive. When Miles returns to pay off the note, Calhoun becomes violent, having learned of the worthless land and having been shadowed by Barrayaran security agents. He tries to have Miles arrested, but is subdued by Elli Quinn. Miles ties him up and locks him in a storage closet, with the complete payment in his pocket. (WA)

Canaba, Hugh:
A doctor and geneticist, he has tan skin, brown eyes, racially indeterminate features, and short, wavy hair graying at the temples. He is to be picked up by Miles and the Dendarii at Jackson's Whole and taken to Barrayar. An arrogant genius, he also has several genetic samples that must be retrieved before he will leave, forcing Miles to infiltrate House Ryoval's laboratories and rescue Taura in the process.

After his rescue, Hugh has a new identity as Vaughn Weddell, and a new life on his adopted planet, where he works in a laboratory at the Imperial Science Institute. He helps diagnose how Simon's memory chip was contaminated, reconstructing the prokaryote organism and also creating the chelation solution to detect its vector encapsulation, enabling the capture of Lucas Haroche. (L, M)

Cappell:
No first name given. The resident mathematician at the Serifosa Dome Waste Heat Management department on Komarr, he is one of Radovas's coworkers that Miles interviews during his investigation. Involved in the jump-point plot, he is in unrequited love with Marie Trogir. When the engineers vote on whether to try to use their hostages to bargain for escape at the jump station or surrender, he votes to keep going, not wanting Marie to have died for nothing. (K)

Captain:
No name given. Simon Illyan's secretary at Imperial Security headquarters during the investigation into his breakdown, he has been there for two years. (M)

Caravanserai:
A very poor and dangerous area of the Vorbarr Sultana on Barrayar, where Bothari lived as a child. When Cordelia arrives on the planet, it is considered a red-light entertainment area. No electricity grid, no comms, no better than slums. Bothari and Koudelka go there one evening to find female companionship, and end up getting into a brawl which leaves Koudelka severely injured. Later, Cordelia, Droushnakova, Bothari, and Koudelka hide out in the area while preparing to

infiltrate the Imperial Residence to find Miles. They also locate Padma and Alys Vorpatril here, and attempt to rescue them as well, but Padma is killed during the improvised operation.

Almost three decades later, when Mark Vorkosigan first visits Barrayar, the area is going through gentrification, and has been greatly improved, although it is still rough in spots. Mark has to fend off local bullies that assault him, almost killing one. A plaque has been placed to mark the exact spot where Padma was killed. (B, MD)

Cavilo:
No first name given. The commander of Randall's Rangers after she had the former leader killed, she is short, attractive, and intense-looking, with close-cropped white-blond hair, elfin-like features, and blue eyes. A sociopath, her only true interest in is herself, and she is adept at using intrigue and seduction to get what she wants.

She first encounters Miles as the arms buyer Livia Nu while he is in his Victor Rotha disguise, and tries to seduce him. She has Sydney Liga, Miles's first contact, killed, and the crime pinned on Rotha. She is working with Stanis Metzov when Miles is recaptured trying to get to Vervain, which has hired the Rangers to protect the planet, unaware that she plans to let the Cetagandans through the wormhole, leaving her to loot Vervain in the confusion afterward.

When Gregor falls into her hands, she tries to seduce and marry him, but is foiled and captured. During the battle with the Cetagandan invasion fleet, she escapes and is raped by Metzov, whom she later

kills while he tries to strangle Miles. Holding Miles
to his promise of safe passage out of the sector, she
accepts a medal of valor on behalf of her ruined
mercenary company, and flees the area. (VG)

Cay, Daryl:
A doctor and the former head of the Cay Project at
Rodeo, he was several years past retirement age, but
was still working when he passed away. (FF)

Cay Project Habitat:
A modular orbital habitat above Rodeo with approximately 1,500 personnel, 494 rotating personnel, and
1,000 permanent inhabitants. Owned by GalacTech,
it can be completely self-sustaining, with hydroponic
gardens and full living facilities. When Leo Graf is
sent there to train quaddies in industrial welding,
he ends up leading a revolution, and the quaddies
disassemble the entire station and jump it through a
wormhole to freedom. (FF)

Cecil:
No first name given. A major in charge of determining
the assignments of Barrayaran Imperial Service recruits.
About fifty years old, he is an excellent teacher and
scholar, lean, even-tempered, and watchful, with a
rare, dry wit. Miles discusses his meteorological officer
assignment with him, and learns it is a test to see
if he is capable of serving on the *Prince Serg*. (VG)

Cee, Terrence:
The man sought by Colonel Millisor and Captain Rau
on Kline Station. Blond-haired, blue-eyed, and in

his early twenties. His official designation is L-X-10 Terran-C. The result of a Cetagandan experiment, he was genetically engineered to possess mental telepathy, and was to be used for covert government work. He tried to escape Cetaganda, along with other telepaths, including his lover Janine and four children, and Doctor Jahar, the founder of the project, but only he survived the attempt. He has kept samples of Janine's tissues, and is trying to raise money to remake her at Jackson's Whole. He spliced his genetic material, including the recessive gene that carries the telepathic ability, into the ovarian cultures that were supposed to be shipped to Athos.

After Millisor is killed, Terrence comes to Athos to be alternate parent to Ethan's children that he intends to father by the EQ-1 line, and earn enough parent credits himself to father his own offspring by Janine's ovarian material. During his first trip to the Cetagandan Empire, Miles overhears Millisor getting permission to pursue Terrence, and sends Elli Quinn to Kline Station to investigate. Doctor Hugh Canaba has a sample of Terrence's genetic material, including his telepathy complex. It is one of the samples that Miles has to get out of Taura on Jackson's Whole. (C, EA, L)

Celestial Garden:
The Imperial residence on Cetaganda, called Xanadu by the galactics. It is covered in a six-kilometer-wide force dome, surrounded by a kilometer-wide park, then a circular street, then another park, then an ordinary street, with eight boulevards radiating outward like wheel spokes, putting the garden right in the center of the city. There are more gardens inside, with white-jade

paved paths for vehicles and guests. Pavilions are scattered throughout the grounds, with simple, tasteful furnishings, including live plants, flowers, and small fountains. The connecting halls are acoustically designed to be hushed overall, yet also carry occupants' voices clearly to each other. In the middle of the dome area are several elaborate towers. Its servants dress in gray and white. Miles, Ivan, and Vorob'yev attend several functions there during the Empress's funeral ceremonies, including the presenting of funeral gifts and the viewing of the body in state, where Miles sees the dead Ba Lura behind the display bier. (C)

Celestial Lady:
An alternate title for the Cetagandan Empress, used mainly by servants. (C)

Celestial Master:
An alternate title for the Cetagandan Emperor, used mainly by servants. (C)

Cenotaph:
A monument honoring the dead who are destroyed or buried elsewhere, often used to commemorate war deaths. Ky Tung suggests they will use one to remember him when he is pulverized to dust fighting the Cetagandans at Vervain. (VG)

Cetagandan Empire:
The Cetagandan Empire consists of eight developed planets, and an equal fringe of allied and puppet dependencies; its homeworld is Eta Ceta IV, with several other planets considered satrapies, which are

ruled by governors. Cetagandans use face paint to denote their rank and clan, which is falling out of favor with the younger generations. They apparently have high artistic tastes, but consider biological childbirth distasteful. They have a complicated system of power involving the ghem and haut castes. The ghem and haut are biological engineers without peer, as evidenced by the otherworldly beauty of their women, but the haut only work in human genetics. Exceptional scientist/artists of the ghem caste are rewarded for their genengineering efforts by having their creations incorporated into the Celestial Garden.

During Piotr Vorkosigan's time, Cetaganda invaded Barrayar, and spent twenty years trying to subjugate the planet. Wanting to control a jump point to the Hegan Hub by conquering Vervain, they suborned Vervain's mercenary hireling Cavilo, who was going to let them in and plunder the planet during the invasion. Held off by the Dendarii and Vervani defense ships, and defeated by the arrival of the *Prince Serg*, they retreat back to their home space.

During his first visit to Eta Ceta IV, Miles stops a plot to create a war between Barrayar and Cetaganda, and saves the Empire from being taken over by Governor Ilsum Kety, who is holding a copy of the haut gene-bank hostage. He visits the Empire again after being infected with deadly parasites by the renegade ba that had stolen a haut-lord gene bank. (BI, C, DI, VG)

Cetagandan ghem-warriors:
Two dozen mercenaries from that planet are recruited by Bel Thorne, Baz Jesek, and Arde Mayhew for the Dendarii Free Mercenary Fleet. Desperate to get off

Tau Verde IV after their contract fell apart, they agree to put aside their differences with any Barrayarans for the duration of the trip. (WA)

Chalopin:
No first name given. The shuttleport administrator on Rodeo, she is well dressed with a swept-back hairstyle. She is displeased about the security incident with Claire and Tony and the additional scrutiny it brings from Vice President Apmad. (FF)

Charles:
No surname given. Chalmys DuBauer's servant. (DD)

Chaste Brotherhoods:
An organization on Athos that abstains from sexual activity of any kind. Ethan Urquhart doubts that his brother Janos will think Terrence Cee is a candidate for membership. (EA)

Chenko:
No first name given. A colonel in the Barrayaran military, he is a neurologist assigned to treat Miles's seizures. A fit and energetic middle-aged man, he and Doctor D'Guise come up with the diagnosis and treatment, although not a cure, to Miles's condition. (M)

Chilian:
No first name given. A ghem-general to Governor Ilsum Kety. His wife is Vio d'Chilian. Chilian is not involved in Kety's plot to take the throne, although his wife is. She and her lover Kety had planned to kill him at their first opportunity. (C)

Chodak, Clive:
A sergeant in the Dendarii Free Mercenary Fleet, he has black, almond-shaped eyes, dark skin, and a square jaw. During Miles's first mercenary run he is a corporal and one of Ky Tung's commandos, and was promoted to his current rank with the renamed Dendarii/Oseran mercenaries. Recognizing Miles on Pol Station Six, he meets with him privately to fill him in on what has happened during the four years he has been away. Under orders from Elena, he saves Miles and Gregor from being spaced by Admiral Oser. For his actions during the battle against the Cetagandans at Vervain, he is taken on a personal tour of the *Prince Serg*, followed by lunch with Aral Vorkosigan. (VG)

Christof:
No first name given. A lieutenant in the Dendarii Free Mercenary Fleet who is excellent at scouting terrain. (BA)

Civilian Defenders of Garson Transfer Station:
Captured Marilacan civilians held in the prisoner camp on Dagoola IV until being rescued by Miles and the Dendarii Free Mercenary Fleet. (BI)

Claire:
No surname given. A quaddie on the Cay Habitat Station, she is slim and elfin-looking, with short, dark hair that frames her face. She has had a baby, Andy, with another quaddie named Tony, and is the first of five quaddie girls to give birth. She was a welder joiner, but was transferred to housekeeping–nutrition tech and hydroponics since giving birth. When she

is told she will not be able to stay in a monogamous relationship with Tony, they both try to escape the Habitat with Andy, resulting in Tony's injury, and Claire being separated from them. When Doctor Curry tries to sedate and sterilize her, she overpowers him and injects him with the sedative instead. She pretends to consider sterilizing him, but leaves him intact. She escapes with Leo and the rest of the quaddies through the wormhole. (FF)

Climbing rose:
A bioengineered, ambulatory rose bush that uses its vines to climb stationary objects, as Ivan finds out at the bioestheties exhibit on Cetaganda. (C)

Clogston, Chris:
A captain in the Barrayaran military, he is the senior fleet surgeon for the military escort of the Komarran trade convoy detained at Graf Station. He confirms that Ker Dubauer is a Cetagandan by analyzing his blood, and also jury-rigs a blood filter to remove the bioengineered parasites from Bel Thorne and Miles, although he eventually has to put both of them into cold stasis to prevent the parasites from killing them. (DI)

Clone:
A perfect copy of a person can be created from the smallest tissue sample of the progenitor, creating an exact physical duplicate. On Jackson's Whole, House Bharaputra runs a thriving business providing cloned bodies for rich, elderly people, who then have their brains transplanted into the new body. The clone created to replace Miles, later named Mark, had to be surgically

altered to resemble his progenitor, as the damage done to Miles's body was teratogenic, which meant a clone of him would have developed to its normal height, and with normal bone strength. (L, BA, MD)

Clone crèche:
A facility owned and run by House Bharaputra on Jackson's Whole where clones are created and raised until they are the proper age for a brain transplant. Mark commandeers the *Ariel* to raid this facility, which also created him, and rescue the fifty clone children there from becoming new bodies for rich clients. He is trapped on the site, and has to be rescued by Miles and the Dendarii, inadvertently causing Miles's death during the operation. (MD)

Cloned organs/tissues:
Replacements for worn or injured organs and tissues may be grown from samples taken from the individual that needs them, assuring rejection-free transplants. It takes an undefined amount of time to grow a cloned organ, and the patient may need artificial life-support or, in extreme cases, cryofreezing to survive until the replacement organ is ready. (All)

Clubhouse:
A hidden meeting area on Cay Habitat created by the quaddies, where they watch forbidden vid dramas and read nonregulation book-discs. (FF)

Collins:
No first name given. A sergeant in the Dendarii Mercenaries, he serves under Bel Thorne and is

killed by Stanis Metzov while escorting Miles to the *Triumph*. (VG)

Comconsole:
A multipurpose communication device that provides telephone/videophone communication, as well as data entry, retrieval, transmission, and storage. Consoles range from low-cost versions to high-end commercial models to secured military versions, each with appropriate degrees of security. Comconsoles also provide access to worldwide sources of information, transfer of documents, and delivery of electronic mail in both printed and video-recording modes. They are able to read and create data cubes or chips, and many also contain a printer allowing the user to make hard copies of documents on flimsies. Programs may be run on the consoles, including image manipulation, computer-assisted design, or entertainment such as designing and viewing a virtual garden. (All)

Comm link:
A small, personal communication device designed to be worn on the wrist or carried in a pocket. Capable of audio transmissions only, one is often keyed to a matching unit as a secured pair. The range varies from a few kilometers to more powerful models capable of surface-to-orbit transmission. With some units, users verbally request the contact number of the person they wish to reach, and calls are readily transferred and can be made into conference calls among multiple participants. (All)

*Commodore Vorhalas*:
An Imperial Cruiser that one of Miles's classmates gets assigned to as a junior weaponry officer. (VG)

Communication:
There is no faster-than-light communication. Communication within a solar system travels by light-speed signal. Interstellar communication must be carried by a ship through a wormhole, either as a physical object or recorded message. The message is then either physically carried by ship to the next jump point or transmitted at light-speed across the system. In high-traffic areas, jump ships may be maintained at jump points to accumulate signals and, at appropriate intervals, jump through the wormhole, then beam or ship the messages to the next jump point. (All)

Constellation:
Cetagandan term for family or clan. (C)

Contingency Blue:
The full retreat orders Aral issues to the Barrayaran fleet after Prince Serg Vorbarra is killed during the war with Escobar. (SH)

Corbeau, Dmitri:
An ensign and jump pilot in the Barrayaran military, he is tall, with an olive complexion, dark hair, and dark eyes. He is at the center of the initial incident that caused the lockdown of the Komarran fleet at Graf Station. Having fallen in love with a quaddie dancer named Garnet Five, he risks a charge of desertion by asking for

asylum there. He is a Sergyaran worm plague survivor, as his parents emigrated there when he was five years old. He volunteers to pilot the *Idris* out of the Union of Free Habitats space, and sends information about Dubauer back to the quaddies on Graf Station. After Corbeau risks his life to stop the renegade Ba, Miles assigns him as the permanent Barrayaran diplomatic consulate officer at Graf Station. (DI)

Couer:
No first name given. A commodore in the Barrayaran military, he is on Aral's second ship during the war with Escobar. (SH)

Council of Counts:
A ruling party on Barrayar similar to a parliament, they are part of the military aristocracy, and wear scarlet and silver robes while in session. With one representative for each District, they have certain gubernatorial powers, such as voting the approval of new counts, or electing a regent. They vote to confirm Aral as Regent of Barrayar. Miles is brought up on charges in front of them more than once, facing a treason charge after he forms the Dendarii Free Mercenary Fleet, and also before Gregor's wedding, when a group of right-wing counts, spearheaded by Lord Richars, tries to charge him with the murder of Etienne Vorsoisson. All charges are dismissed in both cases. (B, CC, SH, WA)

Council of Ministers:
Part of the joint council session convened to confirm Aral Vorkosigan's appointment as Regent of Barrayar.

The ministers wear robes of black and purple with gold chains of office while in session. (B)

Count:
A hereditary title on Barrayar. Counts serve as a combination of ruler and governor of a district, settling disputes among the citizens and representing their district in the Council of Counts. The title was shortened from the word "accountant," as the first "counts" were created by Varadar Tau, an accomplished bandit, to collect taxes during the Time of Isolation. (All except FF)

Crème de meth:
A thick, sweet, green liquor, roughly 60% pure ethanol, that makes the drinker relaxed yet incredibly alert, and also gives a unique sense of confidence and well-being. Miles first tries it at Beta Colony with Arde Mayhew, who had been using it to stay awake for three days. He describes the taste as a cross between horse piss and honey. It also kills hunger and clears the sinuses, but the hangover afterward is terrible, as Miles discovers later. (WA)

Crew, Rosalie:
A wine shop clerk in London who sues Admiral Naismith for a half million credits after she was terrorized and her shop accidentally burned down by three of the Dendarii Free Mercenaries when their credit was denied. When Mark asks about the lawsuit, Miles suggests countersuing for medical damages, as he threw his back out rescuing her. (BA)

"Crossing, The":
A zero-gee ballet about the quaddies' flight to freedom, composed by Aljean, that is performed on Graf
Station while Miles and Ekaterin are there. Normally
Garnet Five dances the part of Silver, but with her
broken arm, she is resigned to watching her under-
study perform the role. (DI)

Croye:
No first name given. A lieutenant in the Barrayaran
Embassy Security on Beta Colony, he is one of the
security detail assigned to watch over Miles, who fears
if Croye finds out he met with Baz Jesek, he'll deport
the deserter back to Barrayar for a swift court-martial
and execution. (WA)

Cryo-chamber:
A portable, emergency medical unit used to preserve
the recently deceased in cryo-stasis for later resuscitation. It enables a medical technician to drain the blood
from a body, replacing it with cryogenic preservation
fluid. Miles is placed in one when he is killed during
the evacuation from the Bharaputra clone facility on
Jackson's Whole. (BA)

Cryo-stasis:
Also known as cryo-freezing, it is a process used to
save victims of severe injury, including death. The
patient's body is drained of all blood, replacing it
with a special cryogenic fluid that preserves tissues
at a low temperature. The body is then placed in a
cryo-chamber and frozen for later revival at a cryo-

revival center. These centers clone tissues and grow needed replacement parts, then transplant them into the person before revival.

The quality of preparation, blood draining, and replacement with cryo-fluid is critical. If the preparation is done by a good medical facility, the chance for successful revival is excellent, though not guaranteed. Major trauma, such as damage suffered in combat and poor or hasty preparation of the body, can let ice crystals form in the tissues during the freezing process, causing varying levels of damage. Excess tissue damage may prevent revival or cause permanent impairment. Tissue damage in the brain can be replaced by cloned neural tissues, but memories, skills, and personality are lost. This may give the resurrected person a range of damage from severe mental disability through loss of personality or skills to varying minor degrees of memory loss. Many cryo patients suffer temporary memory loss due to the procedure. The memory may return slowly or there can be a memory cascade as the associative linkages are recovered.

Cryo-freezing is a last-resort procedure. If the patient can be maintained adequately while replacement organs or tissues are grown, then cryofreezing is avoided. Miles undergoes cryo-stasis after being killed by a needler grenade, and has his heart, lungs, and stomach replaced in the Durona Clinic on Jackson's Whole. (BA, MD)

Crystal Springs:
An area on Athos where Brother Haas lives in a farmer's commune. (EA)

Csurik, Bella:
One of Lem's sisters, she is about to get married.
Lem had promised to haul wood for her new cabin
on the day Raina was killed. (MM)

Csurik, Dono:
One of Lem's younger brothers, he tried to set Miles's
tent on fire after the village celebration, thinking he
was in it. After Miles elicits his confession, he leaves
the boy's punishment up to the family, even though
the attack could have been construed as an assault
on the count himself, and therefore treasonous. (MM)

Csurik, Harra:
A tall, lean, blond hill girl with gray eyes, not unat-
tractive, but also not a beauty. She gave birth to a
daughter, Raina, with a harelip, who was killed four
days later. She accuses her husband of killing the child
and walks for four days to Vorkosigan Surleau to seek
justice. Her father died in the service as District Militia
during the Vordarian Pretendership, and her mother
is her only living relative. Once Miles establishes that
Harra's mother, Mara Mattulich, killed Raina, he assigns
all of her legal rights to Harra, then sends her off
to the Hassadar Teacher's College, ensuring a better
future for the children of Silvy Vale.

When he visits the village ten years later, she is
a teacher at the Silvy Vale school, which is named
for her daughter. She moved Raina's grave when
the valley the town was located in was going to be
flooded for the hydroelectric dam, but left her mother's
grave where it was. Her husband Lem and she have
a four-year-old boy and a one-year-old girl. During

his visit, she advises Miles on how to continue living after enduring what others might think is unendurable shame. (M, MM)

Csurik, Lem:
Harra Csurik's husband, whom she accuses of infanticide. When Miles first meets him, he is twenty years old, a carpenter, and has four brothers and three sisters. He is almost certain it was Mara Mattulich who killed Raina, but does not want to accuse her. Miles interrogates him under fast-penta and confirms his innocence. Afterward, he suggests that Lem go with Harra to Hassadar to gain more experience in carpentry. When Miles visits the village ten years later, he has become Speaker of the Vale. (M, MM)

Csurik, Ma:
No first name given. Lem's mother, she is about fifty years old, little, lean, and work-worn. She has five sons and three daughters. She protests Lem's innocence when she meets Miles at the village celebration. (MM)

Csurik, Raina:
Harra and Lem Csurik's newborn daughter, she was killed by her grandmother, Mara Mattulich, when she was four days old. Her grave was moved, along with the rest of Silvy Vale, before the valley was dammed to create hydroelectric power. The village's two-room school is named after her. (M, MM)

Cultured Furs:
A division of GalacTech Bioengineering, a store where Miles purchased a live fur blanket for Elli. (BA)

Curry:
No first name given. A doctor who works under Doctor Minchenko at the Cay Habitat. He gave Claire drugs to dry up her breast milk and did not inform Minchenko about it. Claire overpowers him when he tries to sterilize her, leaving him sedated and tied up under the sterilization shield. (FF)

•   •   ◨   •   •

D-620 Superjumper:
A large cargo transport ship. When empty it resembles a mutant, mechanical squid. The control room and crew quarters are contained in a pod at the front, with four long, braced arms trailing behind. Two of the arms are normal space thrusters, and the other two are the Necklin field generators. In between the arms is the large space for cargo pods. Leo Graf and the quaddies use a D-620 to escape from GalacTech. Two centuries later, Ekaterin buys Nikolai a model of the ship at Graf Station. (DI, FF)

Daccuto scam:
A shady business deal Mrs. Bianca refers to in which her husband was involved. (DD)

Dag:
No surname given. One of Brother Haas's fellow commune members who chided him for growing his parent beard early. (EA)

Dagger:
A weapon Miles brought to Beta Colony as a memento of his grandfather Piotr. It is a priceless antique on Barrayar, with an unusual watermark on the blade, the Vorkosigan seal inlaid in cloisonné, gold, and jewels on the hilt, and a matching lizard-skin sheath. Almost stolen from Miles by Captain Auson. He recovers it, and uses it to help save Kostolitz and himself in a training simulation at the Imperial Academy. Mark takes it from him when they meet on Earth, but Miles recovers it again and later retires it to his room at Vorkosigan House. (MD, WA)

Dagoola IV Top Security Prison Camp #3:
A Cetagandan prison camp where Miles is interned as part of a mission assigned to the Dendarii Free Mercenary Fleet by Barrayar. It is essentially a holding area encircled by a large force shield that contains latrines and water taps, but nothing else. It has no guards or regulations, and contains 10,214 prisoners. The camp follows the Interstellar Judiciary Commission requirements, but just barely. Each prisoner is implanted with an identification chip that slowly dissolves if they escape the dome, releasing a poison that will kill them in about four hours. Sent to rescue one man, Miles has the Dendarii break in, and saves all but two hundred of the prisoners, most of them lost to a fighter attack that destroyed one of the transport shuttles. (BI)

Dalton Station:
A spaceport where Miles plans to drop off the short-contract personnel the Dendarii Free Mercenary Fleet hired from Tau Verde IV. (WA)

**Damnweed:**
A pest plant on Barrayar, which Miles sees in a new light in Ekaterin's pretty virtual garden, composed entirely of native flora. (K)

**Danio:**
No first name given. A private in the Dendarii Free Mercenary Fleet, he is one of the three arrested soldiers involved in the wine shop standoff in London. Mark bails him out of jail while posing as Miles/Admiral Naismith, and the real Miles thinks he may be useful in their assignment infiltrating a hostage-holding pirate group. (BA)

**Darkoi:**
A province on Barrayar. Its leader, Count Vorlakail, was killed under suspicious circumstances, prompting an investigation. The clerk at Siegling's tries to pass off an inferior swordstick, which he claims is Darkoi craftsmanship, to Cordelia. (B)

**Darla:**
A quaddie who hides video fiction for the group. (FF)

**Darobey:**
No first name given. A thin man, he is one of Radnov's spies in the communication section on the *General Vorkraft*. (SH)

**Data chip:**
A smaller version of the data cube. (All)

Data cube:
An electronic data storage device, similar to the modern flash drive. When the cube is inserted into the proper receptacle on a comconsole, all data contained on it is accessible to the user. It can be secured by encryption programs. (All)

Daum, Carle:
A major in the Felician army, he has dark, almond-shaped eyes, high cheekbones, bright copper hair in tight curls, and coffee-with-cream-colored skin. He hires Miles to smuggle weapons to Felice on Tau Verde IV, and accompanies him on the first run. He calls the Pelians "pelicans," and is killed during one of the ship-to-ship battles over the planet. (WA)

d'Chilian, Vio:
A Cetagandan haut-lady and General Chilian's wife, she has rich, dark chocolate hair, light cinnamon eyes, and vanilla-white skin. Miles and Ivan are invited to an exclusive haut garden party, where Vio is the first haut-lady Ivan sees. She is Ilsum Kety's lover, and is involved in the conspiracy to take the throne. She kills the Ba Lura to move the plan forward. When haut-consort Nadina goes to Kety's ship to order the gene-bank copy returned to the planet, she is captured, and Vio is sent down in her float-chair to impersonate her and capture Ivan. After the plan is foiled, her punishment is to either become a ba servant, which would allow her to live inside the Celestial Garden, as she had desperately wished—although not in the manner she had expected—or commit suicide. (C)

**Dea:**
No first name given. A lieutenant in the Barrayaran military, he is a surgeon, and the assistant to Prime Minister Aral Vorkosigan's personal doctor. He is frustrated because his superior won't let Dea touch their patient. Competent, if not overly imaginative, he performs the autopsy on Raina Csurik, declaring that she was killed by having her neck broken. He saves Fat Ninny by sewing up his neck wound, and also administers fast-penta to Lem Csurik and Mara Mattulich for their interrogations. (MM)

**Deal:**
The proper word for a standard business arrangement between two parties on Jackson's Whole. Of near-sacrosanct importance, it is the only thing that the barons hold mostly inviolate. (L, MD)

**Death-offering:**
A Barrayaran custom to burn an offering for the souls of the deceased; usually friends or relatives, sometimes for enemies so that they do not come back to haunt the offerer. Cordelia burns a lock of her hair at Princess Kareen's funeral. Miles burns a lock of his hair, a lock of Elena Visconti's hair, and a lock of Cordelia's hair for Bothari's death-offering. When Elena brings Mark to Barrayar, she burns a death-offering for her father as well. Miles also burns a death-offering for Piotr consisting of juniper bark, a copy of his officer's commission, and a copy of his three-year Imperial Academy transcripts. Harra Csurik burns one for her daughter as well. (BI, MM, SH, WA)

Deem:
A manager in the Sales and Demonstrations department of House Ryoval, he is a very beautiful, young,
albino man with blue eyes. He notifies Baron Ryoval
of a mauling accident involving Taura, and later speaks
with Miles about selling her before the baron interrupts the call. (L)

Deeva Tau love cults, variant practices of:
A method of lovemaking Miles invents, albeit in name
only, to daunt Mark from trying to sleep with Elli
Quinn while he's impersonating Miles. (BA)

Degtiar, Lisbet:
The late Cetagandan dowager empress, she was a
haut-lady, and the mother of Emperor Fletchir Giaja,
Also referred to as the Celestial Lady, she controlled
the Star Crèche, and with it the genetic heritage and
future of the Empire. Her death brings Miles and
Ivan to Cetaganda to pay their respects on behalf of
Barrayar. Fearing the stagnation of the Empire, her
plan to distribute the haut gene bank to the eight
haut-governors on the satrapy planets backfires into
a conspiracy to overthrow the sitting Emperor. (C)

Degtiar, Rian:
A haut-lady, she is the Servant of the Celestial Lady,
and Handmaiden of the Star Crèche. Essentially a
lady-in-waiting who is related to the late Empress,
three generations removed. She is exceedingly beautiful, with ebony hair, ice blue eyes, and ivory skin. She
contacts Miles to get the Great Key back, then works
with him to recover the real key and discover which

haut governor is behind the plot to take the throne. During the period of mourning for the deceased Empress, Rian acts with the Imperial authority of the Empress, as when she overrides Vio's force screen, something only the Empress could do. She gives Miles a braided lock of her hair to remember her by. During the Dowager Empress's cremation, she is named the next Empress of Cetaganda. (C)

Deleara:
An area on Athos that has a junior, unnamed representative on the Population Council. (EA)

Deleo, Marco:
A lieutenant in the Escobar military, he was twenty-nine years old when he was killed during the Barrayar-Escobar war. His body is recovered by Pilot Officer Ferrell and Medtech Boni. (SH)

Demmi:
No first name given. A pilot with the DFM, he suffered a head wound after the Dagoola IV operation, and gets his jumpset repaired while the Dendarii are on Earth. (BA)

D'Emorie:
No first name given. A Barrayaran major in the Imperial Security division on Komarr, he is in charge of the investigation at the Waste Heat experiment station. He supplies the fast-penta Miles uses to interrogate Doctor Riva. (K)

Dendarii dress uniform:
The standard Dendarii Free Mercenary Fleet dress uniform is a gray velvet tunic with silver buttons on the shoulders and white edging, matching gray trousers with white side piping, and synthasuede gray boots. (L)

Dendarii Free Mercenary Fleet:
The name of Miles's accidental mercenary group, which he came up with while getting a simple weapons-smuggling job to Tau Verde IV from Cârle Daum. During his first adventure as "Admiral Naismith," the outfit swells to three thousand personnel and a fleet of ships, thanks to his brilliant campaïgn to end the war on that planet. Miles is almost brought up on charges of treason for forming his own private army, but suggests that the Dendarii Mercenaries be given to the Emperor Gregor as a secret Imperial force, under titular command of Imperial Internal Security.

When he rejoins them four years later, the fleet has suffered some setbacks, reduced to a dozen ships with about five thousand personnel total. After Admiral Oser regained control in a financial reorganization, he changed the name back to the Oseran Mercenary Fleet, and contracted with Vervain to protect them against the Cetagandans, or anyone else trying to invade. The Dendarii hold off the Cetagandans long enough for the Barrayarans to come to their rescue. With Admiral Oser killed in action while trying to escape, Miles takes over as liaison officer in his Admiral Naismith persona as the Dendarii are secretly assigned as the Emperor's own fleet.

The Dendarii participate in the prisoner-of-war breakout on Dagoola IV, operations to help Marilac defend itself against a Cetagandan invasion, and a layover on Earth afterward, where they almost go broke while waiting to be paid. When Miles must choose between staying with the Dendarii or taking the Imperial Auditor position on Barrayar, he chooses to stay on his home planet, and makes Elli Quinn the admiral in charge of the Dendarii Free Mercenary Fleet. (BA, BI, VG, WA)

Dendarii Gorge:
A deep, narrow, winding gorge near Vorkosigan Surleau, where Aral wrecked his lightflyer after a bout of drinking. When Miles and Ivan were young men, they would challenge each other to tests of piloting skill, taking a lightflyer through it at reckless speeds. Miles finally won the contest once and for all by running the gorge at night with his eyes closed. (SH)

Dendarii Mountains:
A mountain range on the southern border of the Vorkosigans' District, it is inhabited by hardy hill people. The village of Silvy Vale is located here. During the Cetagandan occupation, Piotr Vorkosigan and his men fought a guerrilla war against the invaders, and were based in the mountains. During Vordarian's Pretendership, Cordelia, Gregor, and Bothari hide among the inhabitants while eluding Vordarian's security forces. (B, M, MM)

Department of Sergyaran Affairs:
A new department in Barrayaran Imperial Security, recently created by Simon Illyan at the Viceroy of Sergyar's request. (M)

Designated Alternate:
A term for the second, male parent in a family on the planet Athos. Like having a son, social duty credits are also needed to qualify for this position. D.A.s, as they are referred to, are known by their luxuriant mustaches, instead of a full beard of a father/primary caregiver. (EA)

Deslaurier:
No first name given. An ensign in the Barrayaran military, he is the acting fleet legal officer on the *Prince Xav*. Tall, pale, and wan, with a bit of acne still on his face, he is young to be in the position, but had to replace the senior officer who was sent home on bereavement leave when his mother died. (DI)

Desroches:
No first name given; his nickname is "Roachie." The Chief of Staff of the Sevarin District Reproduction Center, he has dark eyes and a black beard and mustache. A friend and colleague of Ethan Urquhart's, he creates the plan to send Ethan off-planet to acquire the needed ovarian cultures for Athos. (EA)

Destang:
No first name given. Stationed at the Barrayaran Embassy on Tau Ceti, he is a commodore, and the leader of Sector Two Security. About sixty years old, he is shorter than average for a Barrayaran, and lean, with gray hair. A young officer during the Cetagandan invasion, he was a middle-ranking officer during the Komarr revolt. He investigated the destruction of the Halomar Barracks, blown up by Komarran terrorists. Informed by Elena of the problems on Earth,

Destang, who had thought Miles missing for the past two months, arrests the compromised courier, and travels to Earth to restore order, including paying the Dendarii and terminating Ser Galen and Miles's clone if possible. In the end, he gives Miles his orders to take the Dendarii and handle the pirate-hostage incident in Sector IV. (BA)

**Deveraux:**
No first name given. One of the Oseran mercenaries killed in the battle at the ore refinery orbiting Tau Verde IV. (WA)

**D'Guise:**
No first name given. A captain and doctor in the Barrayaran military, he is a cryonicist assigned to treat Miles's seizure problem. Doctor Chenko and he come up with the diagnosis and treatment, and he wants to write up the case in the Imperial Military medical journal. (M)

**d'Har:**
No first name given. A Cetagandan haut-lady, older, with silver hair, she issues Miles and Ivan an invitation to an exclusive garden party, from where Miles is taken to confer with the eight haut-consorts to the satrapy governors about how to halt the plan to distribute the copies of the haut gene bank. (C)

**Diamant:**
No first name given. A general in the Barrayaran military, he was the Chief of Komarran Affairs before

Guy Allegre was promoted to the position. He died two years after his retirement. (M)

Diaz, Carlos:
A private inquiry agent in Rio de Janeiro, he has oily, black hair, an inadequate chin, and a smile like a shark. After losing his license, he is employed by Doctor Bianca of Portobello Pharmaceutical Company to commission a perverted feelie-dream composed by Anias Ruey, which he does, posing as Rudolph Kinney. After it is finished, he sabotages her dream synthesizer to kill her and keep the money he was supposed to pay her. He is lured out to Chalmys Dubauer's home, where Chalmys takes him out to the forest, finds out the true nature of his job, then turns him over to Sheriff Yoder. (DD)

Dimir:
No first name given. A captain in the Barrayaran military, he is Ivan's commanding officer, whom Ivan thinks works for Simon Illyan. He left Beta without Ivan on board, but did not show up at the refinery, as his jump ship was sabotaged, killing everyone aboard. Ivan hitched a ride with a Betan vessel to Tau Verde IV, where Miles figures out what happened to Captain Dimir and his ship. (WA)

District Agricultural Fair:
A large celebration and market show in Hassadar that Miles compares the Cetagandan bioestheties exhibition to, finding them completely different. (C)

Dom:
No surname given. A crewman on the courier run to
Athos, he is Elli's former schoolmate, and is surprised
at her new appearance when he sees her on Kline
Station. (EA)

Donnia:
No surname given. A friend of Sonia's, she brings news
of the coup to Cordelia and Bothari in the Dendarii
Mountains, telling them that Karla Hysopi was taken
by Vordarian's men. (B)

"Doreen's Gift":
Title of a contemporary, popular poem that Carlos Diaz
requests Anias make a feelie-dream of for his aunt so
that Anias will use her sabotaged dream synthesizer.
Anias considers it a saccharine piece of doggerel. (DD)

Dowager Empress:
The proper title for Lisbet Degtiar, Empress of Cetaganda. (C)

Downsider:
A slang term, sometimes derogatory, referring to
anyone born on a planet. (All)

Dream synthesizer:
A neat black box the size of an "antique book," it has
leads that go from the box to circular silver "dreamer
implants" in the user's head. It is used to compose
feelie-dreams, which are stored using a master cartridge.
Just like books, there are a wide range of dreams, from
children's stories to romance to pornography, and they

can be addicting. A diagnostic test kit comes with the set as a precaution against defects. They are not interchangeable without custom adjustments. Carlos Diaz sabotages Anias Ruey's synthesizer, then requests a feelie-dream from her, hoping that she will use it and inadvertently kill herself. Anias tests her synthesizer before using it, setting off the trap, and destroying it in the process. (DD)

Dress greens:
The standard Barrayaran military dress uniform is a forest-green tunic with a high collar, matching green trousers, and cavalry boots. (BA)

Droushnakovi:
No first name given. A sergeant in the Barrayaran army, he is Ludmilla Droushnakovi's father. He is shorter than his children. (B)

Droushnakovi, Ludmilla:
See Koudelka, Ludmilla Droushnakovi

Dubauer:
No first name given. An ensign and botanist with Betan Astronomical Survey, he has brown hair. Shot by Sergeant Bothari with a nerve disruptor, he survives the normally fatal injury, although it leaves him seriously mentally impaired, reduced to the intelligence of an infant, and unable to speak. Cordelia demands that he accompany Aral and her on their trek to the supply cache, and she gets him through the ordeal, although he is tortured by other Barrayaran soldiers during interrogation while in their custody. Repatriated

with the other prisoners of war, he is sent back to Beta Colony, where his mother cares for him. (SH)

DuBauer, Chalmys:
A retired spaceship captain, he is Anias Ruey's closest friend. He is a heavyset man, middle-aged and middle-tall, with sandy hair that's graying at the temples, penetrating gray eyes, and a round face. Made redundant because of wormhole travel technology, he is out of synch with the present time because of the decades of slower-than-light travel for Beta Colony, and his dislocation due to space/light-year travel synchronization. His family passed away long ago, and he has a child on Beta Colony who is now a great-grandmother. Financially comfortable, he lives in an old-fashioned house south of destroyed Cleveland with security gates, protective defenses, a summer house, and a small staff. Indifferent to current culture, he is well thought of in the area and on good terms with local law enforcement. He enjoys gardens, epicurean living, and reconditioning old technical equipment for museums. He interrogates Carlos Diaz to find out the real reason he hired Anias Ruey to create the disturbing feelie-dream. (DD)

Dubauer, Ker:
A Cetagandan Ba passing itself off as a Beta hermaphrodite, it is tall and elegant-looking, with silver hair, dark eyes, and a Betan earring signifying it is romantically attached and not looking. A passenger on the *Idris*, it has a cargo of uterine replicators that it claims are genetically engineered animals, but are really haut fetuses it has stolen from Cetaganda in order to create its own empire to rule over as both Emperor and Empress. It

kills Lieutenant Solian and kidnaps Bel Thorne, using it to gain access to the *Idris* after setting a biological bomb in the Madame Minchenko Memorial Hall to infect hundreds of quaddies as revenge for interfering with its mission. It is stopped by Miles when he recovers its case of genetic samples and destroys them. Taken back to the Cetagandan Empire, it is turned over to haut-lady Pel Navarr's custody, and shall remain a nameless prisoner for the rest of its life. (DI)

Durham:
No first name given. A lieutenant in the Dendarii Free Mercenary Fleet, he is the pilot of Combat Shuttle A-4, which was hit by enemy fire during the Marilac operation. Although mortally injured and in shock, he gets the shuttle back to the *Triumph* for evacuation before dying. Placed in cryo-stasis, he is resuscitated at Beauchene Life Center, suffering amnesia from the process, and also because his neural pilot implants were removed. He recovers from his injuries, although it takes at least a year of intense therapy. (MD)

Durona, Chrys:
Miles's physical therapist, her first name is short for chrysanthemum. A clone of Lilly Durona, she is approximately ten years older than Rowan, with wings of blunt-cut black hair shot with silver, and a more serious attitude. She pushes Miles hard on his physical therapy. (MD)

Durona, Hawk:
A male clone of Lilly Durona, he is about thirty years old, and guards Lilly. When Baron Ryoval's men break

into the Durona Clinic, he tries to stop them, but is stunned before he can do anything. (MD)

Durona, Lilly:
The lead doctor of the Durona group, she is a century old, with the same dark eyes and ivory skin as the rest of her cloned progeny. She was created on Jackson's Whole as a brilliant research doctor by the previous Baron Ryoval before he was killed by the present baron. She plotted her escape with Ryoval's half-brother, Georish Stauber, now Baron Fell, helping him rise to power. In return, he financed the Durona Research Group, which consists of thirty-six clones of Lilly, all trained in medicine. She revives Miles in the hope that he can help them escape Jackson's Whole, but Mark actually brokers the Deal enabling the Duronas to set up their clinic on Escobar. (MD)

Durona, Poppy:
A doctor at the Durona Research Group that works on Miles, she is ten years older than Chrys, with silver-streaked black hair pulled back in a ponytail. Miles evades her during his second escape attempt from the Durona clinic. (MD)

Durona, Raven:
A young man, exact age unspecified, lean with Eurasian features, who is a male clone of Lilly. He is studying to be a doctor, and serves as an intern at the Durona Clinic where Miles is undergoing rehabilitation. (MD)

Durona, Robin:
A slim, ten-year-old Eurasian boy, he is one of Lilly's

two cloned servants who help serve tea to guests. (MD)

Durona, Rose:
Lilly Durona's oldest daughter, and her first clone. Her short hair is almost pure white, and she walks with a carved wooden cane. She oversees the rest of the doctors at the Durona Research Group. (MD)

Durona, Rowan:
The doctor in charge of resuscitating Miles after his death on Jackson's Whole, she is a clone of Lilly Durona. She is Eurasian, tall and slim, with golden skin, black hair, brown eyes, and a coolly arched nose, and wears her hair pulled back in a bun. She falls in love with Miles during his revival and physical therapy, and tries to help him escape Baron Ryoval's men. However, she refuses Miles's order to crash the light-flyer to leave a sign before being captured by Baron Bharaputra's security men. She escapes Bharaputra's security by posing as the clone Lilly, and goes for help, but doesn't return in time to free Miles before he is taken to Ryoval's private laboratory. She decides that a long-term relationship with Miles is not to be, and goes with her clone sisters to Escobar. (MD)

Durona, Violet:
A slim, ten-year-old Eurasian girl, one of Lilly's two cloned servants who help serve tea to guests. (MD)

Durrance:
No first name given. He is the captain of shuttle flight B119 that Ti Gulik copilots. (FF)

Duvallier:
No first name given. A Barrayaran major executed for espionage during one of the riots in Solstice on Komarr. (VG)

Duvi:
No first name given. A sergeant in Barrayaran Imperial Security, he is Vorob'yev's aircar driver on Cetaganda, and drives a bit too adventurously for his superior's taste at times. (C)

Dyeb:
No first name given. A master sergeant in the Dendarii Free Mercenary Fleet, he is prejudiced about female recruits, thinking they're soft. Miles thinks enrolling Taura in his training course would change his mind rather quickly. (L)

• • E • •

Electron orbit randomizer:
An obsolete Beta Colony beam weapon. Miles encounters one during his Tau Verde IV campaign. The best defense against it is to rephase the mass shields, which Baz Jesek does as soon as he learns the Pelians still use them. (WA)

Emma:
No surname given. A pregnant quaddie scheduled to have her baby terminated, she hides in the Clubhouse instead. (FF)

Emperor's Birthday:
One of the highlights of the Barrayaran year, it is a time of feasting and celebration. It is also when all of the Counts renew their oath of fealty to the Emperor, and pay him a symbolic tax in the form of a small bag of gold. The Emperor's Birthday is also the beginning of a new fiscal year for Barrayar, the date of which changes every time a new Emperor takes the throne. Cordelia attends Gregor's first celebration, where Count Vordarian tells her of Aral's bisexual past. Mark presents his family's tithe to Gregor at the Emperor's Birthday celebration while on Barrayar, and also meets Kareen Koudelka during the celebration. (B, MD)

Enforcers:
A name Miles gives to a group of chosen men who keep order during the food drops at the prisoner camp on Dagoola IV once he begins organizing the inmates for the upcoming escape. (BI)

Environmental Impact Assessment form:
A bureaucratic form that George Bannerji insists must be completed before he fires on the Cay Habitat ship during the quaddies' escape. (FF)

Equinox:
One of Komarr's domed cities, known for its population of wild cockatoos. (K)

Escobar:
A rich trading planet located in a heavily populated star system, like Tau Ceti and Orient IV. Barrayar tries to conquer it using the survey planet (Sergyar) where Aral

and Cordelia met as a staging ground, as a wormhole was discovered near it that leads to Escobar, but they are defeated. The Duronas set up their clinic there after leaving Jackson's Whole. (FF, SH, MD)

Estanis:
No first name given. A deceased Cetagandan ghem-general, the official story claims he committed suicide after his Navy's defeat in the Vervain conflict. The rumor is that his "suicide" consisted of thirty-two stab wounds in the back. (C)

Estelle:
A high-end women's clothing store in Vorbarr Sultana for Vor ladies. Alys meets Taura and Roic there to outfit her for Miles's wedding. (WG)

Esterhazy:
No first name given. An armsman at Vorkosigan Sur-leau, he is forty years old, and in excellent physical condition. During Vordarian's coup, Piotr chooses him to assist in taking Gregor into hiding. He brings horses for Piotr, Cordelia, and Gregor to ride into the Dendarii Mountains, and also tells Cordelia that Karla Hysopi and Elena Bothari were taken by Vordarian's men. He has a four-year-old son. (B)

Eta Ceta IV:
The homeworld of the Cetagandan Empire. Miles and Ivan travel there to pay respects to the deceased Empress. Its cities are attractive and brightly lit, although Miles thinks they are gaudy when he first sees them. Its citizens' taxes are only half of Barrayar's,

but Miles's homeworld keeps up with their rival on a military basis with only a quarter of Eta Ceta IV's natural resources. (C, DI)

Euronews Network:
A vidnews network on Earth. Lise Vallerie is one of its reporters. Miles's daring rescue of the clerk from the burning wine shop, along with his interview as Admiral Naismith, is seen by Duv Galeni, getting him in trouble for going absent without leave from the Barrayaran Embassy. (BA)

Explosive ice-die forming:
A real-world technique used by Leo Graf and the quaddies to make a duplicate vortex mirror that matches an existing mirror. First, an ice mold is made by flowing water onto the good mirror in sub-zero refrigeration. Then a metal blank is explosively formed to the ice mold using explosives, which, in Leo's case, is improvised from gasoline. (FF)

• • F • •

Falcon 9 jump ship:
Nikolai owns a model of this fast courier vessel that Miles rode on during some of his Imperial Security missions. He discusses the ship with the boy during their first conversation. (K)

Fallow Core:
A high-tech fortress on Marilac, it was held against a Cetagandan siege by Colonel Guy Tremont and his

men until the base was betrayed to the enemy. The 14th Commandos, among others, were captured and imprisoned at the Dagoola prison camp. (BI)

Farr, Andro:
A good-looking Komarran, he approaches Ekaterin, whom he met at a Winterfair reception for Serifosa terraforming employees, to ask if she knows anything about his missing roommate Marie Trogir, who left all of her personal items and cats behind when she was killed in a test run of the wormhole closer. Ekaterin is unable to help him, and her Uncle Vorthys suggests he contact Security about the matter. (K)

Fast-penta:
A powerful truth drug that renders the subject unable to resist answering questions. Its effects include an overwhelmingly strong feeling of happiness and help-fulness, along with relaxing the body. A subject under fast-penta will answer questions literally, requiring skilled interrogation to elicit the desired information. To ensure security, some couriers, military operatives, and other personnel are given an induced allergy treatment so they will die from anaphylactic shock rather than reveal secret information. It is common to administer a test strip to the subject to determine if a natural or induced allergy exists before using the drug. If allowed, the subject will often babble extrane-ous information that can be embarrassing, as subjects normally remember the interrogation afterward. Some subjects also drool. Due to these embarrassing effects, most people dread being the subject of a fast-penta interrogation. Once the interrogation is complete, an

antidote is usually administered, which neutralizes its effects in a few minutes.

Although fast-penta has no truly harmful side effects, afterward many subjects experience a drug hangover, including headache, dizziness, and muddled thinking. Fast-penta interrogation is sufficiently reliable to be admissible in virtually all courts. A court order or voluntary cooperation is required in most jurisdictions. Miles has an unusual reaction to fast-penta, where he babbles a constant stream of useless information, and can even resist the drug's effects by reciting poetry or lines from a play. (All)

Fat Ninny:
The horse Miles rides to Silvy Vale, a thickset roan gelding that imprinted on him when they were both very young. Not wanting to embarrass himself, Miles decides to call him Chieftain if any of the villagers ask his name. Ninny almost is killed by Mara Mattulich after the celebration, suffering a deep neck cut that Doctor Dea treats. When Mark is on Barrayar, he feeds him sugar at Aral's request, to see if the animal is fooled into thinking he is Miles. The horse isn't fooled, only confused. (MD, MM)

Father Frost:
The mythological being that plays a role in the Winterfair festival on Barrayar, similar to Santa Claus. (MD)

Federstok:
A city on Barrayar where an extremely conservative Vor lord declared himself Emperor after Vidal Vordarian's death, but was defeated in less than thirty hours. (B)

Feelie-dreams:
A form of entertainment, a feelie-dream is a type of prerecorded video that can be played inside a user's mind through a cybernetic implant, in effect putting them into the dream story itself. It can also be used as a weapon, as Anias Ruey discovered hundreds of years earlier. Still manufactured during Miles's time, feelie-dreams are popular among the younger generation of Cetagandans, untitled artists, and the idle rich. (C)

Felice:
A nation on Tau Verde IV, currently at war with the Pelians. Miles's first cargo, weapons disguised as agricultural equipment, is supposed to be delivered there through the blockade. (WA)

Fell Station:
A space station orbiting Jackson's Whole, owned by House Fell. Miles and Bel attend a party there, where they meet Baron Fell, Baron Ryoval, and the quaddie musician Nicol. (L)

Ferrell, Falco:
A pilot officer on the Escobaran Personnel Retrieval and Identification ship, he helps Medtech Sylvia Boni recover bodies after the Barrayar-Escobar war. He thinks she is a deviant when she kisses a corpse good-bye, only to learn the body is that of her deceased daughter. (SH)

Fetaine:
An obsolete mutagenic poison invented as a terror weapon on Barrayar. Normal protective equipment is

not enough to handle it, as it has an incredibly high penetration value. It is the cause of the near-mutiny at Laskowski Base by the technicians when they refuse to clean up a spill of the toxin. (VG)

Firka:
No first name given. One of Russo Gupta's smuggler friends, he was the bookkeeper of the group, handling false passports, easing them around regulations, and taking care of nosy officials. He was killed by Ker Dubauer after transporting his cargo of stolen haut-fetuses. Gupta used his identity while on Graf Station to try to kill Dubauer. (DI)

Five, Garnet:
A quaddie on Graf Station, she is slim and long-limbed, with white-blond hair, leaf-green eyes, and high cheekbones. She is the quaddie Ensign Corbeau was with when he didn't respond to the crew summons from the Barrayaran escort. In the scuffle to retrieve him, her arm was broken, inflaming tensions between the quaddies, the Barrayarans, and the Komarrans. She is a premier dancer in the Minchenko Memorial Troupe that performs zero-gee ballet. She was with Bel Thorne when both of them were gassed unconscious by Russo Gupta, and awoke to find herself in a recycling bin. After the mystery is solved, Ekaterin calls her to help convince Ensign Corbeau to accept the diplomatic officer position on Graf Station. (DI)

Five-space math:
The complex higher math field that governs the science of wormhole jumps and technology. Miles has a

difficult time with his five-space navigation classes at the Imperial Academy, but he passes them. On Komarr, Barto Radovas was a five-space math engineer, as is Doctor Riva. (K, MM)

Flimsy:
The standard means of conveying a hard copy of written or printed documents, the flimsy is a paper-thin sheet of plastic on which text is printed. Most standard comconsoles have built-in printers to create hard copies of documents. (All)

Flipsider:
A derogatory term for a hermaphrodite. (VG)

Float chair:
A device quaddies use to move about more easily in gravity, it is a small, one-person anti-gravity pod. It doesn't have a place for feet, but handles on the floor where the quaddie rests its lower set of hands, with the controls mounted on a central column. (L, DI)

Force screen:
A generated field of pure energy, impenetrable to all physical attacks, and many energy-based ones. The technology behind it is not explained. They are used for defense of ships, buildings, and persons. A force screen can be conformed to the shape of a building or ship or be spherical. A home version may be powerful enough to kill even large insects, and when a larger life-form comes into contact with it, it envelops it in a golden glow. Vehicle-mounted versions provide shielding from debris and radiation for spaceships moving

at high velocity. Chalmys DuBauer traps Carlos Diaz outside of the screen surrounding his property to interrogate him about the feelie-dream he hired Anias Ruey to create. A kilometers-wide force screen over the Cetagandan Emperor's Celestial Gardens requires an entire power plant for its maintenance and provides both military and environmental protection. A spherical force screen over the Marilacan prisoner-of-war camp on Dagoola IV shows above ground as an opalescent dome. Personal defense screens are created by a wire mesh suit that protects against nerve disruptor and stunner attacks, and later a personal plasma mirror shield is created that protects against plasma arc blasts. (All except FF)

Fors, Bern:
A sergeant for GalacTech security. Sent out to recover a stolen shuttle on Rodeo, he and his partner are thwarted by Silver and Ivy Minchenko, who use the shuttle's engines to destroy their ground vehicle. (FF)

Foscol, Lena:
An accountant for the Waste Heat Department of the Komarr terraforming project at Serifosa, she is a middle-aged woman with frizzy, gray-blond hair. Involved in Soudha's scheme to destroy the wormhole to Barrayar, she embezzles the money from the terraforming budget to finance the jump-point plot. She is the one who informs Miles that help will be on the way after Etienne and he are chained outside, and calls Ekaterin to get them. She is noticably upset that Etienne died before help arrived. During the final standoff, she votes to continue the hostage situation,

wanting to use Ekaterin and Helen Vorthys to escape the standoff at the jump-point station. (K)

14th Commandos:
A captured Marilacan military unit held in the prison camp on Dagoola IV until being rescued by Miles and the Dendarii Free Mercenary Fleet. (BI)

4th Armored All-Terrain Rangers:
A captured Marilacan military unit held in the prison camp on Dagoola IV until being rescued by Miles and the Dendarii Free Mercenary Fleet. (BI)

Framingham:
No first name given. A sergeant of Blue Squad in the Dendarii Free Mercenary Fleet, he participates in the mission to rescue Mark and the other Dendarii at the clone facility on Jackson's Whole. (MD)

Franklin:
A representative from Barca on the Population Council, Ethan and Desroches discuss the possibility of sending him on the mission and the potential negative repercussions of it. (EA)

Frill:
A derogatory term for a woman used by Barrayans, implying that they are useless decoration. (B)

Frost IV:
A planet that lost its entire computer network system and records in a tectonic occurrence twenty-eight years earlier. Jackson's Whole, which sells complete

new identities, often uses it as an origin planet if the buyer fits the correct age range. (BA)

Fuzzy crabs:
Animals native to Sergyar that are the size of a pig, with too many hairy black legs, four beady, black eyes set in neckless heads, and razor-sharp yellow beaks. Aral and Cordelia fend off three of them while burying Reg Rosemont. (SH)

•  •  G  •  •

Galen, Rebecca:
One of the two hundred counselors killed in the Solstice Massacre. Her death caused Ser Galen to become a terrorist fighting against Barrayar. In a communiqué between Aral and Simon about Duv Galeni's suitability to join Barrayaran Imperial Security, Aral noted she was one of the few victims who faced her killers when she died. (BA)

Galen, Ser:
The father of Duv Galeni, he is a Komarran terrorist who is behind the plot to replace Miles with Mark, and have him sow chaos on Barrayar. He is about sixty years old, with blue eyes, gray hair, and a thick body, and appears to be an ordinary businessman or teacher. He travels under the name Van der Poole. His sister Rebecca was killed in the Solstice Massacre, and his eldest son died when a bomb Galen made went off prematurely.

Supposedly killed in that incident as well, Galen has

been living on Earth while training the clone Mark to impersonate Miles. He switches the two brothers, then gets Mark released from jail, kidnaps Ivan, and forces Miles and Duv to meet him at the Thames Tidal Barrier to eliminate Miles. Mark kills him with a nerve disruptor when Galen orders him to kill Miles. (BA)

Galeni, Duv:
A captain in Barrayar's Imperial Security, and the senior military attaché for the Barrayaran Embassy at London, Earth. He is also, by default, chief of Imperial Security there as well as Service Security. In his thirties, with dark hair, hooded, nutmeg-brown eyes, a hard, guarded mouth, and a Roman profile, he is an arresting-looking man with blunt, clean fingers. He was born David Galen of the Galen Orbital Transshipping Warehouse Cartel, once a very wealthy, powerful family. His aunt, Rebecca Galen, died in the Solstice Massacre. Duv's father, Ser, became an active member of the resistance, and was thought to have been killed, along with his oldest son, in an accident with one of his own bombs. Because of his Komarran heritage, he has worked very hard to earn his current position. Duv has a doctoral degree in Modern History and Political Science from the Imperial University at Vorbarr Sultana and at age twenty-six turned down a faculty position at the Belgravia College on Barrayar to go back to the Imperial Service Academy.

He is kidnapped by his father, Ser Galen, who tries to turn him against Barrayar and get him to work for Komarr's freedom. Initially prejudicial toward Miles because he is Aral's son, his attitude changes when the two are held prisoner together. During the events at the

Thames Tidal Barrier, Duv takes out two of the Cetagandans sent to kill Miles, and steals their groundcar to
get Miles, Ivan, Elli, Mark, and himself out of the area.

A few years later, he is posted in Vorbarr Sultana
and involved with Laisa Toscane, which goes awry
after Miles invites them to an Imperial State dinner,
where she meets Emperor Gregor. When Duv doesn't
move fast enough, Laisa falls for Gregor instead. Duv
thinks Miles arranged the whole thing, and insults
him, but later comes to his senses and apologizes.
He also lets Miles know when Simon first begins to
exhibit his memory problems. When Haroche can't
make his frame of Miles stick, he tries to frame Duv
instead, but Miles thwarts him, clearing Duv of all
charges. Duv gets over Laisa and falls in love with
Delia Koudelka.

During the preparations for Gregor's wedding, he
has been promoted to the rank of commodore, and is
the Chief of Komarran Affairs for Imperial Security.
He also advises Alys on aspects of Komarran tradition
and etiquette for the Emperor's wedding. He marries
Delia, and they both attend Miles's wedding. (BA,
CC, M, WG)

Gamad:
No first name given. A lieutenant in the Felician
Army, he disagrees with Elena's decision to release
the prisoners when the brig was hit by weapons fire
during a battle with the Pelians. He also informs
Miles that Major Daum was killed during that same
battle, and that he is the senior ranking Felician officer
until relief arrives. Miles finds him to be an irritating
glory-hound. (WA)

Gasoline:
Fuel still used to power land vehicles on more remote planets. When one hundred tons of it is accidentally shipped to the Cay Habitat instead of fuel rods, Leo Graf turns it to his advantage by using the gasoline as an explosive to create a new vortex mirror. (FF)

Gavin:
The head accountant for GalacTech's Operations Department, he appears to be a big, rumpled goon with a broken nose, but speaks precisely, with elegant elocution. During the hearing regarding the Rodeo spaceport security breach, he explains the operational relationship between the Habitat, Rodeo, and Orient IV to Leo. (FF)

Gelle:
No first name given. A Cetagandan ghem-lady, she is beautiful, tall, and elf-like, with blue eyes and blond-white hair that falls halfway to her knees. She talks briefly with Miles and Ivan when they first meet Lord Yenaro, who criticizes her choice of perfume with the outfit she's wearing, irritating her. (C)

General Accounting & Inventory Control:
A bureaucratic office of GalacTech that gives Bruce Van Atta the power to destroy the quaddies by recommending that all "post-fetal experimental tissue cultures" be destroyed by cremation as per IGS Standard Biolab rules. (FF)

Georgos:
No first name given. The Lord Guardian of the Speakers Circle of the Council of Counts, during Vordarian's

coup attempt, he is forced to read a public proclamation declaring Aral a traitor, and Vidal Vordarian the Prime Minister and acting Regent. (B)

Georos:
No surname given. The night shift team leader who works with Ethan at the Sevarin District Reproduction Center. (EA)

Gerould:
No first name given. A colonel in the Barrayaran military, he is a tall man in a black, dirty, wrinkled uniform, his face lined with exhaustion. During the Vordarian coup, he informs Aral that the fighting has gone to house-to-house in Marigrad. (B)

Ghem:
Similar to the Vor-class on Barrayar, they are the aristocratic, military elite of Cetaganda. Referred to as ghem-lords and ghem-ladies, they rank under the haut in social and political status. A ghem-lord can acquire a haut-lady as his wife, if given by the Emperor, an honor that cannot be refused. This is seen as the highest social and political reward by the ghem-lords, but is really a way of keeping them under control by the haut. A ghem-lord may have more than one wife, but the haut-wife automatically outranks the ghem-wife, with the haut heirs supplanting the ghem-lord's blood relations. (C)

Giaja, Fletchir:
The Emperor of the Cetagandan Empire. Tall, lean, and hawkish, with dark hair, he is seventy years old

when Miles first meets him. He ascended to the throne at age thirty, and has ruled ever since. After learning about the Dowager Empress's plan for the copies of the Star Crèche and the governors, he scolds Rian, Nadina, and Pel Navarr for their part in the plan, reiterating that there can be only one interface between the haut-women and the Empire—the Emperor himself. Otherwise unscrupulous people might seek to take advantage of the power afforded by the gene banks. He awards Miles the Cetagandan Order of Merit for his role in stopping the plot, and has him walk in the funeral procession at his left hand, as a pointed message to the other attendees. He also sends a message to Miles via Dag Benin at Gregor's wedding expressing his condolences on the death of Admiral Naismith. When Miles saves the Cetagandan fetal shipment from a renegade Ba at Graf Station, the Emperor sends a personal message of thanks, but no other reward. (C, CC, DI)

Giaja, Slyke:
A Cetagandan prince, he is a cousin of the Emperor. He is tall and hawkish, as are many of the Imperial haut. Rian Degtiar and Miles initially suspect him of being the traitorous governor, but Lord Yenaro clears him when he reveals that Governor Kety is behind the plot. (C)

Gibbs:
No first name given. A colonel in Barrayaran Imperial Security, he is the financial crimes analyst at Solstice, a spare, middle-aged man with graying hair and a meticulous manner. Miles summons him to Serifosa

to track the false accounting on the Waste Heat experiment station. He loves his job, and traces the embezzlement with delight. (K)

Goatbane:
A plant on Barrayar, which Miles sees in a new light in Ekaterin's virtual garden program, composed entirely of native flora. (K)

God the Father:
A religious term used by Athosians. (EA)

"God the Father, Light the Way":
A hymn on Athos that Ethan orders played in a uterine replicator chamber instead of a screechy dance tune. (EA)

Goff:
No first name given. One of the four hired thugs sent to castrate Lord Dono, he is captured by Ivan and Olivia, and is injured in the process. (CC)

Golden Voyage of Marat Galen:
A famous Komarran trade fleet that returned a hundredfold profit to its investors after its run. (K)

Gompf, Laurie:
Hazardous waste management officer on Rodeo. George Bannerji refers to her when he refuses to follow Bruce Van Atta's order to fire on the Habitat ship, saying he should have the proper "hazardous waste disposal" order signed by her first. (FF)

Gonzales, Helmut:
Rio de Janeiro's most successful feelie-dream distributor/marketer, he runs the Sweet Dreams Distributing Company. A large, booming man. Anias describes him as a soulless, inartistic Philistine, but good at his job. He presses her for the sequel to *Triad*, saying that all royalties from that feelie-dream will be applied to repaying the advance for the sequel until she delivers it. (DD)

Gorge:
One of the sub-personalities Mark creates to survive Baron Ryoval's torture, he comes out when Mark is being force-fed. (MD, CC)

Gottyan, Korabik:
An officer in the Barrayaran military, he is Aral's first officer aboard the *General Vorkraft*. Tall, with gray hair, he initially sides with the mutineers, but Aral persuades him to join his side after he returns to camp. He is battle-promoted to captain in the Escobar conflict, just before he is killed. (SH)

Gould, Philip:
The Beta Colony president's press secretary, he organized Cordelia's disastrous welcome home celebration. (SH)

Graf, Leo:
A welding engineer with an eighteen-year career with GalacTech, he teaches quality control procedures in free-fall welding and construction. In his midforties, he's a stickler for procedure and accuracy,

and discovered quality fraud on a previous project. Brought to the Cay Project to teach the quaddies welding techniques, when he learns the entire project is to be scrapped, and the quaddies dumped on Rodeo, he leads a plot to hijack the habitat and take it through the wormhole to freedom. (FF)

Graf Station:
Named after Leo Graf, the space station was originally founded on a small, metallic asteroid, and has been expanded for the past two centuries, including using parts of the original jump ship as construction material. Graf Station is part of a satellite of colonies located within the twin rings of an asteroid belt, collectively known as the Union of Free Habitats. Only Graf Station and a handful of other scattered habitats in the Union maintain gravity and deal with galactics. Along with its Graf Station security force, dressed in slate blue uniforms, it also has Union militia for protection. Sent to the station to investigate a dispute with a Komarran convoy, Miles uncovers a more sinister plot involving a potential war between Barrayar and Cetaganda. (DI)

Grant:
No surname given. Pilot of the shuttle that brings Leo Graf to the Cay Project Habitat. (FF)

Gras-Grace:
No surname given. A stout, red-haired, pleasantly ugly woman, she was the leader of the smuggler crew that included Russo Gupta, Firka, and Hewlitt, and was killed by Ker Dubauer after transporting his cargo of

haut-fetuses. She carried separate sets of identification listing her as Grace Nevatta of Jackson's Whole and Louise Latour of Pol. (DI)

Gravitic explosive:
A powerful munition capable of blowing people to bits. Used by Komarran revolutionaries in their terrorist war against Barrayar. (BA)

Gravitic imploder lance:
A short range ship-to-ship weapon system that causes distortion and rending damage to a targeted area. Its operating technology is not specified. When used in the Hegen Hub conflict, the Barrayaran version had triple the range of the Cetagandan one. It is also mentioned in the scientists' conversation as they try to figure out what the Komarran engineers were up to at the experiment station near Serifosa on Komarr. (K, VG)

Gray, Travis:
A technician in the Dendarii Free Mercenary Fleet assigned to the *Peregrine*, he has been with the mercenaries for six years. He is an expert in communications equipment, and collects classic pre-jump music of Earth origin. Miles mentally reviews his personnel file upon seeing him at a jump-point station near Escobar. (MD)

Great Key of the Star Crèche:
The small rod Miles takes from the Ba Lura when it comes into their ship after landing on the transfer station above Eta Ceta IV. It has decorative glitter on one end that masks dense circuitry, and the other end

is covered with a locked cap bearing the Cetagandan Imperial seal, a clawed, screaming bird. Rian has a necklace that is supposed to open the Great Key, enabling it to be used to access the Star Crèche and its data. The key is the only storage device that has the organized information on the hundreds of thousands of haut genome lines in the Star Crèche. Governor Ilsun Kety makes several copies of the Great Key in a plot to win power. When it appears that Miles, Nadina, and Pel Navarr are about to be killed by Kety, Miles and Pel download the Great Key's data into the Cetagandan communication network. (C)

*Greatest Escape, The*:
A holovid the Marilacans are producing on the prisoner breakout on Dagoola IV. They try to get "Admiral Naismith" to participate as a consultant, but he regretfully refused. (K)

Greenlaw:
No first name given. An older, white-haired quaddie dressed in a velvet-and-silver slashed doublet with matching puffy shorts. She is a Senior Sealer, a minister of downsider affairs that answers to the Board of Directors of the Union of Free Habitats. She has been serving in her position for over forty years and has been all over quaddie space and the two bordering systems. Initially assigned to broker a suitable deal with the Barrayarans regarding the trade fleet and the imprisoned troopers, she doesn't provide a lot of help, and eventually Miles wins the freedom of his men and ships in exchange for the quarantined, contaminated *Idris*. (DI)

Grishnov:
No first name given. A minister and the head of Political Education on Barrayar. He hopes to rule through Prince Serg once the heir is named Emperor, but is killed during Ezar Vorbarra's governmental purge after the Escobar war. (SH)

Groat:
Another name for the hulled and crushed buckwheat that is grown and eaten on Barrayar, often served boiled with syrup at breakfast. Groats are also used in Barrayaran wedding ceremonies, with the Seconds closing a circle of the grain poured on the ground after the bride and groom step inside. After the vows are completed, the groom's Second opens the circle, collecting a kiss on the cheek from the bride as the married couple exits. (All except FF)

Groundcar:
The standard ground transportation vehicle used throughout the galaxy, they range in size from small cars to cargo trucks. A groundcar uses antigravity technology for lift, and is propelled and controlled by fans. Though they are normally close to the ground, a cargo truck on Earth was raised high enough to try to squash Miles during an assassination attempt. (All)

Grunt:
One of the sub-personalities Mark creates to survive Baron Ryoval's torture, he comes out when Mark is being sexually abused. (CC, MD)

Gulik, Ti:
A jump pilot, he is one of Silver's lovers, and also brings her contraband video fiction. Approximately twenty-five years old, he has brown curly hair, and a mostly easygoing temperament. After unknowingly transporting Claire, Tony, and Andy down to Rodeo, he is fired by Bruce Van Atta, and then is cajoled by Leo Graf and Silver into helping the quaddies escape by piloting the jump ship through the wormhole. He also pilots the shuttle down to Rodeo to collect Tony and Mrs. Minchenko. (FF)

Gum-leaf:
A mild stimulant plant that grows on Barrayar. Its leaves are chewed like tobacco and have a pleasantly bitter, astringent taste. Cordelia tries some during Gregor's escape in the Dendarii Mountains. Mara Mattulich also chews gum-leaf. (B, MM)

Gupta, Russo:
A bioengineered amphibious human, he is tall, with pale, unhealthy-looking skin, dark hair shaved close to his skull, leaving patchy fuzz, a large nose, small ears, long, narrow webbed hands and feet, and gill slits under his ribs that need to be regularly sprayed with water when he is on land. Goes by the nickname Guppy. He was created on Jackson's Whole by House Dyan as one of a set of beings that were to be the stage crew for an underwater ballet troupe. House Ryoval acquired him and the others in a hostile take-over and abandoned him.

He joined with the smuggler band of Firka, Gras-Grace, and Hewlitt, and was the only survivor of Ker

Dubauer's attempt to kill them all after they transported his haut-fetus cargo. He tracked Dubauer to Graf Station and tried to kill it with a rivet gun in front of Miles and Bel Thorne. He joined the passenger roster of the *Rudra* after it was delayed at the station, intending to leave as soon as he had killed Dubauer, or follow the Ba if it got away. He sleep-gassed Bel and Garnet Five, but left them where they were. Caught by quaddies after an all-points bulletin was put out for him, he is interrogated by Miles, who gets the whole story, and pieces together the rest of the ba's plot regarding the haut-fetuses. (DI)

Gustioz, Oscar:

A thin man, somewhere between young and middle-aged, he is a parole officer from Escobar who has come to Barrayar to arrest Doctor Borgos on charges of fraud, grand theft, and skipping bail. He also wanted to arrest Mark, but was thwarted by his Class III Diplomatic Immunity. While he is trying to take Borgos into custody, Kareen and Martya Koudelka pelt him first with butter bugs, then with tubs of bug butter, coating him in the stuff. When Miles arrives, he reviews Gustioz's documentation, and refuses to provide the last form he needs to extradite Borgos back to Escobar. (CC)

• • ▌ • •

Haas:

No surname given. He is referred to as Brother Haas. A farmer on Athos, he is a large man, with red skin

from his work and muscular, callused hands. Ethan
Urquhart delivers the bad news that his male fetus,
which was developing in a uterine replicator, is nonviable due to the deteriorating ovarian cultures. He
was hoping for a child from the CJB line to increase
the likelihood of a doctor for his commune in Crystal Springs. Ethan persuades him to go with the JJY
genetic line instead. (EA)

Half-armor:
A less protective, unsealed suit of armor made for
surface encounters on planets with a breathable atmosphere. One of its most useful features is a command
headset with built-in telemetry and a projector to
put vital information in the wearer's field of vision,
controlled by facial movements and voice command.
Half-armor can be combined with anti-nerve disruptor and stunner mesh, as well as a personal plasma
mirror system. Mark takes Miles's personal set during
the clone rescue, leaving Miles with no armor when
he lands on Jackson's Whole to save his brother. (MD)

Halify:
No first name given. A general in the Felician military,
he offers Miles a new mercenary contract to break
the Pelian blockade. (WA)

Handbook:
A portable, electronic document reader commonly
used for day-to-day reading and sharing of information. Books are contained on data cubes or data chips.
Actual paper books are a luxury item. (All)

Hargraves-Dyne Consortium Station:
A space station orbiting Jackson's Whole. Barrayar keeps a consulate there, which Miles calls for help when he escapes Baron Ryoval's guards at his isolated torture facility. (MD)

Haroche, Lucas:
A general in the Barrayaran military, he is the Head of Domestic Affairs in Imperial Security, responsible for uncovering and tracking treason plots and anti-government groups on Barrayar. A graying man in his fifties, with a deep, rich voice and a Western provincial accent, he has served the Empire for thirty years. He sabotages Simon's eidetic memory chip, and tries to frame Miles, then Duv Galeni for the crime because he wants Simon's job, believing he would be a good Chief of Imperial Security. He is devastated to face Gregor after his exposure and arrest, and be branded a traitor. (M)

Hart:
No first name given. A lieutenant in the Dendarii Free Mercenary Fleet and the *Ariel*'s second-in-command, he orders the fast cruiser to dock at Fell Station when driven out of orbit by House Bharaputran security ships. (MD)

Hassadar:
The capital city for the Vorkosigan's District on Barrayar, the city has no strategic military value, and therefore isn't in danger during Vordarian's coup. Piotr transferred the annual tax funds payable to the Imperium by comm link from there to Vorbarr

Sultana. Miles sends Harra and Lem Csurik there to be educated and work so they can return to their village and improve it. (B, MM)

Hassadar Fair:
An annual celebration in the city. Serg Karal saw Miles there with his grandfather several years before Miles traveled to Silvy Vale. (MM)

Hathaway:
No first name given. A friend of Grandmother Naismith, he is in charge of a recycling center. Grandmother sends Miles to him to see if he can help with a squatter, Baz Jesek, who has taken up residence on the property. (WA)

Haut:
The highest Cetagandan social class, haut are below the Emperor, but above the ghem. They control genetic engineering and reproduction for their class. Haut-ladies are sequestered and rarely seen, going out in public in float chairs with protective force screens that allow them to see out, but no one to see them. The force screen can be changed to different colors depending on mood. Haut don't marry, but enter into reproductive contracts with each other. A haut-lady can also be assigned as a wife to a ghem-lord by the Emperor as a high social and political honor. (C)

Hegen Alliance:
The alliance of planets that defeated Cetaganda at the battle of Vervain, including Aslund, Barrayar, Pol, and Vervain, negotiated by Gregor Vorbarra and Aral Vorkosigan. (C, VG)

**Hegen Hub:**
A double star system with no habitable planets and a few space stations and power satellites. More of a route than a place, the Hegen Hub is a vital commerce route to the planets of Aslund, Pol, and Vervain, linking the three planets to Jackson's Whole and the rest of the known universe. It is also of great strategic interest to Barrayar and Cetaganda. When the Cetagandans move against Vervain as a stepping-stone to the Hub, Asland, Barrayar, and Pol come to the planet's defense, defeating the invasion force and setting up the Hegen Alliance. (VG)

**Helda:**
First name not given, only the first letter F on her uniform nametag. Thin and dour, she is the biocontrol warden in Assimilation Station B, and the real culprit behind the loss of Athos's ovarian material shipment. She hates the planet because her son emigrated there to get away from her, and her bitterness drove her to switch the shipment with nonviable tissue samples. She placed them in a long-term storage area, where Ethan finds them by accident while saying good-bye to Teki, and takes them and Terrance Cee with him back to Athos. (EA)

**Helski:**
No first name given. A Barrayaran commodore killed in the Escobar war. (SH)

**Henbloat:**
A plant on Barrayar, which Miles sees in a new light in Ekaterin's virtual garden program, composed entirely of native flora. (K)

Henri:

A research scientist with the Imperial Military Hospital, he is the doctor in charge of the uterine replicator children. At first opposed to the project, he becomes an ardent fan of the technology, and explores using the technology for burn patients. After a visit to check on Elena, Bothari's daughter, he meets Piotr Vorkosigan at Vorkosigan Surleau. He is beaten to death by Vordarian's security forces for not revealing where Miles's replicator is located during the coup. (B)

Hereld, Sandy:

A lieutenant in the Dendarii Free Mercenary Fleet, she is the communications officer on the *Triumph*, and likes to wear unusual hairstyles. She is the first person Mark bluffs past acting as Miles on his way to commandeering the *Ariel*. (MD)

Hessman:

No first name given. An admiral in the Barrayaran Imperial Navy with a questionable budget that attracts Aral's and Koudelka's attention. He sends Ivan to go look for Miles, but intends for him to be killed on the trip. He turns on his co-conspirator, Count Vordrozha, when Miles accuses him of sabotage and murder in the Council of Counts. (WA)

Hewlett:

A short, mahogany-skinned jump-ship pilot killed by Ker Dubauer after his and the rest of the smuggler crew transported his haut-fetus cargo. Russo Gupta had his identification papers while he was on Graf Station. (DI)

Hexapedal grazers:
A six-legged herd animal on Sergyar. Low-slung and thick-limbed, they exist in several different varieties, are coffee-and-cream-colored, and communicate in hisses and whistles. During their journey to the supply cache, Aral and Cordelia manage to kill and eat one. The meat is edible, but gamy and tough, with a bitter undertaste. (SH)

House Bharaputra:
One of the largest criminal factions on Jackson's Whole, its main enterprise is illegal genetics. Its baron, who was captured by the Dendarii during their retreat after the failed clone rescue, is freed, and later his men capture Miles and hold him prisoner before selling him to Baron Ryoval. Mark also leads a rescue operation to free clones raised in one of the House's laboratories, but is surrounded, and has to be rescued by Miles and the Dendarii, leading to Miles's death during the extraction. (L, MD)

House Dyne:
One of the largest criminal factions on Jackson's Whole, its main enterprise is money laundering. (L)

House Fell:
One of the largest criminal factions on Jackson's Whole, its main enterprise is as an arms dealer, the biggest one "this side of Beta Colony." Miles uses buying arms from them as the pretext to smuggle Hugh Canaba off the planet. After Mark kills Baron Ryoval, he makes a Deal for Baron Fell to acquire the assets of House Ryoval. (L, MD)

House Hargraves:
One of the largest criminal factions on Jackson's Whole, its main enterprise is serving as a galactic fence and middleman for ransom exchange. Miles grudgingly admits that most of the victims it negotiates on behalf of do come back alive. (L)

House Ryoval:
One of the largest criminal factions on Jackson's Whole, its main enterprise is creating life-forms for the purchaser's pleasure, deviant or otherwise. House Ryoval purchased Taura from House Bharaputra, holding her prisoner until Miles rescued her. Miles also destroys Baron Ryoval's entire collection of genetic samples on his way out. Baron Ryoval captures Mark when he returns to Jackson's Whole to rescue clone children, and tortures him for five days until Mark kills him and turns the assets of his House over to Baron Fell. (L, MD)

Howl:
One of the sub-personalities Mark creates to survive Baron Ryoval's torture, he comes out when Mark is physically abused. (MD)

Husavi:
No first name given. The head of civilian security on the Komarr jump-point station, he holds the rank of group commander and wears a blue and orange uniform. He has been having problems with Captain Vorgier over how to handle the hostage-holding engineers, which Miles alleviates upon his arrival. (K)

Hysopi, Karla:
A hired caregiver for Konstantin Bothari's child Elena, she is a military widow with three children of her own, and lives in the village near Vorkosigan Surleau. She is taken, along with Elena, by Vordarian's men during the search for Gregor, and held hostage until being released after the coup is put down. (B)

•  •  |  •  •

*Idris*:
A Toscane Corporation cargo and passenger ship that is part of the Komarran merchant fleet escorted by the Barrayarans. It is a utilitarian vessel consisting of seven huge parallel cylinders, one in the middle surrounded by the other six. The central one in devoted to personnel, with two nacelles opposite each other on the outer ring housing the Necklin rods, enabling the ship to travel through wormholes, and the other four cylinders devoted to cargo. Its normal-space engines are mounted in the vessel's rear, and mass shield generators are in the front. The ship rotates around its central axis to bring whichever cargo cylinder is needed into alignment with the docking bay for loading and unloading of cargo.

Docked at Graf Station for adjustments to its jump drive, the ship ran into complications when the replacement parts didn't pass inspection, and was held until the parts could be repaired or replaced. Lieutenant Solian, the Barrayaran security liaison aboard, then turned up missing. The *Idris* is also carrying Ker Dubauer's cargo of haut-fetuses, and it attempts to hijack the entire vessel to retrieve them, but is foiled by Miles, Armsman Roic, and Ensign Corbeau. Afterward, Miles leaves the ship to Senior Sealer Greenlaw as compensation for allowing his men and other ships to leave for Cetaganda to avert the impending war between that empire and Barrayar. (DI)

Illyan, Simon:
A lieutenant in the Barrayaran military and one of the Emperor's personal security staff. When Cordelia first meets him, he is young with brown hair and a "bland, puppy face." He has an eidetic memory chip implanted in his brain by order of Emperor Ezar, allowing him to record anything he sees and hears and play it back with perfect recall. The chip has a ninety percent incidence of introducing iatrogenic schizophrenia in its subjects, although Simon is among the fortunate ten percent.

Assigned to Aral Vorkosigan as his personal spy, he is rapidly promoted through the ranks, becoming Security Commander for Aral once he is appointed Regent, when he heads up the investigation into Evon Vorhalas's assassination attempt on Aral. Twenty years later, Simon is chief of Imperial Security on Barrayar, and Miles's overall superior during his tour of duty in Imperial Security. By this time he is slight and aging, with a round face etched with faint lines, a snub nose, and brown hair turning gray at the temples. He has the unenviable job of requesting Miles's resignation from Imperial Security after discovering his falsification of his report on the recovery of Lieutenant Vorberg, and also his lying to the Imperial Military doctors about his seizures.

Shortly thereafter, Simon begins having what appear

to be mental lapses, which turn severe enough to require him to be forcibly removed from his position and kept sequestered in the ImpSec HQ hospital for review. The memory chip in his head was sabotaged by General Haroche, forcing him to relive events of the past thirty years as if they were actually happening, and he might have died if not for Miles arriving to help him. After removal of the chip renders him unable to return to his former duties, Simon retires, and becomes romantically involved with Alys Vorpatril. He will have some continuing memory difficulties, but Cordelia buys him a map finder data cube and a personal organizer to help him adapt to his new, more sedate life. He accidentally tips Ekaterin off to Miles's secret courtship at the dinner party. Later, he visits Ekaterin at the Vorthys house to apologize, and interrupts Lieutenant Vormoncrief's assault on her and Nikki. He and Alys attend Miles's wedding. (B, CC, M, MD, SH, WG)

Imperial Auditor:
A career on Barrayar that Miles describes as a cross between a Betan Special Prosecutor, an Inspector General, and a minor deity. Appointed for life, they were originally created by Emperor Voradar Tau to audit his counts, and also served as tax collectors for their Districts. Since that time, their position has grown to encompass investigating any situation that cannot be resolved by normal means. There are nine Imperial Auditors, eight permanent positions, with the ninth left permanently open to install men as needed in that position, then releasing them when their specialized services are no longer required. Stymied by Lucas Haroche over visiting Simon after his breakdown, Miles petitions

Gregor, who appoints him as an acting Imperial Auditor. After solving the case, and with the approval of the other four active Auditors, Miles is permanently installed as the eighth Imperial Auditor, the youngest since the Time of Isolation. After that, Miles serves in this capacity on Komarr, Barrayar, and Graf Station. (M, K, CC, DI)

Imperial Military:
Known as ImpMil for short, Barrayar's military force is responsible for carrying out offensive or defensive military campaigns for the Empire. It encompasses both the ground army and the space navy. It is a progressive organization, accepting anyone who can pass the necessary requirements, regardless of their family history or background. Enlisted men often serve in both infantry posts and on warships, as do commissioned and noncommissioned officers. The Imperial Military has defended the planet from invasion by Cetaganda, taken over Komarr, failed to conquer Escobar, and defeated the Cetagandans during the Vervain conflict. (All except FF)

Imperial Residence:
The home of the Emperor on Barrayar, it is a sprawling building that has been added onto in a mix of architectural styles and wings with the succession of new rulers over the centuries. Ludmilla Droushnakova leads Cordelia and Bothari inside to rescue Miles using a network of secret tunnels underneath the structure. (B)

Imperial Security:
Known as ImpSec for short, Barrayar's main law enforcement agency is charged with investigating and neutralizing internal and external threats to the Empire.

Headquartered in a windowless building in Vorbarr Sultana, its members are a combination of intelligence analyst and espionage agent, and are sent to every corner of the known universe. Both Miles and Ivan serve in Imperial Security, with Miles forced to resign after lying about his seizures, and Ivan attaining the rank of captain. During his time of service, Miles saves the Emperor Gregor's life and averts a war with Cetaganda. Duv Galeni also serves in Imperial Security, attaining the rank of commodore and heading the department of Domestic Affairs for Komarr. (All except FF)

Incendiary Cat Plot:
A story alluded to, but not told, by Aral Vorkosigan to Mark as an illustration of Barrayar's long political history. (MD)

Interstellar Judiciary Commission:
A board that acts like the present-day United Nations, they have created rules for the treatment of prisoners of war, which the Cetagandans follow in their own way, creating cruel places like the Top Security Camp #3 on Dagoola IV as a result. (BI)

Investigatif Federale Building:
The headquarters of Escobaran law enforcement, it is a forty-five-story-tall glass building. Simon Illyan tells Mark he came close to emigrating when he visited the building. (MD)

Irene:
No last name given. The first bunkmate Cordelia has on the Tau Cetan passenger liner carrying prisoners

of war back to Beta Colony. She works with the psy-chological officers from Escobar to gather information from the prisoners of war during the trip. Cordelia tries to evade her for most of the journey home. (SH)

IV Thalizine 5:
A truth serum substitute used on Silver to interrogate her about Tony's and Claire's escape from the Cay Habitat. (FF)

Iverson:
No first name given. He is a lieutenant in Barrayaran Imperial Security who responds to Miles's call for help from the Ryoval torture facility. He arrives with a hired security team from House Dyne, and insists on clearing the facility himself. (MD)

•   •   J   •   •

Jackson's Whole:
A planet where corruption and commerce go hand in hand, and anything can be bought for the right price. Located on one of the Hegen Hub jump routes. Five wormholes lead from Jacksonian territory to half the known galaxy. Founded as a hijackers' base two centuries before Miles was born. The old criminal gangs have become criminal syndicate monopolies known as Houses. The only thing sacred to them is the Deal. The houses are run by barons, men who have schemed, clawed, and killed their way to the top. Miles goes there to pick up a defecting genetic scientist, and ends up rescuing Taura from House

Ryoval, destroying Ryoval's private genetic sample collection in the process.

A few years later, Mark commandeers a Dendarii ship and commando team to rescue clones from House Bharaputra, but ends up having to be rescued by Miles, who is killed in the attempt and later resuscitated at the Durona Clinic. After being captured and tortured by Baron Ryoval, Mark kills the baron, and makes a Deal with Baron Fell to acquire House Ryoval's assets in exchange for letting the Duronas leave the planet. (L, MD, SH, VG, WA)

Jahar, Faz:
A Cetagandan geneticist who created the telepathy project that spawned Terrence Cee after finding a homeless woman with the ability and creating children from her genetic tissue. Supposedly blown up in a lab accident, in reality he was killed in the resulting explosion when Terrence and Janine sabotaged the laboratories where they had been created. (EA)

Jamie:
A quaddie killed in an accident before Leo Graf came to the Cay Habitat. It is the first experience the quaddies have with death. (FF)

Janine:
Also known as J-9-X-Ceta-G, she was a genetic experiment like Terrence Cee, and first put the notion in his head to escape. He thought of her as a sort of combination sister and lover, even though they shared very few genetic materials. She was the only other survivor of Doctor Jahar's project to reach puberty,

and was killed by Captain Rau as they tried to escape. Terrence has genetic samples of her, and is trying to have her cloned once he gets to Jackson's Whole. Once Ethan and Terrence recover the ovarian shipment, Terrence agrees to have her genetic samples used for the next generation of children on Athos. (EA)

Jankowski:
No first name given. He is an armsman for Vorkosigan House. His younger daughter found the escaped butter bug queen. He provides security for Miles's wedding and reception. (CC)

Jarlais:
No first name given. A major in the Barrayaran military, he is the officer on duty at Imperial Security headquarters when Miles attempts to visit Simon. He forwards Miles's request to General Haroche. (M)

Jasi:
No surname given. An Imperial Security medic who arrives with Elena to help Aral during his coronary problem. (MD)

Jean:
No surname given. The midwife who delivered Raina, she has a son of her own. (MM)

Jesek, Bazil:
A thin, dark-haired, dark eyed man in his late twenties. He was a former lieutenant and engineer's assistant on jump-drive engines in the Barrayaran military, but deserted in the heat of battle. Miles takes him

off Hathaway's hands, and has him swear fealty to him to get him out of Beta Colony. Baz goes on the Tau Verde IV run, recovers his nerve and composure in the battles that follow, and also falls in love with Elena Bothari, which nearly gets him killed by her father. After initially withholding his permission for them to marry, Miles grants it, also promoting him to commodore and naming him acting commander of the Dendarii Free Mercenaries while Miles goes to clear his name on Barrayar.

He loses command of the fleet when Admiral Oser takes over by subterfuge, and is restored to his position after the Battle of Vervain. Several years later, having secured a lucrative position at an orbiting shipyard at Escobar, he resigns from his post and asks to be released from his armsman's oath to raise a family with his wife Elena, which Miles grants. He comes back to Barrayar with his wife and daughter to attend Miles's wedding. (BA, M, MD, WA, WG)

Jole:
A lieutenant in the Barrayaran military, he is Aral Vorkosigan's aide-de-camp during the Vervain conflict. Blond, good-looking, and brilliant, he was commended for quick thinking during a shipboard accident, and came to Aral's attention soon after. He accompanies Aral on the *Prince Serg* when they arrive at Vervain. (VG)

Jollif:
No first name given. The Barrayaran commodore that Ivan Vorpatril serves under during his first military assignment. (VG)

Jon:
A husky quaddie from the pusher crew who goes along to hijack the shuttle used to retrieve Tony and Mrs. Minchenko. (FF)

Joris:
No first name given. An armsman for Lord Dono Vorrutyer, he is driving the lord's car when the attack occurs, and is stunned during the fight. (CC)

Juan:
No surname given. A servant at the Bianca house, he answers the door for Anias and Lieutenant Mendez. (DD)

Jubajoint:
Similar to a cigarette. Bruce Van Atta smokes one in private after disconnecting smoke alarms in his office. (FF)

Jump-pilot implant:
One of the most common cybernetic systems in the Vorkosigan Saga is the jump-pilot implant, which uses surgically implanted viral circuitry and electrodes at the temples that allow a pilot to jack in to a ship's navigation and guidance systems. Each system has to be calibrated to a particular pilot, and forced removal of the system, as Sergeant Bothari does during inter-rogation of a jump pilot during the Tau Verde IV campaign, can cause mental and physical trauma, and even death. (All)

**Jump-point stations:**
Self-sustaining space stations that exist to monitor ships entering and exiting wormholes. They all look fairly similar, with merchants selling wares, hotels for transients, and their own security forces. Some, like Graf Station or Kline Station, have been heavily modified and built onto over the decades. (All except DD)

**Jupiter Orbital #4:**
A station where Leo had a previous mission training a group of roustabouts. He thinks training the quaddies couldn't be any more difficult. (FF)

·  ·  **K**  ·  ·

**Kanzian:**
No first name given. An admiral in the Barrayaran Imperial Fleet, he is overweight and undertall, with a fringe of graying hair, and resembles a grandfatherly research professor. Assigned to advanced space operations, he is one of two men who Aral considers his superiors in military strategy. During Vordarian's coup, he joins Aral's side. During one of Simon's memory flashbacks, he inquires about Kanzian, who at the time has been dead for five years. Simon had been escorting him out of the capital when Padma Vorpatril was killed. (B, M, SH)

**Kara:**
A quaddie who works as an infirmary aide on the Cay Habitat, she updates Claire on the status of the revolt. (FF)

Karal, Ma:
No first name given. Serg Karal's wife, she has three boys, and rules her home with a firm but not unyielding hand. (MM)

Karal, Serg:
The Speaker of Silvy Vale for the past sixteen years, he is roughly sixty years old, balding, leathery, and worn, and missing his left hand. He is disappointed that Harra went to see the count over her baby's death, not wanting to cause problems over what he tries to pass off as an accident. He was a corporal in the Barrayaran military for twenty years, where he lost his hand. He doesn't provide a lot of help until the attacks on Miles's tent and his horse, which is an insult to the entire village, not to mention an assault against the Voice of Count Vorkosigan. (MM)

Karal, Zed:
One of Serg Karal's children, he is twelve years old, the middle child of three boys. At the village celebration, he claims that Miles is there to kill Lem Csurik, but Miles explains the true reason he has come to Silvy Vale: to administer justice. Zed and his brothers are in the tent when Dono Csurik tries to burn it, but they all escape unharmed. Almost a decade later, Miles encounters Zed again, now a man with a full, neatly trimmed black beard, when he returns to visit Raina's grave. His older brother married a girl from Seligrad, and his parents spend the winters there, helping with their grandchildren. (M, MM)

**Kat:**
No surname given. One of the Dendarii mercenaries who clears booby traps on a captured Pelian warship, she disarms one with three seconds to spare. (WA)

**Kaymer Orbital Shipyards:**
A construction and repair shipyard located in Earth orbit. Miles brings his combat drop shuttles there for repairs after the prisoner breakout on Dagoola IV. He has to settle for placing his payment in escrow until the repairs are made, since the company's representative doesn't quite trust mercenaries. (BA)

**Kee:**
No first name given. A trooper in the Dendarii Free Mercenary Fleet, he is killed in action during the Marilac mission. (MD)

**Keroslav District:**
A district on Barrayar known for its baked goods. After the Singing Open the Great Gates ceremony, Miles makes idle conversation about the district's various baking styles with Voreedi while waiting for his Cetagandan contact to get in touch with him. (C)

**Kesterton:**
No first name given. A trooper in the Dendarii Free Mercenary Fleet, he participates in Mark's clone facility raid at Jackson's Whole. (MD)

*Kestrel*:
The Barrayaran courier ship that delivers Miles's orders to go to Graf Station, and also takes Ekaterin and him to his destination. (DI)

Kety, Islum:
The haut-governor of Sigma Ceta, one of the Cetagandan satrapy worlds. A cousin of the Emperor, he is in his mid-forties, tall, lean, and hawkish, with an artificial touch of gray at his temples. He is behind the conspiracy to overthrow the Emperor, using the power of possessing the Star Crèche and his plan to put a false copy of the Great Key in Miles's possession to provoke a war with Barrayar. He sets up Lord Yenaro to kill Miles and Ivan. His haut-consort is Nadina, whom he kidnaps when she comes to his ship to take back his copy of the Star Crèche. In her place, he sends his mistress, Vio d'Chilian, to capture Ivan. After he is arrested and his plan foiled, he will be forced to retire or commit suicide. (C)

Kevi:
No surname given. An assistant to Emperor Gregor, he is unobtrusive, middle-aged, and intelligent-looking. He shows Ivan and Mark to Gregor's private office in Vorhartung Castle. (MD)

Killer:
One of the separate personalities Mark creates to survive Baron Ryoval's torture. Also known as Other by Mark's various personalities, Killer comes out to murder Baron Ryoval. (MD)

Kim:
No first name given. One of the Oseran mercenaries killed in the battle for the ore refinery orbiting Tau Verde IV. (WA)

Kimura:
No first name given. A sergeant in the Dendarii Free Mercenary Fleet's Yellow Squad, he participates in Miles's attempted rescue of Mark and Green Squad on Jackson's Whole. (MD)

Kitten tree:
A bioengineered tree that sprouts the front half of kittens instead of fruit, on display at the Cetaganda bioestheties exhibit. When Ivan tries to free one of them, he accidentally kills it, as it wasn't designed to survive away from the plant. Vorreedi quietly disposes of the remains. (C)

Kline Station:
A very large space station near a star that has no planets, founded three centuries before Ethan Urquhart first visits it, and built onto ever since. One of the projects the quaddie race was originally created to build, it is within a sub-light boost of six jump points, including to Athos. An independent station, it has a complete internal ecosystem, supplying its own food, heat, light, etc. The station also has environmental police, called biocontrol wardens, who make sure uncleared animals, produce, molds, fungi, and other potentially hazardous material are not brought onto the station. They have pine green uniforms with sky blue accents. Security

personnel wear black and orange. Docks and Locks, or maintenance, wears red uniforms. Ethan Urquhart is sent there to acquire new ovarian tissue cultures for his planet, and runs into the various parties chasing after Terrence Cee. (EA, FF)

Klyeuvi, Amor:
Also known as Kly the Mail, he was a major in the Barrayaran military during the reign of Yuri Vorbarra, and fought against the Cetagandan invasion. He wears a worn Imperial Postal Service jacket and clothes made up of other uniform pieces: black fatigue shirt, ancient dress green trousers, and well-oiled officer's knee boots. He is unshaven, his lips are stained black from chewing gum-leaf, and he's missing several teeth, with the others a uniform yellow brown. A friend of Piotr's, he helps Cordelia, Gregor, and Bothari escape from Vordarian's security men. He has ridden the mail circuit for eighteen years, and was an Imperial Ranger for twenty years before that. He has a niece and was married but no children. After his death, he is buried in the cemetery at Vorkosigan Surleau. (B, MD)

Knolly:
No first name given. An admiral in the Barrayaran Imperial Fleet, he suffers from colitis. Referred to as "Jolly Nolly" by Admiral Kanzian, during Vordarian's coup, he is located at Jumppoint Station One, and hasn't answered any messages from either side. Aral and Kanzian plan a private meeting with him to bring him over to their side. (B)

Komarr:

A planet controlled by Barrayar for forty years, it is near a wormhole nexus with routes to Barrayar, Sergyar, Escobar, Pol, the Cetagandan Empire, and several minor routes. An 0.9 standard gravity planet, with an abundant native supply of gaseous nitrogen and water ice, it has an atmosphere with a high $CO_2$ content, but an inadequate greenhouse effect to retain heat. The population lives in domed cities that receive solar heat from a set of mirrors called a hexagonal soletta array. Breath masks are required to go out on the planet's surface. When Cetaganda invaded Barrayar eighty years before Cordelia met Aral, Komarr let them through the wormhole route. Later, Aral was in charge of the campaign to seize the planet, but he was unjustly given the title "The Butcher of Komarr" when his political officer ordered two hundred people from the planet killed against his orders.

Miles's first official assignment as an Imperial Auditor is to assist in the investigation into an accident at the soletta array, damaged by a collision with an inner system ore freighter, threatening to stop the centuries-long terraforming project. Miles thwarts a plot by renegade Komarran engineers to cut Barrayar off from the galaxy by permanently closing the wormhole. He also meets his future wife, Ekaterin, there. Emperor Gregor's wife, Laisa Toscane, is also a Komarran, and their marriage strengthens the relationship between the two planets. (CC, K, M, SH)

Komarr Revolt:

A military action that Aral Vorkosigan dealt with while serving as the Regent of Barrayar. (WA)

Komarran fleet shares:
A risky form of investment, where a person or company buys shares in a Komarran trading fleet, which goes on an extended trip through the galaxy, with any profits to be distributed upon its arrival back home. Etienne Vorsoisson borrows money and invests his family's entire fortune in a trip that goes wrong, losing three-quarters of the investment. (K)

Kosti:
No first name given. A corporal in the Barrayaran military, he is the gate guard at the empty Vorkosigan House when Miles arrives home. About twenty-one years old, he is a tall, blond-haired young man with sharp features. Against regulations, he has adopted a cat that was rescued from the security system. He has a younger brother, Martin, whom Miles hires as a driver until before he goes into the Military Academy. He also receives lunch every day from his mother, whom Miles hires as House Vorkosigan's cook once he sees it. (M)

Kosti, Ma:
No first name given. Her son guards Vorkosigan House as part of Imperial Security security protocol. After seeing the gourmet spread Corporal Kosti receives every day, Miles hires her to cook at Vorkosigan House. Her culinary reputation spreads so fast that everyone wants to hire her away, including Cordelia, who would like to bring her to Sergyar when Aral and she go back. Ma Kosti joins Mark's company when she comes up with many delicious recipes using bug butter, and is upset when Miles doesn't allow her to serve all of the creations

at his dinner party. She also assists with creating and distributing the maple ambrosia at the Emperor's wedding reception, and prepares the food for Miles's wedding reception. (CC, M, WG)

Kosti, Martin:
Corporal Kosti's younger brother. A tall, blond young man who looks like his older sibling, but with softer features. He is two months away from the mandatory age of eighteen to apply for Imperial service, so Miles hires him in the interim as his driver and batman. Initially, Martin isn't a very good driver, but improves with experience, and grows on Miles as well. He accompanies Miles to Silvy Vale, and teaches city dances to the kids there. (M)

Kostolitz:
No first name given. A fellow officer's school candidate in the Barrayaran military, he is paired with Miles during the initial physical training, when Miles breaks his legs on the obstacle course. Later, Miles has his revenge during officer school, when he keeps cool during a hazardous exercise and saves both of them from getting "killed." (WA)

Koudelka, Clement:
An ensign in the Barrayaran military, he is one of Aral's loyal men during the mutiny on Sergyar. He is tall with a regular, pleasant face. After he is hit with a nerve disruptor while fighting the mutineers, the nerves in his right leg and left arm are replaced by artificial ones, which render him unable to serve in the infantry. After accepting the position of Regent,

Aral promotes him to lieutenant, and makes him his personal secretary.

He carries a spring-loaded swordstick, a weapon of the aristocracy, by Aral's special order. He considers suicide at least once, due to the isolation and prejudice he receives from other Barrayarans. After having sex with Ludmilla Droushnakovi on the night of Aral's assassination attempt, he feels guilty about taking advantage of her, which she proves him wrong about later. His father was a grocer, which enables him to help smuggle Cordelia, Bothari, and Droushnakovi into Vorbarr Sultana to rescue Miles. He is ordered to escort Alys Vorpatril out of the city after they save her from Vordarian's security men.

After the coup is put down, he marries Droushnakovi, and they have four daughters together. He is a commodore by the time Miles becomes an Imperial Auditor, and is very upset at the turn of events between Mark and Kareen, which he finds out in public at the dinner party. With Cordelia's assistance, he agrees to the option arrangement for Mark and Kareen to have a relationship that works for everyone, and even apologizes to Mark for his earlier churlish behavior. He also has to get used to the idea of his daughter Olivia and Count Dono Vorrutyer getting married as well. (B, CC, SH, WA)

Koudelka, Delia:
The first and tallest of Commodore Clement and Ludmilla Koudelka's daughters, she is blond, beautiful, smart, and athletic. Miles escorts her to the Imperial State dinner, as she is quite graceful, and loves to dance. Ivan asks her to marry him, but finds out she

has chosen Duv Galeni, and will be marrying him instead. She attends Miles's dinner party with Duv during their engagement, and also attends Miles's wedding. (CC, M, MD, WG)

Koudelka house:
The Koudelkas live in a large, three-story home on the end of a block row right in the middle of Vorbarr Sultana, with windows overlooking a park, only six blocks away from Vorkosigan House. Clement and Ludmilla purchased it twenty-five years ago, when he had been Aral's aide while he was Regent. (CC)

Koudelka, Kareen:
The fourth daughter of Clement and Ludmilla Koudelka, she is a vivacious eighteen-year-old with short, loose, ash-blond curls, electric blue eyes, and a passionate drive. She plans to study at Beta Colony, courtesy of Cordelia Vorkosigan. Mark meets her at the Emperor's Birthday Celebration, then promises her a dance at Winterfair, if he returns alive from his mission to rescue Miles.

After her first year at Beta Colony, she is in an exclusive relationship with Mark, although she cannot bring herself to tell her parents. She wants to go back to school on Beta, but her family is not wealthy, and asks her to consider attending college in Vorbarr Sultana. To earn money, she accepts shares in Mark's butter bug company, first to keep tabs on Doctor Borgos, then becoming the head of marketing. Her parents disapprove of Mark as a suitor, and Kareen is upset at the limited choices she has as a woman on Barrayar. She prefers life on Beta Colony, but does not want to give up her family either. With Cordelia's help, she works out a mutual option between Mark and herself, and brokers an understanding that her parents can accept. Along with her sister Martya, Kareen helps save Doctor Borgos from the Escobaran parole officers. (CC, MD)

Koudelka, Ludmilla Droushnakovi:
When first assigned to Cordelia, she is the servant of the Inner Chamber in the Imperial Residence, and Princess Kareen's personal bodyguard. She is alert, tall, and heavily muscled, with gold-blond hair and blue eyes. At the time of Vordarian's Pretendership, both of her parents are still alive, and she has three older brothers, all in the military along with her father, and a younger sister. She is instrumental in getting Cordelia and Bothari inside the Imperial Residence using hidden tunnels under the compound that Captain Negri showed to her. After Koudelka deflowered her on the night of Aral's assassination attempt, she works through the guilt of not being officially on duty at the time, and eventually makes up with and marries him. She and Kou have four daughters, Delia, Kareen, Olivia, and Martya, planning to marry them off to the surfeit of Barrayaran Vor males that are being born at the same time. She is one of the first ladies on Barrayar to use a uterine replicator for her two youngest daughters. She feels the same as her husband does about Mark and Kareen, but comes to an understanding on the relationship after Cordelia talks to both of them at Kareen's request. She takes over Alys Vorpatril's duties while Alys is on Komarr playing Baba for Gregor's upcoming wedding to Laisa. She and her husband attend Miles's wedding. (B, CC, M, WG)

Koudelka, Martya:
Another of the Koudelkas' four daughters. Ivan escorts her to the Imperial State dinner. Younger, shorter, and tawnier than her sister Delia, Martya is also more acerbic and direct. After Delia turns down Ivan's marriage proposal, he panics and asks Martya to marry him, but her reply is a succinct, "anyone but you." One of the guests at Miles's dinner party, afterward she is assigned to keep an eye on Kareen, and becomes her sister's go-between with Pym, and also good friends with Ekaterin. When Kareen is banned from working in Vorkosigan House, Martya gets in on the butter bug scheme, where she also meets Doctor Borgos, whom she finds quite interesting. She was to be Ekaterin's Second during the wedding ceremony, but stepped aside to give Taura the honor as a reward for stopping the assassination plot. She also kisses Roic on the cheek for saving them all from the terror Miles would have become if Ekaterin had died. (CC, M, WG)

Koudelka, Olivia:
One of the four tall, blond Koudelka sisters, she has an independent streak, and accompanies Martya to help cheer up Tatya Vorbretten during the Cetagandan bloodline scandal. Later she falls in love and gets engaged to Lord Dono Vorrutyer. She always wanted to be a countess, and will have her chance when Dono wins his petition to inherit his brother's District. She attends Miles's wedding. (CC, M)

Kshatryan Foreign Legion:
A remote mercenary group Ivan considers joining to

avoid Miles's wrath after learning that Alexi Vormoncrief has proposed to Ekaterin. (CC)

Kshatryan Imperial Mercenaries:
A group of about a dozen men recruited by Captain
Thorne, Baz Jesek, and Arde Mayhew on Tau Verde
IV for the Dendarii Free Mercenary Fleet. After
botching a bodyguarding job, they are desperate to
get off the planet. (WA)

*Kurin's Hand*:
Cavilo's flagship of the Randall's Rangers fleet. (VG)

Kush:
No first name given. A soldier in the Barrayaran
military, he is the leader of a patrol on the *General
Vorkraft* that will be part of the attempt to stop the
mutineers. (SH)

Kyril Island:
An arctic, egg-shaped island seventy kilometers wide,
one hundred sixty kilometers long, and five hundred
kilometers from the nearest landmass. At Aral's confirmation ceremony as Regent, Evon Vorhalas mentions
the possibility of getting assigned there as punishment.
Lazkowski Base, used by the Barrayarans for winter
military training, is located there, and is where Miles
is sent for a six-month tour of duty as the Chief
Meteorological Officer. Alexi Vormoncrief is posted
there as punishment for interfering in Miles's and
Ekaterin's relationship. (B, CC, VG)

• • **l** • •

**L. Bharaputra & Sons Biological Supply House:**
Based on Jackson's Whole, it is one of the largest
genetic-engineering companies in the galaxy. Controlled
by the ruthless House Bharaputra, it will take extreme
measures, including murder, to protect itself. When
the Population Council on Athos ordered a supply
of ovarian tissues from them, the order was intercepted and lost on Kline Station. The company was
also cheated by the Cetagandans in a co-sponsored
genetic breeding plot for creating telepathic subjects,
and hired Elli Quinn to eliminate Colonel Millisor
and his men as revenge. Their representatives are
tall, dark-skinned, and wear gaudy, embroidered silk
jackets. A pair of them, one dressed in pink and one
in brown, are sent to retrieve Baron Luigi Bharaputra's
advance payment from Quinn when she takes too long
in eliminating Millisor. (EA)

**Lai:**
No first name given. A lieutenant in the Betan mili-
tary, he is a crew member aboard the *Rene Magritte*.
Slight and thin with a scholarly scoop, he accompanies
Lieutenant Stuben aboard the *General Vorkraft* to
rescue Cordelia. (SH)

**Lairouba:**
A planet that has sent its leader to Earth to participate
in talks about the right-of-passage through the group
of planets known as the Western Orion Arm. Tau

Ceti is the hub of this nexus, and Komarr connects through it by two routes, which is why Barrayar is interested in the discussion. (BA)

Lake:
No first name given. A lieutenant in the Oseran Mercenaries, he is pale, blond-haired, and Admiral Oser's right-hand man. Elena Bothari dislikes him intensely. He supervises the attempt to kill Miles on Oser's orders, but Miles escapes with help from loyal Dendarii men, including Clive Chodak. Captured by Cavilo's men, Lake is severely interrogated on the *Kurin's Hand*. (VG)

Lamitz:
No first name given. A general in the Barrayaran military, referred to as possibly homosexual. (VG)

Lannier, Ma:
No first name given. She taught Harra Csurik reading and writing. (MM)

Lara:
No surname given. A corporal in security on Kline Station, she is average-looking with dark hair. She got her name from her grandmother. When Ethan Urquhart attempts to find out about the attempted attack on him from Colonel Millisor, she thinks he's flirting with her. She is called away to investigate the disappearance of a prisoner, one of Millisor's men who fired a nerve disruptor at Ethan earlier that day. (EA)

Lars:
No surname given. One of two guards Ser Galen used to discipline Mark during his training to impersonate Miles. (MD)

Las Sands:
An area on Athos that has a senior, unnamed representative on the Population Council. (EA)

Latour, Louise:
One of Gras-Grace's aliases, listing her as a citizen of Pol. Russo Gupta carries the identification papers while on Graf Station. (DI)

Lava lamp:
Just like the twentieth-century version. Miles purchases a Jackson's Whole–made one on Komarr as a birthday present for Emperor Gregor. (K)

Lazkowski Base:
Located on Kyril Island on Barrayar, near the Arctic Circle, it is a winter training base for infantry known as Camp Permafrost, with a capacity of six thousand men. After Miles graduates from the Academy, his first assignment is a six-month duty as the camp's Chief Meteorological Officer. Alexi Vormoncrief is posted there as punishment for interfering in Miles's and Ekaterin's relationship. (CC, VG)

Liant:
No first name given. One of the prisoners under Beatrice's command who helps reorganize the prisoners for evacuation on Dagoola IV. (BI)

Liga, Sydney:
An arms buyer on Pol Station Six, he has pale, rabbit-like features, with a protruding lip and dark hair. He meets with Miles, who is posing as the arms dealer Victor Rotha, claiming to need upgraded weapons for his security guards on an asteroid mining facility. He is killed by Cavilo, who tries to pin the crime on Rotha/Miles. (VG)

Lightflyer:
A vertical takeoff and landing aircraft that ranges from one- and two-person versions through bigger passenger vehicles that can carry several passengers to large cargo versions. Antigravity technology is used for lift; however, the method of propulsion is not specified. All lightflyer safety restraints and crash protection systems are very effective, making it possible to survive a lightflyer crash that demolishes the vehicle. (All)

Lightner, Peter:
A Betan pilot in Betan Astronomical Survey, he is known as Big Pete. One of Cordelia's crew who helps rescue her, he pilots the stolen shuttle out of the *General Vorkraft*. (SH)

Lilly Junior:
A tall Eurasian girl unwillingly rescued from the clone crèche on Jackson's Whole, she is a Durona clone meant for Lotus Bharaputra to inhabit. Lotus named her Lilly as revenge on her sister. She escapes from Mark and the Dendarii with Baron Bharaputra and goes back to the Bharaputra residence, where she

meets Rowan and Miles, both prisoners. Her conversation with Miles causes her to question her previously unflagging devotion to Lotus, and she escapes the baron's home by posing as Rowan and going to the Durona Clinic. After Mark makes a Deal for the Duronas' freedom, Lilly travels to Escobar with the rest of her clone sisters. (MD)

Live fur:
Created by GalacTech bioengineering, a live fur is a living organism, like a cat, with none of the defects, like claws or shedding or eating or defecation. It is "fed" by an electromagnetic net in its cellular level, passively gathering energy from the environment. Miles buys one for Elli, and keeps it in his room at the embassy, where it enjoys purring when petted, and snuggling up to his face while he sleeps. It scares Mark when he first stays in Miles's room, and he throws the fur into a closet. Elli sends one to Miles and Ekaterin as a wedding present. (BA, WG)

Liz:
No surname given. A pleasantly plump, middle-aged Komarran, she is the head of the Carbon Drawdown department in the Serifosa branch of the Terraforming Project. Her department has had great success with introducing peat bogs to the planet. (K)

London Municipal Assizes:
Housed in a big, black crystal building two centuries old, it is where all civil criminals are held for processing. Miles, Elli, Ivan, and Duv Galeni go there to try

to get Mark freed into their custody, only to find that Ser Galen has beaten them to him. (BA)

Lord Midnight:
A story Aral relates to Mark about an unusual political benchmark that occurred on Barrayar. During the Time of Isolation, Count Vortala was feuding with his son, so he disinherited him, and persuaded the Council of Counts to approve naming his horse, Midnight, as his heir. The horse died before Vortala, and the son inherited everything anyway. (MD)

Lord Vorloupulous and his 2000 Cooks:
A true story used on Barrayar as an example of violating the letter of the law. When private armies were eliminated by order of Emperor Dorca Vorbarra, Count Vorloupulous called his liveried army "cooks" and armed them with butcher knives. With his army defeated by the Emperor's men, he would have been executed for treason except for the Cetagandan invasion. Vorloupulous's sentence was delayed, he was sent to fight, and he died in battle. (WA)

Lord Vorventa the Twice-Hung:
Miles refers to him during a conversation with Ekaterin about whether criminal charges would be brought against her deceased husband. Vorventa's double demise occurred during the Time of Isolation. (K)

*Love in the Gazebo*:
One of the contraband video fiction titles Ti Gulik brings to Silver. (FF)

Love-Lies-Itching:
A plant on Barrayar, which Miles sees in a new light in Ekaterin's virtual garden, composed entirely of native flora. (K)

*Love's Savage Star*:
A holovid Ethan watches while waiting for Quinn to find out what Colonel Millisor is up to. (EA)

Lubachik:
An ensign in the Barrayaran military, he graduates in Miles's class. Painfully earnest, he is assigned to Imperial Security training to learn advanced security and counterassassination techniques. (VG)

Luigi Bharaputra and Sons Household Finance and Holding Company of Jackson's Whole Private Limited:
A powerful lending company that owns the lease contract on the *Ariel*, and that sends an agent to investigate the insurance claim on the ship. (WA)

Lura:
The Cetagandan Ba, or neuter servant, who enters Miles's ship when he lands at Eta Ceta IV's docking station and leaves him with a fake copy of the Great Key of the Star Crèche and a small nerve disruptor. Hairless, it had disguised itself with a white-haired wig. It was the Dowager Empress's personal attendant for sixty years, but had been tricked by Governor Ilsum Kety into contacting Miles and Ivan and giving up the fake Great Key to provoke a war with Barrayar. It is killed by Vio d'Chilian, and its body left near

the Dowager Empress Degtiar's as she lies in state, made to look like it committed suicide. (C)

Leutwyn:
No first name given. Adjudicator called in on Graf Station to judge if warrants could be issued for arrest and fast-penta interrogation, arrived in time to witness the arrival of Russo Gupta and sanction his arrest and interrogation. He also attends the inspection of the Idris, and escapes the ship with Security chief Venn's help after Dubauer hijacks it. (DI)

L-X-10 Terran-C:
The project name for Terrence Cee, Doctor Jahar's genetic-engineering telepathy subject on Cetaganda. (EA)

●   ●   M   ●   ●

Mail:
Physical delivery of mail on planets is uncommon in major metropolitan areas, replaced primarily by electronic communication. Special messages, such as the invitations to Emperor Gregor's wedding, are written on parchment and hand-delivered. Some mail is sent by small recording or speaker devices. In the backcountry, such as the Dendarii Mountains on Barrayar, mail was delivered via mounted rider during Ezra Vorbarra's time, but has since been replaced by comconsoles. Since some backcountry people were illiterate, particularly during the Time of Isolation,

the mailman might have read the message for the recipient, and written a reply for them as well. (B)

Malka:
One of the four hired thugs sent to castrate Lord Dono, he is captured by Ivan and Olivia, and injured in the process. (CC)

Maree:
No surname given. She is a very pretty clone with blond hair and blue eyes. Her actual age is about ten years old, but she appears to be twenty. She has had surgery done, including giant breast enlargements. After being removed from the clone crèche on Jackson's Whole, she attempts to escape the *Peregrine* and go back with Baron Bharaputra, but is stopped by Mark. Afterward, he attempts to molest her, but suffers a trauma-induced flashback, rendering him nearly cata-tonic. She is one of the clones who is set up with an education from Mark's fund after he makes the Deal to get the Duronas off Jackson's Whole. (MD)

Margara:
No first name given. An administrator at Beauchene Life Center. Doctor Aragones advises Miles to speak to her about recertifying the Dendarii medics in the latest triage and cryo-chamber techniques. (MD)

Marilac:
A planet that is key to Cetagandan plans to expand the Empire because of its location near a jump point to Zoave Twilight. The Marilacans have accepted large amounts of aid from the Empire, which Lord Vorob'yev

thinks is lulling them into a state of complacency, since they don't think Cetaganda will attack an ally. After the invasion, Miles saves almost ten thousand of their soldiers to form a new guerrilla army to continue fighting, and also uses the Dendarii to smuggle aid to the Marilacans during the war. Eventually, the Cetagandans withdraw their forces without gaining control of the planet. (BI, C)

Marilican Embassy:
Miles and Ivan attend a welcoming party at the embassy for the various planetary diplomats at the start of the Dowager Empress's funeral ceremonies, and first meet Lord Yenaro there. The embassy has a large, elaborate, multimedia sculpture in its lobby entitled "Autumn Leaves." (C)

Mattulich, Mara:
Harra's mother, she is tall, stringy, tough, and chews gum-leaf. Harra is her only surviving daughter, but she gave birth to four other children, two stillborn, and two she killed because each was born deformed. Many of the older generation in Silvy Vale, including Mara's own mother, condoned the practice. Miles sentences her to death, but stays the actual execution, stripping her of all legal rights and placing her in the care of her daughter and the Speaker. After her death, Harra doesn't move her grave, leaving it to be covered by the new lake formed by the hydroelectric dam. (MM)

Mayhew, Arde:
A jump-ship pilot officer from Beta Colony. He lets Cordelia stow away on his cargo run off planet, enabling

her to escape to Barrayar. Almost two decades later, he's around forty years old, and is the pilot officer of the jump ship *RG 132*. His jump implants are obsolete and his career will be over when the ship is sold, so he barricades himself inside and threatens to blow it up when Miles first meets him. Miles buys the ship and swears Arde as his armsman. He rams the *Triumph* with the *RG 132* during the Tau Verde IV campaign, and pilots the *Triumph*'s escape shuttle C-2 when saving Miles and Gregor during the Vervain conflict. He comes to Barrayar to attend the wedding, spending much of his time entertaining Nikolai and the other children with tales of his adventures. (SH, VG, WA, WG)

Maz, Mia:
She works at the Vervani embassy on Eta Ceta IV as the assistant chief of protocol specializing in women's etiquette. About forty years old, she has olive skin, dark curly hair, and loves chocolate desserts. She helps Miles with his investigation, giving him information on the Great Seal, and explaining some of the dizzying Cetagandan social customs. After the coup plot is stopped and the funeral of the Empress is over, she accepts Vorob'yev's proposal of marriage. (C)

McIntyre:
No first name given. A doctor on the Betan survey team, he is also known as Mac. One of Cordelia's crew that rescues her from the *General Vorkraft*, he tells her Koudelka was the Barrayaran hit by nerve disruptor fire on Sergyar. (SH)

Medical hand scanner:
A portable device used to scan for injuries of bones and soft tissues, and also to detect physical abnormalities in a subject. Miles was going to equip his Dendarii mercenaries with medical scanners to try to catch Mark, until he realized they both had artificial bone replacement in their legs, making them practically identical again. (BA)

Medical stunner:
Used for pain relief and local anesthetic during medical procedures. Miles has a Dendarii doctor numb his broken hand after he gets out of the prison camp on Dagoola IV. (BI)

Mehta:
No first name given. A doctor with the Betan Expeditionary Force Medical Service, she is a slim, tan-skinned woman about Cordelia's age with drawn-back dark hair, and is dressed in a blue uniform. She uses drugs without Cordelia's knowledge to try and get her to talk about her captivity with the Barrayarans. When she advises that Cordelia undergo long-term therapy, Cordelia attacks and subdues her during her escape. (SH)

Memory chip implant:
Simon Illyan's cybernetic eidetic memory chip is the only mention of brain/computer interaction, other than jump-pilot interfaces and feelie-dreams, in the Vorkosigan Saga. The chip, placed between the hemispheres of the brain, is a multilayer sandwich of organic and inorganic components from which thousands of connections go out to various points in the brain itself.

Sensory signals for sight and sound pass into and out of the chip, and can give eidetic replay of memories on demand. The chip causes a high rate of schizophrenia in its recipients, with Simon being one of the notable, rare exceptions. His chip is sabotaged by a Komarran bioweapon administered by General Lucas Haroche, causing it to randomly dump stored memories into Simon's brain, creating debilitating hallucinations. It is removed, leaving him perfectly functional, although it necessitates his retirement from Imperial Security. (All except CC, DD, DI, FF)

Mendez:
No first name given. A middle-aged, competent police lieutenant in Rio de Janiero's homicide bureau that is investigating the attempted murder of Anias Ruey. He accompanies her to Doctor Bianca's house, standing by while she gets the feelie-dream back. (DD)

Metropolitan Station:
One of the few orbital arcologies in the Union of Free Habitats that maintains gravity and deals with galactics. (DI)

Metzov, Stanis:
A general in the Barrayaran military, he is the commander of Lazkowski Base on Kyril Island when Miles first meets him. A career officer with thirty-five years in service, he is a tall, hard-bodied man with iron-gray hair and iron-hard eyes. Because of his actions in trying to put down the technicians' insubordination during the fetaine spill incident, he is discharged from the military and turns up near Vervain, working with Cavilo as part

of Randall's Rangers. He tries to murder Miles twice, once by shooting him as he is about to board the *Triumph*, and again in Admiral Oser's former quarters. He is killed by Cavilo before he can get his revenge. (VG)

Millifenigs:
The currency of Felice, which government representatives try to use to pay Miles's mercenary contract. Delisted from the Betan Exchange, the slick, colorful bills are practically worthless on the open market, but Miles considers using them as wallpaper for Vorkosgian House. When the Tau Verde IV war is over, Miles checks the exchange rate to find them listed at 1,206 millifenigs to the Betan dollar. (WA)

Millisor, Ruyst:
A Cetagandan ghem-colonel and counter-intelligence agent, he is an average-looking man with a hard body and eyes like gray chips of granite. He has tracked Terrence Cee across the galaxy, and gets permission from haut-lady Rian Degtiar to pursue him to Jackson's Whole. The trail leads him to Kline Station and the order of modified ovarian cultures that was supposed to be shipped to Athos from House Bharaputra genetics company. His cover on the station is ghem-lord Harman Dal, an art and artifacts dealer. He captures and interrogates Ethan Urquhart, then orders the doctor killed when he yields no useful information. His Cetagandan clan face paint is brilliant blue with yellow, white, and black swirls. After he takes Teki hostage, his room is breached by Biocontrol Warden Helga, and he is arrested after attacking her. Freed by one of his men, he captures Terrence, Ethan, and Elli,

and is about to kill the latter two and take Terrence back to the Empire when he is killed by a plasma bolt from the Bharaputran assassins sent to kill him and recover the money the baron paid to Elli Quinn to kill him. (C, EA)

Minchenko, Ivy:
Doctor Minchenko's wife. A frail, silver-haired woman who was a musician on Earth, she loathes Rodeo, in the words of her husband. She plays harpsichord and violin, and begins teaching Silver the latter instrument while waiting for the rescue team to bring Tony back to the shuttle. (FF)

Minchenko Station:
One of the few orbital arcologies in the Union of Free Habitats that maintains gravity and deals with galactics. (DI)

Minchenko, Warren:
The medical/fertility doctor for the Cay Project. Nearing mandatory retirement age, he is old and shrunken, with a leathery face and white hair, but is still vigorous and commanding, and is a reassuring authority figure for the quaddies. He thought he should have been put in charge of the Cay Habitat after Doctor Cay's death. Refusing to evacuate with the rest of the Habitat personnel, he accompanies the fleeing quaddies through the wormhole to freedom. (FF)

Minister of the West:
A title of one of the members of the Council of Ministers on Barrayar. (SH)

Ministry of Political Education:
The official name of the Barrayaran secret police.
Aral killed the Political Officer, from the Ministry's
military branch, aboard his ship during the Komarr
campaign when the man countermanded a direct order
and instigated the Solstice Massacre, impugning Aral's
honor. The Ministry is dismantled and its headquarters
destroyed during Ezar's governmental purge following
the war with Escobar. (SH)

Mirror dance:
A Barrayaran dance in which one partner must copy
the moves of the other partner as accurately as possible, even down to facial expressions. Either partner
can lead, as Cordelia finds out when she tries dancing
it with Aral. (B, MD, SH)

Missile:
Not used as a major element in space battles due
to the effectiveness of defensive force screens. The
one exception is when a sacrifice ship lays down a
"sun wall" of nuclear-tipped missilettes deployed as
a single unit, creating a planar wave that clears the
detonation space of everything, often including the
ship that created the wall. (VG)

Moglia:
No first name given. The chief of security at Ryoval
Biological Laboratories. Miles interrogates him using
fast-penta just before being captured by Ryoval security. Moglia tries to recapture Miles and the rest of
his team, holding Miles hostage, but Taura violently
convinces him to let them go. (L)

Mok:
No surname given. One of two guards Ser Galen used to discipline Mark during his training to impersonate Miles. (MD)

Molino:
No first name given. Middle-aged and dyspeptic-looking, he is the senior cargomaster of the Komarran trade fleet being held at Graf Station. Responsible for the safe passage of the fleet on its route, the incidents at the Union of Free Habitats are giving him quite a headache. When Lieutenant Solian disappears, he tries to get Admiral Vorpatril to order the fleet to disembark for their next destination, but is overruled. He complains about the station personnel trying to fine the Komarran fleet for the Barrayarans' actions, which Miles dismisses. (DI)

Monorail:
A form of land transportation using a series of linked cars mounted either above or below a central rail system. Some long-distance public transportation on Barrayar and Komarr is done by monorail. (B, K)

Moon Garden Hall:
A domed area on Eta Ceta IV, like a smaller version of the Cetagandan Celestial Garden, but not as lush and ornate. It is roughly three hundred meters in diameter, covering steeply sloping ground, with natural paths leading through the hall. The 149th Annual Bioestheties Exhibition, Class A is held there, dedicated by the ghem-ladies to the memory of the Dowager Empress. Miles sets up a meeting in the hall with Rian Degtiar's servant, but cannot keep it due to

meeting Lord Yenaro at his exhibit of perfumed cloth, and thwarting his inadvertent assassination attempt on Miles and Ivan. (C)

Morita Station:
A project that Leo Graf and Bruce Van Atta had both worked on twelve years before their reunion at the Cay Project Habitat. Leo had kicked Bruce into administration to get him out from underfoot during it. (FF)

Mosquitoes:
After a global war, many Earth animals were genetically altered. These new mosquitoes are about five inches long, with powerful venom that would only take a few stings to kill a human. Chalmys traps Carlos Diaz in the forest using a force screen, and questions him about the commissioned feelie-dream while the mosquitoes attack him. (DD)

Mount Sencele:
The mountain where Barrayaran Imperial officer candidates undergo a 100-kilometer endurance march as part of their elimination testing. (WA)

Mourning uniform:
A dress uniform worn by members of the Barrayaran military or Vor Houses when attending an appropriate function. It is like the standard dress uniform, but with the logos and rank insignia stitched in black silk on black cloth. Miles wears his at several functions on Eta Ceta IV. (C)

Mu Ceta:
One of the eight satrapy planets in the Cetagandan Empire. Its forces were defeated when they tried to take Vervain to control the wormhole that connects the Empire to the Hegen Hub. The governor of Mu Ceta is from the Degtiar constellation. He is the present Emperor's half uncle, and much older, although he has been governor for just two years. (C)

Munos:
No first name given. A big man, he is a sergeant in Escobaran law enforcement who assists Gustioz in arresting Doctor Borgos. He is also involved in the bug butter fight. (CC)

Murka:
No first name given. A tall ensign in the Dendarii Free Mercenary fleet, he accompanies Miles to Ryoval's laboratory on Jackson's Whole to try to find Taura. He and the other two Dendarii men are caught while infiltrating the laboratory, but he bluffs his way out, leaving Miles alone inside. Promoted to lieutenant, he is also part of the prisoner rescue on Dagoola IV, and is standing next to Miles when killed by a Cetagandan sniper. Miles pulls his head off while trying to retrieve his command headset, an act that gives him nightmares later. (BI, L)

Mynova:
No first name given. A female trainee on the *Ariel*, she asks about the pay schedule for the Dendarii mercenaries, inadvertently giving Miles yet another headache to deal with for his "fake" mercenary company. (WA)

* * N * *

Nadina:
No first name given. The haut-lady consort to Ilsum Kety, she is an older, silver-haired woman. She knows about the plan to send copies of the Star Crèche to the eight governors, but not about Kety's plot to take over the Empire, and is held prisoner when she goes to retrieve Kety's copy of the genebank. Her long hair is cut by Miles as a necessary sacrifice during her rescue. (C)

Naismith, Cordelia:
See Vorkosigan, (Naismith) Cordelia

Naismith, Elizabeth:
Cordelia's mother, she is a Betan bioengineer, and the co-author of the article "On an Improvement in Permeability of Exchange Membranes in the Uterine Replicator" in the issue of *The Betan Journal of Reproductive Medicine* read by Ethan Urquhart. When Miles and Elena visit her on Beta Colony, she is nearly ninety years old, but still as spry and smart as ever. She asks Miles to help her friend Mr. Hathaway with Baz Jesek, helps Miles manipulate Bothari into letting Elena go on the trip to Tau Verde IV, and also takes in Elli Quinn during her reconstructive facial surgery. When Kareen Koudelka goes to school at Beta Colony, she calls Elizabeth "Gran Tante," and both she and Mark grow close to her during their stay. When Commodore Koudelka finds out what Mark and Kareen have been up to there, he angrily refers to her as a "damn Betan pimp." (CC, EA, WA)

Naru:
No first name given. A Cetagandan ghem-general, he is third-in-command in Imperial Security on Eta Ceta IV. He is working with Ilsum Kety to overthrow the Emperor, and comes to Kety's flagship to assist with reproducing copies of the Great Key. After the plot fails, he will be executed for his attempted treason against the Empire. (C)

Natochini:
No first name given. A commander in the Barrayaran military, he is the executive officer of the *Prince Serg*, and escorts Clive Chodak and Ky Tung on a tour of the ship. (VG)

Navarr, Pel:
The haut-consort of Eta Ceta IV, she is dressed in white, with blond, elaborately braided hair. She takes Miles in her float chair to the Star Crèche, to meet with Rian and the six other haut-consorts to the satrapy governors. She helps Miles to recover the Great Key and rescue the haut-consort Nadina. Miles uses her float chair to broadcast the data in the Great Key and to protect the Key inside until they can be saved by Ivan and ghem-colonel Benin. She attends Gregor's wedding. She helps save Miles's life after he is infected with the bioengineered parasites on Graf Station. (C, CC, DI)

Necklin field generator rod:
The system that generates the warp field used for wormhole jumps. The two rods are placed opposite each other on the sides of the ship. The rods generate the field that twists the spacecraft through the wormhole,

also known as five-space. At the end of each rod is a vortex mirror that helps stabilize and guide the field. The rods and their associated vortex mirrors are inside protective hull structures, often as separate cylinders that are an integrated part of the ship's fuselage. (All)

Needle gun:
A weapon that fires dozens of tiny metal needles that expand on impact and tear through a target's body like razors, causing immense, usually fatal damage. There is also a larger, needle grenade version, capable of injuring multiple targets, or causing extensive damage to one person, as happened to Miles when he was shot in the chest with one. The range is undefined, and it is not stated how effective body armor is against one, as Miles wasn't wearing any when he was killed. (All)

Needle ray pistol:
A small, concealable energy pistol. Carlos Diaz pulls one on Chalmys DuBauer when he is trapped outside the energy screen, but he can't use it, owing to some kind of magnetic resonance from the force screen that would overload the pistol's power pack and make it explode. (DD)

Negri:
No first name given. A hard-faced, hard-bodied, bullet-headed man. Although he holds the rank of captain in Barrayaran Imperial Security, he is actually the head of Emperor Ezar Vorbarra's personal security. While he wields tremendous power, he is completely loyal to the Emperor, and is known as his familiar. He plotted with Ezar and Aral to let Prince Serg get killed in the

battle with Escobar, preventing Barrayar from being ruled by an insane deviant. He dies while saving young Prince Gregor from Count Vordarian's coup attempt, bringing him to Vorkosigan House before succumbing to his wounds. He is succeeded by Simon Illyan. (B, SH)

Nelson:
A security guard at Shuttleport Three on Rodeo. (FF)

Nerve disruptor:
An energy-based beam weapon that destroys nerve cells, it fires a central beam with a surrounding nimbus. A hit to the head usually results in death. A partial hit may just destroy part of the brain, leaving the victim alive but with major cognitive damage. A direct hit to the body may destroy sensory and control nerves, which may be replaced by artificial systems. A partial hit to the body may cause permanent loss of sensation and/or control to the affected area. In a near-miss, the nimbus may just give a tingling or fried feeling to the affected area, leaving a twitchiness that a victim may recover from. Ensign Dubauer suffers a hit to the head from a nerve disruptor that leaves him a conscious vegetable, unable to communicate or perform anything but basic tasks, like walking or eating. While taking the *General Vorkraft* back from mutineers, Cordelia is hit by the nimbus of a disruptor shot that leaves a patch of muscle on her leg permanently numb. Clement Koudelka is hit by a disruptor as well, necessitating the replacement of some of his nerves with artificial networks. A nerve disruptor's range is undefined, but is at least line of sight. Effective defenses include space armor, a half-armor suit with a built-in nerve disruptor/stunner

shield net, or another body, as Cordelia uses when she takes the engineering section of the *General Vorkraft* from the mutineers. (All)

*Nest of Doom*:
A video fiction involving space marines and aliens that Siggy mentions as a possible plan to hijack the shuttle. Silver negates the idea. (FF)

Neuve:
No first name given. A sergeant in the Barrayaran military, he is part of the maintenance detail at Laz-kowski Base. Miles is to report to him to oversee basic labor detail as part of his punishment for damaging a remote weather station to save his life. (VG)

Nevatta, Grace:
One of Gras-Grace's fake identities, listing her as a citizen of Jackson's Whole. (DI)

Nevic:
An ally of Ilsum Kety, he is a Cetagandan ghem-lord who pressed a theft charge on Lord Yenaro. (C)

Newt:
A genetically engineered animal that keeps the oxygen-giving algae in check on Kline Station. Also a primary food source on the station, everyone there is very sick of eating it. It has been made into every recipe imaginable, including newt nuggets. Quinn and Ethan Urquhart swap one hundred kilograms of newts with Okita's body to smuggle it into the waste disposal area of the station. (EA)

Nicol:
No surname given. A quaddie, she has ivory skin, blue eyes, and short, clipped ebony hair. She plays a double-sided hammered dulcimer at the party on House Fell's space station. Tricked into an onerous contract, she wants to hire the Dendarii to smuggle her out of Jackson's Whole. Smitten, Bel Thorne takes the job for one Betan dollar, and they get her out alive. When Miles travels to Graf Station, he finds her living with Bel Thorne, and working as a musician with the Minchenko Memorial Troupe. She is a friend of Garnet Five. (DI, L)

Niels:
No first name given. A Barrayaran soldier who fought in the Escobar war, he thinks Aral Vorkosigan is the most cold-blooded bastard he ever met. Carl and Evon Vorhalas refer to him while discussing Aral at the Regent's confirmation ceremony. (B)

Nilesa:
No first name given. A yeoman in the Barrayaran military, he is the camp cook on the survey planet later known as Sergyar. Not held in high esteem by the other men. Cordelia compliments him on his cooking, which improves his demeanor considerably. He repays her kindness by helping her during the mutiny aboard the *General Vorkraft*. (SH)

Nim:
No first name given. A sergeant in the Dendarii Free Mercenary Fleet, Miles assigns him as back-up during

the chase and escape with Mark, Ivan, and Duv Galeni
at the Thames Tidal Barrier. (BA)

*Ninjas of the Twin Stars*:
Title of a video fiction enjoyed by some of the quaddies and Ti. (FF)

Norris:
No first name given. He is the operations manager for
GalacTech in Rodeo's local space, but is attending a
materials development conference on Earth during the
quaddie revolt, which leaves Administrator Chalopin
officially in charge. (FF)

Norwood:
No first name given. A medic in the Dendarii Free
Mercenary Fleet, he prepped Trooper Philippi's body
for cryo-stasis, and refuses to remove it from the
chamber when Miles is killed. He helps Elli Quinn
prep Miles's body, then ships the entire cryo-chamber
to the Durona Clinic. Unfortunately, he is killed shortly
thereafter, before he can report exactly what he had
done to his superior officer. (MD)

Nout:
No first name given. One of the *Ariel*'s crewmen.
Miles puts him in charge of securing the worthless
Felician millifenigs. On Jackson's Whole, he has been
promoted to corporal, and lets Nicol in to see Miles
and Bel Thorne. He also participates in the prisoner
rescue on Dagoola IV. (BI, L, WA)

Nuovo Brasilian Military cloning fiasco:
Referred to by Bruce Van Atta in reference to the quaddie program on Cay Habitat. Although not clearly defined, the incident led to a general hysteria and mistrust of many planets regarding genetic manipulation on sentient creatures. (FF)

* * 0 * *

Oil cakes:
A Barrayaran breakfast dish. (MM)

Okita:
No first name given. One of Millisor's men, he is average-looking, but with dense muscles. He is to kill Ethan after the interrogation by Colonel Millisor and make it look like an accident. Quinn kills him while saving Ethan, ironically in the same fashion that Okita intended to kill Ethan, by pitching him over a catwalk to the floor. (EA)

Ola Three:
One of the Cetagandan satrapy planets, it is near a wormhole to Vega Station. (MD)

Oliver:
No first name given. A burly sergeant in the 14th Commandos, he was captured at Fallow Core, and has spent his time caring for the catatonic General Guy Tremont. He tells Miles that Fallow Core wasn't taken on October 6th, it was betrayed on October 5th.

He helps Miles organize the prisoners, and agrees to serve in the new Marilac Army. (BI)

Olney:
No first name given. A corporal of the motor pool at Lazkowski Base, he is tall with black hair and a Greek accent. One of two men who played a dangerous prank on Miles. As punishment he was assigned to clean the recovered scat-cat, then assist Miles and Pattas in cleaning out various drains around the base. (VG)

Olshansky:
No first name given. A colonel in the Barrayaran military, he is the first Head of Domestic Affairs for the planet Sergyar. (M)

120-Day War:
The term used by Escobarans referring to the brief war between Barrayar and their planet. (SH)

Orb of Unearthly Delights, The:
A pleasure dome on Beta Colony. Its services are not quite as wide-ranging as Jackson's Whole, but varied enough to entertain a broad spectrum of guests. Commodore Koudelka is very upset when Doctor Borgos mentions that Mark and Kareen visited the Orb. Miles and Ekaterin also visit the Orb during their stay at Beta Colony during their honeymoon. (CC, DI)

Orbital solar mirrors:
A large array of enormous solar mirrors above Komarr to reflect extra sunshine onto the planet's surface. The increase in solar flux to Komarr's surface is increased

by an undefined percentage, adequate to help warm the planet and foster plant growth over a period of centuries. The orbital location of the array is not specified (though it sets after sunset) but seems not to be in Komarran orbit nor as far away as the L5 stable orbit point. The station-keeping method is not specified. (K)

Orient IV:
The planet with whose government GalacTech had entered into a ninety-nine-year lease on Rodeo. When rich mineral deposits were discovered thirty years later, the Orient IV government initiated stricter taxes and other economic penalties to drive GalacTech off-planet and take it back. (FF)

Orient Station:
A space station owned by the government of Orient IV. GalacTech leases about one-quarter of it from them while working on Rodeo and the Cay Habitat Project. (FF)

Oser, Yuan:
Admiral and the commanding officer of the Oseran Free Mercenary Fleet, he has graying hair, a beak-like nose, and a penetrating stare. Miles describes him as having a look that makes junior officers search their consciences. He loses Ky Tung to the Dendarii when he chews him out over losing the *Triumph* in battle and denies him another command. When Miles breaks the blockade of the wormhole and puts the Oseran mercenaries at odds with their employer over nonpayment of salary, Oser offers to join the Dendarii Mercenaries.

When Miles rejoins the Dendarii four years later, Oser has taken over the Dendarii from Baz Jesek in a bloodless financial reorganization coup and renamed them the Oseran Mercenaries. After capturing Miles, he orders him killed, but then has to work with him against the Cetagandans. When Miles can't convince him to fight, Elena injects him with fast-penta, and they lock him up before the upcoming battle. During combat, he escapes the brig and tries to flee with a few others to the *Peregrine*, but his shuttle is destroyed by the Cetagandans. (VG, WA)

Oseran Free Mercenary Fleet:
A mercenary group under contract with the "legal" government of Pelias on Tau Verde IV to blockade the wormhole near their planet and search all inbound cargo ships for contraband. After Miles defeats them and breaks the blockade by interrupting the payroll between Pelias and the mercenaries, their leader, Admiral Yuan Oser, offers the rest of his force to the Dendarii Free Mercenary Fleet. (WA)

Other:
Another name for Mark's sub-personality Killer, it comes out to kill Baron Ryoval. (MD)

Outlands:
An area on Athos with no rules, and inhabited by "outlaws," men who have turned their backs on regular society. Janos, Ethan's former partner, goes there to live while Ethan is on his mission to Jackson's Whole. (EA)

Ovarian tissue cultures:
Used to populate Athos with exclusively male citizens. Genetic designations of the various lines include CJB, JJY, LMS, EEH, and others, with a number following the three letters. Doctor Ethan Urquhart is a CJB-8. The initials CJB stand for Cynthia Jane Baruch, a doctor who was hired to create Athos's ovarian cultures, and who used her own genetic material to help start the planet's population. Elli Quinn donates one of her ovaries to the planet, which will be designated EQ-1. (EA)

Overholt:
No first name given. A sergeant in Barrayaran Imperial Security, he is a very large man who escorts Miles home after the Laskowski Base incident. Miles dubs him Overkill. Assigned as Miles's bodyguard during the Hegen Hub mission. They are separated when Miles is captured by Jacksonian Consortium security, and when they are reunited, he's assigned to guard Emperor Gregor until Gregor is safely under Barrayaran protection again. (VG)

• • P • •

Padget:
No first name given. A member of the Dendarii Free Mercenary Fleet, he is the jump pilot of the *Ariel* and pilots the craft while Miles talks to Baron Ryoval as they leave Jackson's Whole. (L)

Parchment:
A rare paper used on Barrayar for three types of

messages: Imperial edicts, official edicts from the Council of Counts and the Council of Ministers, and orders from the Council of Counts to their own members. This last group is tied with a particular color of ribbon to denote what type of order it contains. Miles figures out that the order delivered to Captain Dimir to arrest him was tied with a black ribbon, and through that backtracks to the plot to destroy his father by charging him with the violation of Vorloupulous's Law against raising a private army. (WA)

Parnell:
No first name given. The pilot officer of Cordelia's bulk freighter during her decoy run against the Barrayan patrol blockading the wormhole to Escobar. (SH)

Pattas:
No first name given. A technician in the Barrayaran military, he works in the motor pool at Lazkowski Base. One of two men who played a dangerous prank on Miles. As punishment, he was assigned to clean the recovered scat-cat, then assist Miles and Olney in cleaning out various drains around the base. (VG)

Patty:
A pregnant quaddie who was scheduled to have her baby terminated, she hides in the Clubhouse instead. (FF)

Pearson:
No first name given. An engineer in the Dendarii Free Mercenary Fleet, he is promoted to Fleet Engineer as Baz Jesek's replacement, per his recommendation. (M)

Peat bog:
A successful introduction to the Komarran ecology during its terraforming. The bioengineered strain there gives off six times more oxygen than its Earth counterpart. Miles, Ekaterin, Etienne, Vorthys, Venier, and Nikolai all see it while on a tour of the region around Serifosa. (K)

Pel:
No first name given. A prisoner at the camp on Dagoola IV who assists in the Dendarii rescue mission. (BI)

People's Defense League:
A Barrayaran political splinter group that wants to get rid of the aristocracy, by assassination if necessary. Aral suggests eliminating their platform by making everyone on Barrayar a Vor. (SH)

*Peregrine*:
A ship in the Dendarii Free Mercenary Fleet whose captain is arrested when he fails to join Miles against the Cetagandan attack on Vervain. The captain and Admiral Oser were trying to reach this ship when their shuttle is destroyed by the Cetagandans during the battle. (VG)

Peritaint:
An artificial poison or biological weapon created by the Durona Research Group for House Fell, which made money selling it, then made even more by selling the antidote. (MD)

Peruvian Moral League:
A citizens' group that condemned Anias Ruey's feelie-dream, *Triad*, boosting its sales. (DD)

Philip:
No surname given. He heads the Microbial Reclas-sification Department at the Serifosa branch of the Komarr Terraforming Project. He tracks natural and mutated bacteria, but wants to introduce higher organ-isms to help stabilize the planet's environment. (K)

Phillipi:
No first name given. An air-bike trooper in the Dendarii Free Mercenary Fleet, she dies during the clone raid on Jackson's Whole, but her body is frozen in cryo-stasis. She is dumped by Elli so Miles can be saved, permanently killing her. (MD)

Pitt:
No first name given. Leader of a small group of about fifteen men in the prison camp on Dagoola IV, he and four others beat up Miles upon his arrival, taking everything he has. Pitt has committed other crimes, including rape and murder, but no one is able to hold him accountable. Miles achieves both revenge and a strategic distraction when he falsely accuses him of being a Cetagandan spy, carving the title on his back with a broken water cup. The other prisoners beat him to death. (BI)

Pitt's lieutenant:
A Marilacan, no name given. He acts as Pitt's second-in-command at the Dagoola prison camp and attempts to

kill Miles after Pitt's death. Miles shows him mercy and he ends up being rescued along with the others. (BI)

Plasma arc:
A standard military energy-beam weapon, suitable for melting and/or burning. Personal versions range from pistol and rifle-size weapons, powered by self-contained power packs, to large, portable plasma arc systems that can damage vehicles and ships from thousands of meters away. A plasma arc power pack can also be jury-rigged to overload, creating a crude explosive device, as Aral does on Sergyar to start a fire. A wound from a plasma arc can be devastating, like what Elli Quinn suffers during the Tau Verde IV campaign, when a plasma arc shot burns off her face. (All except FF)

Plasma cannon:
A ship-to-ship version of the plasma arc, it is immensely more powerful, with a range of several thousand kilometers. Miles places one in the corridor of the *Ariel* to neutralize Cavilo's holding Gregor as a hostage. (VG)

Plasma mirror field:
A ship-mounted plasma mirror field that absorbs and reflects an incoming beam, sending it back to hit the attacking vessel. It allows a shuttle to take on a warship and defeat it, as the Escobarans did to the Barrayaran navy during the 120-Day War. (SH)

Plasma mirror field pack:
A self-powered, personal deflection energy field capable of absorbing approximately thirty to forty hits before

burning out. During the clone rescue mission on Jackson's Whole, Mark uses his plasma mirror field pack to shield Elli during the extraction. (B, MD)

Plause:
No first name given. An ensign in Miles's class, he is assigned to languages school to learn galactic languages since he already speaks all four native Barrayaran ones perfectly. (VG)

Plumbing:
Frictionless (waterless) or sonic toilets are found in self-contained settings, such as space habitats. In lower-tech settings or in planetary facilities, traditional water-based plumbing is still used, with accompanying pipes and potential drain problems, as occurred when Doctor Borgos tried to dispose of forty kilograms of bug butter by washing it down the sink. Bathing facilities range from historic bathtubs, such as the one in Vorkosigan House where Ivan dunks Miles to snap him out of his depression, to traditional water showers and sonic showers, which use sound waves to remove dead cells and dirt. (All)

Pol:
A neighboring planet of Barrayar, it connects that planet to the Hegen Hub by way of the Komarr nexus. A republic, it joins the Hegen Hub Alliance after the Vervain conflict. (VG)

Pol Station Six:
A jump-point station between Pol and the Hegen Hub. Miles goes there in his Victor Rotha disguise to

gather intelligence on the various ship buildups near the Hegen Hub. (VG)

Population Council:
The organization responsible for ensuring safe reproductive ability for Athos's all-male population. They accepted the lowest bid for a new batch of ovarian material from L. Bharaputra & Sons, and received a shipment of nonviable tissue cultures. Their solution is to send Ethan Urquhart into the galaxy to acquire viable cultures. (EA)

Portobello Pharmaceutical Company:
The large company that both Doctor and Mrs. Bianca work in and own. (DD)

Power armor:
A self-contained combat suit used in ship-to-ship boarding and combat in space or other hostile environments. Each armored suit augments the user's physical strength, contains its own power, environmental, and weapons systems, is impervious to stunner and nerve disruptor fire, and can withstand plasma arc fire for a short time. A suit is also capable of being remote-piloted from a central command. Miles and Auson tap into the Oseran suits during the assault on the refinery at Tau Verde IV, programming error codes into the enemy suits to sabotage them. Later during that same campaign, Miles finds one that will fit him, but is rendered incapable of using it by his ulcer. (WA)

Pramod:
A quaddie at the Cay Habitat, he is a striking boy with aquiline nose, brilliant black eyes, wiry muscles, and dark mahogany skin. One of the quickest learners in the engineering class, he is instrumental in helping Leo create the new vortex mirror for their cargo ship. (FF)

*Prince Serg*:
A new Imperial Cruiser and the most powerful ship in the Barrayaran fleet. If Miles can survive six months at Lazkowski Base, he will be transferred to it. The dreadnought reinforces the Dendarii forces in the fight against the Cetagandans at Vervain. Its gravitic imploder lances have three times the range of the Cetagandan ones. (VG)

*Princess Olivia*:
An unarmed ship that was hijacked using Lord Vorbataille's yacht. All of the passengers aboard were killed. (WG)

*Prisoner of Zenda, The*:
A video that Siggy brings to the rest of the quaddies. (FF)

Projector:
A cloaking device Stuben and Lai use to hide their Betan Survey ship from the *General Vorkraft*'s sensors and rescue Cordelia. Later, an improved version is used to project the image of a Betan warship to lure the Barrayaran vessels away from guarding the wormhole so supply ships can reach Escobar. (SH)

Prole:
A slang term, shortened from the word "proletariat," used by the Vor to refer to anyone that isn't in their class. (CC)

Ptarmigan:
No first name given. A lieutenant and shuttle pilot in the Dendarii Free Mercenary Fleet, he takes all orbit-to-surface flights at combat-drop speed. (BA)

Pym:
No first name given. A retired sergeant in the Barrayaran military, he is an armsman to Aral Vorkosigan, and Bothari's replacement. A tall, habitually fit man graying at the temples, he is always dressed in the brown and silver house uniform. He served twenty years in the Imperial Guard, meeting his wife while on security duty at Vorhartung Castle. Afterward he joined the House Vorkosigan staff, aided by a recommendation from Simon Illyan. He accompanies Miles to solve the infanticide case at Silvy Vale. He escorts Mark and Elena in Vorbarr Sultana to protect Mark after Ivan failed to keep him out of trouble. He also tries to help Miles in his pursuit of Ekaterin, and also feeds information about Mark to Kareen after their forced separation. He is highly insulted by Doctor Borgos's genetic modification of his butter bugs with the Vorkosigan family crest. During Miles's wedding and celebration afterward, he feels so bad about missing the toxic pearls that he gives Roic time off with double holiday pay while he works the night shift. (CC, MD, MM, WG)

Pym, Miss:
No first name given. A daughter of Armsman Pym, she is Ekaterin's personal maid, and is sent to Barrayar while Miles and Ekaterin go to Graf Station. (DI)

* * 0 * *

Quaddie:
An unofficial nickname for the bioengineered workers on the Cay Project. They are genetically engineered humans with a second set of arms and hands instead of legs and feet. They are literally owned by GalacTech, which tries to dump them on Rodeo when the Cay Project is shut down. Doctor Cay dubbed them *Homo quadrimanus*. Bruce Van Atta refers to them by the derogatory nickname "chimps." They prefer living in zero-gee, but can move about in artificial gravity with the help of float chairs. After Leo Graf leads the first group to freedom, they establish the Union of Free Habitats in an asteroid belt, and grow to a population of more than a million. Miles meets several during his adventures, including Nicol, a quaddie musician, and Garnet Five, a zero-gee ballet dancer. (DI, FF)

Quaddie approved fiction:
Video fiction approved for the quaddies' viewing by GalacTech personnel. As seen by the titles (*The Little Compressor That Could*, *Bobby BX-99 Solves the Excess Humidity Mystery*, *Bobby BX-99 and the Plant Virus*), they are educational in nature. The quaddies pass them up in favor of more escapist fare. (FF)

Quartz:
A Betan city, of which Cordelia says the president can "put on falsies and go woo the hermaphrodite vote" there before she'd become a government representative. (SH)

Quinn, Elli:
A mercenary in the Dendarii Free Mercenary Fleet, she begins as a recruit-trainee, and ends up as admiral in command of the entire organization. Slim but curvy, she has short-cropped, dark, curly hair, a fine, chiseled nose, large eyes, and white skin. Her face was burned off by a plasma arc blast at Tau Verde IV, but Miles paid for reconstructive surgery on Beta Colony.

She was born and raised on Kline Station. Miles sends her there to find out what Colonel Millisor is chasing after, a task she covers by also accepting a contract to eliminate him from House Bharaputra. It is her first intelligence assignment, and while she succeeds in her primary mission, she is unable to convince Terrence Cee to join the Dendarii mercenaries. She donates one of her ovaries to Athos to be the start of a new genetic line: EQ-1.

During the prisoner rescue at Dagoola, she infiltrates the Cetagandan forces, posing as part of the prisoner observation teams. She is one of only three people outside Barrayar who know Miles's true identity, and often serves as his bodyguard. She and Miles fall in love, but she turns down his marriage offer, preferring a mainly physical relationship with Miles in his Admiral Naismith persona rather than the hopeless complications of marrying Lord Vorkosigan. During the incident at the Thames Tidal Barrier she is stunned unconscious, and must be rescued by Miles and Ivan.

She leads the rescue mission for Mark on Jackson's Whole, and almost scuttles the deal to get Miles's cryo-chamber from Baron Bharaputra by threatening him with multi-planet retaliation if the chamber isn't returned. She also accompanies Mark on the trip to the Durona complex to recover Miles, and goes into Ryoval's secret laboratory to find him.

After Elena and Baz resign from the Dendarii, she is promoted to commodore and fleet-second in Baz's place by Miles. However, he also alienates her when he gets his new orders to return to Barrayar, first by not revealing his seizures to Imperial Security, and second by choosing Sergeant Taura to escort him to Tau Ceti. She is very upset at Miles's deception of Simon Illyan, and the increasing uncertainty of their relationship.

When she does see Miles again, he offers her the choice of becoming his wife and joining him on Barrayar, or becoming the admiral of the Dendarii. She chooses the promotion, but asks him to join her instead, and leave Barrayar behind. Miles regretfully declines, accepting his role as Lord Vorkosigan and Imperial Auditor. She is unable to attend Miles's wedding, and a pearl choker arrives supposedly as a wedding gift from her, but she had already sent a living fur along with a naughty limerick. The jewelry is actually an assassination attempt by another party using a neurotoxin to kill Ekaterin and destroy Miles, but the plot is stopped before it can succeed. (BA, BI, CC, EA, M, MD, WA)

Quintillan:
The Minister of the Interior on Barrayar, he works
with Aral Vorkosigan. One of the men Aral suggests
to be the Regent of Barrayar until Gregor comes of
age to rule, he is not a serious candidate because he
is not Vor. Two decades later, Aral Vorkosigan is ready
to give him the Prime Minister position, but he died
in a lightflyer accident before it could be arranged.
(MD, SH, WA)

• • R • •

Racozy:
No first name given. Cordelia tells Simon he is one of
three men that could replace Aral as Prime Minister.
Racozy assumes the position when Aral retires. (MD)

Radials:
A class of animal that lives on Sergyar. One is an
aerial, gas-filled jellyfish that lands on the hexapeds
and takes blood from them with tendril-like appendages
tipped in poison. Others are little, round, underground
creatures that move on cilia-like legs. One of the
"vampire balloons," as Aral describes them, attacks
Dubauer during the trek to the supply cache. (SH)

Radnov:
No first name given. A lieutenant in the Barrayaran
military, he is Aral's political officer on the *General
Vorkraft*, and leads a mutiny while Aral is on the
survey planet, later named Sergyar. He escapes capture when Aral returns to the on-planet base, and is

brought back to the ship by the crew of the *Rene Magritte* when they rescue Cordelia. He and his men take over the engineering section, and threaten to turn off life-support unless Aral and his officers surrender. Cordelia stuns him and his co-conspirators with help from Nilesa and Tafas. (SH)

Radovas, Barto:
A five-space math engineer, he was hired by Administrator Soudha as part of the terraforming project on Komarr, although he is actually involved in the plan to close the wormhole to Barrayar. After his disappearance, rumors spread that he ran off with Marie Trogir, even though he was married and had three children. He turns up dead in the Soletta Station wreckage, even though he wasn't supposed to be up there. He and his wife are a part of the jump-point plot, and his death was actually part of the Soletta accident, when one of their experiments with the wormhole-closure device caused an ore ship to crash into the mirror array. (K)

Radovas, Mrs.:
No first name given. The widow of Barto Radovas, she is in her late fifties, although she appears fifteen years younger, and is slender and well dressed. When notified of her husband's death, she feigns ignorance of what he was doing, and would have been a penniless widow if not for Miles ordering that she receive survivor's benefits even though Radovas resigned his post five days before dying. She is a leader of the jump-point plot, which Miles discovers just before his capture at the Waste Heat experiment station. During

the standoff on the jump station, it is her deciding vote that induces the conspirators to surrender and release their hostages. (K)

Randall's Rangers:
A mercenary group hired by Vervain for protection, unaware that the group's commander, Cavilo, plans to use the mercenaries to rob the planet after letting the Cetagandans into Vervain space. Cavilo changes the uniforms to black and tan after she has Randall murdered. (VG)

Rappelling harness:
A climbing tool consisting of a self-powered spool of drop-wire with retractable handles, a ribbon harness for the user, and a gravitic grappling hook that will attach to just about any surface. Miles uses it several times at the Thames Tidal Barrier on Earth. (BA)

Rathjens:
No first name given. A general in Barrayaran Imperial Security, he is the chief of Imperial Security on Komarr, and is middle-aged, alert, and busy. He dresses in Komarran civilian wear instead of his Barrayaran uniform. Miles calls him at his office in Solstice to discuss the identification of the unknown body found in the solar-array wreckage. (K)

Rau:
No first name given. A Cetagandan ghem-captain working with Colonel Millisor at Kline Station, he kidnaps Ethan Urquhart and brings him to the colonel for interrogation. He is so average-looking Ethan has

a hard time remembering his face even when Rau is right in front of him. When dressed as a Cetagandan, his face paint is base red with slashes of orange, black, white, and green. He is killed by assassins from Bharaputra House. (EA)

Razor-grass:
A plant on Barrayar that is not actually a grass, which Miles sees in a new light in Ekaterin's virtual garden, composed entirely of native flora. (K)

*Reddi-Meal!*:
A prepackaged, self-heating meal sold in Vorbarr Sultana and other Barrayaran cities. Miles lives on them in the first few days after his return to Barrayar before he hires Ma Kosti as Vorkosigan House's cook. (M)

Reed:
No first name given. An investigator with Eurolaw in London, he is charged with looking into the attempted murder of Admiral Naismith at the shuttleport. He interrogates Mark while he is in his Lieutenant Vorkosigan persona, and releases him into Ser Galen's custody before Miles can get him. (BA)

Reformation Army:
The unit title Miles gives the prisoners on Dagoola IV, once he starts reorganizing them for the coming escape. (BI)

*Rene Magritte*:
A Betan scientific survey ship with a crew of fifty-two, commanded by Cordelia Naismith and sent to

a survey planet that has attracted the attention of Barrayar as well. Her crew risks their lives to free Cordelia, bringing a group of Barrayaran mutineers on board the *General Vorkraft*. (SH)

*RG 132*:
An obsolete but operational jump-capable cargo ship that Arde Mayhew threatens to destroy at Beta Colony. Miles buys the ship and uses it to transfer weapons to Tau Verde IV. It is damaged beyond repair when Arde uses it to ram the *Triumph* into the ore refinery, bending the Necklin rods and peeling half the hull off. (WA)

RG Freighter:
On Komarr, Nikolai has a model of this antique cargo-hauling jump ship, which reminds Miles of the *RG 132*, which he owned briefly when he was seventeen years' old. (K)

Rho Ceta:
One of the eight satrapy planets in the Cetagandan Empire, and Barrayar's nearest unallied neighbor. It would expand toward Komarr, except that Barrayar holds two-thirds of the jump points between the two planets. Its governor is Este Rond, and its unnamed Imperial consort has brown hair. (C)

Rigby:
No first name given. A Group-Patroller, or civilian peace officer, on Komarr, she accompanies Miles, Vorthys, Etienne, and Tuomonen to inform Doctor Radovas's wife of his death. (K)

Ritter:
No first name given. The surgeon who performs
Cordelia's placental transfer, assisted by Doctor Vaagen
and Doctor Henri. Tall, dark-haired, with olive skin
and long, lean hands. (B)

Riva:
No first name given. A professor of five-space math
at Solstice University, she is called in as a consultant
by Imperial Auditor Vorthys to help figure out what
the Waste Heat engineering group were building
with all of the money siphoned off the project. She
is about fifty years old, and is a thin, intense, olive-
skinned woman with bright black eyes who paces
endlessly while solving a problem. Miles interrogates
her under fast-penta when he thinks she is withholding information. Her answers let them discover that
the engineers have built a wormhole destroyer, and
are planning to close the wormhole to Barrayar. She
also figures out that there is a very good chance the
device will backlash, and destroy whatever vessel or
ship it is on, and it is that sort of backlash that caused
the solar-array collision. (K)

Rivek:
No first name given. A commodore in the Barrayaran
military stationed in Sector Four, he was concerned
with the rescue of Lord Vorvane's wife and children,
which Miles handled with the Dendarii a few years
earlier. Simon brings it up during one of his flashback moments caused by his malfunctioning memory
chip. (M)

River barge:
A large, flat-bottomed boat that carries cargo on a river. Used on Barrayar throughout the Time of Isolation, river barges established the location of Vorbarr Sultana, as the rapids there defined the limits of barge traffic. Afterward, a dam and lock system allows barge traffic to continue upriver from the city. (B, CC)

Road:
In most modern cities, a regular city grid of streets provides organized transportation and defines blocks of property. During Barrayar's Time of Isolation, transportation reverted to horses and mule-drawn carts and wagons. In the old part of some cities, networks of winding streets with very narrow lanes and alleys defy modern traffic, such as in Vorbarr Sultana's Caravanserai district. Country and backcountry roads range from paved highways to dirt paths. Modern cities use automated traffic grids. Barrayar, barely a century past the Time of Isolation, is still improving its infrastructure. It's not until the time of Gregor's wedding that the capital, Vorbarr Sultana, starts implementing automated traffic grids for groundcars and lightflyers. (All)

Rodeo:
A marginal world, home to GalacTech mining and drilling operations. Its surface consists primarily of harsh desert and mountains. GalacTech owns Rodeo on a ninety-nine-year lease with Orient IV, but large mineral deposits make the planet much more interesting to the Orient IV government. GalacTech had planned to dump the quaddies on planet if they were not profitable. (FF)

Roic:

No first name given. An armsman at Vorkosigan House, he usually works the night shift, but is pressed into day duty when Ekaterin first arrives at the house. He is awoken to intervene during the butter bug fight, and greatly embarrassed to be caught in the foyer covered in bug butter and wearing briefs, a backward stunner holster, and nothing else.

Assigned to assist Taura while she's visiting Barrayar, he is intrigued by her and becomes smitten. He proves his loyalty to Vorkosigan House and redeems his honor, which he felt was questioned during the butter bug battle, when he and Taura figure out the assassination plot aimed at Ekaterin, saving her life and Miles's sanity. As his reward, Pym takes over his night shift duty for the next week, while Roic romances Taura after the wedding reception.

He accompanies Miles and Ekaterin on their honeymoon as bodyguard and batman. A former municipal guardsman in Hassadar on Barrayar, he assists in the investigation at Graf Station, and helps Miles take the *Idris* back from the renegade Cetagandan ba that hijacked it. (CC, DI, WG)

Rond, Este:

The haut-governor of Rho Ceta, he is middle-aged, tall, heavy, and vigorous, with a bullish demeanor. Miles considers him an early suspect in the plot to overthrow the Emperor, but eliminates him in favor of either Slyke Giaja or Ilsum Kety (C)

Rose:
A gentle mare Cordelia rides during Gregor's escape into the Dendarii Mountains. (B)

Rosemont, Reg:
A lieutenant and member of the Betan Astronomical Survey team, he had blond hair and a long body. He was killed by the Barrayarans in the assault on Base One. Cordelia buries him on the planet, and is almost unable to imagine her ship operating without him. She makes sure there is a marker placed at his grave on Sergyar. (SH)

Rotha, Victor:
Miles's cover name for his mission to the Hegen Hub, posing as a weapons procurement agent from Beta Colony. (VG)

Rudy:
A male quaddie at Cay Habitat, he is designated to mate with Claire next. (FF)

Ruey, Anias:
A feelie-dream composer, she has lank, black hair, alive dark eyes, and soft, pale skin. She lives in a Rio apartment with a good view of the sea. She refers to an ex-husband, an ex-guardian aunt, and an ex-boyfriend who works in journalism. Carlos Diaz commissions a dark, violent feelie-dream from her on behalf of his employer, Doctor Bianca. After it is completed, she learns her dream synthesizer has been sabotaged to kill her, and turns amateur detective to figure out who would wants her dead and why. (DD)

Ruibal:
No first name given. A colonel in Barrayaran Imperial Security, he is a neurologist on the team helping Miles to treat Simon. A short, round-faced man, he provides the initial evaluation summary and assists with Simon's case. (M)

Rule 27B:
As defined by Miles: Never make key tactical decisions while having electroconvulsive seizures. (VG)

Ryoval, Ry:
The baron of House Ryoval on Jackson's Whole, a rival of House Bharaputra. He inhabits a clone body, and looks to be in his mid-twenties, with smooth, dark olive skin, a high-bridged nose, and long, shining black hair in a braid. He has a large bodyguard who is biologically enhanced to be an unarmed killing machine. His House's specialty is genetically created slaves made to order for whatever illicit pleasure the buyer has in mind. Baron Fell is his younger half brother. Ryoval killed Fell's clone to take over his House. He wants genetic samples from Miles, Bel Thorne, and Nicol, and offers to trade Taura for them. Instead, Miles steals Taura and Nicol, and destroys his vast library of genetic samples as well. Ryoval has sent several bounty hunters after the admiral. He captures Mark, thinking he is Naismith, and puts him through physical, psychological, and sexual torture. Mark gets revenge by killing Ryoval just before he is going to remove one of Mark's eyes. (L, MD)

* * **S** * *

S.A.H. Pesodoro:
A South American monetary unit. Carlos Diaz offers
to pay Anias Ruey twenty thousand pesodoros to make
a violent, disturbing feelie-dream. (DD)

Sahlin:
No first name given. A captain in the Felician military, he accompanies General Halify, and is supposed
to take the ordnance shipment Miles brought to Tau
Verde IV planetside. (WA)

Saint Simon:
No first name given. A lieutenant in the Barrayaran
military, he is part of the engineering staff on the
*General Vorkraft*. Aral authorizes his plan to stop the
mutineers. (SH)

Saltpetre Plot, The:
A plot on Barrayar during the Time of Isolation that
caused the death of Count Vorvayne, who was hung
in stocks until he died. His wife, the sixth Countess
Vorvayne, sat at his feet in a hunger strike and died
of exposure. Ekaterin remembers this example of a
Vor wife's faithfulness to her husband. (K)

Sanctuary Station:
One of the few orbital arcologies in the Union of
Free Habitats that maintains gravity and deals with
galactics. (DI)

Sardi:
No first name given. A Barrayaran soldier who thinks
Aral is a strategic genius. Carl and Evon Vorhalas refer
to his opinion while discussing Aral at the Regent's
confirmation ceremony. (B)

Satrap governor:
Each of the eight satrapy worlds controlled by the
Cetagandan Empire is ruled by a governor, all of
whom are chosen from Imperial relations. Each has
a haut-lady consort, who keeps an eye on things on
each planet for the Empress. They also each have a
ghem-general to oversee their planetary armed forces.
At the Dowager Empress's funeral, each one has
received a copy of the Star Crèche gene bank from
the deceased Empress, but none of them has the true
Great Key. One governor, Ilsum Kety, had planned
to take the throne of the Empire for himself, but his
plan is foiled by Miles and Ivan. (C)

Scat-cat:
A small, teardrop-shaped vehicle used to travel around
Lazkowski Base and Kyril Island. Miles accidentally
sinks one in mud when he is given bad directions
during his assignment as Chief Meteorological Officer.
Recovered by Lieutenant Bonn, Miles is forced to
oversee its cleaning as part of his punishment. (VG)

Schriml:
No first name given. A deputy, he is with Sheriff
Yoder at Chalmys DuBauer's house. (DD)

Scrubwire:
A low, round Barrayaran plant with a spicy scent and a dull color. Ekaterin includes it in the display garden near Vorkosigan House for its pleasant smell. (CC)

Seal of the Star Crèche:
The screaming bird sigil on the end of the Great Key that Miles has Mia Maz identify for him. It is used to seal reproductive contracts between Cetagandan haut-lords, indicating the contract has been approved by the Empress. (C)

Second:
The Barrayaran term for best man or maid of honor at a wedding. Miles serves as Gregor's Second during his wedding. For Miles's wedding, Ivan serves as his second, and for saving the bride's life Taura is elevated to Ekaterin's Second in place of Martya Koudelka. (CC, WG)

Senden:
No first name given. A ghem-lady, she is the sister of Lady Benello, and invites Ivan to a court-dance practice during his stay on Eta Ceti IV. (C)

Sendorf:
One of the three men Cordelia tells Simon could be a potential Prime Minister replacement for Aral. (MD)

Sens:
No first name given. One of Radnov's mutineers, he is captured during Aral's return to their camp on Sergyar. (SH)

Sergyar:
Barrayar's colony planet, named after the vile Prince
Serg Vorbarra, which was first explored by Cordelia
and Aral before they were married. Only inhabited
for the past thirty years, there are about one million
colonists on-planet. Aral is the Viceroy of Sergyar and
has requested a separate Imperial Security Office of
Domestic Affairs be created for the growing colony.
Sharing their dual appointment with equal political
authority, Cordelia is Vicereine of Sergyar in her own
right; hers is not a mere courtesy title as Aral's wife.
The colony had a problem with an infectious worm
plague, but that has been brought under control. Aral
and Cordelia return home from the planet for Gregor's
wedding. Ensign Dmitri Corbeau is originally from
Sergyar. (CC, DI, M)

Serifosa:
One of Komarr's domed cities, it is where the inves-
tigation into the solar mirror accident takes place.
The Vorsoissons live there until Etienne's death. (K)

Setti:
No first name given. A Cetagandan, he is one of
Millisor's men. Quinn kills him in the shuttle bay by
tossing him the booby-trapped reader given to Ethan
by a Bharaputran assassin. (EA)

Seven Secret Roads of Female Pleasure:
A fictional method of lovemaking Miles invents to
prevent Mark from sleeping with Elli Quinn while
he's impersonating Miles. (BA)

Sharkbait One:
A jumpscout ship with the Dendarii Free Mercenary Fleet. It scouts for Cetagandans during the Vervain conflict. (VG)

Sharkbait Three:
A jumpscout ship with the Dendarii Free Mercenary Fleet. During the Vervain conflict it announces that help is arriving, and the wormhole must be cleared. (VG)

Ship knits:
Casual wear worn on spaceships, they are like sweat suits, consisting of shapeless, loose, comfortable shirt and pants. (All)

Shock stick:
A melee energy weapon that imparts an electric shock when it hits a target. Often used as a control or punishment device, it has adjustable power settings that cause varying levels of pain. At higher settings, repeated hits can shock a subject unconscious. Ser Galen used a shock stock to punish Mark during his training, and Miles is hit by them several times, including once to the face on Ilsum Kety's ship during his mission in the Cetagandan Empire. (BA, C, MD, VG)

Shuttle:
A small, self-powered, environmentally sealed transport craft used for surface-to-orbit transportation. The means of power and propulsion is not specified. Anti-gravity is used for liftoff and touchdown, so there are no blast effects from a propulsion system. Reentry friction does cause hull heating. Shuttles come in many models, from

simple drop versions that carry passengers and cargo, to armed and armored military models capable of transporting fifty to sixty soldiers or civilians, as during the prisoner-of-war breakout on Dagoola IV. (All)

Shuttle A-4:
A fully loaded combat shuttle destroyed by a Cetagandan fighter during the prisoner rescue on Dagoola IV. (BI)

Shuttle B-7:
An empty combat shuttle destroyed by a Cetagandan fighter during the prisoner rescue on Dagoola IV. (BI)

Shuttleport Locks:
An import and shopping district in Serifosa Dome on Komarr. Ekaterin takes Miles shopping there, where he purchases Gregor's lava lamp, and the miniature planet jewelry for Delia Koudelka and Laisa Toscane, along with the miniature Barrayar pendant he gives to Ekaterin after she helps foil the Komarran engineers' wormhole plot. (K)

"Siege of the Silver Moon, The":
A Barrayaran childhood ballad and drinking song about a Vor lord and a witch woman who ride in a magic mortar and pestle, which they use to grind their enemies' bones. Miles hums a bit of it while first talking to Arde Mayhew on Beta Colony. (WA)

Siegel:
No first name or rank given. A soldier in the Barrayaran military, he is the leader of a patrol on the *General Vorkraft* that attempts to stop the mutineers. (SH)

**Siegling's:**
A high-class weapons store in the Vorbarr Sultana, where Cordelia buys Koudelka a swordstick. Thickly carpeted, with wooden paneling. The smell inside reminds her a bit of the armory aboard her Betan survey ship. The clerk tries to sell her an inferior weapon, but Cordelia demands and receives the very best. (B)

**Siembieda, Ryan:**
A hazel-eyed engineering tech sergeant with the Dendarii Free Mercenary Fleet, he was killed at Mahata Solaris during an assault by a Cetagandan hit team trying to kill Miles. Cryogenically frozen, he was thawed and resuscitated on Earth. Miles fills him in on what had happened on their way back to the Dendarii fleet at the spaceport. (BA)

**Siggy:**
A quaddie who brings contraband video fiction to Claire and Silver. He discusses a potential plan to take the jump ship based on what he saw in another video, *Nest of Doom*, involving space marines against aliens, but Silver scuttles his idea. (FF)

**Sigma Ceta:**
One of the eight satrapy planets in the Cetagandan Empire, it borders the Vega Station group. Its governor is Ilsum Kety, much like Slyke Giaja, and cousin to him through their mothers, who were half sisters through different constellations. (C)

Silica:
One of the main cities on Beta Colony, it is known for its university. (B, WA)

Silica Hospital:
A medical facility on Beta Colony. Elizabeth Naismith is employed there as a medical equipment and maintenance engineer. (B)

Silica Zoo:
Located on Beta Colony, the Silica Zoo maintains habitats underground for humans and animals alike. (WA)

Silver:
A quaddie on the Cay Project Habitat, she is one of the ringleaders in the revolt against GalacTech. She has medium-length, platinum-blond hair, a sharp facial-bone structure, and works in hydroponics. A good friend to Tony and Claire, she has a purely sexual relationship with Van Atta, which she uses to get information from him. She's also sleeping with Ti, the shuttle pilot, and leverages their relationship to involve him in the quaddie revolt. She accompanies Ti to transfer Mrs. Minchenko and rescue Tony from Rodeo. Silver begins learning how to play the violin, taught by Mrs. Minchenko, while waiting for the rescue party to return to the shuttle. Two centuries later, she is a heroine to countless quaddie descendants, and her relationship with Leo and the flight to free space has been immortalized in zero-gee ballet. (DI, FF)

Silvy Vale:
A small village in the Dendarii Mountains on Barrayar. Miles first visited it to solve the murder of the infant Raina Csurik. He goes back after resigning from Imperial Security to try to get some perspective on his life by visiting Raina's grave, only to find the graveyard has been moved owing to flooding caused by their new hydroelectric dam. The village now has reliable power, and the citizens are building a new clinic and will soon have a full-time doctor on site supplied by Countess Vorkosigan's Hassadar medical program. (M, MM)

Sim:
No first name given. A trooper in the Dendarii Free Mercenary Fleet who participates in the prisoner rescue on Dagoola IV. (BI)

Simka, Sri:
A military historian, he wrote two books on military tactics about campaigns on Walshea and Skya IV. Ky Tung mentions his work during his first conversation with Miles. (WA)

Sinda:
A female quaddie at the Cay Project, she is scheduled to mate with Tony next. (FF)

Singing Open the Great Gates:
A Cetagandan ceremony featuring a large chorus of several hundred female and male ghem, who sing an incredible, multipart song that lasts about thirty minutes. Miles and Ivan attend the performance during the Dowager Empress's funeral ceremonies. (C)

Sink of Sin:
A religious term on Athos that refers to a man's soul being drained away when he looks at a woman. Ethan is concerned that he might feel its effect when he looks upon the faces of the female doctors in an issue of *The Betan Journal of Reproductive Medicine*. (EA)

*Sir Randan and the Bartered Bride*:
One of the contraband video fiction titles Ti Gulik brings to Silver. (FF)

*Sir Randan's Folly*:
One of the contraband video fiction titles Ti Gulik brings to Silver. (FF)

Sircoj:
No first name given. A major in the Barrayaran military, he oversees gate security at the Tannery Base shuttleport after Vordarian's coup attempt, and notifies Cordelia of Doctor Vaagen's arrival. (B)

Sixteen, Pramod:
A quaddie airseal technician on a work crew in Freight Bay Two on Graf Station who helps catch Russo Gupta. (DI)

Skellytum:
A tall maroon-colored plant with a barrel-shaped trunk and raised tendrils that is native to Barrayar. Ekaterin owns a bright red miniature one that is seventy years old. She inherited it from her grandmother many years ago, and uses bonsai techniques to keep it small. Etienne smashes it when Ekaterin tells him

she is leaving, and Miles salvages it, although she will have to repot a cutting from it instead of trying to save the entire plant. Ekaterin plants the salvaged cutting in the garden near Vorkosigan House before quitting as Miles's designer. She returns to find him watering it the wrong way, not having read her detailed instructions. (CC, K)

Sleep gas:
A standard tranquilizer gas that can be administered by grenade or in an aerosol spray. Safe and effective, it is often used in police or hostage situations. (All)

Sleeptimer:
A time-release sleep aid that can be calibrated for varying durations of effect. Cordelia suggests Miles use one to snatch some sleep before his wedding. (WG)

Smetani:
No first name given. A corporal in Barrayaran Imperial Security, he mans the front desk when Miles brings his little group to headquarters to arrest Lucas Haroche. Miles orders him not to inform Haroche about his appearance there, which is seconded by Simon Illyan. (M)

Smolyani:
No first name given. A lieutenant in the Barrayaran military, he pilots the courier jump ship *Kestrel*, and delivers Miles's orders to go to Graf Station in the Union of Free Habitats. He also transports Miles, Ekaterin, and Roic to the station. (DI)

Social duty credits:

Part of a government program on Athos, social duty credits are earned via volunteer work and service to society, to be used toward gaining sons and becoming a designated alternate parent. They can also be used to pay fines, as Janos does when he is arrested for destruction of public property and assault and battery on his boss. (EA)

Soletta Station:

The name for the orbital solar mirror array, and the space station that supports it, in orbit around Komarr. The station was damaged, and six technicians were killed as a result of Barto Radovas and Marie Trogir's experiment with one of the wormhole-closing devices, which created an energy backlash that drove an ore freighter into the solar mirrors, rendering four of the seven panels inoperable. As his wedding present to Komarr, Gregor funds the repair of the station, as well as expanding the solar program to aid the terraforming process. (CC, K)

Solian:

No first name given. A Komarran serving as the Barrayaran security liaison aboard the trade ship *Idris*, he went missing while the ship was docked at Graf Station. Captain Brun thinks he deserted, because some personal effects and a valise are missing but uniforms were left. About four liters of blood, presumably his, were found in an airlock, so he is assumed dead. The blood was planted by Russo Gupta to try to draw attention to the *Idris*, so that Ker Dubauer wouldn't get away. Solian fell victim to the same deadly biotoxin that killed the smugglers, administered by Dubauer. His remains are found in another body pod on the *Idris*. (DI)

Solstice:
The domed capital city of Komarr, it is occasionally rocked by riots caused by Komarrans protesting Barrayar's control of their planet. It is where the infamous Solstice Massacre occurred, with a plaque erected in the martyrs' honor on the site. (K)

Solstice Massacre:
Occurring during the conquest of Komarr, it saddled Aral Vorkosigan with the nickname "The Butcher of Komarr." Two hundred Komarran counselors, including Ser Galen's sister Rebecca, were killed by order of Aral's political officer, who was then killed by Aral when he found out what had happened. A plaque memorializes the site in Solstice. Miles visited the site with Duv Galeni, who burned a death offering for his aunt there. (BA, K, VG)

Solstice University:
The main university on Komarr. Imperial Auditor Vorthys once taught a course there, and he requests the assistance of a university professor, Doctor Riva, while investigating the solar mirror array accident at the Waste Heat experiment station. (K)

Soltoxin:
The poison gas used in an assassination attempt against Aral by Evon Vorhalas, which caught Cordelia as well. Soltoxin is a slow-acting poison that will turn

the lungs to jelly within an hour if the antidote is not quickly administered. A delaying first-aid treatment is to wash the gas from the skin and mouth to minimize absorption. The antidote is an inhaled gas that is a violent teratogen, destroying bone growth in a fetus. The antidote damages the fetal Miles, weakening his skeleton, and causing him to be transferred to a uterine replicator for regenerative calcium treatments. In adults, since their bones have already reached maturity, the antidote induces a tendency toward arthritic-like breakdowns that are treatable. Soltoxin also causes testicular scarring in males on the cellular level, often rendering survivors sterile. (B)

Sonia:
No surname given. Amor Klyeuvi's niece, she is an aged woman, with gray hair in a long braid down her back. She gives sweet cakes to the boy who brings Kly's mount back to his hiding place. (B)

Sonic grenade:
An airtube-launched grenade that killed Aral's mother when one was shot into her stomach during Yuri Vorbarra's Massacre. It is also used in an assassination attempt against Aral's motorcade in Vorbarr Sultana after he is named Regent. Although the technology isn't defined, the weapon is powerful enough to make a large hole in the street after missing the armored groundcar. The weapon might have been older ordnance with a possibly defective tracker, as the security didn't detect a ranging pulse before the attack. (B, SH)

Sonic toilet:
A standing lavatory disposal device on jump stations that uses sound waves to break apart waste matter. Ekaterin tries to clog one using her shoes while being held prisoner to cause a maintenance alert, but it disposes of her footwear without any problem. (K)

Soudha:
No first name given. He is an administrator and the department head of Waste Heat Management at the Serifosa branch of the Komarr Terraforming Project. A big, square-handed man in his late forties, he gives Andro Farr the runaround about Marie, then spreads the story that she ran off with Barto Radovas. He is siphoning money from the terraforming project by creating a fake experimental department and employees, then using the funds to build a wormhole-destruction device that will collapse the jump point between Komarr and Barrayar, leaving the latter planet cut off from the rest of the universe. Along with Barto and Madame Radovas, Marie Trogir, Lena Foscol, Cappell, and Arrozi, he considers himself to be a Komarran patriot doing what is best for his planet, with humane limits on loss of life, but a previous test of the device caused the Soletta Station accident, and the group doesn't realize that their device has a very good chance of destroying them and the entire jump-point station. After their device is destroyed by Ekaterin, he votes to stop the standoff, and surrender to the authorities. (K)

South Province:
An area on Athos where Ethan Urquhart's family comes from. (EA)

Soya oatmeal:
One of the two provisions at Base One that weren't
destroyed in the Barrayaran attack. Cordelia, Aral,
and Dubauer survive on it during their trip to the
supply cache. (SH)

Spacer's Union:
A galaxywide union for the men and women who work
on projects in near and deep space. Leo Graf sees
potential problems with them when the effectively
enslaved quaddies arrive to compete for work. (FF)

Spaceship:
A powered, self-contained vehicle capable of traveling between planets or stars. The propulsion system
is not specified, and neither is the fuel that powers
the ships. The fuel used is sufficiently compact that
refueling does not affect most trips, and multiple jumps
between solar systems are possible without refueling.
Fuel cost and efficiency are important to the economy
of commercial ships. Acceleration forces are high,
ranging from 15g to 100g, and are compensated for
by artificial gravity so the crew and passengers only
feel one-gee during that time. There are many different kinds of ships, some that lack jump capacity, and
are designed solely to travel within one solar system,
and others equipped with Necklin field generators to
travel through wormholes, enabling them to cross vast
distances quickly. Interstellar ships need a jump pilot
with a cybernetic link to the ship to control the jump,
in effect making them part of the ship while they are
jacked in. The jump pilot's cybernetic link includes
expensive micro-viral circuitry implanted by delicate

surgery into the pilot's brain. Metal contact points for the control headset show on the forehead. The jump can take several subjective hours for the pilot, but little or no subjective time for the passengers. If a person feels unusual subjective effects during jumps, it may be appropriate to screen them to see if they can be jump pilots. (All)

Speaker:
The title for the leader of any village in the Dendarii Mountains. Serg Karal is the Speaker of Silvy Vale when Miles first visits, and is replaced by Lem Csurik when he returns ten years later. (MM, M)

Sphaleros:
No first name given. A ground-captain in Imperial Security, he comes to the Vorthys house to assist Nikolai after he calls Emperor Gregor for help when Vassily and Hugo try to remove him. He escorts everyone in the house to Vorhartung Castle to meet with Gregor personally. (CC)

Sprague, Joan:
A commodore in the Escobaran military and Irene's boss, she is a steady-eyed older woman who is a psychiatrist. After interviewing Cordelia, she recommends further therapy. Her reports arrive too late to prevent Cordelia's disastrous homecoming at Beta Colony. (SH)

Star Crèche:
The Cetagandan haut caste's gene bank, which contains the genetic information on every haut-lord and lady.

It is what the haut use to procreate, with great ceremony and detailed contracts between the two parties. Births are carried to term by uterine replicator. The Empress has the ultimate approval over every new child, and she can decide to terminate contracts as well. Any child born becomes, in effect, the property of the father's constellation (i.e., clan). (C)

Stauber, Georish:
The baron of House Fell, he is a surprisingly old, fat, jovial man, balding with liver spots and a white fringe of hair, and red cheeks. Baron Ryoval is actually his older brother, who had Stauber's clone killed before he could be transplanted. Stauber is very interested in the Betan rejuvenation treatment Admiral Naismith is rumored to have undergone. He trades information to let Miles and the *Ariel* leave Jackson's Whole unmolested. Later, he assists Mark, who is posing as Miles, to broker a trade for Miles's cryo-chamber with House Bharaputra. He is also the founder of the Durona Group, and knows Lilly Durona quite well. After Ryoval's death, Mark negotiates a Deal with Stauber that gives House Fell control of House Ryoval's complete assets in exchange for letting the Durona Group go, along with a significant payment to Mark as the negotiating agent. (L, MD)

Steady Freddy:
No last name given. The public's nickname for the Betan president. Lots of people did not vote for him and like to say so. Cordelia accidentally kicks him in the groin during her homecoming on Beta Colony. (SH)

Strangle vine:
A hardy weed that grows wild on Barrayar's southern continent. Ekaterin suggests that Doctor Borgos
modify the butter bugs to eat it, providing him with
a potentially lucrative market. (CC)

Stuben:
No first name given. A lieutenant in the Betan Expeditionary Force, he is the chief zoologist of the survey expedition on Sergyar. Shorter than Aral, with
shoulder-length brown hair that is later cut very short
for the rescue attempt. When Cordelia orders him to
head back to Beta and report about Barrayar's plans
to invade Escobar, he disobeys and launches a rescue
mission for her instead. (SH)

Stunner:
An energy weapon firing a beam that knocks a target
unconscious upon impact. A stunner produces a central
beam with a surrounding nimbus that can affect one
to three victims. A near-miss may cause tingling or
numbness. It doesn't cause permanent harm unless a
victim has an underlying health problem like a heart
condition. Recovery symptoms include nausea, vomiting,
and headache, which can be minimized by administer-
ing synergine. A stunner's range is undefined, but is
at least line of sight. Space armor or half armor with
a built-in nerve disruptor/stunner shield net protects
against it. (All)

Suegar:
No first name given. A prisoner for three years in the
camp at Dagoola IV, he has seen much and is now

starving and borderline insane. A self-styled prophet, he carries a torn piece of paper that he calls scripture, which he got during the fighting at Port Lisma. He is looking for someone he calls "The One," who will help all of the prisoners escape. Miles seizes on this to formulate a plan, and enlists Suegar to help him by being his guide. He takes a bad beating, but escapes with Miles in the end. (BI)

Sumner:
No first name given. A trooper in the Dendarii Free Mercenaries who participates in the clone raid. (MD)

Sun wall:
A combat tactic of taking a wormhole involving a sacrifice ship that lays down a wall of nuclear-tipped misslettes, creating a planar wave that eliminates anything in the local space, including the ship that created the wave. (VG)

Surgeon:
No name given, he is one of four men over forty years old serving on the *General Vorkraft*. He treats Dubauer and Aral in Sickbay. (SH)

Sweet Dreams Distributing Company:
The company that Anias Ruey is under contract with for her feelie-dreams. It is owned and operated by Helmut Gonzales. (DD)

Sword Swallower:
The nickname for the first plasma mirror system, invented by Beta Colony, which turns an attacker's

energy weapon against the attacking ship. The Escobarans used it to repel the Barrayaran invasion. (SH)

Swordstick:
A personal weapon on Barrayar, it is a hardwood cane
that conceals a spring-loaded sword blade. It can be
carried only by a member of the Vor class. Cordelia
buys one for Koudelka, which Aral allows him to
carry as a weapon issued by the Regent. During the
mission to rescue Miles in the Imperial Residence,
Bothari uses it to decapitate Vordarian. (B)

Sylveth:
No last name given. The blond, lovely daughter of the
Lord Mayor of London and his formidable wife, whom
Miles escorts to an embassy function. Miles uses Ivan
and her to leave the Barrayaran embassy unnoticed
to attend to the wine shop incident, and later teases
Ivan, who may have bought her lingerie. (BA)

Synergine:
A general stabilizing drug used to counteract a variety
of injuries, including shock. Miles suggests it be given
to Ivan to counteract the aftereffects of the drug Vio
used to paralyze him during the Great Key plot. (All)

Szabo:
No first name given. A white-haired, grim-looking man
dressed in a blue and gray uniform, he is the senior
armsman for Count Vorrutyer. After Count Pierre's
death, and upon hearing Lady Donna's plan to gain
control of her brother's district, he gave his personal

word to assist her, and escorted her to Beta Colony for the sex-change operation. Although he was escorting Lord Dono on the night of the attempted assault, he was stunned before he could stop the attackers. (CC)

• • T • •

Tabbi:
One of the welding quaddies at Cay Station that Leo trained.

Tabor:
A ghem-lieutenant military attaché of Cetaganda's Earth embassy. A young man. His face is painted yellow and black, befitting his military rank. Miles meets him at the ·Barrayaran Embassy, and is warned by Duv Galeni that he is spying on them. He is involved in the incident at the Thames Tidal Barrier, ostensibly sent to kill Miles, and is subdued by Duv Galeni, who drops him and his partner off at the Cetagandan embassy, but takes their groundcar. (BA)

Tacti-Go:
A strategy game that has no unexpected variables or random factors, popular with Barrayaran children. Gregor brings a set to play with Miles during his house arrest. Miles, bored with the game by age fourteen, handicaps himself to not insult his Emperor by beating him too quickly. (VG)

Tafas:
No first name given. A Barrayaran crew member on the *General Vorkraft*, he works with Radnov, but ultimately helps Cordelia stop the mutiny. (SH)

Tailor, William:
A commodore in the Betan Expeditionary Force, he introduces Doctor Mehta to Cordelia. (SH)

Tanery Base Shuttleport:
A military shuttleport on Barrayar. During Vordarian's coup attempt, Piotr theorizes Aral will go there to open communications with the Imperial space fleet to try to bring them over to his side. After their stay in the Dendarii Mountains, Cordelia is brought there, as Aral made it his base of operations while he fights Vordarian. (B)

Tangle field:
Used by police for arresting or restraining suspects, it is a grenade-sized device that can be thrown at a fleeing target. Upon impact, it tangles around the person's limbs, effectively restraining them while also imparting a burning sensation to inhibit further resistance. (VG)

Tarpan, Luca:
The true brains behind the assassination attempt on Ekaterin, he has ties to the House Bharaputra syndicate on Jackson's Whole. He ordered the attempt on her life to sow confusion and cover his escape from Barrayar, leaving Lord Vorbataille as a sacrificial goat. (WG)

Tarski:
No first name given. An officer in the Barrayaran
military. Baz Jesek mentions him as an example of
someone who was infuriatingly correct all the time.
(WA)

Tatya:
One of Ivan's many girlfriends, she brings flowers to
his flat in Vorbarr Sultana. (VG)

Tau Ceta V:
One of the Cetagandan satrapy planets. (C)

Tau Ceti:
A star roughly 11.9 light-years away from Earth, it is
a common jump point for spaceships on their way to
more distant outposts. (SH, M)

Tau Verde IV:
A planet containing the two warring nations of Felice
and Pelias. Miles accepts a weapons-smuggling job
to pay off Arde Mayhew's debt, and his involvement
in ending the war also leads to the creation of the
Dendarii Free Mercenaries. (WA)

Taura:
A genetically engineered super-soldier created by
Hugh Canaba, she is the only one of her kind. Sixteen
years old when Miles first meets her during his first
mission to Jackson's Whole, she is eight feet tall and
weighs roughly three hundred pounds. She is human-
oid, with ivory skin, dark curly hair with burgundy
highlights, claws, and fangs. Her face is lupine, with

a long jaw, flat nose, light hazel eyes, ridged brows, and high cheekbones. She is very intelligent, with an IQ of 135. Although she is very strong, her metabolism runs very fast, which causes problems with her appetite and energy. Originally known as Nine, as she was the ninth out of ten test subjects. Miles renames her Taura when he rescues her from House Ryoval. She joins the Dendarii Free Mercenary Fleet, whose doctors work on slowing her metabolism. After their first sexual encounter on Jackson's Whole, they have a brief romantic reacquaintance during the escape trip.

Eventually she becomes the sergeant in charge of Green Squad during Mark's raid to free the clone children. She is a sometime, if not constant, lover of Miles before his relationship with Elli Quinn. She is Miles's bodyguard on the trip to Tau Ceti when he heads back to Barrayar. Miles makes Elli promise to let him know when her time is up as they still have not found a way to slow her metabolism any further. He wants to be there when she dies to fulfill the promise he made to her long ago.

During her first visit to Barrayar, she is twenty-six, and has been told for the past four years that each one will be her last. She has gray hairs, but dyes them to match her natural color. She has come to attend Miles's wedding, and is a bit melancholy over the match but approves. When the gift of pearls, supposedly from Elli Quinn, is presented to Ekaterin, Taura sees they appear dirty with her enhanced vision. When Ekaterin becomes sick, she realizes the problem but is afraid Elli will be blamed, not knowing she would never have sent such a murderous gift. Roic catches her trying to borrow the pearls for analysis and convinces her to let Imperial

Security do the job, which is fortunate for Ekaterin. She gets to be Ekaterin's Second as her reward, and after the reception is over, she and Roic retire for a private celebration of their own. (L, M, MD, WG)

Teddie:
A quaddie on Cay Habitat who trades shifts with Silver so she could see Claire after Andy was taken from her. (FF)

Teki:
A cousin of Elli Quinn's who works on Kline Station, and who helps her expose one of Colonel Millisor's men. Ethan meets him later, and finds out his helpfulness was not accidental. He gets snatched by Millisor and worked over, but is rescued by Elli when she calls Biocontrol to Millisor's room. When Helda is dismissed for misconduct, he becomes the temporary head of Assimilation Unit B on the station. Through him, Ethan and Terrence Cee find the missing ovarian cultures meant for Athos. (EA)

Tesslev:
No first name given. Piotr Vorkosigan refers to him as the best lieutenant he ever had. The son of a tailor, he fought in the guerrilla campaign against the Cetagandans in the Dendarii Mountains, and was killed in action. (WA)

Thames Tidal Barrier:
Also jokingly known as the King Canute Memorial, it is a huge dike that protects London from the sea. Watchtowers spaced a kilometer apart house engineers

and technicians who watch for damage to the massive seawall. Ser Galen locks Ivan in a pumping station access well, to be killed when the high tide comes in, and has Miles and Duv Galeni meet him and Mark in Section Six, among the auxiliary pumping stations. Miles, Duv, and Mark must navigate their way through the section to rescue Ivan and Elli, avoid the Barrayaran and Cetagandan hit squads, and get out alive. (BA)

Thermal mine:
A portable munition that releases a large amount of thermal energy upon detonation. During the clone rescue mission on Jackson's Whole, House Bharaputra guards used a thermal mine to completely destroy a Dendarii combat shuttle's cockpit and kill the pilot. (MD)

*Thin Blue Line, The*:
A holovid documentary made on Beta Colony of the Barrayaran invasion of Escobar nineteen years ago, when Aral re-met Cordelia. Named for the blue uniforms of the Betan Expeditionary Force, of which Cordelia was a member during that time. Elena sees it and is very upset at what she terms the "fictions" perpetuated by the Betans. (WA)

3rd Armored All-Terrain Rangers:
A captured Marilacan military unit held in the prison camp on Dagoola IV until being rescued by Miles and the Dendarii Free Mercenary Fleet. (BI)

Third Cetagandan War:
A military action that Aral Vorkosigan participated in while serving as the Regent of Barrayar. (WA)

Thorne, Bel:
A Betan hermaphrodite, it has soft, short brown hair, and a chiseled, beardless face. Formerly a lieutenant in the Oseran Mercenary Fleet, it starts over as a trainee-ensign in the Dendarii Free Mercenary Fleet. It gains a brevet promotion to captain after successfully leading the ore refinery takeover operation at Tau Verde IV.

Four years later, while on picket duty near Vervain, Bel rescues Miles after he is freed by Cavilo to infiltrate the Dendarii. It is instrumental in assisting Miles in retaking the Dendarii from Admiral Oser. It also participates in the prison break on Dagoola IV. During the mission to Jackson's Whole, Bel is attracted to Nicol at first sight, and is furious when Barons Fell and Ryoval discuss selling her, or selling a genetic sample of her. Bel agrees to smuggle Nicol out of Jackson's Whole for one Betan dollar, on Miles's condition that the operation be kept top secret. During the Dendarii's time on Earth, Bel is sent to testify on Private Danio's behalf in London.

When Mark impersonates Miles to launch his mission to Jackson's Whole, it is not fooled, but goes along with his plan because it wants to rescue the clone children too. For its error, Miles makes it resign from the Dendarii, but he suggests it apply to Imperial Security for an undercover position. Bel has had a crush on Miles for a long time, and kisses him passionately before leaving.

Later, Miles learns Bel has become the assistant portmaster at Graf Station, and also the Imperial Security civilian employee/informer on Graf Station. It is considering becoming a permanent civilian and wants Miles to relieve it of its Imperial Security duties. Kidnapped by Ker Dubauer, Bel takes the ba aboard the *Idris* to retrieve genetic samples of the haut-fetuses; then the ba infects Bel with the same biotoxin it used to kill the smugglers. Found by Miles, Bel is cured of the poison at the last minute, leaving permanent injuries. Bel receives a Warrant of the Celestial House from the Cetagandans in acknowledgment of the actions in saving the haut-lords' children. (BA, BI, DI, L, MD, VG)

Time of Isolation:
A period on Barrayar that occurred after the first wave of fifty thousand colonists arrived, only to find that the wormhole they had used to get there had mysteriously closed. Their terraforming project collapsed, and the intervening period degenerated into a time of near-feudalism and violent wars. Approximately seventy-five years before Aral and Cordelia met on Sergyar, the Time of Isolation ended when a new wormhole was discovered and Barrayar rejoined the rest of the galaxy, catching up with the rest of the inhabited planets as quickly as possible. (MM, SH)

Timmons:
No first name given. A customs agent on Beta Colony, he repeatedly catches Bothari trying to smuggle assorted weapons past the security checkpoint. (WA)

Tonkin:
No first name given. A trooper in the Dendarii Free
Mercenary Fleet, he participates in the rescue mission
on Jackson's Whole, and is with Medic Norwood and
Mark when Norwood sends Miles's cryo-chamber to
the Durona Group, although he doesn't know what
the medic did with Miles's body. Mark uses Tonkin's
helmet recorder to figure out what happened to his
brother. (MD)

Tony:
Also known as TY-776-424-XG, he is a pink-faced
quaddie with tight, blond curls. He is a grade-two
welder and joiner, and a permanent resident on the
Cay Project Habitat. He is Claire's mate, and Andy's
father. He tries to escape Cay Habitat with both of
them, but is shot during the attempt, and hospitalized.
He is rescued by Ti and Doctor Minchenko. (FF)

Toranira:
A planet that controls the other end of one of the
jump points from Vega Station. Sometimes it is Cetaganda's ally and sometimes the Empire's enemy, but
is currently upholding the arms embargo imposed on
Vega Station by the Cetagandans. Miles's plan had
been to smuggle three warships from the Dendarii
fleet there, and leave them to pick up three brand-
new warships at Illyrica, but Mark has derailed his
scheme by stealing the *Ariel*. (MD)

Toscane, Anna:
Laisa's aunt, a sixty-year-old, married, gray-haired
heiress whom Ivan must escort to the Komarran

delegation welcoming party. She thinks he is a nice young man, and shows him a picture of her seven-year-old granddaughter, on whom she dotes, boring Ivan. (CC)

Toscane, Laisa:
See Vorbarra, Laisa Toscane.

Tractor beam:
A ship-mounted directed-gravity beam that can be used to seize and immobilize vehicles, and pull or push them as necessary. Primarily used as a tool rather than a weapon, but the pilot of a Dendarii combat shuttle uses its tractor beam to slam a pursuing aircar into the ground. (L)

"Tragedy of the Maiden of the Lake":
A Barrayaran legend. When Vorkosigan Surleau was besieged by the forces of Hazelbright, they held out as long as they could, but before the town could fall, the unnamed Maiden of the Lake asked her brother to kill her so she wouldn't suffer abuse at the hands of the invaders. He did so, not knowing that the siege would be lifted the next day by her betrothed, General Count Selig Vorkosigan. Many poems, plays, and songs about the event have been written and performed on Barrayar. Ekaterin ponders the story while being held prisoner by the Komarran engineers. (K)

Transient:
Term used by space station inhabitants for anyone from off-station. (All)

Translator earbug:
A small device, designed to be worn in a person's ear,
that can instantly translate a spoken language into
the wearer's native tongue. Miles attends a dinner on
Earth that is made more difficult when the earbugs
do not arrive in time for the event. (BA)

Trans-Stellar Transport:
Also known as TST, it is a transport company Galac-
Tech works with. Ti wanted to be a jump pilot for
them. (FF)

Tremont, Guy:
The commanding officer of the 14th Commandos
Division and the hero of the siege of Fallow Core,
he is the man at the prison camp on Dagoola IV that
Miles came to rescue. When Miles finds him, he is
lying in his own waste, catatonic and emaciated, and
dies soon afterward. (BI)

*Triad*:
The title of Anias Ruey's romantic feelie-dream. She
has been commissioned to make a sequel to it, as it
has sold quite well. (DD)

Tris:
No first name given. The leader of the women prisoners
at Dagoola, she is a former frontline trooper, well-
muscled, with dark, rage-filled eyes. Miles convinces
her to help organize the camp around the ration
drops in preparation for the Dendarii breakout. He
also recruits her in the end for the new Reformation

Army. She escapes with the rest of the prisoners when the Dendarii arrive. (BI)

*Triumph*:
A Betan-built ship, it is classed as a pocket dreadnought, with a crew of sixty. Under the command of Captain Ky Tung, the ship is disabled when Arde Mayhew uses his freighter to ram it into the ore refinery supplying Tau Verde IV. When it is freed, it is given to Captain Auson to command after the battle. It participates in the prisoner escape on Dagoola IV. Later, it is the flagship of the Dendarii Free Mercenary Fleet. Miles has to take out a loan against it while on Earth to cover payroll and expenses. (BA, BI, WA)

Trogir, Marie:
An engineering technician in the Waste Heat Management department at Serifosa on Komarr. She lives with Andro Farr and has gone missing. Rumors supported by Soudha claim she ran off with Doctor Radovas. One of the Komarrans that created the jump-point destruction device, she died in the Soletta Station accident, but her body, crushed into the wreckage, wasn't found until after the case was wrapped up, and the other engineers are stopped from setting off the device. (K)

Truzillo:
No first name given. An officer in the Dendarii Free Mercenary Fleet, he is the captain-owner of the *Jayhawk*. Miles asks Baz to convince him to trade his ship for a brand-new Illyrican-made warship, part of a solution to an arms embargo at Vega Station. (MD)

Tsipis:
No first name given. The Vorkosigan family business
manager, he handles the household accounts. He sets
up Miles's accounts to handle the day-to-day operation
of Vorkosigan House, and would like to discuss a more
aggressive investing strategy with him as well. (M)


Tung, Ky:
The captain of the *Triumph* when Miles first meets
him at Tau Verde IV, he is a squat, hard-edged
Eurasian, about fifty years old. He and his crew are
captured at the refinery after Arde Mayhew rams
the *RG 132* into his warship. He is a citizen of the
People's Democracy of Greater South America. A
military history buff, he was a junior lieutenant in the
Selby Fleet at Komarr, and a great admirer of Aral
Vorkosigan, having read Aral's report on Komarr eleven
times. After being reprimanded by Admiral Oser in
front of his crew, and not given another command,
the angry Tung leaves the Oseran fleet and joins the
Dendarii Mercenaries.

Demoted to personnel officer by Admiral Oser after
he retook the Dendarii four years later, Tung helps
rescue Miles and Gregor. Arrested by Oser for his
actions, he is freed by Miles again in exchange for
restoring him to command. For his actions during the
Vervain conflict, he is taken on a personal tour of the
*Prince Serg*, followed by lunch with Aral.

Promoted to commodore in the Dendarii Mercenaries, he leads the rescue of Miles and the prisoners on
Dagoola IV. He has a daughter on Earth who has a
new first grandson. His sister is from Brazil and he
visits her and her family during the fleet's layover. He

turns in his resignation there to marry to his second
cousin, once removed, and retire. (BA, BI, VG, WA)

Tuomonen:
No first name given. A captain in Barrayar Imperial
Security, he is the head of the Serifosa office. He is
in his late twenties and fit, with dark hair and brown
eyes. He married a Komarran woman five years ago,
one year after his posting to the planet, and has one
daughter.

He is a smart, conscientious man, and he and Miles
get along well, but he is very upset when Miles ends
up hurt at the experimental plant after neglecting
to tell him that Etienne was taking him there. He
interrogates Ekaterin about her husband's death with
skill and grace, although he does have to bring up
an embarrassing theory about Miles possibly eloping
with Ekaterin after killing her husband. Facing a black
mark on his record because he didn't uncover the
conspiracy to close Barrayar's wormhole, he's told by
Miles to look him up if his military career ever comes
to a standstill, as he could use a good assistant. (K)

•  •  U  •  •

Ullery:
No first name given. A physician and the senior officer
of the survey party, directly under Reg Rosemont in
the chain of command, who fills Cordelia in on what
happened at Base One. (SH)

Undress greens:
A casual Barrayaran military outfit, consisting of a
high-collared tunic, side-piped trousers, and half-
boots. Miles and Ivan wear undress greens to the first
party they attend on Eta Ceta IV in the Cetagandan
Empire. (C)

Ungari:
A captain in Imperial Security, he is bland like Illyan,
but attractive, and somewhat stockier. About thirty-five
years old, he has been working as a galactic operative
for ten years. He is in charge of the mission to gather
intelligence regarding the activity around the Hegen
Hub with Miles, but everything goes awry, and nearly
ruins his career. (VG)

Unicorn and Wild Animal Park:
A division of GalacTech Bioengineering, it is an animal
park that Ryan Siembieda toured during his time on
Earth after being revived from cryo-preservation. (BA)

Union of Free Habitats:
Located on the edge of Sector V, it is a group of space
habitats located in the ring of one of two asteroid belts
circling their star. Contains the arcologies Graf Station,
Metropolitan Station, Minchenko Station, Sanctuary
Station, and Union Station. Emperor Gregor sends
Miles there to adjudicate a dispute between Graf
Station and the Barrayaran escort ships accompanying a Komarran trade fleet, and he uncovers a plan
to spark a war between Cetaganda and Barrayar in
the process. (DI)

Union Station:
One of the few orbital arcologies in the Union of Free Habitats, or Quaddiespace, that maintains gravity and deals with galactics. (DI)

United Brethren String Chamber Orchestra:
A classical orchestra on Athos, one of their hymns is "God the Father, Light the Way." Ethan orders this song played in one of the uterine replicator chambers instead of a screechy dance tune. (EA)

Upsider:
A term used to refer to someone born on a space station. (All)

Urquhart, Bret:
Ethan Urquhart's youngest brother, he plays piccolo in the army regimental band on Athos. (EA)

Urquhart, Ethan:
A doctor and the Chief of Reproductive Biology at the Sevarin District Reproduction Center on Athos. Six feet tall with dark hair, he is constantly mistaken for a twenty-year-old due to his lack of a beard. He was raised by his father and his designated alternate parent on a fish farm in the South Province, and is the eldest of five male children, followed by Steve and Stanislaus from the D.A.'s genetics, then Janos, also from the D.A.'s genetics, and last is Bret from his father. He served in Athos's military as a master sergeant in the Medical Corps. Sent by the Population Council of Athos to replenish their ovarian cultures to maintain their population, he encounters women for

the first time, and risks his life to recover a shipment of cultures for his planet's future. (EA)

Urquhart, Janos:
Ethan Urquhart's brother, three years younger than him. He is the son of Ethan's father's D.A., and he and Ethan have a sexual relationship. Irresponsible and reckless, he destroys Ethan's brand-new lightflyer in an accident, damaging a tree in the process. After Ethan goes on his mission, Janos runs off with his friend Nick to the outlands. (EA)

Urquhart, Stanislas:
Ethan Urquhart's brother, created from his father's designated alternate parent's genetic material. (EA)

Urquhart, Steve:
Ethan Urquhart's younger brother, created from his father's designated alternate parent's genetic material. (EA)

Ushakov:
No first name given. A colonel in Imperial Security Operations, he is Alexi Vormoncrief's commanding officer. Simon Illyan tells Vormoncrief that Ushakov will be hearing from General Allegre about the altercation with Ekaterin at the Vorthys's house. (CC)

Uterine replicator:
An artificial womb used to carry and develop human embryos to full term. Invented on Beta Colony. The use of replicators has spread to several planets across the galaxy, including Barrayar, Cetaganda, Jackson's

Whole, and Athos. It is a portable container that replicates the functions and use of a natural womb, and frees women and babies from the hazards of natural gestation and birth. The fetus may be grown from blastocyst to birth in the replicator. Small enough to be carried by one person if necessary, the replicator has a containment membrane, nutrient tanks, filters for waste products, and its own power unit. It is necessary to service the replicator periodically, discarding the waste products and ensuring that the systems are running efficiently. Since gestation takes place outside the body, it is standard practice to certify that the blastocyst implanted into it for gestation is free of genetic defects before transfer to the replicator. Replicators are also used for bioengineering experiments, most notably to create the quaddies.

Aral Vorkosigan introduces the technology to Barrayar when he takes seventeen of these Betan inventions home with him after the Escobar War, all containing the offspring of rapes by Barrayaran soldiers on captured female opposition soldiers. These replicators become important in the series. After the soltoxin attack on Aral and Cordelia Vorkosigan, the only way their unborn son Miles can survive is through the use of one of these replicators. Cordelia gave permission for his fetus to be transferred to one for experimental calcium treatments to stimulate his bone growth, which was impaired by the antidote to the poison. After Cordelia, Droushnakovi, and Bothari sneak into the Imperial Residence and kill Vordarian, they carry Miles's replicator out with them through the secret tunnels. (All)

• • V • •

Vaagen:
No first name given. A captain in the Barrayaran Imperial Military and doctor of Biochemistry, he is introduced as the research facility's expert on military poisons. Cordelia promises him a research center if he can save Miles after the soltoxin attack. He is beaten by Vordarian's guards because he won't reveal where Miles's replicator is after the coup. When they find the replicator anyway, he's released, and makes his way to Cordelia and Aral to let them know that Vordarian has their son. (B)

Valentine:
No first name given. A retired admiral in the Barrayaran military, he is one of the nine Imperial Auditors, although he has been too frail for years to actively carry out the duties of his position. (M)

Vallerie, Lise:
A reporter with the Euronews Network on Old Earth. Miles makes up a story that Admiral Naismith is a clone of him during an interview with her after she sees him in both his identities. He's pleased with his story, figuring it will throw the Cetagandans and anyone else who might be looking for him off the real scent. The reporter obligingly spread the news. She also knows Investigator Reed at Eurolaw. (BA)

**Van Atta, Bruce:**
The supervisor of the Cay Project on Rodeo. He is about forty, tall, pale, dark-haired, with spots on his hands. He was once a subordinate to Leo Graf and then became his boss on the CPH. Divorced, he has a sexual relationship with Silver. Leo punches him after the escape incident with Tony and Claire. He leads the attempt to retake the station, and commands the security shuttle crew to fire on the fleeing habitat ship, but they do not obey his orders, with Doctor Yei even trying to knock him out with a spanner. (FF)

**Vandermark, Jan:**
The alias Mark Vorkosigan used the longest in the two years after he gained his freedom back on Earth. (MD)

**Varusan Crotch Rot:**
A sexually transmitted disease mentioned by Quinn as part of her ploy to bring biocontrol wardens down on Colonel Millisor at Kline Station. (EA)

**Vatel:**
A quaddie on pusher duty, he catches the out-of-control pusher after it damages the vortex mirror. (FF)

**Vaughn:**
The code name for Doctor Hugh Canaba during the Jackson's Whole mission to pick him up. (L)

**Vega Station:**
A space station with three jump points, one into the Cetaganda Empire through its satrapy Ola Three, one blocked by Toranira, and the third held by Zoave

Twilight. Miles's original mission, before going to rescue Mark, was to take the *Ariel*, the *D-16*, and the *Triumph* to the station and leave them there, picking up three brand-new Illyrican-made warships for the Dendarii in trade. (MD)

Venier, Ser:
An assistant to Etienne Vorsoisson at the Serifosa branch of the Komarr Terraforming Project. He is a short, slight man, with brown eyes, a weak chin, and a nervous air. Miles thinks he resembles a rabbit. He is not involved in the plot to close Barrayar's wormhole. After Etienne is killed, he proposes marriage to Ekaterin, but she turns him down. (K)

Venn:
No first name given. The crew chief of Graf Station security, he does not care for downsiders and Barrayarans. He coordinates the investigation on the station side, and attends the interrogation of Russo Gupta and the inspection of the *Idris*. He helps Sealer Greenlaw and Adjudicator Leutwyn escape the ship after Dubauer hijacks it. (DI)

Venne:
Commander of the Tactics Room on Vorrutyer's ship. He sends hourly updates of the Escobar battle to Aral, and tells him of the messages coming in about the fleet being defeated. (SH)

Vervain:
A wealthy and technologically advanced planet near a wormhole to the Cetagandan Empire. Mu Ceta's forces

were badly beaten when they tried to take Vervain and the wormhole by a combination of subterfuge and force, thanks to the intervention of Miles and Aral Vorkosigan. The planet has two jump exits, one to the Hegen Hub, the other into the sectors controlled by the Cetagandans. In the subterfuge part of the plot, Cavilo plans to turn on her Vervani employers and raid their planet, then fence the loot at Jackson's Whole. She is also employed by the Cetagandans, and was planning to run a double double cross by letting them into Vervain space to take over, with Vervain becoming another satrapy of the Cetagandan Empire. (C, VG)

Vibra-knife:
A personal melee weapon, it is a blade with its own power source that makes it vibrate at very high speed, greatly increasing its damage potential. (All)

Vifian:
No first name given. A tech in the Dendarii Free Mercenary Fleet, she is from Kline Station. Injured in the Marilacan mission, she was treated at Beauchene Life Center, and has amnesia as a result of the cryo-stasis and treatment. (MD)

Villanova, Elizabeth:
A plump, pleasant downsider matron who oversees the quaddie children's crèches on the Habitat. Known as Mama Nilla by the staff and children. Elects to remain with the quaddies instead of evacuating off the station. (FF)

Virga, Valeria:
Author of Rainbow Illustrated Romances, including *Love in the Gazebo*, *Sir Randan's Folly*, and *Sir Randan and the Bartered Bride*, all of which are among the contraband video fiction Ti Gulik brings to Silver. (FF)

Visconti, Elena:
Elena Bothari's mother, she is a beautiful, dark-haired woman. She served in the Escobar War, was taken prisoner by the Barrayarans, and was raped by Sergeant Bothari under the orders of Admiral Ges Vorrutyer. After peace was declared, the resulting fetus was transferred into a uterine replicator, and was born as a daughter, Elena Bothari, who was raised by her father on Barrayar. Visconti was given a memory wipe to save her from the nightmares that could result from her experiences as a prisoner of war, but gradually recovers some of those memories. A banking security technician, she is trapped on Tau Verde IV when a new war breaks out there, and is recruited for the Dendarii by Arde Mayhew. When she realizes who Sergeant Bothari is, she kills him in front of Elena. Initially not wanting anything to do with her daughter, she grants Miles a lock of her hair as a death-offering for Bothari before he leaves for Barrayar, and eventually manages to reach a rapport with her daughter. (MD, SH, WA)

Vogti:
No first name given. One of Aral's armsmen. His wife and elderly mother were taken hostage by Vordarian's men. (B)

Vone:
A slang term for a videophone, it enables users to see and hear each other. (DD)

Voraronberg:
No first name given. A minor Barrayaran lord, he is the Imperial Residence's food and beverage manager. (MD)

Vorbarr Sultana:
The capital of Barrayar, and the planet's largest city. It is home to the Imperial Residence, Vorhartung Castle, the Council of Counts, several excellent universities and colleges, the headquarters of Imperial Security, and the Imperial Military Hospital. The Vorkosigans have a home there, which Miles lives in after he resigns from Imperial Security. (All except FF)

Vorbarr Sultana Hall:
One of the cultural highlights of the capital city on Barrayar. Tickets for performances are often sold out as far as two years in advance. Martya Koudelka gets four tickets to the Imperial Orchestra that plays there, and persuades the Vorbrettens to accompany Olivia Koudelka and herself to the performance. (CC, M)

Vorbarra, Dorca:
The father of Yuri and Xav Vorbarra by different mothers and kinsman of Ezar, he is known as Dorca the Just. He ended the period of internal strife on Barrayar during the Time of Isolation, uniting the counts under one imperial banner. When the Time of Isolation ended, he was the Barrayaran Emperor

as the Barrayaran/Cetagandan war broke out. He promoted twenty-two-year-old Piotr Vorkosigan to the rank of general for his guerrilla campaign in the Dendarii Mountains. Aral thinks his father was spared during Yuri Vorbarra's Massacre because Piotr wasn't blood-related to Dorca. His house colors are red and blue. (All except FF)

Vorbarra, Ezar:
A relative of Emperor Yuri Vorbarra, Ezar served alongside Piotr Vorkosigan during the Cetagandan War. Between them, Ezar and Piotr ran the Cetagandans off Barrayar, though the resistance cost five million Barrayaran lives. When it became clear that Yuri was mad and unfit to be Emperor, Ezar and Piotr rebelled and put Ezar on the throne. Ezar married the sister of Mad Emperor Yuri, just before he was killed. He is the Emperor of Barrayar at the start of the war between Barrayar and Escobar. His son, Serg, is as unfit as old Yuri was to take the throne, so Ezar ruthlessly arranges for his only child's assassination during the course of the Escobaran War. He appoints Aral Vorkosigan Regent until Serg's son, Gregor, comes of age to take the throne. Aral says that Ezar was the man who stabilized the old way and new way on Barrayar. When Cordelia meets Ezar on his deathbed he is very white, with white hair, and hazel eyes—which he passed on to his son and grandson. He dies shortly after Aral is approved as Regent by the Council of Counts. (B, SH)

Vorbarra, Gregor:
The grandson of Emperor Ezar Vorbarra, and the son of the deceased Crown Prince Serg Vorbarra and

Princess Kareen, the current Emperor of Barrayar is tall, dark-haired, and pensive, with piercing hazel eyes. He ascends to the throne at the age of five, upon the death of his grandfather and mother, and is raised by Aral and Cordelia Vorkosigan. Cordelia oversees Gregor's education until he is twelve, when he is sent for the appropriate Imperial military school training.

Thanks to the Vorkosigans' careful oversight, he is a very effective ruler when he takes the reins of the Imperium at twenty-one, except for falling for an internal plot to discredit Aral through Miles's accidental creation of the Dendarii Free Mercenary Fleet. Once Miles is cleared of the charges, he suggests that Gregor use the mercenary unit as the Emperor's Own, which Gregor takes him up on. He also goes through a difficult period when he discovers that the reputation of his father—the "gallant" Prince Serg—is a myth, and that his progenitor was a monster.

Depressed and despondent while attending trade negotiations on Komarr, Gregor attempts to commit suicide when drunk by falling off a high balcony, but ends up climbing down the vines on the side of the building and running away. He found passage on a ship off-planet, and eventually ended up in a Jackson Consortium prison cell with Miles, whom he grew up with back home. When both men are captured by Cavilo, she tries to seduce Gregor into marrying her for her protection. Gregor plays along with her long enough to escape, then leads the Barrayaran reinforcements back through the wormhole to relieve the Dendarii.

Through the course of the series from this point onward, Gregor grows steadily more able and mature, and his judgment becomes increasingly acute. When it becomes clear that Mark Vorkosigan will be accepted as the son of Aral and Cordelia, Gregor insists on meeting Mark to take the clone's measure. Satisfied that Mark is a true Vorkosigan, Gregor gives him a comm card that enables Mark to contact the Emperor whenever he wishes. Over Simon's disapproval, Gregor gives Mark the final permission to try to locate Miles on Jackson's Whole.

He appoints Miles as acting Imperial Auditor when Simon Illyan develops serious mental problems as a result of the failure of his memory chip, turning Miles loose to find out what happened, and who is responsible. He personally interviews General Lucas Haroche after his arrest, and solicits a full confession. Impressed with Miles's work on the case, he calls the other four active Imperial Auditors together to review it, and they all vote to offer Miles the permanent position of Imperial Auditor, with Gregor also promoting Miles retroactively to the rank of captain per his request.

After Miles returns from his mission to Komarr, Gregor surprises everyone by falling in love with a Komarran, Doctor Laisa Toscane, and asking her to marry him. While going through the amazing preparations for his wedding, Gregor makes time for a meeting with Nikolai Vorsoisson, the son of Etienne, in which he tells the boy as much of the truth of his father's death as can be allowed without compromising security. Later, he also puts Vassily Vorsoisson and Hugo Vorvayne straight as to Nikolai's safety, and assures them of the ludicrousness of Vormoncrief's plot against Miles. Gregor is safely and happily married to

Laisa Toscane, and Gregor's heirs, Miles among them, breathe a sigh of relief and wish him many happy years, and even more healthy offspring. He interrupts Miles's own honeymoon to send his Imperial Auditor to sort out the problem of the Komarran trade fleet at Graf Station in Sector V. (All except EA, FF, SH)

Vorbarra, Kareen:
The wife of Prince Serg, after his death she becomes Princess Dowager, and mother of the new Emperor, Gregor. She is a thin, strained-looking woman of thirty with beautiful, dark hair. The strain is a result of her marriage—Crown Prince Serg was a monster—and the dynastic politics of the Imperium that threaten her life and that of her child every day. Kareen kisses Cordelia's hand when they first meet, thinking that she killed Ges Vorrutyer. She assigns Droushnakova as Cordelia's bodyguard when Cordelia admits to missing the bright women friends that were so dear to her back on Beta Colony. During Vordarian's failed attempt to take the Barrayaran throne, he claims Kareen as his wife to try to solidify his claim to power. After Cordelia proves to Kareen that Vordarian lied to her about Gregor's death during the coup, Kareen attempts to kill Vordarian. She is shot and killed by one of the Residence guards. (B)

Vorbarra, Laisa Toscane:
A woman Duv Galeni is seeing until Emperor Gregor becomes entranced by her and they become engaged to be married. She is short, a bit plump but attractively so, with brilliant blue-green eyes, glowing milky skin, a lovely face, and short, light brown hair with silvery

blond highlights. She is a daughter of the Toscane family on Komarr, which cooperated with the Barrayaran conquest, and now holds a lot of influence on the planet. She is a trade lobbyist at Vorbarr Sultana, and has a doctorate in business theory. In an effort to court her, Gregor gives her a horse ride at their first private luncheon. She is appalled by some of the more traditional terms of the wedding contract, but Lady Alys helps reinterpret some old, embarrassing customs to put her more at ease. She marries Gregor, and becomes the Empress of Barrayar. Her family owns a fifty percent share of the Komarran trade fleet impounded at Graf Station in the Union of Free Habitats. (CC, DI, M, WG)

Vorbarra, Serg:
The son of Emperor Ezar, he is the crown prince of Barrayar, and the next in line to the throne. He is co-commander of the Barrayaran armada during its attempt to invade Escobar. He is about thirty years old, with a square face, black hair, hooded hazel eyes, and thin lips. A vain, pompous, deviant man, he is goaded into personally leading the attack on the Escobar fleet, and is killed in the ensuing battle. His death is part of a plan hatched by Emperor Ezar, Captain Negri, and Aral to save Barrayar from Serg's insanity, since he is manifestly unfit to rule. After his death he is hailed as a hero on Barrayar. The planet of Sergyar is named after him. (SH)

Vorbarra, Xav:
Aral's grandfather, he was the ambassador to Beta Colony when he was a youth, where he met Aral's Betan

grandmother. While the assassins sent by Yuri Vorbarra (his half brother) missed him during the Massacre, his wife was killed, leading Xav to side with Ezar in the civil war that resulted in Ezar becoming Emperor. (SH)

Vorbarra, Yuri:
An Emperor of Barrayar who went mad in his later years, despite, or perhaps because of, his heroic earlier role resisting the Cetagandan invaders. He is related to Prince Xav Vorbarra (half brother). He was deposed by an army headed by Piotr Vorkosigan and Ezar Vorbarra. During Yuri's ritual death of a thousand cuts, Aral Vorkosigan, though only thirteen years old at the time, was offered the first cut. (SH)

Vorbarra-Vorkosigan, Olivia:
Daughter of Xav Vorbarra, and the mother of Aral Vorkosigan, she was killed by one of Emperor Yuri's assassins, who shot a sonic grenade into her stomach in front of Aral when he was eleven years old. (SH)

Vorbataille:
No first name given. A count's heir in the southern districts of Barrayar, he is entangled in criminal activity involving Jackson's Whole, including using his private yacht to insert a hijacking team onto the *Princess Olivia*. He is betrayed when Luca Tarpan sets him up to take the fall for the assassination of Ekaterin. (WG)

Vorberg:
No first name given. A lieutenant in Barrayaran Imperial Security, he is a courier officer who was captured and held for ransom. Illyan sends the Dendarii Free

Mercenaries to rescue him. During his rescue, Miles accidentally cut his legs off with a plasma arc while suffering a seizure. Vorberg's legs are fortunately salvageable, though he lost a bit of height in the accident. He later meets Miles back on Barrayar, but doesn't know Miles was the one who maimed him. Understandably, he speaks disparagingly of the Dendarii Mercenaries. While convalescing he is given a job as night guard commander for the security at the clinic where Simon has been placed. When Miles doesn't respond to Simon's repeated requests to see him, Vorberg finds Miles to chastise him, inadvertently letting him know something is wrong, and putting the whole chain of events that leads to Miles's appointment as Imperial Auditor into play. (M)

Vorbohn:
No first name given. A lord on Barrayar, he is the head of the Vorbarr Sultana Municipal Guard. He helped Officer Gustioz with obtaining permissions to arrest Doctor Borgos. He is also waiting to arrest Lord Richars when the Council of Counts finishes voting on Lord Dono's claim to his brother's District. (CC)

Vorbretten House:
The Vorbretten ancestral manor was so badly damaged during the fighting over Vordarian's Pretendership that the family demolished the remains and built anew. Protected by force screens, the new mansion is modern, light, and airy, perched on a bluff overlooking the river, nearly opposite Castle Vorhartung, and with excellent views of the Vorbarr Sultana cityscape both up and down river. (CC)

Vorbretten, René:
A count on Barrayar, he is the epitome of the modern
Vor class; tall, athletic, and handsome. He speaks four
languages, plays three musical instruments, and has
perfect singing pitch. His house colors are dark green
and bittersweet orange. He is the son of Commodore
Lord Vorbretten, who had been a star protégé of Aral
Vorkosigan until he was killed at the Hegen Hub
during the Cetagandan takeover attempt a decade
ago. When his grandfather died, René gave up his
military career and assumed the count's duties. He
married Tatya, the eighteen-year-old daughter of
Lord Vorkeres, in a love match. While the couple
was preparing for starting their first child in a uterine replicator, the gene scan revealed that Rene is
one-eighth Cetaganda ghem-lord by an alliance of his
great-grandmother during the Occupation. This means
the seventh Vorbretten count was not the true son of
the sixth, which could cut René out of the succession in favor of the true lineage by a descendant of
the sixth count's younger brother, Sigur Vorbretten,
the son-in-law of Count Boriz Vormoncrief, who has
filed claim on Sigur's behalf to the Vorbretten district.
With help from Miles and Lord Dono Vorrutyer, René
fends off the claim to his district, and is confirmed
as the true count by a majority of the Council. (CC)

Vorbretten, Sigur:
A descendant of the sixth Count Vorbretten's younger
brother, he has had a claim filed on his behalf by
Count Vormoncrief on the Vorbretten District due to
René Vorbretten's Cetagandan heritage. René wins the

vote, and a gracious Sigur accepts defeat with what appears to be relief. (CC)

Vorbretten, Tatya Vorkeres:
Countess, and the wife of René, she has bright hazel eyes, wide set in a heart-shaped face with a foxy chin and ringlets of ebony hair. She and Olivia Koudelka went to school together, and Olivia and Martya visit the Vorbrettens during the Cetagandan bloodline scandal to cheer her up. Her cousin Stannis is a directing officer in the fife and drum corps of the City Guard. Withdrawn and depressed about the scandal, she attends the Council of Counts meeting that will decide her husband's fate, unwilling to wait for the news. (CC)

Vordarian, Vidal:
A commodore and count of Barrayar, he is a staunch conservative who disapproves of Aral's progressive ideas. About forty years old, he is neither handsome nor ugly, with dark hair and a dished-in face, a prominent forehead and jaw, and a mustache. He told Cordelia during the Emperor's Birthday celebration that Aral was bisexual, making her realize Vordarian was not to be trusted, and resulting in her telling Simon Illyan to watch him. His district has four major manufacturing cities and some military ports, with one being the largest shuttleport and supply depot. After Ezar's death, he attempts to overthrow the current government and install himself as Emperor, holding Kareen hostage in the Imperial Residence and declaring himself Prime Minster and acting Regent of Barrayar. He is killed by Bothari at Cordelia's command. His house colors are maroon and gold. (B)

**Vordarian's Pretendership:**
What Barrayarans call the attempted coup that occurred when Aral first became Regent. (B, WA)

**Vordrozda:**
A Barrayaran count who arrives at Vorkosigan House with Admiral Hessman during Piotr's funeral. Cordelia distrusts him. When he learns of Miles's formation of a mercenary army at Tau Verde IV, he tries to bring charges of treason against Miles to discredit Aral, in hopes of eliminating a potential rival to the Emperor's throne. He is uncovered by Miles, who accuses him at the Council of Counts, and forces him into revealing his sedition. (WA)

**Vorfemme knife:**
A small knife, often decorated, that is traditionally carried by all woman of the Vor class on Barrayar, ostensibly to defend themselves if necessary. Helen Vorthys remembers that she had been carrying an enameled one in her boot, which she had unfortunately thrown at one of the engineers. Ekaterin wasn't wearing hers, in an attempt to appear more modern. Vorthys mentions her grandmother and Ekaterin mentions her great-aunt in reference to the knives, implying that Vor women have used them for more than decoration in the past. (K)

**Vorfolse:**
No first name given. A count on the south coast of Barrayar who started his own political party. He is a man with very few assets, as his family consistently sided with the wrong people at the wrong

time throughout the previous century, including the Cetagandans and Vordarian. He currently rents out his family mansion to a prole with ambition, and has only one servant. Lord Dono, Olivia, Ivan, and Szabo all showed up at his flat to gain his vote regarding Dono's suit at the Council when they are attacked by Richars' men, who attempt to castrate Dono. Count Vorfolse is so incensed by the assault happening on his property that he verbally admonishes Richars in the Council chamber before voting in favor of Lord Dono. (CC)

Vorgarin:
No first name given. One of the undecided counts that Miles thought he brought to René Vorbretten's side, although not to Lord Dono's. (CC)

Vorgier:
No first name given. A captain in Imperial Security, he is in charge of the Komarr jump station security. He wants to make an aggressive raid to end the hostage standoff with the Komarran engineers, but Miles overrides him in favor of negotiation. (K)

Vorgorov, Cassia:
A slim girl, eighteen years old, with dark brown hair, a slightly long face, and pretty eyes. She runs into Ivan, whom she's had a long-standing crush on, and Mark at the Emperor's Birthday celebration. Ivan knows her, as his mother wishes him to consider her as a possible match, but he does not appreciate her as Mark does. She seems unsettled by Mark, however, and when left alone with him, excuses herself and

leaves him as quickly as possible. She later marries Lord William Vortashpula, Count Vortashpula's heir, and discreetly rubs it in Ivan's face. (CC, MD)

Vorgustafson, Vann:
A Barrayaran Imperial Auditor, he was recently appointed by Emperor Gregor. A retired industrialist and noted philanthropist who doesn't dress according to his lofty social status; in fact, his wardrobe lacks color coordination. Shorter and stouter than Vorthys, he has a bristling gray beard and a pink, choleric face that can alarm those who first meet him, since he appears to be on the verge of stroke or heart attack. Along with the other Auditors in attendance, he approves Miles for the eighth Imperial Auditor position. (M)

Vorhalas:
No first name given. A count on Barrayar, he is a staunch Conservative, and a linchpin in the party, due to his reputation for integrity. He did not rebel against Aral's Regency government when one of his sons was put to death for participating in an illegal duel. When word of Richars's bungled assault on Lord Dono gets back to him, he leads Counts Vorkalloner, Vorpatril, and Vorfolse in switching their vote against Richars. (CC)

Vorhalas, Carl:
Son of Count Vorhalas, Carl is a Barrayaran lord and Evon Vorhalas's younger brother. Early in Aral Vorkosigan's Regency government, he is publicly executed by beheading after he kills someone in a

duel. Afterward, Evon Vorhalas attempts to kill Aral because he wouldn't stop the execution. (B)

Vorhalas, Evon:
Carl Vorhalas's brother, he attempts to assassinate Aral using the soltoxin in revenge for Carl's execution. During the coup, he escapes to Vordarian's side and is put in charge of commanding ground troops in Vorbarr Sultana. He is shot by his own men when he won't surrender after Vordarian's death. (B)

Vorhalas, Rulf:
Admiral in the Barrayaran fleet, he is a friend of Aral's, and brother to Count Vorhalas. Roughly fifty years old, he is subordinate to Prince Serg during the war with Escobar, and is killed when the prince's ship is destroyed. (SH)

Vorharopulous:
No first name given. One of the counts involved in voting on the René Vorbretten and Lord Dono Vorrutyer cases. His house colors are chartreuse and scarlet. (CC)

Vorhartung Castle:
An old, rambling castle located on a bluff above the river rapids that divide the city of Vorbarr Sultana. It is where the Council of Counts convenes to handle the governmental business of Barrayar. It is also the site of Gregor's Imperial offices. It incorporates a museum open to the public when the counts are not in session, containing such exhibits as the preserved scalp of Mad Emperor Yuri Vorbarra. (All except FF, SH)

Vorhovis:
No first name given. A Barrayaran Imperial Auditor, he is the youngest of the seven Imperial Auditors before Miles joins, and one of the best. A cool, lean, sophisticated man, he is the model of the modern Vor lord. He has been a soldier, diplomat, planetary ambassador, and one time assistant to the Minister of Finance. Miles had requested to work with him before Gregor makes him an acting Imperial Auditor. Along with the other Auditors in attendance, Vorhovis approves Miles for the eighth Imperial Auditor position. (M)

Vorinnis:
No first name given. A Barrayaran count whose district has remained neutral during the War of the Vordarian Pretendership, and who was heavily courted by both sides. Piotr thinks he is playing both ends against the middle, and wants Aral to hang him if he doesn't choose soon. Cordelia plans to travel through his district during her rescue mission to save Miles. (B)

Vorinnis:
No first name given. A Barrayaran count who would be backed by the military right if he ever attempted to claim the throne. Despite his conservative bent, he votes for both René Vorbretten and Lord Dono Vorrutyer at the Council of Counts meeting, thanks to some back-door politicking by Alys Vorpatril. (CC)

Vorkalloner:
No first name given. An Imperial Auditor in the more traditional mold, having been appointed straight out of

the military, where he was an admiral. Tall and thick, he seems to take up a lot of space. He had a long, distinguished military career, is socially bland, and does not affiliate himself with any political party. Along with the other Auditors in attendance, he approves Miles for the eighth Imperial Auditor position. (M)

Vorkalloner:
No first name given. A Barrayaran count, he is one of the Conservative members who changes his vote from Richars Vorrutyer to Lord Dono Vorrutyer. (CC)

Vorkalloner, Aristede:
A lieutenant commander in the Barrayaran military, he is Aral's second officer on the *General Vorkraft*. Promoted to commander, he is killed during the Escobar conflict. His body is later retrieved by an Escobaran Personnel Retrieval Team. (SH)

Vorkosigan, Aral:
The second son of General Piotr Vorkosigan, Aral is a lifelong soldier in the Barrayaran military. In his early forties, he is slightly taller than Cordelia Naismith, but stocky and powerful. He has untidy, dark hair tinged with gray and intent gray eyes, with a heavy jaw, a straight, broad nose, and a faded, L-shaped scar on left side of his chin. His house colors are brown and silver.

When Cordelia meets him on the planet later named Sergyar, he is the captain of the Imperial war cruiser *General Vorkraft*. He is known as "the Butcher/Hero of Komarr," depending on who is referring to him. He had an older brother who was killed by Mad

Emperor Yuri when Aral was just eleven. His mother was half Betan, and was killed in front of him during Yuri Vorbarra's Massacre. His maternal grandfather is Prince Xav Vorbarra, who served as ambassador to Beta Colony, and his grandmother, the prince's wife, was in the Bureau for Interstellar Trade.

Aral has faithfully served the Imperium for most of his life. He has had an amazing military career, and is a superb strategist responsible for pushing back multiple expansion attempts by the Cetagandans. He oversaw the conquest of Komarr, which would have been bloodless except for the Solstice Massacre, where he earned his nickname. He was involved in the plot to eliminate Prince Serg during the war with Escobar, and organized the Imperial Fleet's withdrawal afterward. He served as Regent of Barrayar during Emperor Gregor's youth, and was forced into a brief civil war with Vidal Vordarian when he attempted to overthrow the Regency. When Gregor took his throne, Aral served him as Prime Minister, and eventually accepted the position of Viceroy of Sergyar.

Aral married twice. His first wife died young, committing suicide by plasma arc. His second wife, Betan Commander Cordelia Naismith, is the love of his life. He has two sons, Miles and Mark. (All except FF)

Vorkosigan (Naismith), Cordelia:
At the beginning of the Vorkosigan saga, she is the commander of a Betan Astronomical Survey team, an astrocartographer, and the captain of the Betan scientific vessel *Rene Magritte*. Thirty-three years old, she has copper hair and gray eyes. Her immediate family includes a brother who just purchased a second

child permit and a mother who specializes in medical engineering. Her father, also a Betan Survey officer, died in a transport accident when she was a child. Her first true adult romance was with a man who emotionally manipulated her to the point of abuse, and then maneuvered her out of a captaincy. She has had no lovers since that emotional and career disaster.

She is captured by Aral Vorkosigan while surveying the planet later known as Sergyar. As his prisoner, she discovers that there is much to admire in her putative enemy. Before they have reached his ship, the two have fallen in love. Back at Aral's ship, she is instrumental in stopping a mutiny before being rescued by her crew. Afterward, she serves in the Betan Expeditionary Force, commanding a bulk freighter used as a decoy to lure Barrayaran warships away from a wormhole to Escobar. After being captured by the Barrayarans again, she is interrogated/tortured by Admiral Ges Vorrutyer before he is killed by Sergeant Bothari. Aral comes to her rescue, only to discover that she has already rescued herself. He hides her in his cabin while Vorrutyer's death is investigated. Cordelia is then sent to a prison camp, where she is repatriated back to her home planet of Beta Colony and treated as a hero. But her government suspects her of having been suborned by the Barrayarans. Their attempts to cure her almost cause her to have a nervous breakdown. When she discovers that she is suspected of being a deep-cover spy, she escapes, travels to Barrayar, and marries Aral.

Soon she is pregnant with Miles. After an assassination attempt on Aral using soltoxin gas, Cordelia's fetus is severely damaged, and must be removed and placed in a uterine replicator. During the coup attempt by Vidal Vordarian, Cordelia becomes the de facto protector of Gregor while they are in hiding in the mountains near Amie Pass. Once Gregor and Cordelia are safe again, they learn that Vordarian is holding Miles's replicator hostage. Cordelia leads Bothari, Droushnakovi, and Koudelka on a mission to save her son. After saving Alys Vorpatril from Vordarian's goons and helping deliver her son Ivan, Cordelia continues on to the Emperor's Residence, where she finds Miles's replicator. Captured by Imperial Security guards, they escape with Vordarian as a hostage, until Cordelia orders Bothari to execute him, which he does with Koudelka's swordstick. Cordelia takes Vordarian's head back to Aral, and tells him to end the war.

As Aral serves as Regent of Barrayar, Cordelia sees to the raising of Gregor and Miles, as well as doing her best to bring Barrayar into the modern age without losing its virtues, or her own. Among her other ventures, she helps fund the medical facility in Hassadar. Half the people there are oath-sworn to her in exchange for their schooling. Even after her children are grown, she frequently serves as a voice of reason for them. She accepts her clone-son Mark as her and Aral's own, and tries to help him assimilate to his new life. She also buys Mark a ship to go and rescue Miles from Jackson's Whole after his cryo-revival.

When Miles nearly destroys his relationship with Ekaterin, she gives him relationship advice that gets him back on track. She invests in Mark's bug butter business, and brokers an agreement between Mark and the Koudelkas after his relationship with Kareen becomes difficult.

Cordelia's name and title keep changing throughout the Vorkosigan sagas. She begins as Commander Cordelia Naismith, then becomes Captain Cordelia Naismith. When she marries Aral Vorkosigan, her name/title becomes Lady Vorkosigan. When Aral is appointed Regent, she becomes Regent-Consort Lady Vorkosigan. After Piotr's death, she becomes Regent-Consort Countess Vorkosigan. Then Aral and she move to Sergyar, where Aral becomes viceroy, and Cordelia becomes Vicereine Countess Vorkosigan. (All except FF)

Vorkosigan, Countess, the fifth:
No first name given. An ancestor of Miles's who suffered under the periodic delusion that she was made of glass. One of her irritated relations eventually dropped her off a twenty-meter castle turret, killing her. (BA)

Vorkosigan crest:
A stylized maple leaf in front of three triangles, which represent the Dendarii Mountains, it was originally used to seal the bags of District tax revenues. In an attempt to curry favor with Miles, Enrique Borgos gene-splices the Vorkosigan crest onto the back of a group of butter bugs, not realizing it's a terrible insult to the family. (CC)

Vorkosigan, Ekaterin Nile Vorvayne Vorsoisson:
A Barrayaran from the South Continent, she is the wife of the administrator for the Serifosa division of the terraforming project on Komarr. She has rich brown hair with amber highlights and light blue eyes, and is withering under the stress of her unhappy

marriage. She has three older brothers and lost her
mother when she was a teenager. She lived with her
Aunt Helen and Uncle Vorthys in Vorbarr Sultana for
two years before marrying Etienne Vorsoisson and, a
decade later, is living in Serifosa, on Komarr.

Ekaterin feels closer to her aunt and uncle than to
her father. She has a passion for growing plants and
is very intelligent. She is not happy with her husband,
and when she finds out he has taken bribes, lost most
of their savings and pension on a Komarran trade
fleet, and is still not going for help for his illness as
well as blocking her son's treatment, she leaves him.
After his death, she gets Nikolai into a hospital for
treatment of his Vorzohn's Dystrophy, and prepares
to leave Komarr to travel back home to Barrayar. At
the jump-point station to pick up Helen Vorthys, they
are both taken hostage by Arozzi, and held prisoner
where the engineers are planning to try to close the
wormhole. Ekaterin escapes and ends up breaking the
wormhole-closing device. She and Helen are put into
an airlock, with the engineers threatening to space both
of them, until Miles convinces them to surrender. She
ends up going back to Barrayar, with the promise of
seeing Miles again very much on her mind.

When she and Nikolai arrive on Barrayar, they live
with her Aunt and Uncle Vorthys in Vorbarr Sultana
and she plans to attend school. Despite Miles trying
to keep her under wraps, she is inundated by gentleman callers, but has no intention of getting married
again. Miles gives her a garden design job and she
enjoys her time with him, but just as she is letting
her guard down, he is forced to propose to her in the

middle of his disastrous dinner party, and she storms out, thinking he was trying to manipulate her.

She accepts work from Mark and Kareen redesigning the butter bugs to be more consumer-friendly. Eventually she comes to realize, after carrying around Miles's heartfelt letter of apology and listening to the slander of him by her suitors, brother, and former brother-in-law, that she is in love with Miles.

Brought to Castle Vorhartung by Gregor so he can protect her son from her overbearing relatives, she attends the Council of Counts vote, and when the false charge that Miles murdered her husband is made by Richars, she proposes to Miles to prove that he is not manipulating her into an unwanted marriage. During the preparations, she is naturally jittery about marrying again, but forges onward. When a poisoned gift choker of pearls makes her very ill, at first she thinks it is nerves, and is relieved to find the illness stemmed from poison. Rather than feeling frightened at the assassination attempt, she continues with the wedding, wearing the now-clean pearls in defiance of her husband's enemies.

While honeymooning with her husband, Miles is sent to Graf Station to adjudicate a dispute between the station security and the Barrayaran fleet escort. She assists where she can, especially at the end, where Miles must reach Cetagandan space with the haut-fetuses to return them back to the Empire, and also be treated for the parasites that are killing him. She receives a Warrant of the Celestial House from the Cetagandans in acknowledgment of her actions in saving the haut-lords' children. (K, CC, DI, WG)

Vorkosigan House:

A large, gray stone mansion that is more than two centuries old. Built by Miles's great-great-great grandfather, it was one of the reasons he went bankrupt. Approximately four kilometers from Imperial Security HQ, it is a four-story building with two wings plus a few other odd architectural bits added over the decades. A semicircular drive leads up to the house, with a strip of lawn and a garden setting the house off from the street. A stone wall topped by black wrought-iron spikes surrounds the grounds. There is a force screen inside the wall for true protection. It's a big house, meant to be lived in by multiple generations at once, along with armsmen, servants, and staff.

It is where Evon Vorhalas tries to assassinate Aral, and catches Cordelia in the soltoxin attack. Almost thirty years later, Miles moves in after resigning from Imperial Security, and takes over his grandfather Piotr's former suite of rooms after his confirmation as Imperial Auditor.

There is an empty lot adjoining the house where a house was demolished long ago and Imperial Security did not want anything new built, as it would have blocked their field of fire as they protected Count Vorkosigan. Miles has Ekaterin build a native Barrayaran display garden there. Vorkosigan House is the initial site of Mark Vorkosigan's butter bug industry. But several of Doctor Borgos's butter bugs escaped the lab in the basement, and later Borgos tries to dump fifty kilograms of bug butter down the sink drain, which clogs the main drain, leaving Miles to go in and fix the problem. The house is also the site of the bug butter war, where Kareen and Martya try to save Doctor Borgos from the Escobaran parole officers by pelting them with tubs of bug butter. (B, CC, M)

Vorkosigan, Mark Pierre:
Miles's clone, he was created from stolen tissue samples on Jackson's Whole, financed by a hostile Komarran faction to create a copy of Miles to kill Aral and take over the Barrayaran throne. Mark was raised with other clones in Jacksonian clone crèches until he was fourteen, when he was taken by Ser Galen for more intensive training to impersonate Miles and in espionage and assassination. Galen's training regime for Mark was filled with torture and abuse.

Six years younger than Miles, he is a nearly exact physical duplicate, right down to the plastic replacement bones in his legs. He doesn't suffer from the brittle bone syndrome that Miles has, but is as intelligent as his brother, and comes up with the plan to have Miles kidnap himself so they can insert Mark into the Dendarii and the Barrayaran Embassy in London. Mark is obsessed with Miles, who nearly talks him into coming back to Barrayar as his true brother. Arrested on suspicion of hiring assassins to kill Admiral Naismith, Mark is freed by Ser Galen, who tries to get him to kill Miles at the Thames Tidal Barrier. Mark shoots Galen instead, and takes Miles to where Ivan is trapped in a pumping chamber. Miles gives Mark a half-million-mark credit chit, and tells him he's free to do whatever he wishes with his life.

Four years later, Mark pretends to be Admiral Miles Naismith again to gain control of the *Ariel* and a squad of Dendarii commandos to rescue a group of fifty clones from House Bharaputra on Jackson's

Whole. After the events in London, Cordelia is aware of his existence and has read the intelligence reports concerning him. Mark's attempt to rescue the clones fails, leading Miles to come to Jackson's Whole to save him. Miles is killed during the rescue and cryogenically frozen in front of him. Mark is sent to Barrayar, where he meets Aral and Cordelia, who tell him if Miles is dead, he is the Vorkosigan heir. Not wanting to get enmeshed in Barrayaran politics or family trees, Mark figures out where Miles is, and goes to rescue him with help from Cordelia, Elli Quinn, Bel Thorne, and Elena Bothari-Jesek. He is captured by Baron Ryoval's men and tortured, causing his personality to fracture. One of his personalities, Killer, kills Ryoval. Mark then negotiates a deal with Baron Fell to let the Duronas leave Jackson's Whole and goes back to Barrayar with Miles, two million Betan dollars richer, and ready to plan his new life as Mark Vorkosigan.

He stays with Aral and Cordelia for a time, and then moves on to Beta Colony to go to school at the University of Silica, studying accounting. He is getting acquainted with his grandmother, Elizabeth, and is also involved with Kareen Koudelka. Elli Quinn doesn't like him, blaming Mark for Miles's seizures, and calling him a "fat little creep." Mark is a potential suspect in Simon Illyan's breakdown, but his alibi of being on Beta Colony rules him out. In an attempt to differentiate himself from Miles, Mark gains an enormous amount of weight.

After a year of university study and therapy, Mark returns to Barrayar. His latest capital venture is an offshoot of a visit to Escobar to get powerful weight-loss drugs. He also takes an Escobaran scientist,

Doctor Enrique Borgos, under his wing to develop a bioengineering program to convert Barrayaran native plants to human edible food. The butter bug scheme turns Vorkosigan House on its ear.

Mark's relationship with Kareen Koudelka progresses well, but runs into difficulty with Kareen's return to Barrayar. He becomes quite desperate about potentially losing Kareen, until his mother Cordelia helps allay her parents' concerns about her relationship with Mark. He also seems to be bonding more with people, particularly with Miles. Mark is engaged in a valiant struggle to become a functional, if never quite normal, human being, and seems to be succeeding.

The butter bug maple ambrosia is a hit at the Emperor's wedding reception, and Mark also brokers a deal with Count Vorsmythe for start-up capital for his company, the profits from which he plans to use to explore alternate longevity techniques other than brain transplants. (BA, CC, DI, K, M, MD, WG)

Vorkosigan, Miles Naismith:
The hyperactive, physically deformed, genius son of Aral Vorkosigan and Cordelia Naismith. As a result of the soltoxin attack on his mother while she is pregnant, Miles is born with severe teratogenic, though not genetic, damage. In particular, his bones are brittle, misshapen, and prone to breakage. Miles was not able to walk until he turned five, after which he never slowed down. He has dark hair, gray eyes, a bit of a humpback, and is short for his age, approximately four foot ten inches tall. His appearance, on mutation-phobic Barrayar, is a problem that requires constant vigilance to contain. Miles reaches adulthood only

because of his father's position, his intelligence and ability to charm those around him, and the watchful eye of Sergeant Bothari, who keeps enemies at bay.

Miles tries to commit suicide at age fifteen while attending school on Beta Colony, but Bothari prevents him from succeeding. Two years later, he washes out of the Imperial Military Academy when he breaks both his legs during a physical trial. His grandfather Piotr, Miles believes, dies from the shame of this. Miles accidentally forms the Dendarii Free Mercenaries while on a trip to Beta Colony to visit his grandmother. He ends the blockade of Tau Verde IV, and averts a plot to discredit his father and family back on Barrayar. After these adventures, Gregor realizes that Miles is a loose cannon, and appoints him to the Military Academy by Imperial fiat.

Miles's first assignment after graduating from the Imperial Academy is to replace the chief meteorology officer on Lazkowski Base. After trying to prevent the slaughter of technicians who refuse an order to clean up a dangerous poison, he is shipped back to Vorbarr Sultana, where he offers to resign his commission to save the rest of the men from standing trial. After a period of house arrest, he is seconded to Imperial Security and assigned to gather information on increased activity around the Hegen Hub. Miles poses as an arms dealer, and is framed for murder. While fleeing the charges, he finds the Emperor of Barrayar, Gregor, who has escaped his security detail, and is also in prison. The two uncover a plot by the psychotic mercenary Cavilo to let Cetaganda invade Vervain. When Cavilo learns she has the Emperor of Barrayar in her clutches, her thoughts turn to a marriage alliance, and Miles has to rescue his ruler and prevent an interplanetary war from breaking out. He manages both, with a bit of help from his father, Aral, and the Dendarii Free Mercenaries.

Promoted to lieutenant in Imperial Security, he travels under the cover identity of a courier officer, but actually is a galactic Special Operations agent who reports directly to Simon Illyan, who reports directly to Gregor. While attending the funeral of the Dowager Empress on Eta Ceta IV, in the Cetagandan Empire, Miles solves the murder of the ba Lura, foils a plot against the Cetagandan Emperor, and stops a war between Cetaganda and Barrayar. Miles also falls in love with the haut Rian Degtiar, knowing there is no conceivable way they ever could be together. After risking his life to recover the missing Great Key of the Cetagandan Star Crèche regalia in time for the funeral of the Emperor's mother, and recovering copied Cetagandan gene banks from the eight satrap governors, Miles is awarded the Order of Merit by the Cetagandan Emperor.

Next, he is sent to Jackson's Whole to pick up a genetic scientist to work on some interesting new biological strains that Imperial Security has secured. Miles gets tangled up in rescuing a quaddie musician and a bioengineered super-soldier from the two wealthiest Houses on the planet. He earns the wrath of Baron Ryoval when he destroys the genetic samples library in Ryoval's laboratory during his escape.

Miles next earns the enmity of the Cetagandan Empire by using the Dendarii to stage a daring rescue of 10,000 Marilacan prisoners from Dagoola IV, a prison camp. Miles goes in under cover as one of the prisoners. He combines psychology and a bit of religious persuasion to organize the prisoners for escape. He is almost killed before he can pull off the rescue, in the course of which he loses 207 prisoners, along with two shuttles, plus four dead and sixteen wounded Dendarii.

Miles was supposed to report to Tau Ceti after the mission, but the Cetagandans put a large price on his head, forcing him and the Dendarii to lay low on Earth to repair the fleet and get needed medical attention for his crew. Miles and Elli fall in love during this time, but she turns down his offer of marriage. She wants to be Admiral Quinn in space, not Lady Vorkosigan stuck on Barrayar. While coming to terms with this, Miles is kidnapped as part of a Komarran plot to replace him with a clone, Mark, who will destabilize the Barrayaran government and open an opportunity for Komarr to break free of the Imperium—or so the Komarran plotters hope. Escaping from his captors with Elli's help, Miles also gives Mark his freedom, and gets a new mission to rescue Barrayaran hostages from some mercenaries turned pirates.

Four years later, Miles learns that Mark posed as Admiral Naismith and commandeered the *Ariel* to go to Jackson's Whole and rescue clones there who are about to be killed to provide donor bodies to wealthy and amoral elderly clients. Miles follows Mark with the intention of rescuing his brother, if necessary. During the mission, Miles is killed by a needler grenade to the chest, but cryogenically preserved for later resuscitation. He ends up a patient at the Durona clan medical facility, with a replacement heart, lungs, and stomach, but missing his memory, and must undergo rehabilitation there, where he falls in love with his doctor, Rowan Durona. Captured by Baron Fell's men just before he was about to be rescued by Mark, Miles is sold to Baron Ryoval, but arrives at the compound after Mark had already killed Ryoval. He contacts Imperial Security, which comes to get him, and watches as Mark consummates a deal with Baron Fell to get the Duronas off Jackson's Whole, and make a million Betan dollars in the process. Miles escorts his brother back to Barrayar.

Miles recovers from his cryo-stasis. During his revival his spine was straightened and he gained a centimeter of height, but he has some bad news to go along with the good. He now suffers from seizures that he has not reported to either Imperial Security or Elli Quinn, his second-in-command among the Dendarii. Miles's pride crashes and embarrassment peaks with a crucial accident on a rescue mission when he has a seizure and accidentally cuts off the legs of the Barrayaran courier they were rescuing. Miles does not report all the details of the accident or his health woes to Imperial Security, not wanting to be removed from active duty. Miles gets orders to return immediately to Barrayar, where, instead of a mission, he gets a medical discharge and is forced to resign after Simon catches him in his lies and falsified reports. After he suffers through his depression, the incident with Simon Illyan's memory gains him an acting Imperial Auditor post from Gregor to find out what's really going on. Miles discovers that General Haroche, the acting chief of Imperial Security, is the culprit. The Emperor offers Miles the chief of Imperial Security position, but he declines, not wanting a desk job. Miles does accept the position of the eighth Imperial Auditor, with a request to be promoted to captain post-career. He regretfully decides to not join Elli in the Dendarii Free Mercenary Fleet, but asks her one last time to marry him. She declines, but accepts the position as Admiral of the Dendarii. Miles gets medical aid and is able to control the seizures so he can function normally.

Three months after his appointment as a full Imperial Auditor, Miles travels with Imperial Auditor Vorthys to investigate a Soletta Station accident at Komarr. He meets Ekaterin, Vorthys's married niece, when staying with her family, and falls in love with her. With Vorthys and help from Doctor Riva, Miles figures out the plot rebellious Komarrans had concocted to close Barrayar's wormhole, and moves to stop the Komarran engineers from setting off the device, knowing that it will probably destroy the jump-point station. Unfortunately, Ekaterin's husband is one of the casualties of the plot. Miles convinces the Komarrans to surrender and release their hostages. Despite her very recent widowhood, and his part in the husband's death, Miles begins making plans to make Ekaterin his as soon as he possibly can, before some other Vor lord can snatch her away.

Having returned from his successful mission on Komarr, Miles is now on a personal mission to woo and win Ekaterin Vorsoisson. Gregor also gives Miles the task of managing René Vorbretten's problem with succession—the count has discovered he is part Cetagandan, and not a direct descendant of the sixth count. Miles also has to handle the Vormiur uterine replicator case of his 122 daughters as well. But his work does not keep Miles from trying to win Ekaterin over by being friends. He plans to court her without telling her. In his first salvo, he gives her the job of designing a garden near Vorkosigan House. The entry of multiple suitors for her hand sends Miles into overdrive, however, and he is suddenly plotting as if she has become a military objective. He tries to put on an elegant dinner party, but it ends in disaster when the butter bugs are released into the house, and his intent to marry Ekaterin is accidentally exposed by Simon Illyan. Miles proposes to her in front of everyone, but she storms out of the house, enraged by his deception. He must then apologize and lay his true feelings bare to her. In the end, Miles helps René Vorbretten win his case, assists Lord Dono Vorrutyer to inherit his brother's title and District, and wins Ekaterin over, leading her to propose to him at the Council of Counts meeting with his delighted parents watching from the balcony behind her.

As Miles is anxiously awaiting his upcoming wedding, he is determined for everything to go well, but worried that his bride-to-be is getting cold feet. Then Ekaterin gets sick—very sick. When Miles finds out that Ekaterin's illness is caused by a murder attempt using poisoned pearls that appear to be from his ex-lover Elli Quinn, he is furious, not at Elli, since he knows she would never do something like this, but that an attempt was made on the love of his life. Even after the plot is foiled and the perpetrators are caught, Miles is still so anxious about the marriage that Aral ends up tranquilizing him so he will be calm enough to get through the ceremony. Everything goes fine, and Miles and his new wife are whisked off to Vorkosigan Surleau for their honeymoon.

Happily wed, Miles and Ekaterin celebrate their first anniversary by starting two children in replicators and then going on a galactic honeymoon. The children will be a boy named Aral Alexander and a girl named Helen Natalia. They are on their way home from that honeymoon when Miles gets a message to go to Graf Station and sort out the mess caused by the confiscation of a Komarran space fleet and its Barrayaran armed escort. But events soon transpire that lead to attempted and actual murder, and could cause another war between Cetaganda and Barrayar. Though it nearly kills him, Miles is able to straighten out everything and make it home in time for the births of his children. (All except FF, SH)

Vorkosigan, Piotr:
Aral's father, and a general in the Barrayaran military, Count Piotr Vorkosigan's life bridges the planet's history from the Time of Isolation to the modern era. At twenty-two, he became a general in the Barrayaran army that expelled the Cetagandan invaders after two decades of resistance. When it became apparent the Mad Emperor Yuri Vorbarra was unfit to rule, Piotr led a civil war that deposed and executed Yuri and placed Ezar Vorbarra on the throne. As Emperor Ezar ruthlessly turned Barrayar into a government of laws for all, Piotr was the backbone of the Conservative party in the Council of Counts, with his fingers in the pies of numberless political intrigues. As his son Aral became a political player for the Progressive party, Piotr swallowed his pride and his political leanings and followed. When Aral married a galactic woman, Piotr struggled, but tried to cope. When Cordelia became pregnant, Piotr was beside himself with joy, having almost given up hope that Aral would have sons. Although Piotr attempts to

have Miles aborted after the soltoxin attack, and tries
to kill him after he is born, he warms to Miles as the
boy proves to be as smart and fearless as Piotr himself.
But after he learns that Miles has washed out of the
Imperial Academy, Piotr dies in his sleep. Miles burns
a death-offering to him after graduating from Imperial
Academy. (B, MM, SH, WA)

Vorkosigan, Selig:
One of Miles's ancestors, he broke a siege of Vorkosigan
Surleau using a handful of retainers and subterfuge.
The dagger that Miles carries, formerly Piotr's, is
supposed to date back to his time. (VG)

Vorkosigan Sousleau:
Prime Minister Vortala tells Aral that he heard the village near his summer home was going to be renamed
this in honor of his habit of capsizing his sailboat. (SH)

Vorkosigan Surleau:
The Vorkosigan summer residence on the Long Lake,
near the Dendarii Gorge. It was once a guards' barracks. After the Cetaganda War resulted in Vorkosigan
Vashnoi being turned into an irradiated nuclear bomb
crater, it became the main Vorkosigan residence in
the District until the official home in Hassadar was
completed. The old guard house has been refurbished
and modernized since its original days. It sits near
the ruins of the great castle, a low, stone residence
artistically landscaped and bright with flowers. Defensive arrow slits have been remodeled into large glass
windows that give a view of the lake, and there is a
modern comm-link antenna on the roof. A modern

guards' barracks is farther down the hill, hidden among the trees.

Aral lives at Vorkosigan Surleau after his resignation from the military, and Cordelia goes to finds him there after she arrives on Barrayar. Miles loved growing up there, enjoying riding horseback and swimming in the lake. He retreats there whenever the stresses of Vorbarr Sultana get to be too much for him. (All except FF)

Vorkosigan Vashnoi:
The old district capital of Vorkosigan's District. It was bombed with atomic weapons by the Cetagandans during the war, killing thousands. Its irradiated ruins make up much of the Vorkosigan family's holdings. (All)

Vorkosigan's Leper Colony:
The term given to Aral Vorkosigan's command during the time when he's out of favor. His fleet superiors sent him all of the screw-ups, incorrigibles, and near-discharges, which Vorkosigan manages to turn into a proper military force. (SH)

Vorlakail:
No first name given. A deceased Barrayaran count, he is one of the everyday matters that Aral deals with as Regent. There is suspicion that the count was dead before his palace was burned to the ground in Darkoi, prompting an investigation. (B)

Vorlakial:
No first name given. An officer in the Barrayaran military, he is one of the men Aral believes is a better military strategist than himself. (SH)

Vormoncrief, Alexi:
A lieutenant in the Barrayaran military, he works in the operations department of Imperial Security, He is distantly related to the Vorvaynes through his grandmother and is also a nephew of Count Boriz Vormoncrief. He tries to court Ekaterin, sending a Baba to her family to open negotiations, which fails. He intimidates and interrogates Nikolai, and assaults Ekaterin, earning himself a broken nose for his efforts, and a reprimand from Simon Illyan. Finally, after he attempts to have Ekaterin's relatives take Nikolai away from her, Gregor posts him to Camp Lazkowski on Kyril Island for the duration of his military career. (CC)

Vormoncrief, Boriz:
A Barrayaran count, he is the current head of the weakened Conservative Party. He is also part of the Vorbretten issue, having filed the claim on behalf of his son-in-law, Sigur Vorbretten. (CC)

Vormuir, Helga:
A Barrayaran countess and the wife of Tomas Vormuir, he of the 122 replicated daughters. Because of the uterine replicator business, she refuses him when he comes to call for a conjugal visit, dumping a bucket of water on his head and threatening to warm him up with a plasma arc. Later, thanks to an aphrodisiac supplied to her by Count Dono, her husband misses the vote on Count Dono and René Vorbretten. (CC)

Vormuir, Tomas:
A Barrayaran count. His house colors are carmine and green. In an effort to stem the loss of citizens from

his district, he obtained thirty uterine replicators and has fathered 122 daughters without his wife's consent, using eggs from the local fertility clinic without the donors' permissions. Assigned to investigate as Imperial Auditor, Miles can't find a way to punish Vormuir, until Ekaterin suggests that, as they are legally the count's bastard children, by law the Emperor can order Vormiur to give a dowry with each daughter's hand in marriage, which Gregor puts into effect immediately. The count misses the vote on Lord Dono due to the aphrodisiac slipped to him by his wife. (CC)

Vormurtos:
No first name given. A Barrayaran lord and one of Richars's supporters, he drunkenly accosts Miles and Ekaterin after a social function, only to be verbally defeated by Miles. (CC)

Vorob'yev:
No first name given. The Barrayaran ambassador to Cetaganda, he is a stout solid man, about sixty years old, with sharp eyes. He wears the Vorob'yev house uniform, wine red trimmed in black. Appointed to the position by Aral Vorkosigan, Vorob'yev retired from the military, and has held this position for six years. He tries to keep Miles out of trouble and prevent an interstellar incident, but is unable to contain him. In the end, having survived his run-in with Miles and having kept relations between the two planets more or less intact, he asks Mia Maz to marry him, which she accepts. (C)

Vorparadijs:
No first name given. A general in the Barrayaran military, he is the last surviving Imperial Auditor appointed by Emperor Ezra Vorbarra. He is ancient, skinny, and uses a cane. Although he is technically the senior Auditor, the others don't let him know when they are meeting. Laisa wants to meet him at the Imperial State dinner, but Miles warns her off, letting her know that the office is the interesting part, and the man himself is a terrible bore. He is not at the meeting to confirm Miles as an Imperial Auditor. (M)

Vorpatril, Alys:
Wife of Captain Lord Padma Xav Vorpatril, she is the very pattern of a proper Vor woman. She has long, dark hair, and is accustomed to being in charge, although not overbearingly so. She is pregnant at the same time as Cordelia, and assists her in integrating into Barrayaran society. Her house colors are blue and gold.

During the War of Vordarian's Pretendership, her husband and her unborn child are on Vordarian's assassination lists, because their blood right to the Barrayaran throne is better than his. She and Padma hide in the caravanserai section of town during the coup attempt, but they are discovered, and Padma is killed. Cordelia is able to rescue Alys. In the confusion of their escape, Alys goes into labor, delivering her son, Ivan, that same evening. After the coup is put down, Alys oversees Koudelka's and Droushnakovi's wedding preparations.

She eventually becomes Gregor's official hostess, and handles his social calendar. She organizes the Imperial state dinner where Emperor Gregor first meets Laisa Toscane. She takes Laisa under her wing, and makes sure the Komarran heiress is accepted as Empress by all the old Vor families. During Simon Illyan's illness, she stays by his side, and then helps take care of him during his convalescence afterward. The two of them embark on a romance, much to her son Ivan's dismay. When Miles is courting Ekaterin, she is quite appalled at the disintegration of his infamous dinner party, but sympathetic to his plight as well. A veteran of Vorbarr Sultana politics, she assists greatly with René Vorbretten's and Dono Vorrutyer's cases, confirming counts that will vote for them, and removing a few that won't. She is also Byerly Vorrutyer's contact to Imperial Security. (All except FF, SH)

Vorpatril, Falco:
A count, he is a member of Barrayar's Conservative Party. He is one of Ivan's relatives. Despite Falco's exasperation at Ivan's inability to get married, Ivan tries to persuade him to vote for René Vorbretten's and Dono Vorrutyer's petitions at the Council of Counts. Initially against Dono's case, Falco comes over to their side when Richars attempts to castrate Dono. It is not known how he voted on René Vorbretten's case. (CC)

Vorpatril, Ivan:
Miles's cousin, he is tall, fit, easygoing, handsome, a bit lazy, and—after a successful but not outstanding pass through the Imperial Academy—a model Vor military officer. He makes a career of slipping through life nearly invisibly, doing just enough to succeed, and reserving his real efforts for his social life and

for dealing with Miles, who is the closest thing to a brother Ivan has.

As children together, Ivan and Miles set the pattern of their adult relationship. Miles came up with wild ideas, and then coerced Ivan into helping him carry them out. The two of them, Miles and Ivan, engage in an underground game of one-ups-manship whenever they are together, but Ivan picks his ground carefully whenever he decides to challenge Miles. The first serious challenge Ivan issued to Miles—not intentionally, for a change—came when Ivan was accepted into the Barrayaran Imperial Military Academy at the same time that Miles failed the physical qualification test after acing all the written examinations. Miles traveled to Beta Colony to visit his grandmother, but seemingly vanished in midroute. Ivan was sent to find Miles by Admiral Hessman, but his mission was part of an intricate plot to bring down Prime Minister Aral Vorkosigan. Ivan was not supposed to survive the trip. In spite of the odds stacked against him, Ivan survives and finds Miles, who uncovers the plot against his father based on the information Ivan gives him.

After Miles is admitted to the Imperial Academy in spite of his physical limitations, Ivan and he routinely end up on the opposite side in undergrad war games, and Miles savors his frequent victories over his taller and better-looking cousin. Upon graduation, Miles gets sent to the worst posting in all of Barrayar's army—to Kyril Island as a weatherman. Ivan can't help but grin. But he's in position to help Miles research his new and psychotic commander's sealed military files, and the two ensigns inadvertently uncover a hole in Imperial computer security.

Ivan rises through the military ranks steadily, and is next promoted to the rank of lieutenant. But he still retains his responsibilities as a Vor and close relation to Emperor Gregor. Because of those connections, he accompanies Miles on the diplomatic mission to the Cetagandan Empire to attend the Dowager Empress Lisbet Degtiar's funeral on Eta Ceta IV. Ivan is entirely smitten by all the beautiful ghem-ladies, and they seem to return his regard, especially after a practical joke results in Ivan being slipped an anti-aphrodisiac before two ghem-women seduce him. Ivan concocts a story about Vor lords having to pleasure their women multiple times before the Vor lord is free to participate himself. He then delivers on that promise, making his popularity explode after that. Ivan also comes up with the idea to have eight haut gene banks, distributed by the Dowager Empress in a plot that has fallen apart with her death, recalled from the satrap governors' ships. But his good looks nearly get him killed. The haut-lady Chilian d'Vio thinks Ivan is the brains behind Miles's attempts to save Lisbet's heir, the haut Rian Degtiar, from a murderous conspiracy that could eventually plunge Cetaganda and Barrayar into war. Miles rescues Ivan, but is captured in the process of retrieving the last gene bank and the Celestial Great Key that opens it. Ivan finds ghem-Colonel Benin, and leads a rescue party to save Miles and his Cetagandan helpers from satrap governor Ilsum Kety.

His next run-in with Miles occurs when Ivan is stationed on Old Earth, serving as the second assistant military attaché at Barrayar's embassy in London. His cousin is also on Earth in his persona of Admiral

Naismith of the Dendarii Free Mercenary Fleet. But Lord Miles Vorkosigan also has to report in to Earth's Barrayaran embassy. Ivan covers for Miles when he goes to recover his three Dendarii, who have torn up a wine shop in the city. Ivan is captured by Ser Galen as part of a power play to force Miles to come to Ser Galen. Galen has arranged for a clone to be made of Miles, and he wants the chance to substitute that clone, later known as Mark, for Miles. Galen and the clone, now known as Mark, capture Ivan and lock him in an underwater pumping station, giving him an acute case of claustrophobia. But Miles is able to win the clone's trust, and they rescue Ivan, with the clone killing Galen along the way. Ivan, along with two Cetagandans, sees the two Vorkosigans, Miles and Mark, together, with Mark dressed as Admiral Naismith. The sight gets the Cetagandans off Miles's back for a considerable amount of time.

Ivan is given the task of introducing Mark to Barrayar after Miles turns up missing, and possibly dead, in the process of trying to extract Mark from a mission on Jackson's Whole. Since Ivan is still upset with Mark for giving him that claustrophobia complex back on Earth, he takes on the mission with a larger than usual lack of grace, resulting in Mark almost killing a bully in the Caravanserai.

After he's promoted to captain, Ivan helps Miles get through his forced resignation from his Imperial Security career, invading Vorkosigan House and dumping Miles into an ice bath to break him out of his near-catatonia. He then moves in, enjoying the delightful meals that Ma Kosti provides. Ivan is appointed to be Miles's assistant when Miles is promoted to the position of acting Imperial Auditor to investigate Simon Illyan's memory loss. He ultimately finds the bioengineered weapon that disables Simon. But Ivan's fondness for Simon doesn't stifle his dismay when he discovers his mother and Simon are having an affair.

About this time, Ivan's own marital prospects are looking grim, thanks to a Vor preference for producing boy children rather than girls around the time of Ivan's birth. There aren't a lot of eligible Vor women still unmarried, and Ivan begins to believe he's out of time to find his own wife. In a panic, Ivan asks Delia to marry him. In typical fashion, when Delia turns him down flat, Ivan asks Martya to marry him on the same day, and she turns him down even flatter. Then Ivan's worst nightmare comes true when his mother, Lady Alys, becomes his commanding officer while she arranges Gregor's wedding. Peeved at Miles's declaring Ekaterin off-limits to his cousin's courting, Ivan tells Alexi Vormoncrief about her, so Miles won't lack for competition. His meddling launches a string of unintended results, including Miles's disastrous dinner party.

Afterward, Ivan is still feeling like the last Vor in his generation to be married, and starts seriously looking for his future bride. When he hears his former lover Lady Donna Vorrutyer is available again, he sets his sights on her, and then is dismayed to learn she has undergone a sex-change operation in order to inherit her brother's title of count along with the district. Ivan is also out of luck with former girlfriend Olivia Koudelka, as she has already fallen in love with Lord Dono. Ivan proves his worth when he helps thwart an assault on Lord Dono, then brings four Conservative counts on the Council to Dono's side, assuring him the vote and his countship.

Ivan then serves as Miles's Second during his wedding. Several days before the ceremony, Aral takes Ivan aside to warn him not to do anything to spoil the ceremony. But Ivan can't resist after decades of twitting his cousin Miles at every opportunity. His addition to the winter garden wedding decorations is to slip in an ice sculpture of two grinning rabbits copulating under a bush. (C, CC, M, MD, VG, WA, WG)

Vorpatril, Padma Xav:
A captain in the Barrayaran military, he is also the husband of Lady Alys Vorpatril, and Ivan's father. In his middle thirties, he is a big, cheerful man. He is Cordelia's escort during Aral's confirmation ceremony at the Council of Counts. Padma is Aral's first cousin via his mother's younger sister, and is Aral's closest living relative other than Piotr. Although Padma and Alys, who is heavily pregnant with Ivan, evade the roundup of the counts during the initial stages of Vordarian's War of Pretendership, Padma is discovered while trying to find a doctor to aid his wife, who is in labor. He is killed by Vordarian's guards, but Alys and Ivan are rescued by Cordelia. Alys arranges to have a memorial plaque inserted into the street on the exact spot where Padma died. (B)

Vorreedi:
No first name given. The protocol officer assigned by Barrayar to Cetaganda, he is actually an Imperial Security colonel and the chief of Imperial Security on Cetaganda. Middle-aged, middle-sized, he often wears a

loose bodysuit and the well-cut robes of a Cetagandan ghem-lord. The Cetagandans know his true position in Intelligence, but politely do not acknowledge it, just as the Cetagandan officers of similar status are known on Barrayar. Vorreedi is supposed to oversee Miles and Ivan's stay on Eta Ceti IV, but is kept in the dark for much of the time by Miles. He finds out what was happening under his nose only after Miles spells out what he's done during an audience with the Cetagandan Emperor. (C)

Vorrutyer, Byerly:
Known as "By," he is a Vor "town clown," or social gadfly, and has a sarcastic tongue and wicked commentary on the social and political intrigues of Barrayar. He also has a secret career in Imperial Security as a Domestic Affairs civilian contract employee with a rating of IS-8. He's first introduced when he appears to court Ekaterin, although he may in fact have been working. A cousin to Miles and Ivan by way of Aral Vorkosigan's first marriage. He has a cousin, Richars Vorrutyer, and a recently deceased cousin, Pierre, who died from a heart attack at barely fifty. By pretends to help both Dono and Richars, but he is actually on Dono's side. His machinations help Lord Dono by manipulating Richars's assault on him, which firmly turns the Council of Counts against Richars. By's Imperial Security drop contact is Lady Alys Vorpatril. His house colors are blue and gray. (CC)

Vorrutyer, Donna/Dono:
Count Pierre's younger sister, she is forty years old. When Pierre dies, Donna decides to block her despised

cousin Richars from inheriting Pierre's District by having a sex change on Beta Colony, becoming Lord Dono Vorrutyer. He is an athletic-looking and handsome man of middle height, more lithe than muscular, with dark hair, a groomed, glossy mustache and beard, and electric brown eyes.

Ivan Vorpatril had a fling with Donna several years earlier, and the newly minted Lord Dono uses that relationship to help smooth the way to receive Gregor's approval and win the vote to make his countship official at the Council of Counts. Dono hates Richars because he tried to rape Donna when she was twelve, and when she stopped him he drowned her puppy and blamed her for it. Donna has been previously married three times, an early, arranged marriage that she behaved badly during to escape, a second marriage that both parties soon agreed was a mistake, and a happy third marriage that ended in tragedy when her new husband was killed in a sporting accident. Dono has remained a virgin in his new gender, and is looking forward to a very unusual marriage night first. Although set upon by thugs hired by Richars to castrate him, the attack is foiled by Ivan Vorkosigan and Olivia Koudelka, who use it to bring more counts over to Dono's side. At the Emperor's reception, Dono and Olivia announce their engagement. The couple attends Miles's wedding. (CC, WG)

Vorrutyer, Dono:
Not to be confused with his later namesake Donna/Dono. Mad Emperor Yuri's Imperial architect, and uncle to Vice Admiral Ges Vorrutyer. He designed the Imperial Security headquarters, which resembles

a giant, windowless concrete box with oversized stairs that exhaust anyone trying to climb them. But when Miles is forced to examine all of Imperial Security from top to bottom, he realizes Yuri's architect might have designed hideously ugly buildings, but he knew how to make safe ones. After Emperor Yuri's death, Dono retired to his son-in-law's estate and went mad himself. He designed and built a bizarre set of towers there, which his descendants now charge the public to see. (MD)

Vorrutyer, Ges:
A vice admiral in the Barrayaran Navy, he is co-commander of the Barrayaran armada sent to conquer Escobar, and is on the ship that captures Cordelia's shuttle. Roughly Aral's age, he is a bit taller and stocky, with dark, curly hair with only a little gray in it, and beautiful deep, velvet brown eyes with long, black lashes. He is slated to be Minister of War once Prince Serg Vorbarra takes the throne. He went to school with Aral, and was the elder brother to Aral's young first wife. Ges had a homosexual relationship with Aral, during the distraught period after Aral's wife's death, and he still harbors an obsession with his ex-lover. Vorrutyer is a sadist, a fan of the writings of the Marquis de Sade, and abuses the privileges of his rank. He enjoys torturing people, both men under his command and any prisoners who take his fancy. Bothari kills Vorrutyer to stop him from raping Cordelia. (SH)

Vorrutyer House:
A generation older than Vorkosigan House, it is much more fortress-like, star-shaped with thick stone walls

and no windows on the ground floor, only gunslits. The main gate to the ground is made of thick, iron-bound planks. The house hasn't been cleaned since Count Pierre's death, and when Lord Dono moves in, he is less than pleased with its current condition. (CC)

Vorrutyer, Pierre:
Also known as "Le Sanguinaire," he is a noted count in Barrayaran history. He was Emperor Dorca's trusted right arm/head thug in the civil war that broke the power of the independent counts just before the end of the Time of Isolation. The Cetagandans killed him after an infamous and costly siege. His oldest daughter married an earlier Count Vorkosigan (they became Piotr's parents), which is where Mark gets his middle name of Pierre. (CC)

Vorrutyer, Richars:
A cruel, petty man, he lodges a suit to inherit his deceased cousin Pierre's District and become a count, but is thwarted by Miles working with Lord Dono after Richars threatens to bring a murder charge against him. Richars is a notable sadist and a slickly believable sociopath. He attempted to rape his cousin Lady Donna when she was twelve, and when he failed, killed her puppy. He later thwarted two marriages for Pierre, and then possibly had Pierre's third fiancée killed to prevent his cousin from producing an heir. After ordering thugs to castrate Dono, Richars is found out when the plot fails. Denounced publicly at the Council by several former allies, he is arrested after the rest of the counts vote in Dono as count. (CC)

Vorsmythe:
No first name given. One of the former Imperial
Auditors who used to hand in illegible reports that
were never longer than two pages. (M)

Vorsmythe:
No first name given. A Barrayaran industrialist attending
the Winterfair Ball that Mark wishes to talk to about
investing his newly acquired wealth. (MD)

Vorsmythe:
No first name given. A countess on Barrayar, she
assures Alys Vorpatril that both René Vorbretten and
Dono Vorrutyer have her husband's vote. (CC)

Vorsmythe:
No first name given. A count on Barrayar and husband to Alys's friend, he helps Mark learn how the
food-service distribution works locally, and becomes
an investor in the butter bug business. Not to be
confused with the industrialist or the Auditor. (CC)

Vorsmythe *Dolphin*-class 776 jump ship:
The jump ship that carried the Vorsoisson family
to Komarr, it has quadruple-vortex outboard control
nacelles, dual norm-space thrusters, and can carry
one hundred passengers. Nikolai loved the ride, but
caused some distress when he flushed his shoes down
the toilet. He owns a model of the ship, and Miles
and he discuss it during their first conversation on
Komarr. (K)

Vorsmythe, Helga:
One of the formerly eligible Vor women that Ivan
does not have the chance to marry. (M)


Vorsoisson, Etienne:
Ekaterin's husband, also known as Tien, is an administrator at the Serifosa division of the terraforming
project on Komarr. He has brown eyes, is overly
status-conscious, is quick to take offense at the most
innocuous comments, and frequently puts his foot in
his mouth.

A disaster both as a husband and as an employee,
he's had thirteen jobs in ten years, and has moved
his family all over the Barrayaran Imperium and
finally to Komarr. Tien is from the South Continent
of Barrayar, and served in the military for ten years
prior to his civil career. Tien is ten years older than
his wife, and is a distant, selfish, and emotionally
abusive husband.

Both he and his son have a genetic disease—a Barrayaran mutation called Vorzohn's Dystrophy. He has
the typical Barrayaran prejudices against mutation, and
wants to keep his condition secret, worried news of
the condition will cramp his chances for advancement.
By doing so, he has put his son at risk by shutting
them both off from any possibility of treatment. Tien
keeps promising his wife he'll get treatment off-world,
but puts it off as too expensive.

He is also up to his neck in illegal activity, knowing about the peculation scam at waste management,
but not about the plot to destroy the wormhole to
Barrayar. He has taken bribes from Soudha, losing the

money in Komarran trade fleet speculations. When Ekaterin finds out about all of this, she leaves him.

To make amends, he finds Miles and tries to bluff him into thinking he has just found out the graft in his department. He takes Miles to the Waste Heat experimental site, where they are both captured by the Komarrans plotting against Barrayar. Because he didn't check his breath mask, which wasn't fully charged, before going outside the dome, he dies horrifically in the unbreathable atmosphere while he and Miles are chained to a fence, even though the plotters had summoned help for them before leaving. Because of his connection to the plot to destroy the wormhole to Barrayar, the true nature of his death remains classified. Only Ekaterin, Miles, Vorthys, the plotters, Gregor, Imperial Security, and eventually Nikolai know the truth. (K)

Vorsoisson, Nikolai:
The only son of Ekaterin and Etienne, he is nine years old, with brown eyes and hair that is darkening to his mother's shade of brown. Called Nikki for short, he is a growing boy, almost as big as Miles when they first meet, and would like to be a jump-ship pilot. He finds out about his Vorzohn's Dystrophy after his father dies, and receives treatment for it before leaving Komarr. He is a bit worried about what other kids will think of him, but Miles helps him deal with it.

Nikki does not seem to have been very close to his father, but he has begun to forge an excellent relationship with Miles. When rumors surface that Miles murdered his father, Ekaterin and Miles take Nikki to see Emperor Gregor, who gives Nikolai as

much of the truth as he can, and puts to rest his
fears that Miles murdered Etienne. When Vassily
Vorsoisson and Hugo Vorvayne come to take custody
of him because they are worried that Vorbarr Sultana
will be embroiled in a war, Nikki calls Gregor. The
Emperor's solution is to bring everyone in the house
to Vorhartung Castle for a personal meeting, where
he guarantees Nikolai's and his mother's safety to her
irritating but worried relatives. Nikki is pleased that
his mother has proposed to Miles, and wants Miles
to make her happy. At the wedding reception, he and
his friends latch on to Arde Mayhew to hear all about
the pilot's adventures. (CC, DI, K, WG)

Vorsoisson, Vassily:
Ekaterin's cousin-in-law, he is a lieutenant in the Barrayaran military, with a job at Orbital Traffic Control
at Fort Kithera River. As Etienne's cousin he is the
Vorsoisson male next in line to inherit the official
guardianship of Nikolai. He allows the transfer of
guardianship to Ekaterin. But when Alexi Vormoncrief sends him news that Miles supposedly murdered
Etienne, he comes to town with Hugo Vorvayne to
take Ekaterin and Nikolai back home. Nikolai calls
Gregor, who has them all brought before him, and
puts an end to the idea. Vassily meets the family of
his new in-laws, and reconciles the idea of having the
Vorkosigans as relatives. (CC)

Vorsoisson, Violetta:
One of the formerly eligible Vor women that Ivan
does not have the chance to marry. (M)

Vortaine:
The Barrayaran count that is Ivan's heir. If he dies, his daughter will receive his assets, but his hereditary titles would go to Count Vordrozda. (WA)

Vortaine:
No first name given. A count on Barrayar, he is involved in the water boundary rights case with Count Vorvolynkin. He will not vote for either René Vorbretten or Dono Vorrutyers. A later generation than the previous Vortaine. (CC)

Vortala:
No first name given. A colonel in Imperial Security, he takes over Simon Illyan's internal security jobs while Simon is hospitalized. (M)

Vortala:
No first name given. The Prime Minister of Barrayar during Ezar Vorbarra's reign and the beginning of Aral Vorkosigan's Regency. A lean man, wrinkled and shrunken with age, he has clipped white hair fringing a bald and liver-spotted head, and can be very obnoxious even without swearing. He uses a walking stick, mainly for show. He tries to form a progressive political party, but only with the higher Barrayaran classes. Prince Serg wants Aral and Vortala dead when he is in power. Vortala summons Aral to the meeting where Ezar names him Regent. When Vordarian tries to overthrow the government, he escapes house arrest to join Aral at Tanery Base. (B, SH)

Vortala the Younger:
No first name given. A colonel in the Barrayaran military, he is the head of the Imperial Security task force assigned to provide security for the Emperor's wedding. (CC)

Vortalon:
No first name given. A captain in the Barrayaran military during the Time of Isolation, his life is fictionalized and he becomes a holovid hero that Nikolai watches. The boy refers to him when discussing how the character settles a debt of honor against villains who attack his father. He thinks he might have to kill Miles if Miles had killed Etienne Vorsoisson. (CC)

Vortashpula, Irene:
One of the eligible young ladies at the Emperor's Birthday celebration that Alys Vorpatril tried to get Ivan to consider as a possible marriage candidate. (MD)

Vorthalia the Bold:
A childhood obsession of Miles's. He was a holovid character supposedly based on a historical character. When Miles looked him up in the Imperial Archives he learned the truth about his idol, who wasn't as heroic as the vids made him appear. (CC)

Vorthalia the Brave and the Thicket of Thorns:
A metaphorical example of a liege lord cutting through the red tape of government that Miles uses in his initial conversation with Arde Mayhew. (WA)

**Vorthys, Georg:**
A Professor Emeritus of Engineering at Vorbarr Sultana University, Imperial Auditor, and Ekaterin's uncle. One of Emperor Gregor's civilian Imperial Auditor appointees, he is stout, white-haired, and smiles often. He is the Barrayaran expert on engineering failure analysis, and has written the standard texts on the subject. He became interested in the connections between sociopolitical and engineering integrity late in life. Along with the other Auditors in attendance, he approves Miles for the eighth Imperial Auditor position. Three months later, he and Miles go to Komarr to investigate the Soletta Station accident, and they visit Ekaterin and her family while there. Vorthys has been married for forty years to Helen, also a professor. After thwarting, along with Miles, Helen, and Ekaterin, the rebellious Komarran engineers' plot, he and his wife take Ekaterin and Nikolai in until she can settle herself on Barrayar. (CC, K, WG)

**Vorthys, Helen:**
A Professora of History at Vorbarr Sultana University, and a notable expert on Barrayaran political infighting, she is Imperial Auditor Georg Vorthys's wife and Ekaterin's aunt. Ekaterin lived with the Vorthys couple while she was going to university in Vorbarr Sultana, and again after her return from Komarr. She and Ekaterin are kidnapped by Komarran revolutionaries determined to cut off Barrayar's wormhole access. Both women are instrumental in ending the plot safely. She is scheduled to have replacement heart surgery to correct her congestive heart failure, but even while ill she gently guides Ekaterin's love life. She suspects Miles is in love with

Ekaterin, and sees that Ekaterin returns his regard long before she has any inkling of her own feelings. Helen approves of the match, and is one of the most favored guests at the wedding. (CC, WG)

Vortienne:
No first name given. A Barrayaran count, referred to in conversation between Aral and Cordelia as ready to retire in favor of his son. Has unusual, unnamed proclivities that he exercises with his guards. (MD)

Vortrifani:
No first name given. A Barrayaran count who would be backed by the "far right, blow-up-the-wormhole, isolationist loonies" if he attempted to claim the throne. When he plotted with extremists to drop a ship called the *Yarrow* onto the Imperial Residence, the plot was stopped by Imperial Security. Vortrifani distanced himself from the plan, but his power was severely weakened. Simon Illyan lauded Colonel Haroche's work on the case as superb. (M, VG)

Vortugalov:
No first name given. A Barrayaran count who would be backed by the Russian-speaking populace if he attempted to claim the throne. (VG)

Vorvane:
No first name given. A Barrayaran, she is the wife of the Minister of Heavy Industries. She and her three children are part of a group of 216 kidnapped people that the Dendarii Free Mercenaries are ordered to free by any means necessary. (BA)

Vorvayne brothers:
Ekaterin's four brothers. Hugo is the oldest; he supported her in many ways during her unhappy marriage to Etienne, but is stirred up by the gossip surrounding Miles and tries to keep his sister from marrying him. But once he realizes that the rumors are gross exaggerations and that Miles and Ekaterin truly love each other, he once again gives her his full support. Will, the youngest, takes pictures at the births of his sister's first children. The middle two brothers are not named. All four attend their sister's wedding. (CC, DI, K, WG)

Vorvayne, Rosalie:
The wife of Ekaterin's oldest brother, Hugo, she is in her forties, with dark hair and olive skin. She has three children, two sons and a daughter. She comes to Vorbarr Sultana to tell Ekaterin about Alexi Vormoncrief's marriage offer. (CC)

Vorvayne, Sasha:
Ekaterin's father, he has a modest flat in the small South Continent town where he retired. Before his retirement he was an officer in his district government on Barrayar. He knew Etienne slightly through his work. After his wife's death, he wanted to remarry a woman named Violie, and wished to have Ekaterin "settled" before doing so. To him this meant properly married off to a Vor, so he supported Etienne's courtship of Ekaterin. (CC, K)

Vorventa, Edwin:
A captain in the Barrayaran military, he accosts Mark in the garden at the Imperial Residence. Mark finds it disturbing that he knows so much about his relationship

with Miles. But the chain of evidence proves Vorventa got the information from his younger brother, who was Simon's Galactic Operations supervisor's adjutant, and who as a result is demoted and transferred out of the department. (MD)

Vorventa, Tatya:
One of the formerly eligible Vor women that Ivan does not have the chance to marry. (M)

Vorville:
No first name given. A Barrayaran count, at the time of the Hegen Hub war, he is described as a man who would be backed by the French-speaking populace if he attempted to claim the throne. At the time of the Emperor's wedding, he'll vote for René Vorbretten because of his friendship with René's late father. (VG, CC)

Vorville, Mary:
A Barrayaran noblewoman, she ensures that her father, Count Vorville, will vote for René Vorbretten due to a friendly relationship between him and René's late father. (CC)

Vorvolk:
No first name given. A Barrayaran countess, and wife of Lord Henri Vorvolk, she dances with Miles at one of the Imperial parties. (M)

Vorvolk, Henri:
A friend and contemporary of Gregor's, he was pulled out of classes at the Imperial Academy three times

during the events of Miles's first off-planet adventure to attend secret committee sessions of the Council of Counts about the pending charges. At the time of Gregor's wedding, Miles spends much of the night before the votes on René Vorbretten's and Dono Vorrutyer's countships arguing with Henri's friends about the merits of the individual cases. Henri has an office in the old dungeon area of Vorhartung Castle. (CC, MD, WA)

Vorvolynkin:
No first name given. A count on Barrayar, he is involved in a water boundary lawsuit with Count Vortaine, and will vote for René Vorbretten and Dono Vorrutyer just to irk his opponent. (CC)

Vorvolynkin, Louisa:
A Barrayaran noblewoman, she is the daughter-in-law of Count Vorvolynkin, who is involved in a boundary water rights dispute with Count Vortaine, and whom she has persuaded to vote for both René Vorbretten and Dono Vorrutyer in the Council of Counts meeting to antagonize his legal enemy. (CC)

Vorzohn's Dystrophy:
An adult-onset disease, the result of a mutation that arose on Barrayar, it first appeared in Vorinnis's District during the Time of Isolation. Its symptoms include a bewildering variety of physical debilitations that set in during middle age, and ends with the unfortunate gene carrier's decline in mental activity and death. It can be cured if caught early enough. It runs in

the Vorsoisson family, and has already manifested in Etienne, causing uncontrolled muscle tremors, and his brother, who committed suicide. Etienne's son, Nikolai, has the gene complex as well, but hasn't shown any symptoms yet. Regardless, Etienne doesn't want him treated, for fear it will expose his own disease. Only after her husband's death can Ekaterin take her son to be cured. She does so with a little assistance from Miles in his Imperial Auditor mode. (CC, K)

* * W * *

Wah-wah:
The slang term for a gale-force wind at Lazkowski Base, which can reach speeds of 160 kilometers per hour. When the wind siren sounds, anyone outside must take cover immediately. Miles watches a vid on the subject that features a flying latrine. (WA)

Watts, Boss:
A middle-aged quaddie male, dressed in a conservative slate blue uniform, he is the supervisor of Graf Station Downsider Relations, and is in the party that greets Miles, Ekaterin, and Roic when they arrive at Graf Station. He is involved in the negotiations with the renegade ba, and threatens to destroy the *Idris* if it looks like it's going to ram the station. (DI)

Weddell, Vaughn:
See Canaba, Hugh.

**Wedding of Vlad Vorbarra le Savante to Lady Vorlightly, The:**
An event that occurred during the gaudy, archaic period of the Time of Isolation. Both the bride and groom had to strip naked in front of witnesses to prove neither had any genetic mutations. (CC)

**Wilstar:**
No first name given. A person Vorob'yev goes to talk with at the Mariliacan embassy party, leaving Miles to chat with Mia Maz. (C)

**Winoweh's 2nd Battalion:**
A captured Marilacan military unit held in Dagoola Top Security Camp #3 until being rescued by Miles and the Dendarii Free Mercenary Fleet. (BI)

**Witgow trans-trench monorail tunnel:**
An engineering project mentioned by Doctor Yei when comparing the different emphases in the quaddies' education to Leo Graf. (FF)

**Worley:**
No first name given. A trooper in the Dendarii Free Mercenary Fleet that participates in the clone raid on Jackson's Whole. (MD)

**Worm plague:**
A disease on Sergyar that causes uncomfortable and unsightly bloating of its victims, it has just recently been brought under control on the colony planet. Dmitri Corbeau is a worm plague survivor, and has the scars to prove it. (DI, K)

Wormhole:
A shortcut that connects two distant points in space by traveling through a different physical dimension, reducing the travel time from decades to a few days or weeks. Traveling through wormholes is known as "jumping," and is accomplished by Necklin rods, which create a field that enables jump ships to pass through the wormholes. All of the settled planets in the Vorkosigan universe are connected by at least one wormhole, and some have several in their local space. Although wormholes are generally stable, there have been variances, such as when the one to Barrayar closed due to a gravitational anomaly, leading to the Time of Isolation on that planet. Wormholes are economically and strategically vital for all of the planets in the Vorkosigan Saga, and access to and control of them has been fought over many times. (All)

Wyzak:
The airsystems maintenance supervisor on Cay Habitat. He leads a search for Silver when she goes to steal the shuttle for the rescue mission to Rodeo. (FF)

• • X • •

Xaveria:
No first name given. A private in the Dendarii Free Mercenaries, he is one of the three arrested soldiers involved in the wine shop standoff in London. Mark bails him out of jail while posing as Miles/Admiral Naismith. (BA)

Xerxes:
A planet one jump away from Graf Station, Ker Dubauer was headed there when his Komarran cargo ship was impounded at the space station. (DI)

Xi Ceta:
One of the eight satrapy planets in the Cetagandan Empire, it is Marilac's neighbor. Its governor is Slyke Giaja. (C)

Xian:
No first name given. A Marilacan general who fled the fighting at Fallow Core. He had promised to return, but was killed in the fighting at Vassily Station. (BI)

•  •  **Y**  •  •

Yalen:
No first name given. A private in the Dendarii Free Mercenaries, he is one of the three arrested soldiers involved in the wine shop standoff in London. Mark bails him out of jail while posing as Miles/Admiral Naismith. (BA)

Yaski:
No first name given. A lieutenant in the Barrayaran military, he is the fire marshal at Lazkowski Base. After filling in Lieutenant Bonn on the situation in the fetaine stockpile, he agrees to destroy it using plasma mines. (VG)

Yegorav:
No first name given. A lieutenant in the Barrayaran military, he serves on the *Prince Serg*, and escorts Elena and Miles to Aral for debriefing after the battle. He does not know Elena's and Miles's real identities until they are all in Aral's office. (VG)

Yei, Sondra:
A doctor, she is the head of psychology and training for six years on the Cay Project. Pushing middle age, she is pleasantly ugly, with bright mongolian eyes, a broad nose and lips, and coffee-and-cream skin. A company woman, she initially butts heads with Leo over the quaddies. Evacuated with the rest of the staff during the simulated hull breach on the Habitat, she tries to knock Van Atta unconscious with a spanner when he orders the shuttle crew to fire upon the escaping cargo ship. (FF)

Yenaro:
No first name given. A minor Cetagandan noble about Miles's age, he is tall and lean, with a square skull and prominent, round cheekbones. He wears a small face paint decal designating his rank and clan instead of applying the full pattern. The grandson of ghem-General Yenaro, who fought opposite Miles's grandfather Piotr during the Cetagandan Occupation, he inherited his family's estates, but not the means to keep them up.

He created the Autumn Leaves sculpture for the Marilacan Embassy, and has a strong interest in chemistry/perfumes making. He is a pawn in the plot to overthrow the Emperor, and is manipulated into playing tricks on Miles and Ivan, then unknowingly trying to kill them at the bioestheties display. He tells Miles that Ilsum Kety is behind the plot, and the Emperor rewards him by appointing him a ghem-lord-in-waiting, tenth rank, sixth degree. (C)

Ylla:
On Leo Graf's return trip from this planet, he changed ships on the Morita transfer station on his way to Earth. (FF)

Yoder, Bill:
A sheriff in Ohio. Chalmys DuBauer knows him well, and turns Carlos Diaz over to him after extracting his confession to attempting to murder Anias Ruey. (DD)

Youth:
No name given. He owns a rickety lightflyer, and takes Cordelia, Bothari, and jugs of maple syrup out of the Dendarii Mountains to a small market town. (B)

Yuell:
No first name given. A math professor at Solstice University, he is a stout, sandy-haired young man with very high intelligence. He accompanies Doctor Riva to the Waste Heat experiment station to assist her, and is one of the few people who can argue math with her and be right. He is disappointed there will be no dinner at the Top of the Dome restaurant in Serifosa on this trip. (K)

Yuri Vorbarra's Civil War:
The battle between Yuri Vorbarra and his kinsman Ezar for the throne of Barrayar. Ezar wins, and during the campaign, Aral helps kill Yuri. (SH)

**Yuri Vorbarra's Massacre:**
The term Barrayarans use to refer to the night Mad Emperor Yuri sent out death squads to assassinate all of his relatives, including Aral. For some unknown reason, he didn't send one for Piotr, but his men kill Aral's mother with a sonic grenade in front of him. (SH)

· · Z · ·

**Zai:**
No first name given. An armsman whom Esterhazy hopes warned the village near Vorkosigan House about the Imperial troops searching for information about Gregor's location. (B)

**Zamori:**
No first name given. A major in the Barrayaran military, he is a heavyset fellow who works in operations, and was once a student of Professora Vorthys. He tries to court Ekaterin, with no success. (CC)

**Zara:**
A quaddie who pilots the cargo pusher around the Transfer Station, she has dark hair and copper skin, and is dressed in the purple T-shirt and shorts of the pusher crew. She has a top rating among the pusher pilots. (FF)

**Zeeman, Dale:**
A technician working in Kline Station atmosphere control, he unknowingly helps Quinn dispose of Okita's body by giving her a hundred kilograms of newts to take with her when she leaves. (EA)

Zelaski:
No first name given. A trooper in the Dendarii Free Mercenary Fleet, she is killed in action during a mission to Marilac. (MD)

Zipweed:
A Barrayaran plant with blond and maroon stripes that has a slightly sweet odor. Ekaterin plans to use some of them in the Barrayaran display garden near Vorkosigan House. (CC)

Zlati ale:
A pale ruby, alcoholic liquid. Lord Yenaro offers it to Ivan and Miles during the party at his home. Ivan's drink is laced with an anti-aphrodisiac as a prank to embarrass him. (C)

Zoave Twilight:
A planet with several jump points, among them the third jump point from Vega Station. It is mentioned by Vorob'yev as being the ultimate goal of the Cetagandans in their dealings with the planet Marilac. It is unwillingly abiding by the arms embargo placed on Vega Station by the Cetagandan Empire. Later, Miles and three ships from the Dendarii fleet are orbiting this planet after their mission to recover the Barrayaran courier being held hostage. (C, M, MD)

*Appendices*

# Topology of the Wormhole Nexus

## CRYSTAL CARROLL AND SUFORD LEWIS

The next page shows a map of the topology of the wormhole nexus. No attempt has been made to indicate where in the galaxy these systems and stations lie or how far apart they are; only the wormhole connectivity is shown. Actual locations and the five-dimensional wormholes connecting them would be impossible to show on a two-dimensional page. The wormhole connectivity, however, can be nicely arranged into this flat diagram.

This diagram contains all the systems and stations with specified locations as revealed so far. Other systems, stations, wormholes, and connections exist. Below is the list of the systems we know exist without knowing their relationship to the ones shown on the map.

# Systems of Unspecified Location:

| | | |
|---|---|---|
| Beni Ra | Kshatria | Skya |
| Frost | Minos | Varusa Tertius |
| Hespari | Nuovo Brasil | Walshea |

| | | |
|---|---|---|
| **MAP KEY** | ● | System |
| | ◆ | Space Station |
| | ○ | Wormhole to Unspecified Connection |
| | ——— | Direct Route (may still require several jumps) |
| | – – – – | Known, Unspecified Intermediate Points |
| | ·········· | Sub-light Route |

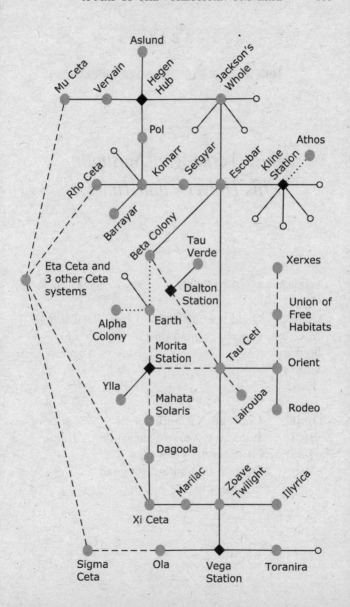

# Miles Vorkosigan/Naismith: His Universe and Times

| Chronology | Events | Chronicle |
|---|---|---|
| Approx. 200 years before Miles's birth | Quaddies are created by genetic engineering. | *Falling Free* |
| During Beta-Barrayaran War | Cordelia Naismith meets Lord Aral Vorkosigan while on opposite sides of a war. Despite difficulties, they fall in love and are married. | *Shards of Honor* |

| Chronology | Events | Chronicle |
|---|---|---|
| The Vordarian Pretendership | While Cordelia is pregnant, an attempt to assassinate Aral by poison gas fails, but Cordelia is affected; Miles Vorkosigan is born with bones that will always be brittle and other medical problems. His growth will be stunted. | *Barrayar* |
| Miles is 17 | Miles fails to pass physical test to get into the Service Academy. On a trip, necessities force him to improvise the Free Dendarii Mercenaries into existence; he has unintended but unavoidable adventures for four months. Leaves the Dendarii in Ky Tung's competent hands and takes Elli Quinn to Beta for rebuilding of her damaged face; returns to Barrayar to thwart plot against his father. Emperor pulls strings to get Miles into the Academy. | *The Warrior's Apprentice* |

| Chronology | Events | Chronicle |
|---|---|---|
| Miles is 20 | Ensign Miles graduates and immediately has to take on one of the duties of the Barrayaran nobility and act as detective and judge in a murder case. Shortly afterwards, his first military assignment ends with his arrest. Miles has to rejoin the Dendarii to rescue the young Barrayaran emperor. Emperor accepts Dendarii as his personal secret service force. | "The Mountains of Mourning" in *Borders of Infinity*<br><br>*The Vor Game* |
| Miles is 22 | Miles and his cousin Ivan attend a Cetagandan state funeral and are caught up in Cetagandan internal politics. | *Cetaganda* |
| | Miles sends Commander Elli Quinn, who's been given a new face on Beta, on a solo mission to Kline Station. | *Ethan of Athos* |

| Chronology | Events | Chronicle |
|---|---|---|
| Miles is 23 | Now a Barrayaran Lieutenant, Miles goes with the Dendarii to smuggle a scientist out of Jackson's Whole. Miles's fragile leg bones have been replaced by synthetics. | "Labyrinth" in *Borders of Infinity* |
| Miles is 24 | Miles plots from within a Cetagandan prison camp on Dagoola IV to free the prisoners. The Dendarii fleet is pursued by the Cetagandans and finally reaches Earth for repairs. Miles has to juggle both his identities at once, raise money for repairs, and defeat a plot to replace him with a double. Ky Tung stays on Earth. Commander Elli Quinn is now Miles's right-hand officer. Miles and the Dendarii depart for Sector IV on a rescue mission. | "The Borders of Infinity" in *Borders of Infinity*<br><br>*Brothers in Arms* |

| Chronology | Events | Chronicle |
|---|---|---|
| Miles is 25 | Hospitalized after previous mission, Miles's broken arms are replaced by synthetic bones. With Simon Illyan, Miles undoes yet another plot against his father while flat on his back. | *Borders of Infinity* |
| Miles is 28 | Miles meets his clone brother Mark again, this time on Jackson's Whole. | *Mirror Dance* |
| Miles is 29 | Miles hits thirty; thirty hits back. | *Memory* |
| Miles is 30 | Emperor Gregor dispatches Miles to Komarr to investigate a space accident, where he finds old politics and new technology make a deadly mix. | *Komarr* |
| | The Emperor's wedding sparks romance and intrigue on Barrayar, and Miles plunges up to his neck in both. | *A Civil Campaign* |

| Chronology | Events | Chronicle |
|---|---|---|
| Miles is 31 | Armsman Roic and Sergeant Taura defeat a plot to unhinge Miles and Ekaterin's midwinter wedding. | "Winterfair Gifts" in *Irresistible Forces* |
| Miles is 32 | Miles and Ekaterin's honeymoon journey is interrupted by an Auditorial mission to Quaddiespace, where they encounter old friends, new enemies, and a double handful of intrigue. | *Diplomatic Immunity* |
| Miles is 39 | Miles and Roic go to Kibou-daini. | *Cryoburn* |

# 800 Years in Barrayaran and Galactic Human History

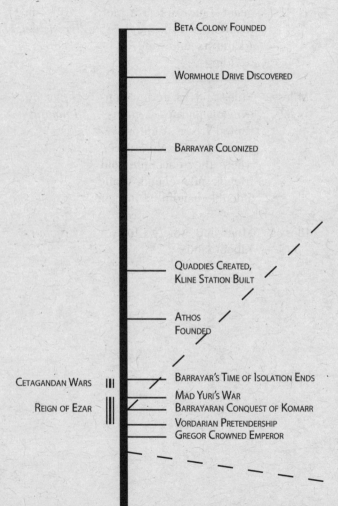

BETA COLONY FOUNDED

WORMHOLE DRIVE DISCOVERED

BARRAYAR COLONIZED

QUADDIES CREATED,
KLINE STATION BUILT

ATHOS
FOUNDED

CETAGANDAN WARS     BARRAYAR'S TIME OF ISOLATION ENDS

MAD YURI'S WAR

REIGN OF EZAR     BARRAYARAN CONQUEST OF KOMARR

VORDARIAN PRETENDERSHIP

GREGOR CROWNED EMPEROR

# 60 Years in Barrayaran and Galactic Human History

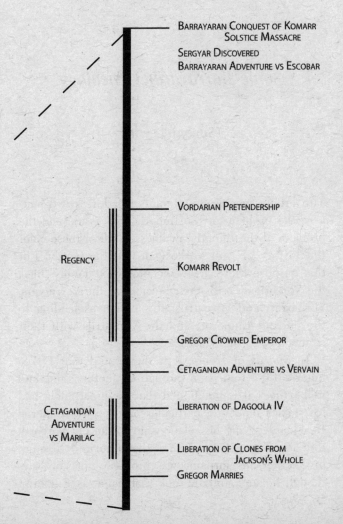

BARRAYARAN CONQUEST OF KOMARR
SOLSTICE MASSACRE

SERGYAR DISCOVERED
BARRAYARAN ADVENTURE VS ESCOBAR

VORDARIAN PRETENDERSHIP

REGENCY

KOMARR REVOLT

GREGOR CROWNED EMPEROR

CETAGANDAN ADVENTURE VS VERVAIN

CETAGANDAN
ADVENTURE
VS MARILAC

LIBERATION OF DAGOOLA IV

LIBERATION OF CLONES FROM
JACKSON'S WHOLE

GREGOR MARRIES

# Some Barrayaran Genealogy

## SUFORD LEWIS

This article specifically attempts to address two matters: the problem of the Imperial succession and the problem of the Imperial madness. Both of these color the history of Aral Vorkosigan and his family. For this purpose there are three important family lines: the Vorkosigans with their linkages to the Vorrutyers, Vorbarras, and Vorpatrils; the Vorbarras leading to the current Emperor; and the Vorpatrils with their connection to the Vorbarras.

In *Shards of Honor* it is mentioned that Dorca inherited the Imperium through his mother's line and in *Barrayar* it is mentioned that his great-uncle had his stables built in a particular place in the Imperial Residence, giving his relationship to the old Vorbarra line more specifically. Since he inherited through his mother, his surname was probably not Vorbarra, though he undoubtedly took that name as Emperor.

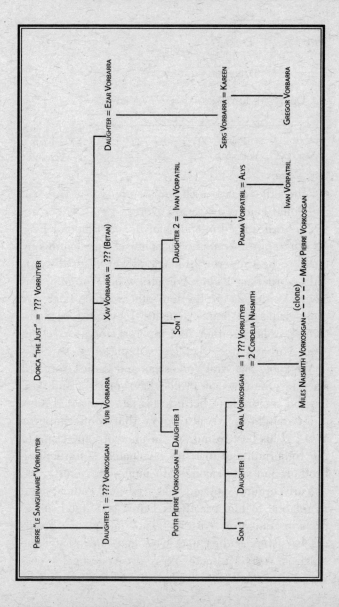

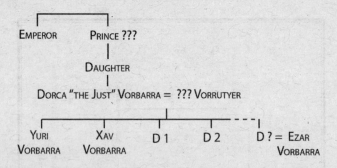

On the other hand, Ezar apparently was a Vorbarra and some kind of cousin to Dorca.

On his deathbed in *Shards of Honor*, Emperor Ezar says there are five men with better claims than his by blood to be Emperor. Aral Vorkosigan heads this list. Vidal Vordarian, Padma Vorpatril, Lord Vortaine, and Count Vordrozda are the four others. Since Ezar says their claims are better than his, they must be more directly related either to Emperor Dorca or to the "true Vorbarra line" that Dorca replaced.

We know that Aral Vorkosigan and Padma Vorpatril are the grandsons of Prince Xav Vorbarra and Aral has the senior claim because his father married Xav's older daughter. We also know that Mad Emperor Yuri did his best to murder anyone with any claim to the Imperium and that this eliminated Aral's mother, brother, and sister along with numerous others.

Yuri certainly noticed that Aral and Padma stood in relation to him exactly as Dorca had stood to the previous emperor. We don't know about any brothers or sisters Padma may have had, only that none survived Yuri's Massacre. We know Aral's uncle, Xav's son, was also killed. So, although Aral may claim Salic

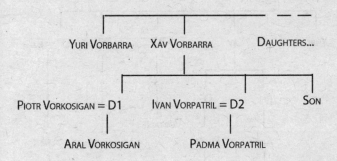

Law bars him from the Imperium, this is a legalistic argument that has had little practical force in the past.

In *The Warrior's Apprentice* Miles Vorkosigan mentions that Ivan Vorpatril, his second cousin, is his heir. Likewise, Ivan is very aware of Lord Vortaine as heir to his title and of Count Vordrozda as heir to Lord Vortaine. Indeed, Miles works out that this relationship is Count Vordrozda's motivation for charging him with treasonous intent in raising an armed force and for Admiral Hessman sending Ivan with the doomed courier supposedly sent to fetch Miles to answer this charge. It is also mentioned that Lord Vortaine's daughter, unmarried and fiftyish, would get her father's money but Count Vordrozda would get any title. This makes it obvious that Lord Vortaine has no sons. Vordrozda's maneuverings are aimed eventually at the Imperium. Since Ivan is not that close in line for the Vorpatril countship, what other title could be relevant? It is the Vorbarra heritage that is of interest relative to Lord Vordrozda.

What can we figure out about Lord Vortaine? As heir to Ivan, he must relate into Ivan's line to Prince Xav through a daughter of Xav younger than Ivan's

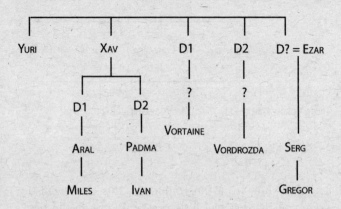

grandmother or a daughter of Dorca. It has to be a daughter, because Vortaine inherits from Ivan rather than the other way around. All we need for Count Vordrozda to be Lord Vortaine's heir is for Vordrozda to similarly inherit from the same line via a yet younger daughter.

Vortaine and Vordrozda were heirs to Miles's and Ivan's fathers similarly, and figured in Ezar's calculations as potential successors to Yuri. It is their ages, as closer contemporaries to Aral, that make it more likely that they are grandsons of daughters of Dorca rather than of other daughters of Xav. Confirming this, all the rest of Xav's descendants were eliminated by Yuri's Massacre. The most distant Vortaine can be is third cousin, because if he were a fourth cousin, Gregor would be Ivan's heir before him. In the diagram above, Vortaine and Vordrozda are second cousins to Miles's and Ivan's fathers, thus second cousins once removed to Miles and Ivan. Note that Gregor is also a second cousin once removed.

Padma Vorpatril had no siblings that survived Yuri's

Massacre. This also means that Ivan has no first cousins younger than himself on his father's side. Indeed, he seems not to have any first cousins at all, but that may only reflect his mother's attitude about her own family. That Alys Vorpatril chose to maintain very close ties to the Vorkosigans, incidentally thus to the Regent of Barrayar, rather than to other relatives, probably says more about her political interests than about the existence of first cousins to Ivan on his mother's side. However, any first cousins Ivan might have, related to his mother's line, would not be his heirs relative to any titles he might inherit through Prince Xav.

Just the information that Aral "heads the list" eliminates the possibility of any male children of Yuri or any brothers of Yuri and Xav, at least any surviving ones or ones with surviving male children. Aral and Padma, sons of Xav's first and second daughters, respectively, are also mentioned as the only descendants of Xav to survive Yuri's massacre.

We never find out much about Vidal Vordarian's claim. We only know that he spent a lot of time contemplating his genealogy. This implies that there was some problem about his claim, too, but he managed to convince himself of its justice. In order to convince himself that his claim was comparable to Aral Vorkosigan's, his claim needed to differ from Aral's by more than just which of Xav's siblings it derived from. Vordarian may have been the sort of stolid conservative type who could have been convinced simply by the fact that his own line contained no tainted off-worlders. However, Vordarian cannot trace to a brother of Yuri and Xav since none and no heirs of any survived Yuri's Massacre. Possibly he could trace back to a sister, as

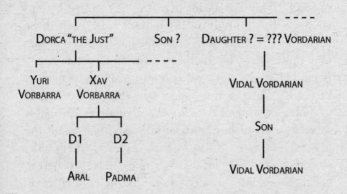

Vortaine and Vordrozda do. However, let's give him more credit than that, and look at another option.

Say Dorca's sister married a Vordarian from which the descent went straight to Vidal. With Aral appointed as Regent and Vidal Vordarian fearing that Aral would seize the Imperium, Vordarian can argue that his claim is just as good as Aral's (ignoring that Aral has not yet claimed the Imperium) and make his own preemptive strike. The subtle point of which relationship takes precedence, besides depending on precisely what the Barrayaran rules are, is also exactly the sort of thing that often gets decided by strength of arms and spinelessly rubber-stamped by legitimizing bodies afterward.

Without going back to Dorca's great-uncle and what siblings *he* might have had, just going back to Dorca himself and looking at Dorca's siblings opens up a new set of possible claimants to the Imperium. Actually, these would hardly be new; Yuri must have thought of them, too, and killed as many of them as he could. However, it is also known that he did not get all of them.

If Dorca had a brother whose daughter married a Vordarian, the effect would be essentially the same. We know that there is a female link somewhere just because Vidal is a Vordarian rather than a Vorbarra. So we can easily generate a relationship that gives Vordarian a claim. Obviously a claim that goes through two females is not as good as a claim that goes through only one. Perhaps that is why there are only five contenders. Everyone else who might have a claim has two or more females in the linkage.

The other consideration that determines how good a claim is is how far back you have to go to get to an emperor. The fewer generations you have to go back, the better. By that token, Vordarian's claim is not as good as any of the others as he has to go back to the generation before Xav. However, perhaps he has convinced himself that this is really better, as it harks back to a "better" age.

What about Ezar? Since Aral claims that Salic Law bars him (and thus everyone else we know of), there is an implication that Ezar has male line descent that legitimizes his claim. It does not have to be more legitimate than that of Yuri or Xav; just by being through the male line, it is automatically better than the rest. Piotr, when he persuaded Ezar to assume the throne, probably just made the argument that Ezar would make a better ruler and he, Piotr, and all his troops wanted him. A glance at the possibilities and Piotr's encouragement—these were all his relatives; he knew them pretty well, remember—should have been enough to convince him.

For instance, say Ezar's great-grandfather was the youngest brother to the emperor who was Dorca's

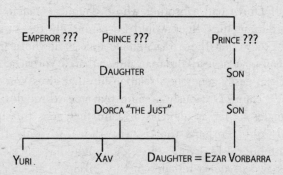

great-uncle. This would make Ezar a third cousin to Yuri and Xav. Now, if Ezar's son Serg's madness has the same source as Yuri's, Ezar's relationship to Dorca could be irrelevant to it. It is only necessary that Ezar marry a sister or daughter of Yuri. Indeed, if the madness descends from a Vorrutyer source, as has also been hinted, Yuri likely inherited it through his mother and Serg from his mother, making Ezar's relationship to Dorca—second cousin, once removed—irrelevant.

In *The Warrior's Apprentice* Miles remarks that he is related to Mad Emperor Yuri through two separate lines of descent. He is contemplating the likelihood that he may go mad. We can identify one line easily through Prince Xav. Yuri's madness could have come from his mother, who seems to have been a Vorrutyer. In *Shards of Honor*, Aral mentions this same Prince Xav as having married a Betan, so that means the other line of descent must be through Piotr.

Since Piotr is ninth-generation Vorkosigan, it must be through Piotr's mother or grandmother. If we assume Piotr Pierre was the first son, this makes Pierre the first name of his mother's father, who was likely a Vorrutyer. In *A Civil Campaign* we learn of

Pierre "le Sanguinaire" Vorrutyer, who was Emperor Dorca's strong right arm and whose eldest daughter married a Vorkosigan. This is very likely the second link. This would be like Miles's thoroughness and, further, like his fatalism to note that whichever line Yuri got it from, Miles is related to both, and to the more likely Vorrutyer line, twice.

If the genetic disposition to madness comes from the Vorrutyers, Yuri's, Serg's, and Ges Vorrutyer's madness could then all have a common origin. During the reigns of Dorca, Yuri, and Ezar, the Vorrutyers were very close to the emperors. The terrible architecture of the government buildings built during Yuri's reign is attributed to a crazy Vorrutyer architect in Yuri's favor. Dorca married a Vorrutyer. Piotr's father married a Vorrutyer. The Vorrutyers are apparently very thorough in consolidating alliances with everybody of any note. Aral and Ges Vorrutyer were probably second cousins and childhood friends just as Miles and Ivan are second cousins and childhood friends and similarly with Gregor as well. Further, Aral's first wife was apparently a Vorrutyer and Ges's sister—that would have boded very ill for their children and probably for their home life if she had become mad in time.

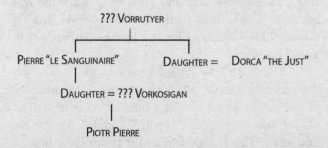

This easily gets us to Vorrutyers and madness through the Vorkosigan line. Should we suspect that Dorca and Pierre "le Sanguinaire" were also cousins? Or that Dorca married Pierre's sister (possibly his own cousin)? Alternatively (or even, in addition), Pierre could have been related to Dorca's father, who might have been a Vorrutyer, since Dorca inherited through his mother, and thus she was a Vorbarra. Any of these possibilities make Miles's second connection with Yuri's line less direct than his first, but if the connection with Yuri's line that we want is actually to a Vorrutyer madman, then this can do it. With the Vorrutyer penchant for marrying their daughters to powerful families, sometimes several generations in a row, the deleterious effects of cousin marriages alone should have made many of the "best" families somewhat barmy even without a specific tendency to madness.

Since Mad Yuri did not count Piotr as a Vorbarra descendant, these links through Piotr Pierre to the Vorrutyers meet the need to get to the "mad" part of Yuri's inheritance without getting to the Imperial part. Miles certainly has two separate links if one link is through his grandfather Piotr, and the other is through his great-grandfather Xav. Let us not quibble about whether this is really "Yuri's line," since the real worry is in inheriting Yuri's madness. "Yuri's line" is a reasonable shorthand for the blood that resulted in Yuri's madness.

In *The Vor Game* Miles mentions six factions on the succession issue, although it is not clear whether or not he is making them up for Cavilo's benefit. The old list was: Vorkosigan, Vorpatril, Vortaine, Vordrozda, Vordarian. This is only five and it is not clear that all actually have surviving claimants. It is also possible that Lord Vortaine's daughter, said to be in her fifties in *The Warrior's Apprentice*, did marry and have children, providing a continuing Vortaine-derived line. Yes, this is rather late, but my great-grandmother had her last child at fifty-two and some women continue to be fertile even later. Vordrozda could have had brothers or sisters and continuing lines through them. Just because no one is mentioned as linked to Vordarian does not mean that the line of descent he based his claim on has to have ended with his death.

But who would be the sixth? Given the many connections of the Vorrutyers to the Vorbarras, there could be a Vorrutyer claim. There could still be descendants of not only the "true Vorbarras" Dorca supplanted (besides Ezar and his heir, Gregor), but also of who knows how many Vorbarras supplanted in the same way even earlier in Barrayar's turbulent history. Thus there is little problem coming up with six factions. It is more of a question of whom to leave out of the list: Vorkosigan, Vorpatril, Vordarian, Vortaine, Vordrozda, Vorrutyer, and "true" Vorbarra.

This doesn't include the possibility that someone thought to be dead might be alive, or that someone thought to have died unmarried and without issue might have secretly married and had legitimate issue. Nor is it impossible that illegitimate issue might make a claim, too. The Barrayarans have not progressed to the complete and certain census of citizens that Beta Colony has, and there could be more than just a few hiding out from past wars or from sweeps such as Yuri's through all rivals. They could also be patriotically, for the good of Barrayar, refraining from upsetting what appears to be a reasonable order. Ezar's father could probably have made a claim when Dorca seized the Imperium, but did not. He could have had many possible reasons for refraining—such as being only seven years old, for instance. Finally, they might be as nutty as fruitcakes, true to their Vorrutyer heritage, and not know that the Imperium could be theirs. What a wealth of opportunity!

Can't you just see it? Somewhere, some father is passing on the True Talisman of the Vorbarras so that, should the Imperium falter, his son can present this talisman to make his claim. Meanwhile, he is to cultivate his skills and knowledge, practice virtue, and support order. Oh yes, and when the time comes, pass on this duty to his sons.

—Suford Lewis

The following is an excerpt from:

# CRYOBURN

## LOIS McMASTER BUJOLD

Available from Baen Books
November 2010
hardcover

# CHAPTER ONE

Angels were falling all over the place.

Miles blinked, trying to resolve the golden streaks sleeting through his vision into mere retinal flashes, but they stubbornly persisted as tiny, distinct figures, faces dismayed, mouths round. He heard their wavering cries like the whistle of fireworks from far off, the echoes buffeted by hillsides.

*Ah, terrific. Auditory hallucinations, too.*

Granted the visions seemed more dangerous, in his current addled state. If he could see things that were not there, it was also quite possible for him to not see things that *were* there, like stairwells, or broken gaps in this corridor floor. Or balcony railings, but wouldn't he feel those, pressing against his chest? Not that he could see anything in this pitch darkness—not even his hands, reaching uncertainly before him. His heart was beating too fast, rushing in his ears like muffled surf, his dry mouth gasping. He had to slow down. He scowled at the tumbling angels, peeved. If they were going to glow like that, they might at least illuminate his surroundings for him, like little celestial grav-lights, but no. Nothing so helpful.

He stumbled, and his hand banged against something

hollow-sounding—had that bit of wall *shifted*? He snatched his arms in, wrapping them around himself, trembling. *I'm just cold, yeah, that's it*. Which had to be from the power of suggestion, since he was sweating.

Hesitantly, he stretched out again and felt along the corridor wall. He began to move forward more slowly, fingers lightly passing over the faint lines and ripples of drawer edges and handle-locks, rank after rank of them, stacked high beyond his reach. Behind each drawer-face, a frozen corpse: stiff, silent, waiting in mad hope. A hundred corpses to every thirty steps or so, thousands more around each corner, hundreds of thousands in this lost labyrinth. *No—millions*.

That part, unfortunately, was not a hallucination.

*The Cryocombs*, they called this place, rumored to wind for kilometers beneath the city. The tidy blocks of new mausoleums on the city's western fringe, zoned as the Cryopolis, did not account for all the older facilities scattered around and underneath the town going back as much as a hundred and fifty or two hundred years, some still operational, some cleared and abandoned. Some abandoned without being cleared? Miles's ears strained, trying to detect a reassuring hum of refrigeration machinery beyond the blood-surf and the angels' cries. Now, there was a nightmare for him—all those banks of drawers bumping under his fingertips concealing not frozen hope, but warm rotting death.

It would be stupid to run.

The angels kept sleeting. Miles refused to let what was left of his mind be diverted in an attempt to count them, even by a statistically valid sampling-and-multiplication method. Miles had done such a back-of-the-napkin rough calculation when he'd first arrived here on Kibou-daini, what, just five days ago? *Seems longer.* If the cryo-corpses were stacked up along the corridors at a density, on average, of a hundred per ten meters, that made for ten thousand along each kilometer of corridor. One hundred kilometers of corridors for every million frozen dead. Therefore, something between a hundred and fifty and two hundred kilometers of cryo-corridors tucked around this town somewhere.

*I am so lost.*

His hands were scraped and throbbing, his trouser knees torn and damp. With blood? There had been crawlspaces and ducts, hadn't there? Yes, what had seemed like kilometers of them, too. And more ordinary utility tunnels, lit by ceiling tubes and not lined with centuries of mortality. His weary legs stumbled, and he froze—um, *stopped*—once more, to be sure of his balance. He wished fiercely for his cane, gone astray in the scuffle earlier—how many hours ago, now?—he could be using it like a blind man on Old Earth or Barrayar's own Time of Isolation, tapping in front of his feet for those so-vividly-imagined gaps in the floor.

His would-be kidnappers hadn't roughed him up too badly in the botched snatch, relying instead on a hyposprary of sedative to keep their captive under control. Too bad it had been in the same class of sedatives to which Miles was violently allergic—or even, judging by his present symptoms, the identical drug. Expecting a drowsy deadweight, they'd instead found themselves struggling with a maniacal little screaming man. This suggested his snatchers hadn't known everything about him, a somewhat reassuring thought.

Or even anything about him. *You bastards are on the top of Imperial Lord Auditor Miles Vorkosigan's very own shit list now, you bet.* But under what name? *Only five days on this benighted world, and already total strangers are trying to kill me.* Sadly, it wasn't even a record. He wished he knew who they'd been. He wished he were back home in the Barrayaran Empire, where the dread title of Imperial Auditor actually *meant* something to people. *I wish those wretched angels would stop shrieking at me.*

"Flights of angels," he muttered in experimental incantation, "sing me to my rest."

The angels declined to form up into a ball like a will-o'-the-wisp and lead him onward out of this place. So much for his dim hope that his subconscious had been keeping track of his direction while the rest of his mind was out, and would now produce some neat inspiration in dramatic form. Onward. One foot in front of the other, wasn't that the grownup way of solving problems? Surely he ought to be a grownup at his age.

He wondered if he was going in circles.

His trailing hand wavered through black air across a narrow cross-corridor, made for access to the banks' supporting machinery, which he ignored. Later, another. He'd been suckered into exploring down too many of those already, which was part of how he'd got so hideously turned around. Go straight or, if his corridor dead-ended, right, as much as possible, that was his new rule.

But then his bumping fingers crossed something that was not a bank of cryo-drawers, and he stopped abruptly. He felt around without turning, because turning, he'd discovered, destroyed what little orientation he still possessed. Yes, a door! If only it wasn't another utility closet. If only it was unlocked, for a change.

*Unlocked, yes!* Miles hissed through his teeth and pulled. Hinges creaked with corrosion. It seemed to weigh a ton, but the bloody thing moved! He stuck an experimental foot through the gap and felt around. A floor, not a drop—if his senses weren't lying, again. He had nothing with which to prop open the door; he hoped he might find it again if this proved another dead end. Carefully, he knelt on all fours and eased through, feeling in front of him.

Not another closet. Stairs, emergency stairs! He seemed to be on a landing in front of the door. To his right, steps went up, cool and gritty under his sore hand. To his left, down. Which way? He had to run out of up sooner, surely. It was probably a delusion, if a powerful one, that he might go down forever. This maze could not descend to the planet's magma, after all. The heat would thaw the dead.

There was a railing, not too wobbly, but he started up on all fours anyway, patting each riser to be sure the step was all there before trusting his weight to it. A reversal of direction, more painful climbing. Another turning at another landing—he tried its door, which was also unlocked, but did not enter it. Not unless or until he ran out of stairs would he let himself be forced back in there with those endless ranks of corpses. He tried to keep count of the flights, but lost track after a few turnings. He heard himself whimpering under his breath in time with the angel ululations, and forced himself to silence. Oh God, was that a faint gray glow overhead? Real light, or just another mirage?

He knew it for real light when he saw the pale glimmer of his hands, the white ghosts of his shirtsleeves. He hadn't become disembodied in the dark after all, huh.

On the next landing he found a door with a real window, a dirty square pane as wide as his two stretched hands. He craned his neck and peered out, blinking against the grayness that seemed bright as fire, making his dark-staring eyes water. *Oh gods and little fishes let it not be locked* ...

He shoved, then gasped relief as the door moved. It didn't creak as loudly as the one below. *Could be a roof. Be careful.* He crawled again, out into free air at last.

Not a roof; a broad alley at ground level. One hand upon the rough stucco wall behind him, Miles clambered to his feet and squinted up at slate gray clouds, a spitting mist, and lowering dusk. All luminous beyond joy.

The structure from which he'd just emerged rose only one more storey, but opposite it another building rose higher. It seemed to have no doors on this side, nor lower windows, but above, dark panes gleamed silver in the diffuse light. None were broken, yet the windows had an empty, haunted look, like the eyes of an abandoned woman. It seemed a vaguely industrial block, no shops or houses in sight. No lights, security or otherwise. Warehouses, or a deserted factory? A chill wind blew a plastic flimsy skittering along the cracked pavement, a bit of bright trash more solid than all the wailing angels in the world. Or in his head. *Whichever.*

He was still, he judged, in the Territorial Prefecture capital of Northbridge, or Kitahashi, as every place on this planet seemed to boast two interchangeable names, to ensure the confusion of tourists no doubt. Because to have arrived at any other urban area this size, he would have had to walk over a hundred kilometers underground in a straight line, and while he would buy the hundred kilometers, considering how his feet felt right now, the straight line part was right out. He might even be ironically close to his downtown starting point, but on the whole, he thought not.

With one hand trailing over the scabrous stucco, partly to hold himself upright and partly from what was by now grim superstitious habit, Miles turned—right—and stumbled up the alley to its first cross-corri—corner. The pavement was cold. His captors had taken away his shoes early on; his socks were in tatters, and possibly also his skin, but his feet were too numb to register pain.

His hand crossed a faded graffiti, sprayed in some red paint and then imperfectly rubbed out, *Burn The Dead*. It wasn't the first time he'd seen that slogan since he'd come downside: once on an underpass wall on the way from the shuttleport, where a cleaning crew was already at work effacing it; more frequently down in the utility tunnels, where no tourists were expected to venture. On Barrayar, people burned offerings *for* the dead, but Miles suspected that wasn't the meaning here. The mysterious phrase had been high on his list of items to investigate further, before it had all gone sideways . . . yesterday? This morning?

Turning the corner into another unlit street or access road, which was bounded on the opposite side by a dilapidated chain-link fence, Miles hesitated. Looming out of the gathering gloom and angel-rain were two figures walking side-by-side. Miles blinked rapidly, trying to resolve them, then wished he hadn't.

The one on the right was a Tau Cetan beaded lizard, as tall, or short, as himself. Its skin rippled with variegated colored scales, maroon, yellow, black, ivory-white in the collar around its throat and down its belly, but rather than progressing in toad-like hops, it walked upright, which was a clue. A real Tau Cetan beaded lizard, squatting, might come up nearly to Miles's waist, so it wasn't *exceptionally* large for its species. But it also carried sacks swinging from its hands, definitely not real beaded lizard behavior.

Its taller companion . . . well. A six-foot-tall butterbug was definitely a creature out of his own nightmares, and not anyone else's. Looking rather like a giant cockroach, with a pale pulsing abdomen, folded brown wing carapaces, and bobbing head, it nonetheless strode along on two stick-like hind legs and also swung cloth sacks from its front claws. Its middle legs wavered in and out of existence uncertainly, as if Miles's brain could not decide exactly how to scale up the repulsive thing.

As the pair approached him and slowed, staring, Miles took a firmer grip on the nearest supporting wall, and essayed cautiously, "Hello?"

The butterbug turned its insectile head and studied him in turn. "Stay back, Jin," it advised its shorter companion. "He looks like some sort of druggie, stumbled in here. Lookkit his eyes." Its mandibles and questing palps wiggled as it spoke, its male voice sounding aged and querulous

Miles wanted to explain that while he was certainly drugged, he was no addict, but getting the distinction across seemed too much of a challenge. He tried a big reassuring smile, instead. His hallucinations recoiled.

"Hey," said Miles, annoyed. "I can't look nearly as bad to you as you look to me. Deal with it." Perhaps he had wandered into some talking animal story like the ones he'd read, over and over, in the nursery to Sasha and little Hellion. Except the creatures encountered in such tales were normally furrier, he thought. Why couldn't his chemically-enchanted neurons have spat out giant kittens?

He put on his most austere diplomat's tones, and said, "I beg your pardon, but I seem to have lost my way." *Also my wallet, my wristcom, half my clothes, my bodyguard, and my mind.* And—his hand felt around his neck—his Auditor's seal-ring on its chain. Not that any of its overrides or other tricks would work on this world's com-net, but Armsman Roic might at least have tracked him by its ping. If Roic was still alive. He'd been upright when Miles had last seen him, when they'd been separated by the panicking mob.

A fragment of broken stone pressed into his foot, and he shifted. If his eye could pick out the difference between pebbles and glass and plastic on the pavement, why couldn't it tell the difference between people and huge insects? "It was giant cicadas the last time I had a reaction this bad," he told the butterbug. "A giant butterbug is actually sort of reassuring. No one else's brain on this planet would generate butterbugs, except maybe Roic's, so I know exactly where you're coming from. Judging from the decor around here, the locals'd probably go for some jackal-headed fellow, or maybe a hawk-man. In a white lab coat." Miles realized he'd spoken aloud when the pair backed up another step. What, were his eyes flashing celestial light? Or glowing feral red?

"Just leave, Jin," the butterbug told its lizard companion, tugging on its arm. "Don't talk to him. Walk away slowly."

"Shouldn't we try to help him?" A much younger voice; Miles couldn't judge if it was a boy's or a girl's.

"Yes, you should!" said Miles. "With all these angels in my eyes I can't even tell where I'm stepping. And I lost my shoes. The bad guys took them away from me."

"Come on, Jin!" said the butterbug. "We got to get these bags of findings back to the secretaries before dark, or they'll be mad at us."

Miles tried to decide if that last remark would have made any more sense to his normal brain. Perhaps not.

"Where are you trying to get to?" asked the lizard with the young voice, resisting its companion's pull.

"I . . ." *don't know*, Miles realized. *Back* was not an option till the drug had cleared his system and he'd garnered some notion of who his enemies were—if he returned to the cryonics conference, assuming it was still going on after all the disruptions, he might just be rushing back into their arms. *Home* was definitely on the list, and up till yesterday at the top, but then things had grown . . . interesting. Still, if his enemies had just wanted him dead, they'd had plenty of chances. Some hope there . . ."I don't know yet," he confessed.

The elderly butterbug said in disgust, "Then we can't very well send you there, can we? Come *on*, Jin!"

Miles licked dry lips, or tried to. *No, don't leave me!* In a smaller voice, he said, "I'm very thirsty. Can you at least tell me where I might find the nearest drinking water?" How long had he been lost underground? The water-clock of his bladder was not reliable—he might well have pissed in a corner to relieve himself somewhere along his random route. His thirst suggested he'd been wandering something between ten hours and twenty, though. He almost hoped for the latter, as it meant the drug should start clearing soon.

The lizard, Jin, said slowly, "I could bring you some."

"No, Jin!"

The lizard jerked its arm back. "You can't tell me what to do, Yani! You're not my parents!" Its voice went jagged on that last.

"Come *along*. The custodian is waiting to close up!"

Reluctantly, with a backward glance over its brightly-patterned shoulder, the lizard allowed itself to be dragged away up the darkening street.

Miles sank down, spine against the building wall, and sighed in exhaustion and despair. He opened his mouth to the thickening mist, but it did not relieve his thirst. The chill of the pavement and the wall bit through his thin clothing—just his shirt and gray trousers, pockets emptied, his belt also taken. It was going to get colder as night fell. This access road was unlighted. But at least the urban sky would hold a steady apricot glow, better than the endless dark below ground. Miles wondered how cold he would have to grow before he crawled back inside the shelter of that last door. *A hell of a lot colder than this*. And he *hated* cold.

He sat there a long time, shivering, listening to the distant city sounds and the faint cries in his head. Was his plague of angels starting to melt back into formless streaks? He could hope. *I shouldn't have sat down*. His leg muscles were tightening and cramping, and he wasn't at all sure he could stand up again.

He'd thought himself too uncomfortable to doze, but he woke with a start, some unknown time later, to a shy touch on his shoulder. Jin was kneeling at his side, looking a bit less reptilian than before.

"If you want, mister," Jin whispered, "you can come along to my hide-out. I got some water bottles there. Yani won't see you, he's gone to bed."

"That's," Miles gasped, "that sounds great." He struggled to his feet; a firm young grip caught his stumble.

In a whining nimbus of whirling lights, Miles followed the friendly lizard.

Jin checked back over his shoulder to make sure the funny-looking little man, no taller than himself, was still following all right. Even in the dusk it was clear that the druggie was a grownup, and not another kid as Jin had hoped at first glance. He had a grownup voice, his words precise and complicated despite their tired slur and his strange accent, low and rumbly. He moved almost as stiff and slow as old Yani. But when his fleeting smiles lifted the strain from his face it looked oddly kind, in an accustomed way, as if smiles were at home there. Grouchy Yani never smiled.

Jin wondered if the little man had been beaten up, and why. Blood stained his torn trouser knees, and his white shirt bore browning smears. For a plain shirt, it looked pretty fancy, as if—before being rolled around in—it had been crisp and fine, but Jin couldn't figure out quite how that effect was done. Never mind. He had this novel creature all to himself, for now.

When they came to the metal ladder running up the outside of the exchanger building, Jin looked at the blood-stains and stiffness and thought to ask, "Can you climb?"

The little man stared upward. "It's not my favorite activity. How far up does this castle keep really go?"

"Just to the top."

"That would be, um, two stories?" He added in a low mutter, "Or twenty?"

Jin said, "Just three. My hideout's on the roof."

"The hideout part sounds good." The man licked at his cracked lips with a dry-looking tongue. He really did need water, Jin guessed. "Maybe you'd better go first. In case I slip."

"I have to go last to raise the ladder."

"Oh. All right." A small, square hand reached out to grip a rung. "Up. Up is good, right?" He paused, drew a breath, then lurched skyward.

Jin followed as lightly as a lizard. Three meters up, he stopped to crank the ratchet that raised the ladder out of reach of the unauthorized and latch it. Up another three meters, he came to the place where the rungs were replaced by broad steel staples, bolted to the building's side. The little man had managed them, but now seemed stuck on the ledge.

"Where am I now?" he called back to Jin in tense tones. "I can feel a drop, but I can't be sure how far down it really goes."

What, it wasn't *that* dark. "Just roll over and fall, if you can't lift yourself. The edge-wall's only about half a meter high."

"Ah." The sock feet swung out and disappeared. Jin heard a thump and a grunt. He popped over the parapet to find the little man sitting up on the flat rooftop, fingers scraping at the grit as if seeking a handhold on the surface.

"Oh, are you afraid of heights?" Jin asked, feeling dumb for not asking sooner.

"Not normally. Dizzy. Sorry."

Jin helped him up. The man did not shrug off his hand, so Jin led him on around the twin exchanger towers, set atop the roof like big blocks. Hearing Jin's familiar step, Galli, Twig, and Mrs. Speck, and Mrs. Speck's six surviving children, ran around the blocks to greet him, clucking and chuckling.

"Oh, God. Now I see chickens," said the man in a constricted voice, stopping short. "I suppose they could be related to the angels. Wings, after all."

"Quit that, Twig," said Jin sternly to the brown hen, who seemed inclined to peck at his guest's trouser leg. Jin shoved her aside with his foot. "I didn't bring you any food yet. Later."

"You see chickens, too?" the man inquired cautiously.

"Yah, they're mine. The white one is Galli, the brown one is Twig, and the black-and-white speckled one is Mrs. Speck. Those are all her babies, though I guess they're not really babies any more." Half-grown and

molting, the brood didn't look too appetizing, a fact
Jin almost apologized for as the man continued to peer
down into the shadows at their greeting party. "I named
her Galli because the scientific name of the chicken is
*Gallus gallus*, you know." A cheerful name, sounding like
*gallop-gallop*, which always made Jin smile.

"Makes . . . sense," the man said, and let Jin tug him
onward.

As they rounded the corner Jin automatically checked
to be sure the roof of discarded tarps and drop cloths
that he'd rigged on poles between the two exchanger
towers was still holding firm, sheltering his animal family.
The tent made a cozy space, bigger than his bedroom
back before . . . he shied from that memory. He let go of
the stranger long enough to jump up on the chair and
switch on the hand light, hanging by a scrap of wire from
the ridge-pole, which cast a bright circle of illumination
over his secret kingdom as good as any ceiling fixture's.
The man flung his arm up over his reddened eyes, and
Jin dimmed the light to something softer.

As Jin stepped back down, Lucky rose from the bedroll
atop the mattress of shredded flimsies, stretched, and
hopped toward him, meowing, then rose on her hind
legs to place her one front paw imploringly on Jin's
knee, kneading her claws. Jin bent and scratched her
fuzzy gray ears. "No dinner yet, Lucky."

"That cat does have three legs, right?" asked the man.
He sounded nervous. Jin hoped he wasn't allergic to cats.

"Yah, she caught one in a door when she was a kitten.
I didn't name her. She was my Mom's cat." Jin clenched
his teeth. He didn't need to have added that last. "She's
just a *Felis domesticus*."

Gyre the Falcon gave one ear-splitting shriek from his

perch, and the black-and-white rats rustled in their cages. Jin called greetings to them all. When food was not immediately forthcoming, they all settled back in a disgruntled way. "Do you like rats?" Jin eagerly asked his guest. "I'll let you hold Jinni, if you want. She's the friendliest."

"Maybe later," said the man faintly, seemed to take in Jin's disappointed look, and after a squinting glance at the shelf of cages, added, "I like rats fine. I'm just afraid I'd drop her. I'm still a bit shaky. I was lost in the Cryocombs for rather a long time, today." After another moment, he offered, "I used to know a spacer who kept hamsters."

This was encouraging; Jin brightened. "Oh, your water!"

"Yes, please," said the man. "This is a chair, right?" He was gripping the back of Jin's late stepstool, leaning on it. The scratched round table beside it, discarded from some cafe and the prize of an alley scavenge, had been a bit wobbly, but Custodian Tenbury had showed Jin how to fix it with a few shims and tacks.

"Yah, sit! I'm sorry there's only one, but usually I'm the only person who comes up here. You get it 'cause you're the guest." As the man dropped into the old plastic cafeteria chair, Jin rummaged on his shelves for his liter water bottle, uncapped it, and handed it over. "I'm sorry I don't have a cup. You don't mind drinking where my mouth was?"

"Not at all," said the man, raised the bottle, and gulped thirstily. He stopped suddenly when it was about three-fourths empty to ask, "Wait, is this all your water?"

"No, no. There's a tap on the outsides of each of these old heat exchanger towers. One's broken, but the custodian hooked up the other for me when I moved all my pets up here. He helped me rig my tent, too. The secretaries wouldn't let me keep my animals inside anymore, because the smell and noise bothered some folks. I like it better up here anyway. Drink all you want. I can just fill it up again."

The little man drained the bottle and, taking Jin at his word, handed it back. "More, please?"

Jin dashed out to the tap and refilled the bottle, taking a moment to rinse and top up the chickens' water pan at the same time. His guest drank another half-liter without stopping, then rested, his eyes sagging shut.

Jin tried to figure out how old the man was. His face was pale and furrowed, with sprays of fine lines at the corners of his eyes, and his chin was shadowed with a day's beard stubble, but that could be from being lost Below, which would unsettle anybody. His dark hair was neatly cut, a few gleams of gray showing in the light. His body seemed more scaled-down than distorted, sturdy enough, though his head, set on a short neck, was a bit big for it. Jin decided to work around to his curiosity more sideways, to be polite. "What's your name, mister?"

The man's eyes flew open; they were clear gray in color, and would probably be bright if they weren't so bloodshot. If the fellow had been bigger, his seedy looks might have alarmed Jin more. "Miles. Miles Vo— Well, the rest is a mouthful no one here seems able to pronounce. You can just call me Miles. And what's your name, young...person?"

"Jin Sato," said Jin.

"Do you live on this roof?"

Jin shrugged. "Pretty much. Nobody climbs up to bother me. The lift tubes inside don't work." He led on, "I'm almost twelve," and then, deciding he'd been polite enough, added, "How old are you?"

"I'm almost thirty-eight. From the other direction."

"Oh." Jin digested this. A disappointingly old person, therefore likely to be stodgy, if not so old as Yani, but then, it was hard to know how to count Yani's age. "You have a funny accent. Are you from around here?"

"By no means. I'm from Barrayar."

Jin's brow wrinkled. "Where's that? Is it a city?" It wasn't a Territorial Prefecture; Jin could name all twelve of those. "I never heard of it."

"Not a city. A planet. A triplanetary empire, technically."

"An off-worlder!" Jin's eyes widened with delight. "I never met an off-worlder before!" Tonight's scavenge suddenly seemed more fruitful. Though if the man was a tourist, he would likely leave as soon as he could call his hotel or his friends, which was a disheartening thought. "Did you get beaten up by robbers or something?" Robbers picked on druggies, drunks, and tourists, Jin had heard. He supposed they made easy targets.

"Something like that." Miles squinted at Jin. "You hear much news in the past day?"

Jin shook his head. "Only Suze the Secretary has a working comconsole, in here."

"In here?"

"This place. It was a cryofacility, but it was cleared out and abandoned, oh, way before I was born. A bunch of folks moved in who didn't have anywhere else to go. I suppose we're all sort of hiding out. Well, people living around here know there's people in here, but Suze-san says if we're all real careful not to bother anyone, they'll leave us be."

"That, um, person you were with earlier, Yani. Who is he? A relative of yours?"

Jin shook his head emphatically. "He just came here one day, the way most folks do. He's a revive." Jin gave the word its meaningful pronunciation, re-vive.

"He was cryo-revived, you mean?"

"Yah. He doesn't much like it, though. His contract with

his corp was just for one hundred years—I guess he paid a lot for it, a long time ago. But he forgot to say he wasn't to be thawed out till folks had found a cure for being old. Since that's what his contract said, they brought him up, though I suppose his corp was sorry to lose his vote. This future wasn't what he was expecting, I guess—but he's too old and confused to work at anything and make enough money to get frozen again. He complains about it a lot."

"I . . . see. I think." The little man squeezed his eyes shut, and open again, and rubbed his brow, as if it ached. "God, I wish my head would clear."

"You could lie down in my bedroll, if you wanted," Jin suggested diffidently. "If you don't feel so good."

"Indeed, young Jin, I don't feel so good. Well put." Miles tilted up the water bottle and drained it. "The more I can drink the better—wash this damned poison out of my system. What do you do for a loo?" At Jin's blank look he added, "Latrine, bathroom, lavatory, pissoir? Is there one inside the building?"

"Oh! Not close, sorry. Usually when I'm up here for very long I sneak over and use the gutter in the corner, and slosh it down the drainpipe with a bucket of water. I don't tell the women, though. They'd complain, even though the chickens go all over the roof and nobody thinks anything of it. But it makes the grass down there really green."

"Ah ha," said Miles. "Congratulations—you have reinvented the garderobe, my lizard-squire. Appropriate, for a castle."

Jin didn't know what kind of clothes a *guarding-robe* might be, but half the things this druggie said made no sense anyway, so he decided not to worry about it.

"And after your lie-down, I can come back with some food," Jin offered.

"After a lie-down, my stomach might well be settled enough to take you up on that, yes."

Jin smiled and jumped up. "Want any more water?"

"Please."

When Jin returned from the tap, he found the little man easing himself down in the bedroll, laid along the side wall of an exchanger tower. Lucky was helping him; he reached out and absently scritched her ears, then let his fingers massage expertly down either side of her spine, which arched under his hand. The cat deigned to emit a short purr, an unusual sign of approval. Miles grunted and lay back, accepting the water bottle and setting it beside his head. "Ah. God. That's so good." Lucky jumped up on his chest and sniffed his stubbly chin; he eyed her tolerantly.

A new concern crossed Jin's mind. "If heights make you dizzy, the gutter could be a problem." An awful picture arose of his guest falling head-first over the parapet while trying to pee in the dark. His *off-worlder* guest. "See, chickens don't fly as well as you'd think, and baby chicks can't fly at all. I lost two of Mrs. Speck's children over the parapet, when they got big enough to clamber up to the ledge but not big enough to flutter down safely if they fell over. So for the in-between time, I tied a long string to each one's leg, to keep them from going too far. Maybe I could, like . . . tie a line around your ankle or something?"

Miles stared up at him in a tilted fascination, and Jin was horribly afraid for a moment that he'd mortally offended the little man. But in a rusty voice, Miles finally said, "You know—under the circumstances—that might not be a bad idea, kid."

Jin grinned relief, and hurried to find a bit of rope in his cache of supplies. He hitched one end firmly to the metal rail beside the tower door, made sure it paid out all the way to the corner gutter, and returned to affix the other end to his guest's ankle. The little man was already asleep, the water bottle tucked under one arm and the gray cat under the other. Jin looped the rope around twice and made a good knot. After, he climbed back onto the chair and dimmed the hand light to a soft night-light glow, trying not to think about his mother.

*Sleep tight, don't let the bedbugs bite.*

*If I ever find bedbugs, I'll catch them and put them in my jars. What do bedbugs look like, anyway?*

*I have no idea. It's just a silly rhyme for bedtimes. Go to sleep, Jin!*

The words had used to make him feel warm, but now they made him feel cold. He hated cold.

Satisfied that he'd made all safe, and that the intriguing off-worlder could not now abandon him, Jin returned to the parapet, swung over, and started down the rungs. If he hurried, he would still get to the back door of Ayako's Cafe before all the good scraps were thrown out at closing time.

—end excerpt—

from *Cryoburn*
available in hardcover,
November 2010, from Baen Books